# CASTLE OF NEVERS AND NIGHTMARES

Cover Design and Map Art © Lana Pecherczyk 2024
www.lanapecherczyk.com

eBook ASIN: B0CKX6T4WD

Paperback Print Edition ISBN: 978-1-922989-29-1
Hardcover Print Edition ISBN: 978-1-922989-30-7

Interior character art by Jaqueline Florencio
Half title art by Salome Totladze

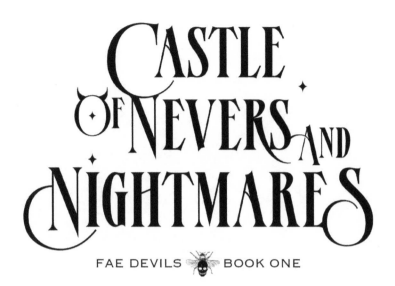

# CASTLE OF NEVERS AND NIGHTMARES

FAE DEVILS 🐝 BOOK ONE

## LANA PECHERCZYK

ADULARIA
HOUSE OF MOONLIGHT

WULFENITE
HOUSE OF EMBERS

CONNEMARA
HOUSE OF TIDES

HELIODOR
HOUSE OF STONE

THE NEXUS

SHADOWFALL KEEP
HOUSE OF SHADOW

AVORLORNA CITY
COURT OF DREAMS

AVORLORNA
THE COMMONWEALTH OF DREAMS

AIRALUDA
HOUSE OF FEAR

ETINEFLUW
HOUSE OF PREY

ARAMENNOC
HOUSE OF BLOOD

THE SCHISM

RODOILEH
HOUSE OF FLESH

THE DARK TOWER
HOUSE OF OBLIVION

NOCTURNA CITY
COURT OF NIGHTMARES

NOCTURNA

THE SUBTERRANEAN OF NIGHTMARES

*To those who dream*

*of a villain*

*who waits for them*

*to say, "When."*

# PROLOGUE

"The bonding ritual isn't working," the druid announces.

"What do you mean, it's not working? It always works." Titania, the ancient queen we despise, attempts to wriggle her power into our hive's collective soul, but we have changed much since she first put us in chains.

All she can do now is force us to bow beneath her command. It won't last.

*Together, we are infinite.*

The Keepers of the Cauldron surround us. Their druidic chant bleeds into our ears, adding to the power of her quelling spell.

"Kneel." Her command vibrates through our being, bouncing around to consume every sense of ownership in our blood. Our legs fold. Our knees crack against the rocky, moss-ridden surface. Our necks lower until our noses are mere inches from the ground, and yet we hold our resistance, trembling under our primal urge to be free of this suffering.

"Bow to my will," she demands.

Never.

*We fight. Thrash. Gnash.* Our hive stands united. We are not six. We are not Legion, Bodin, Emrys, Varen, Fox, and Styx. We are one mind, one soul, one hunger split into six bodies. And we are not the monsters she once enslaved. We have tasted a drop of precious life from the other side of death, and now we hunger for more.

Our hive stands united.

"Why are they acting like this?" Titania asks the druids. "Why do they speak with one voice?"

The archdruid turns pages in his book but won't find the answer. His masked, hooded face shakes in disbelief. "It is a fresh development. Perhaps another trait they've taken from a different queen."

The invisible collar around our neck hisses, cutting our skin with the strength of the sun. We burn. We agonize. We wish upon wishes that we weren't wrong. That freedom is still held in the stars for us, waiting to shine upon our faces from the dark.

"Where is it?" Titania demands, pacing around us as the chanting drones on. "Where is the Wild Hunt?"

"Somewhere you will never find," we answer in unison.

Eye-watering pain lashes through our minds. A part of us relishes it. Some of us feed on it. We pray for more to build a wall around our secrets and protect the star whose existence has given us hope.

Through the chanting, a male druid's harsh voice grates our nerves. "This is not the same as before. The link isn't working."

"Don't you think I know that?" Her footsteps circle us. "Our slumber was never meant to last for thousands of years. The world has changed. They have evolved, but one thing is for certain: they still require a queen to stop them from descending into the Morrigan's chaotic clutches."

"What is that blue, glowing teardrop beneath their left eye?"

This female voice is lighter, musical. Not like the others. "What does it mean?"

The harsh male replies, "Are you an imbecile? It means the same bonding ritual won't work."

Silence. The weight of eyes scores into us in the dark. The drone of druids continues. Cut after cut of judgment leaves scars on our souls. We have been here before, on our knees, oppressed. We hear thoughts run circles in their mind.

*Monsters.*

*Abominations.*

*They should be wiped out of existence.*

The only difference is that this time around, we understand what those words mean, and we are wounded for it. We did not wish for this existence. We have wished for oblivion.

Until her.

A falling star born to be our queen and equal at once. The first and last of her kind. Our fated mate.

"The mark is a blessing," the lyrical voice whispers reverently. "We all know it."

Titania scoffs, "How can nightmares be blessed? The Morrigan does not play well with the other Cauldron deities. Why would she approve such a blessing? All she wants is domination and chaos."

"As do her creatures," the archdruid adds. "They are the same monstrous evil as before. They want us dead. What more proof do you need?"

"I just thought . . ." Her lyrical tone wilts.

"You are here because we lost Keepers during slumber. Do not presume to know what is needed. We need time to adjust, to come up with another solution, that is all."

"The archdruid is correct," Titania replies, a note of panic in her voice. "We cannot risk it. Oberon has arisen, too. He must not learn they have survived all these years. He must *never* learn."

"On this, we agree. Always."

It was only hours ago that our life's dream became a nightmare. Only hours since our star realized her full potential, battled another slaver queen, and bled for us . . . scarred for us . . . but when she laid eyes on what she'd claimed, she called us monsters like so many before.

Our anguish is strong enough to pierce our hearts.

"Oh my," Titania coos and slows her pacing to stare at us. "My my my . . ."

"Your Radiance?" the archdruid asks.

"This might be easier than we thought. All these years, under the guidance of weaker queens, these monsters finally dared to dream . . . now I glimpse the fault in their hearts. Now I know which walls to crumble so this collective state falls." She strokes one of us on the jaw. "Show me her face."

"NO," we bellow as one, surging against our restraints. Our fated queen might not want us, but we would rather die than give her up.

The druidic chanting increases in intensity. The fire against our throats flares, but our defiance grows hotter, too. For her, for our true queen, we will enter oblivion. We will grow dark enough to swallow every other star, so she burns brighter.

As one, the hive strains against our leash. We each rise onto trembling feet and glimpse the terror in Titania's face.

"Yes, you should be afraid," we hiss, cackling with triumph. "Before, we did not know what we missed . . . but now . . . now we have tasted freedom, and she is magnificent."

A bloody, fanged grin splits across each of our faces. Our skulls illuminate beneath our skin, flickering with the urge to release our wraith forms and consume their souls, but her power infuriatingly blocks us.

"Start!" Titania screeches, backing up. "Start the binding ritual."

Robed and masked druids bustle around us, lighting candles, setting herbs on fire. They call on the feylines beneath the earth's crust streaming directly from the Cauldron's Wellspring.

They place a stone disc at the First's feet, sealing the door on his hive-mind space. With one door closed, we are no longer united. The hive is broken. We are thrown back into our individual bodies.

*Fox*

I AM MYSELF AGAIN. IT TAKES A MOMENT TO ACCLIMATE, TO acknowledge the skin I exist within—a tail lashes behind me. My tattered, taloned wings expand to fill the dark cave with increasing shadow. My mind gropes for the hive space, wanting to fling open the mental door and unite us once more. Together, we are invincible. Alone, we drift.

The hive space is just out of reach. If only I could grasp the doorknob and yank it open, we could break the seal blocking Legion from the rest of us. But he stands in our circle, confused. Dark, long hair falls from a widow's peak, hiding his face. His wings are gone. His eyes have switched from wholly black to white with an iris and pupil.

A druid's robe brushes my tail in passing. My taloned wing slices like a blade, aiming for the head. The queen's collar restricts my range. I miss. A squeak behind the druidess's wooden mask is satisfying. She almost drops her stone disc.

*"Fox!"* Varen's voice punches into my mind. *"Listen to me. We have but moments to plan before our minds are not our own."*

My gaze whips to the left. Beside me, inches of dark hair veil his eyes as he hunches. He hides something. I look harder and glimpse white, meaning he ransacks timelines of the future . . . searching for a path to freedom.

His slumped weight presses his neck into the invisible collar restraining him. Blood oozes from his throat, pooling on the ground. When he enters this state, he forsakes his well-being. I must protect him. I claw at my choker, heedless of pinpricks of metaphysical fire stabbing into my bones.

*"I'm coming,"* I send him, mind-to-mind. We, Sluagh of the Morrigan's first hive, are almost impossible to kill, but we can grow weak. We can suffer, oh yes, we can suffer.

*"One of us must retain the truth in order to catch our falling star,"* he sends privately. *"One who must hide in plain sight, take sustenance to feed the others, and protect our secrets until she arrives to complete her claim on us. To free us, once and for all."*

Bodin's steady presence evaporates when another door slams closed in the hive-mind space. A blanket of normalcy hides his monstrous side. Long braids sway as he cranes to check where his wings have gone.

*"Fox,"* Varen urges. *"We are almost out of time."*

With horror, I realize he intends for me to be the sole member of our hive to retain memory.

*"Wait for her,"* he urges. *"Wait and prepare. She will come."*

*"Our fated queen hates us,"* I reply. *"She called us monsters. What if Emrys is right, and she's no better than the others?"*

*"She doesn't know us."*

*"But she rejected us."*

His face tilts a fraction and his eyes lock with mine. The soul-crushing hole in my heart grows deeper as a seal is placed at Emrys's feet. His presence winks out. Oblivion nips at our heels.

*"When she comes,"* Varen murmurs into my mind. *"When her*

*heart opens to ours, we will walk in her light for eternity. For this, I make the sacrifice."*

"Sacrifice?"

Varen breaks eye contact to watch another seal being laid on the ground. Styx's blue-pink skin pulls taut in fear. His long, curved horns slowly diminish. His tail and wings evaporate.

Dread knots in my stomach. His presence winks out, and his otherness disintegrates into the mundane.

*"Your faith in me is misplaced,"* I send to Varen, struggling against my restraints. *"I am the Fifth. Give this responsibility to someone else. Make me the sacrifice."*

*"Don't let them see your true self,"* he instructs. *"Feed within the smoke. Keep the Wild Hunt hidden. Follow the rules, no matter how painful. And above all else, wait."*

*"Why me?"*

*"You may be the Fifth, Fox, but you were the first to understand true freedom."* A smirk touches Varen's lips as a seal is placed at his feet. *"Catch our falling star, give her your heart, and she will guide us home."*

I am alone.

Druidic chanting rises to a crescendo. A stone seal lowers into my field of vision, and my death rattle rages. I don't want this. It shouldn't be me—the one who recklessly heads into danger, who acts first and thinks last. So I lash out—wings, tail, and stubby horns that never quite grew as long as Styx's.

I clash with a nearby druid. It takes Titania by surprise. She fumbles. The final seal spills from her fingers and rolls left to thud against Varen's disc. He frowns in confusion, fathomless eyes now human.

But the disc is right there. I lurch forward, reaching with taloned black fingertips. To my shock, my metaphysical leash gives, and I almost connect with the disc.

"Get the seal!" Titania shrieks, turning the full effect of her power back toward me, reining me in. Her magic smells familiar, yet foreign. I am yanked harshly back into place and forced to my knees. Dainty fingers with colorful nails place the final seal before my feet.

The chanting stops. Everyone holds their breath.

"Is it done?" someone dares to ask.

"Wait," another snaps. "We must be sure."

Wait . . . that is what Varen instructed.

Varen, whose disc now sits beneath my face, somehow mixed up during my attack. They believe I am sealed, yet he has been twice bound instead.

*Don't let them see your true self.*

Yes, we have changed. Titania was our first queen, but we have had many since. We have taken on a magical trait from each. Before, we could only wear glamour. Now . . . I shift my monstrous parts into myself, hiding the truth from judgmental eyes. Horns, tail, wings, talons. It all melts beneath my skin.

Relief exhales around the cave.

"It is done," Titania says with a sigh.

# PART ONE

# ELPHYNE

# CHAPTER
# ONE
## WILLOW

I shouldn't be doing this.

I'm hanging upside down from a rope around my waist, peering through the third-story window of the Order of the Well's chief mana stone maker. It's broad daylight. Anyone can see me if they walk into the yard, but the inhabitants are nocturnal and should be fast asleep. As long as my lookout remains alert, I should be fine.

*Relax, Willow. Relax.*

I puff a lock of long hair from obscuring my vision and check for movement inside. I see a workbench covered with various gemstones, jars of glowing manabeeze, and tools of the trade. Piles of maps battle for supremacy with books on a desk. Grinding offcuts litter the floor. Damn, my Aunt Peaches is messy. Hopefully, that means she won't notice a few valuable items missing.

Leaves rustle behind me, and my pulse quickens. Only an amateur would turn to check. Instead, I study the window's reflection to avoid rousing suspicion that I've noticed an interloper. But my only companions are shrubs, flowers, and a glimpse of the poisonous forest canopy over the yard's boundary wall. No one sane would dare sneak in here when Haze, Peaches' mate, is a seven-foot vampire Guardian with a shadow that kills as much as he does.

Shuffling on the roof draws my gaze as miniature antlers loom over the gutter's edge. One tine is broken. A floppy-eared rabbit's head is next, followed by chicken wings ruffling with nervous anticipation. Tinger huffs and bares tiny fangs.

"Okay, I get it," I grumble to my lookout. "You're so impatient in your old age."

He gives me a familiar warning look I read as, *Don't fuck with me, female, or maybe I'll finally shift into a monster and steal you as my bride.*

Except he's been robbed of magic, like me—so no shifting for us. Since no fae wants to be reminded they're mortal, I salute him, place my palms on the window, and close my eyes to listen with my sixth sense. I might not have magic now, but I once did. Protection wards would feel like ants crawling over my skin. I only sense a sweet, daisy-scented breeze, so I take my dagger from my boot and use it to jimmy open the window.

No security whatsoever. It's almost like they're asking to be robbed.

The smell of stone masonry wafts out, along with perfume and chemicals I'm unfamiliar with. My nose tingles, and I hold back a sneeze. Well-dammit. Being stuck with wolf biology without the perks of shifting sucks.

When my control returns, I maneuver inside like a gymnast, twisting until my feet land on the wooden floorboards. Still crouched, I stretch my awareness for sounds or changes in the atmosphere.

Haze's shadow can act independently, so I'm worse than toast if he's left it to guard these valuable stones. Vampires are also obsessively territorial when protecting their roost, and

Jasmine, their halfling teenage daughter, is showing signs of a sanguineous diet like her dad.

I poke my head through the window and signal the all-clear to Tinger. He descends in a loud gust of flapping wings and knocks an antler against the sill as he enters. I slap my palm to my face and check for signals we've been made. Nothing. Thank fuck.

"You're lucky you're cute," I whisper through gritted teeth, then untie myself from the rope but leave it dangling outside the window for our escape.

Together, we hunt through the treasure trove of mana stones. I'm not exactly sure what types I want, but they're the only source of magic a mortal can use. Spending half my life locked away with exiled humanity in Crystal City has taught me there's always another way. Admittedly, it's not always the right way, but beggars can't be choosers.

Corked jars filled with glowing, swimming manabeeze sit on a table by the wall. The balls of energy erupt from fae bodies and hold memories of the host. We're not supposed to kill to harvest these, but if the fae creature dies for survival reasons, and a prayer of thanks to the Well is offered, repurposing manabeeze to enhance life is permitted. Especially since the fallout two thousand years ago, the Well refuses to flow where metal and plastic are used. Manabeeze and specific elven runes help revive old-world advancements like plumbing, heating, and strengthening.

They also act as a substitute for innate magic.

I slot a full jar into my leather satchel and scour the remaining collection. Each type of mana stone has a different purpose. Proximity stones will alert me of danger nearby. Low-dose heat stones won't do much apart from warming my bed or womb when it cramps before my wolfish heat. However, portal stones are expensive in the market in Cornucopia. It's the only place outside the Order campus I visit. My next trip will mark my fourth solo trip. Not bad, considering my mother only gave me the go-ahead to join supply runs six months ago. Before that, the idea of venturing into crowded public places alone gave me the shakes. Being locked up in a tower for a decade will do that to a person.

My satchel is almost full when I walk past a row of small bowls labeled with old-world names.

Exhaling, I trace the labels. Why do they seem so familiar? One is inscribed as an Australian Opal. The other is called Irish Jade. I was given the green one shortly after being taken from Elphyne. I hated sleeping alone—shifters like company. Humans in Crystal City didn't get it. So I cried every night until someone sat with me. Once the woman I eventually grew to love and call Aunty Rory tucked me in.

*"Here," she says, handing me a small green stone with a groove worn into it. "The Tinker left this behind when she betrayed us and joined your parents. She said rubbing it made her feel less worried or something."*

*My tiny, trembling hand encloses around the cool stone. "You're giving me a present?"*

*"It's nothing."*

Blinking away the memory, I pick up the jade. It's warm to the touch, so must be primed with mana and ready to activate. Drop a few manabeeze onto the surface, and a portal will open to the location the rock was mined from. I sift through the mess on Peaches's desk until I find an old-world map. I tap the land called Ireland. It's next to England, where the Tinker originated.

This is definitely the same stone Rory gave me. How it arrived here in Elphyne, though, is a mystery. Maybe I brought it into the battle where I lost my magic.

Nero, humanity's president, intended to harvest manabeeze floating up from soldier's corpses via airships. He thought he could force me to raise an army of the dead and reclaim Elphyne for the human minority. But the land only flourished after the fallout because magic flows here without metal and plastic—one of the vital rules the Order of the Well upholds.

Nero picked the wrong battle to start his harvesting campaign. I had intended to escape and find my family, but an unexpected urge came over me that I'm still trying to make sense of. Nothing else mattered except for me killing the Unseelie Queen. I was possessed. The berserker instinct had been engraved into my soul. I ended up raising an undead army anyway. People died. My inner well dried out. And six creepy fae boogeymen tried to claim me as their queen.

It's all so much of a blur now. My fingers gravitate to the thin scars along my jaw. The temptation to run away is strong. I could find somewhere no one knows about my shame.

"Tinger, look," I murmur, tapping the map and showing him. "What's the bet Irish Jade will take us to Ireland?"

He sniffs the parchment, then hops away, unimpressed.

"You're right," I reply, as if he's spoken to me. "If this stone sits here unused, chances are that faraway place is uninhabitable."

Feeling nostalgic, I rub my thumb along the worn green groove, for a moment wishing it was a djinn bottle and I could wish to turn back time. Invisible, tingling ants scamper up my hand as the magic awakens, looking for a connection it won't find in me.

Something thuds downstairs.

*Shit.* Someone's awake. I drop the stone into my bag, hoist Tinger by his broken antler, and toss him through the open window. He flutters off into the yard. I'm out next, using the rope to climb to the roof where I lie flat against the tiles, willing my pulse to slow.

No more thuds, but that doesn't mean I'm safe from capture.

I've been back in Elphyne for five years, but everyone still looks at me like the enemy.

In my peripheral vision, Tinger hops into the shadow of a neighboring oak tree. At least he's safe. Me? I'll be fine.

*Oh fuck, did I close the window?*

I scamper along the rooftop to an overreaching oak bough, then swing to the ground at the front of the house and hightail it across campus. I don't slow until two blue-robed Mages further down the path spot me, then I pretend I'm on my mid-morning stroll. "Fake it until you make it," my mother always told me. The Mages cross to the other side of the path, avoiding me like I'm a bad smell.

It's business as usual, then. My confidence returns as I head home. A triumphant grin threatens to stretch my lips. Stepping back onto the path, I open my satchel to check my loot, so I'm not paying attention when I collide with a hard, leather-clad chest.

Glass breaks. I quickly drop the flap, praying a manabee won't buzz out and give me away.

*Avoid scrutiny. Apologize and move on. Quick.*

My fist rubs a circle over my heart in the fae hand sign for an apology.

A handsome blond Guardian smiles at me as though I've made his day. His leather battle gear is squeaky clean. The blue, glowing teardrop beneath his left eye sparkles. His skin is deeply tanned, and he has pointed ears—clean, no furry tips like my father and brother. Must be an elf, then. A vampire would sweat buckets walking around this time of day.

"Willow, right?" His smile turns into a broad grin.

Behind him, two more Guardians approach. One is a crow shifter with black feathered wings, and the other is a wolf shifter. I've seen them around campus. They have the ambition to rise to the elite ranks of the Cadre of Twelve alongside my father and brother. They think fucking me will get them there. My family will rip out their throats first.

There's no point engaging in conversation. I give a tight-lipped smile and continue walking, tensing as I catch their mumbled words behind me.

"See?" one of them says. "I told you she's not worth the effort. As frigid as the dead she brought to life."

I stop but don't look back.

"That was her? But she's the Prime's daughter."

The reply is in a hushed tone. "They say the Well *unmade* her as punishment."

"I heard the Six were obsessed with her."

"I heard she's in cahoots with the evil traitors."

"Nah, they're dead. Or . . . I don't know. Maybe they ran away."

"Yeah," one laughs cruelly. "She was too much of a freak for the boogeymen."

They know I hear better than most. They want me to witness their disdain. I should be used to the gossip by now.

Hugging the satchel to my chest, I walk away until my house comes into view. It's creepy, needing renovations, and belonged to the six Sluagh who were obsessed with me as a child. It's because of them I was kidnapped, held hostage by humanity, and trained as a weapon. It's their fault there was a war in the first place. But as those Guardians said, the Six are gone now.

When I returned, this was the only vacant house on campus for my parents to move into.

The glass windows are cracked. Paint peels from the wooden slats. Thick deciduous trees perpetually keep the mini mansion in shadow.

I was naïve to swoon over their beautiful faces. How my heart soared when I thought they fought through hordes of undead to rescue me. But then one touched me and declared me nothing. So I called them monsters and ran away.

But I won't make the same mistake if I see them again. I'll kill them.

I find a dark spot beneath a skeletal tree to check my bag. Holding my breath, I open the flap and dart back as a horde of manabeeze swarms out.

When the last one escapes, I close my eyes and bump my head against the tree trunk. *I'm so stupid.* I should have held the satchel at my back, not my front. Now I've got nothing to activate the mana stones. This morning's expedition was a failure. With a heavy sigh, I head up the creaky porch steps to my house. When I open the door, my older brother growls, "Where the fuck have you been?"

The scowling blue-eyed, silver-haired Guardian is in his leather battle gear, his giant ax strapped between his shoulder blades. Must be about to head out on a mission. His left eye twitches when hysterical squeals filter down the stairs, followed by the rapid thudding of little feet, glass breaking, and distraught, childish crying.

He hands me two stuffed dolls and then pats me on the shoulder. "Your turn, sis."

"But—"

"I have more important things to do than play with dolls."

My cheeks heat. "Noted."

His tone fills with pity. "I didn't mean it that way."

"Yes, you did."

"Willow—"

"It's fine." I force a smile. "I'll entertain the twins."

Seems like it's all I'm good for.

"Hazel and Holly love spending time with you." His brow lifts as he surveys the area behind me. "Where's your little shadow?"

"Tinger?"

"He's getting old. Maybe don't let the girls tie ribbons to his antlers this time."

"I think Tinger can make his own choices."

Another flash of pity hits his eyes. He tugs me into the embrace of powerful arms and mumbles how much he loves me. It's meant to be comforting, but I only feel stiff and cold. When he's gone, and I'm still staring at the closed door, I wonder how long I'll keep pretending I'm fine.

Sometimes, rage fills me so much that I want to tear my hair out. Once, I had a purpose. Even if that purpose was to raise an army of undead for the enemy, I was wanted. Needed. People killed to have me in their possession. Now, I'm empty as a desert, and all I'm needed for is babysitting and the occasional supply run.

My gaze sharpens on something I never noticed before on the door. Thousands of tiny vertical scratches are gouged into the wood from top to bottom. They're clumped into groups of five and cover the entire surface. One of the Six must have made them . . . perhaps with their talons. Hatred burns the back of my throat like bile. They bargained with the Well for a queen, and they got me. For hundreds of years, they murdered, manipulated, and maneuvered people like chess pieces to ensure everything was in the right time and place for my birth. And then they had me kidnapped by the enemy so I could learn to kill. It was sick, selfish, and twisted. It all amounted to nothing, anyway.

They're cowards.

I rub my thumb over the grooves and wonder what they counted. Whatever it was, they waited a long time. Years. Maybe even decades. One of them was psychic, like my mother. They probably counted the days until they ruined my life. Or these marks are the amount of innocent souls they consumed.

Scratching outside prompts me to open the door. Tinger sits

on the mat, my dagger between his little fangs. I must have dropped it during the escape. Smiling, I let him inside.

"You're a good friend." I ruffle his ears, sheath the dagger inside my boot, then show him what happened to our stash. Only four manabeeze are left trapped between shards of broken glass. "We'll have to source more for a trip to Cornucopia outside a normal supply run."

He blinks at me. Then at the satchel.

"Yeah, I know," I reply with a sigh. "What's the point of selling portal stones? It's not like we're saving for anything."

Little girls squeal upstairs and then giggle. The playroom is probably covered in paint or smelling like a toilet by now. Where I've never been able to shift completely into a wolf, they have since they were two. They can be quite disgusting sometimes, but I don't blame them. It's natural.

Just not for me.

My gaze returns to the scratches on the door and then to the dolls. I may not know my purpose anymore, but it's not to be stuck here babysitting while my new mortal body withers away with age. The Six stole so much from me already. I can't let them take my youth.

"Hey, Tinger," I ask. "How do you feel about a little excursion?"

# CHAPTER
# TWO
## WILLOW

"What do you think, Ting?" I stare at my hastily built cage rigged to a bough over the gully dwarfed by poisonous trees. "It's the perfect place for hunting monsters, right?"

My wolpertinger friend flutters down and sniffs the dirt beneath our trap. I toss down Hazel and Holly's dolls so he can drag them into position beneath the cage.

Before I left home, I made sure the twins were fast asleep, surrounded by their toys. Knowing they'd be out for a few hours, it was the perfect time to duck into the forest outside the Order campus.

When Tinger excitedly binky-hops back to me, we set up a perimeter in the underbrush. I drop a manabee onto each proximity stone to activate it. A slight chemical smell tells me it's worked, but I touch them to make sure. Fire and ants zip up my skin and I gasp, snatching my fingers back.

Definitely working. When a monster crosses this boundary, the matching stone in my hand will vibrate.

I toss a few chunks of fresh meat just inside the barrier as a sweetener, then return to where Tinger awaits by an oversized oak, half shrouded with ferns and taking his job very seriously. I don't have the heart to tell him it could be a while before a monster stumbles across us, even with the bait. An army of monster-hunting Guardians living nearby is a great deterrent.

Careful not to touch the poisonous foliage, I settle beside Tinger and cross my legs.

"If we don't see action in an hour," I say, "we'll head home. The twins will be awake, and I'm sure they'll be pissed I took their dolls as monster bait."

The scent of innocent pups is all over them. One whiff, and a monster will come running for an easy dinner.

I take a stick of dried meat from my bag and raise it to my mouth, but the sound of licking stops me. Tinger has shuffled out from the shelter of his fern and now stares at the food with big, liquid eyes. His forked pink tongue darts out to lick his fangs, and my lips curve.

"I guess you earned some yum-yums." I toss him half, pop the remainder into my mouth, and then draw my short, serrated bone sword from my baldric. "Nothing left to do now but wait."

Having finished his mouthful, Tinger ruffles his feathers and puffs out his chest. He settles back into his shady spot beneath the fern and glares at the area beneath the cage. I hate to admit it, but signs of his aging are becoming obvious. White hairs blend with the creamy gray around his muzzle. His feathered wings are growing sparse. But his eyes are still shrewd.

Wolpertingers don't have females of their kind, so they mate with females from other species. After luring a maiden in with their cuteness, they shift into a giant bipedal creature to complete the coupling, then protect their mate and unborn child with as much violence as any other fae. It doesn't sound so bad, except for the part where the newborn wolpertinger eats its way out of the womb.

I scratch behind his floppy ears, silently glad he's lost that ability to shift. He'd be on the monster-hunting squad's most wanted list, and I'd hate to lose my only friend. He gives me an annoyed side-eye as though I'm disturbing his work.

"Fine." I show him my palm. "Don't ask for a scratch later."

Cracking my neck, I try to sit patiently, but the silence leaves me alone with my thoughts.

"What monster do you think we'll lure?" I ask. "Will it be something newly sprung from the Well after the taint or an oldie but a goodie?"

He doesn't answer.

"Shall we place a bet? Five strips of dried meat say it's not even a monster. I'll bet we lure a dumb warada." He twitches, unwilling to engage. "Okay, fine, you drive a hard bargain. How about I write a number down, slide it across the dirt, and you tell me if you're willing to pay it?"

I continue chatting for half an hour, and no sign of action. But I'm reluctant to leave. Something about the serenity here calls to me. Perhaps it's my wolf DNA, wanting me to be free and to run wild. My dad and brother often shift and disappear into the woods to hunt. I never experienced that joy. Unwittingly, my mind drifts to the six reasons why.

That battle is still murky, but my memory of them is not. I shiver as I recall how hard it had been to look at their stunning faces without my stomach fluttering.

"No one should be that pretty, right?" I ask Tinger quietly. Only here, alone with him, do I dare approach the darkest thoughts circling my heart. "Their magnetism is obviously one of those evolutionary lures, kind of like your cute bunny form. I almost fell for their trap, too." Maybe that's what shames me the most. For a brief moment, before I lost all sense and commanded the corpses to rise, I locked eyes with one of them and felt a connection. Something sad and lonely in his eyes lifted when he looked at me. Had I imagined that? Or was it my brain's way of excusing the things I did?

I'm just a halfling. I don't even have magic anymore, so why would they have wanted me?

Maybe it was all just a dream. A fucking nightmare.

Glancing at the sun's position through the leaves, I stand and dust my hands on my pants. "I think we need to call it a day and head home."

Tinger scampers down to the gully bed and circles the dolls. He drags them out from beneath the cage and takes their place.

My brows lift. "You want to be the bait?"

He glances at me, and I swear he nods before looking at the forest's darkness. Suddenly, the danger is real—an ache blooms in my chest.

"I don't think Peaches will like me putting you in danger like this."

She rescued him from The Unseelie High Queen Maebh—the one I tried to murder even though we've never met.

It's one thing for me to drag Tinger around when he's old, but deliberately putting him in harm's way isn't right. A defiant growl and a flash of fangs punctuate the next look he gives me. I don't see an old, frail creature anymore, but one who still knows what he wants.

"Okay," I agree. "People keep telling us what we're not capable of. So, if you want to sit there as bait, be my guest. We have another fifteen minutes, then we'll—"

The alarm stone vibrates. The top right corner heats, and I snap my gaze northeast. I steady my grip on my sword's hilt and search the ferns in that direction. Was that a frond twitching?

The stone buzzes again, but this time, the lower corner heats. I whip around and glimpse the red curly hair of a four-year-old between the green. Holly and Hazel pounce from the darkness a second later and flash their wolfish fangs.

"Found you!" Hazel snarls.

My heart leaps. "What are you doing here?"

They should be sleeping.

"Tinger!" Holly squeals, noting the fluff ball sitting beneath the cage. She makes grabby hands and bolts down, her red hair flying behind her like a flag.

The stone in my palm vibrates again. That's odd. The twins are inside the proximity barrier, so how is the alarm still sounding? A sizzle erupts somewhere in the trees. My blood runs cold. We're not alone.

"Get up the tree," I shout, dropping the stone and sword. Holly cries when I hoist her by the arm. She's much heavier than I remember and in no way clever enough to climb the nearest oak for safety. I desperately search for another haven and land on the cage. It's not the best, but it will hold the girls while I dispatch the Well Hound circling the gully.

Holly wails when I lift her on top of the swinging cage, but Hazel's eyes are full of mischief and excitement. She scrambles to the edge and looks down. "We hunting?"

"No," I gasp. "*I'm* hunting. You're holding onto the bars and not coming down, understood? Whatever you do, promise me you won't shift. Please?"

They must scent my fear and nod. I reach down to lift Tinger next, but he gnashes his teeth. Message received.

A whiff of sulfuric acid gives me a moment of regret, and then a Well Hound stalks from the shadows. Its head comes up to my ribs—no way my dumb cage would have contained it. Blistered skin shines through patches of matted black fur. Blue, glowing acid drips from its eyes and maw as it targets my sisters, lifting its nose to sniff. It gives me an assessing look, dismisses me and surges for the cage.

A hoarse battle cry rips from my throat as I run to intercept, sweeping up my sword. *Look here! Not them.* Dropping to a knee, I slide beneath the beast as it soars upward, over my head, toward the cage. I raise my sword, intending to disembowel, but a drop of acid hits my cheek. I flinch, and my sword glances off a rib.

But it's enough to let the monster know I'm the problem, not the twins. It twists as it lands and attacks before I can formulate a plan.

*"Your plan is your muscle memory."* Rory's voice cuts deep from my past.

Except I haven't practiced in a while. I've been lazy. My muscles barely remember how to work. The hound's paws hit my chest, and we soar backward—my spine jars against the damp earth and rotten leaves. The sword is knocked from my hand. More acid flicks from its eyes, splashing my face, searing pain into my body. I wrap my hands around its neck, holding the immense weight back with shuddering arms. *I'm too weak.* A moment of panic turns my bones to ice. Bleak thoughts try to push through.

*Dagger. Sword. Grab something.* My gaze flicks to the side. A haunting howl cuts through the air, diverting the Well Hound's attention. I retrieve my boot-strapped dagger and plunge it into the mangey beast's heart. A muffled gurgling sound spills from its throat and then fire explodes over my hand when it bleeds acid. Gasping, I drop the dagger and try to shove the body away, but I'm too clumsy with a blistering hand. Burning leather at my chest means the acid has reached the armor beneath my shirt. I can't let it get further. A surge of adrenaline allows me to heave the body off. It scampers to the side, panting, looking at me with disbelief.

I scramble to retrieve my sword just as something large and white crashes into the gully. Knowing I can only face one target at a time, I choose the hound to finish off but find it collapsed on its side.

Quickly twisting back to face the newer threat, I lower my

sword and exhale as his calming scent hits me. Dad. He sniffs and snarls at what he's assessed but then paces to the cage's base. Holly clings to the rope. Hazel's eyes flare wide, like she's having the time of her life.

"Daddy!" she squeals, tilting the cage in her haste to get down. "We hunting!"

The air shimmers around the wolf, and he shifts into a nude, powerfully built male with long silver hair and a scruffy dark beard. He glares down at me, hands flexing, veins in his warrior's arms bulging. The luminescent, Well-blessed mating marks on his arm remind me that my mother is psychic. She would have seen this problem and sent him here to intervene.

I swallow. "Hey, Dad."

"What were you *thinking*?" he growls, gesturing to the twins and then behind me. "Taking children on a *hunt*!"

"They followed me."

"Followed you?" His eyes widen. "Who was babysitting?"

Defiance builds like a volcano about to erupt. Sizzling behind me tugs my gaze around—white fangs flash amidst a black face, coming straight at me. Shit. *Not dead.* The Well Hound is very much alive. Time slows. My life flashes before my eyes, and instead of attacking, I only think that I'm not done yet. I'm not finished with this world. I have a purpose—I just haven't found it yet.

Tinger vaults from the side, stabbing antlers into the monster's flank, knocking it off course. Sharp teeth snap the air beside my ear. I slice its carotid clean through, then dart away from the acidic spill of blood. It dies so rapidly that manabeeze erupt before it hits the ground. The gully fills with soft, ethereal light as tiny portions of its soul hunt for freedom through the leaves, searching for the path to rejoin the Cosmic Well.

My heart pounds so fast that I feel woozy. But I came here for one thing, and even though I fucked everything else up, I'll be damned if I leave without it. Ignoring my father's wrath, I scramble to find my discarded satchel, pull an empty jar from the bag, and return to the hound.

"Willow!" Dad calls.

"The twins are fine!" I shout back, determined to catch every last floating manabee before they're gone for good.

I am a trembling cocktail of guilt, adrenaline, and triumph as I fill one jar and start on a second.

*"Willow!"*

"They followed me here!" I shriek, gathering as many glowing balls as possible without one hitting me in the chest. "For Crimson's sake," I continue. "I didn't *ask* them to come, and when they turned up, I kept them safe. And I fucking killed the hound!"

*You should be proud of me.*

"Squirt," he murmurs. "It's Tinger."

I tense. Hold my breath. His tone changed. I glance at a small cream shape motionless at the base of his fern. *No.*

"NO!" I drop the jar and run to my furry friend. My *only* friend. Bright-red dots spot his fur. Where is the wound? I can't find the wound. He pants hard and fast. Still alive, but—my throat constricts as his eyes meet mine, and I see everything reflected in the dark, shining depths. No longer sharp and shrewd, but fading.

I failed.

"You saved me, Ting," I cry. "Don't go. I need you."

*Need you to keep saving me.*

"Help him," I beg, glancing at my father as he lowers my sisters from the cage. "Please, Dad. He doesn't deserve to die for my mistake. Heal him."

Sad yellow eyes meet mine. I know the answer before he speaks, but hearing it still hurts.

"I don't have that kind of healing gift," he reminds me.

When I turn back, Tinger's little chest no longer inflates. His tiny-lashed eyes are closed. Tears blur my vision. I can't focus. Can't think. Can't deal. The last of the Well Hound's manabeeze are gone. We're left in dank, acid-scented gloom.

"There's no wound," I mutter, running my fingers over his frail body. "How can I stop the bleeding if there's no wound?"

"He's old." My father's soft tone cuts me like a knife. "His heart probably gave out."

"No."

"Willow . . ."

"He *saved* me," I whisper harshly. "He never stopped protecting me."

After my horrendous battle mistake, Rory helped me escape on an airship. But Cloud, a psychopathic Guardian chased us down. They used to be star-crossed lovers, but something happened to make them enemies. Somehow Rory and I ended up overboard.

Cloud caught us, one in each hand, but he wasn't strong enough to lift us both onto the deck. Rory knew he would never let her go, for my sake. So she stabbed his hand. He let go, and she fell into the deep ceremonial lake, never resurfacing. I don't remember him flying me to shore with his crow shifter wings. I only remember the rain of blood after he killed every human on that airship in retaliation.

And I remember Tinger bravely hopping across the sand to keep me company until my family arrived. He's hardly left my side since.

"What have I done?" My words are ash on my tongue.

Nothing is worth this. *Nothing.*

A drifting ball of light breaks through my blurry tears. I wipe my eyes, clearing my vision to ensure I'm not dreaming. We all thought Tinger was mortal, but a single manabee has popped from his body. It's tiny, but it's something.

*He's something.*

I scramble to find the fallen jar and toss the hound's manabeeze like garbage. With all the care in the world, I gently coax Tinger's precious floating memory into the jar and secure the cork lid. Then I collapse by his side and weep.

My emotions are flayed as I return home later that evening. Even the acid burns on my body don't hurt as much as my heart.

Candlelight flickers in the windows. My parents must be waiting.

I sit on the porch settee, my head in my hands.

I fucked up. They don't need to tell me again. The last hour was filled with Haze berating me while Peaches cried over Tinger's wrapped body. Both victims of the Unseelie High Queen, Peaches found solace in Tinger's friendship and quirky little ways before I did. She wasn't afraid of him like most fear wolpertingers. She claimed him as her own and helped him escape. She once told me she'd caught him rolling in her underwear when they lived at the Obsidian Palace. When I discovered him doing the same thing to mine, Peaches and I giggled over how gross that was.

But now Tinger is gone, it seems funny. Cute. Sad. I keep remembering the adorable, quirky things he used to do. He'll never do them again.

The shame of telling Peaches what I'd done, to see the disappointment in Haze's eyes, the devastation in hers, was something I'll never forget.

*"I'm so sorry,"* I'd croaked, offering my apology for them to claim as a debt.

Haze loomed over his petite mate as she sobbed. She never looked so fragile as in that moment. Never so helpless as she silently stroked the tiny, swaddled form. Peach-colored hair stuck to her tear-stained pale cheeks, but neither Haze nor their daughter moved to interrupt the grieving woman.

Jasmine, five years younger than me but already taller, glared at me with such hatred for my negligence—at least, that's what I saw. And they didn't even know I'd robbed them this morning.

I offered Tinger's manabee to Peaches.

*"He had mana,"* I explained. *"He wasn't as old as we assumed. Wasn't completely mortal."*

I intended it to be a consolation, but all it did was make my mistake seem so much worse. Tinger had *mana* left. He might have seemed old, but that tiny drop of magic proved he might have lived for decades.

I press my hand against my shirt. Beneath it, a new glass vial containing his spark dangles from a cord around my neck. They refused to accept the manabee, instead telling me to hold onto it. They never outright blamed me.

Which is why it's all on me.

I should have known better.

The front door opens, and my father sticks his head out. Now fully clothed, he looks at my raw, wounded face and frowns. "You didn't see a healer."

"I washed my wounds in the temple fountain."

The water is infused with mana. It helps heal. Soaking in it would have been better, but I haven't taken a swim or a bath since Rory died.

His frown deepens, and he gestures for me to come inside. I sigh and get to my feet. Time to face the firing squad. How much worse can it get?

When I shuffle into the kitchen, I find my mother sitting at the small wooden dining table. My stolen mana stones are laid out before her.

*Shit.*

I drop onto a chair opposite her. My father lurks in the doorway. Even in casual clothes, he is a menacing presence.

"Rush," my mother chides, eyes glued to the stones. "Join us."

He grumbles but strides over, scrapes a chair across the floor, and sits. They cut an imposing sight with matching blue fated mate marks on their arms. His shirt can't contain his broad shoulders. His long silver hair is pulled back to reveal tufted shifter ears that twitch in vexation. His alpha gaze is impossible to hold for long.

Next to him, my mother seems delicate, with long fiery hair that's always disheveled. She was in her mid-twenties when the nuclear winter froze everything, including her, two thousand years ago. Freckles sprinkle her flawless skin. She's stunning, tenacious, and loyal. When my father found her thawed and washed up on the shores of a lake, he was covered in curse marks and invisible to everyone but her.

I was conceived during that curse, and even though they're now blessed, I'm far from it.

She stares at the collection of stones with a far-off look in her eyes.

"Clarke?" my father prompts.

"Hmm?" She moves the stones around, sorting them into collections. Her mind has wandered. We're used to it. Sometimes she's here, sometimes distracted—deep within a psychic vision or on her way to receiving one.

Dad's dark brows lower, and he turns the full force of his displeasure on me. "What do you have to say for yourself?"

Despite his ageless appearance, his tone reminds me that he's not twenty-five. He's a few centuries old, has seen many wars, and suffered much.

"Are the twins okay?" I ask.

"They're fine," he grits out. "That's not the point, and you know it."

That wasn't what I was getting at, but it's useless to defend myself now.

I have millions of questions. Why me? What did I do to deserve being curse-born to two perfectly heroic parents? Why was I chosen from millions as the obsession for six soul-stealing, freakishly beautiful, and corrupt males? Why did Rory sacrifice her life for mine? Why did she think I was worth saving when the Well decided I wasn't, when it took back the power it gifted me at birth?

But I hold my tongue. I always do with them. Tinger was my only confidant.

"Can I go to bed now?"

"Go to . . .?" Dad is baffled, his mouth agape.

My muscles cramp under the strain of stifling the urge to fight. The only trait worth anything in my soul is resilience—this strange ability to wake up day after day, to push back when someone holds me down. With the rate things are going, I'm not sure how much longer it will last.

"What about these stones?" He gestures roughly at the collection. "Why are you stealing when you could have just asked? We're all on the same side here, Willow."

How do I tell him that I can't trust anyone? How do I tell him that my decade with the enemy was filled with Nero repetitively tampering with my thoughts, so I would forget the trauma of killing, only to bring them back to life and be attacked all over again? Sometimes, the victims were animals, sometimes innocent humans dragged from the streets. I still feel sick when I remember them walking into the garden with grubby, awe-struck faces, thinking they'd won a prize to meet their president.

There is much about my time in Crystal City I don't reveal. Some of it is too painful to relive. But mostly, I know my parents blame themselves for not seeing the depraved depths of the Six's plan to claim me as their queen.

I tell myself it was the taint on the Well that blocked my mother's magic from working clearly. She had to trust six Guardians who were supposed to be heroes. But it was all lies. The six Sluagh who lived in this house were villains in sheep's clothing.

I might have escaped being their queen, but it wasn't without a cost.

I frown when I notice more gouges on the table top. More counting. The air thickens with alpha power and tastes like a storm. My father sees me swipe one of the marks and must know who made them.

He snarls, "If I ever see them again, I'll kill them."

"Good," I return. "I'll help you."

"No, you won't," he growls. "Because I forbid you to go anywhere near them again. Right, Clarke?"

My mother finally looks up. Something in her eyes gives me pause. Then she glances at her mate and sighs. "You both know they're gone."

Dad's jaw clenches. He hates not knowing how to fix something.

"I'm throwing this out." He jabs a finger on the table. "We've been busy after the twins were born, but it's time. The sooner we erase all evidence of their existence, the better."

"Is that what you want me to do?" I whisper. "Erase my past too?"

"Are you telling me you *want* to keep reminders of them?" Disgust rolls off his tongue. He'd probably burn the house down if he knew what's hidden in my room.

"Why this one?" My mother holds up the jade.

I shrug. "Why not?"

She places it down. "You'll return these to Peaches."

"Fine."

"Have a little respect, Willow." Dad's voice is deep and full of reproach. "Why can't you find something useful to do with your time?"

Harsh. And unfair. "Because I'm only good at one thing, and you won't let me do it."

"Surely there's something meaningful around here you can do. Stealing is not the answer."

"It was good enough for Mom."

His eyes flash with a feral light. "It was different in the old world. She was alone, manipulated, and homeless. Don't compare her situation to yours."

"I guess two out of three isn't so bad, right?"

A puzzled look enters his eyes, swiftly followed by hurt.

My chair scrapes the wooden floorboards as I stand. "I'm tired."

Mom joins me while Dad storms off with a haggard expression. I swear the air parted to avoid his wrath. He's slain more souls than I have, eaten his prey, and ripped out their throats, yet I baffle him. I want to go to him, to hug him and tease him, to wrestle and play with him like I did as a child. Things were so much simpler then. We had a few good years and then I ruined it by getting kidnapped. Now he finally has the chance of happiness with two perfect little girls who can actually shift into wolves like him.

I'm ruining that, too.

"Willow."

My mother's voice stops me at the door. I turn, surprised to find her holding the green stone.

"Keep this one." She places it in my palm. Warmth radiates through my cold, tired bones. The blisters left from the acid seem to ache more beneath her scrutiny.

"Why?"

She tenderly wipes messy hair from my face, focusing her healing gift on my wounds. The pain starts ebbing but then suddenly returns. She gives a self-deprecating shake of her head and steps away.

"I shouldn't have done that without your permission." She then asks hopefully, "Do you want me to heal the wounds?"

I blink rapidly, unsure how to reply. She's never asked before; honestly, I expected the same reaction from her as my father. I expected more . . . I don't know . . . more chastisement over my recklessness.

"My mom never believed in me," she says softly. "My visions embarrassed her. Back then, magic was a trick from charlatans and performers. It made me doubt myself. When I foresaw my father growing ill, I failed to push him to get help. He died. When you came along, I promised myself I would never ignore my instincts again. I tried everything to keep you safe—to be the opposite of my mother."

"I know." I shake my head. "You're both doing your best to support me."

She takes my good hand. "What I'm trying to say is that I fucked up."

I lift my gaze. "What?"

"We're still doing too much for you. Even Thorne tries to stop you from hurting yourself by refusing to let you in his squad. But I see now that the only way to show belief is to support you while you learn from your mistakes, not stop you from making them."

Tinger's face flashes in my mind, and I wince.

My throat clogs. "My mistakes ruin lives."

"Oh, honey." She pulls me into her embrace like a child. And damn, I lean into her warmth, craving the touch of kin I'm so used to holding at arm's length.

"I'm sorry you hurt like this," she mumbles. "Being a parent sucks and growing up sucks too. I keep forgetting that in my time, someone your age was living out of home and well into her career—often with her own family. It's different for fae. Now that I am one, time has slowed for me. But for you, it's sped up. We're crowding you, blocking you from the sun."

*It is not night when we see your face.*

That's what the Sluagh said to me on the battlefield. Was that before or after they called me nothing? My mind races. Fear wraps around my lungs, squeezing until I can't breathe.

"Nothing grows in the shade, Willow. Your father and I need to step back."

Does she want me to leave? For a split second, I wonder if this is her way of getting rid of me—an excuse to be free of the burden of having a daughter like me. I don't belong here any more than I did in Crystal City. No one understands me.

"I'm not good at making my own choices," I whisper, looking into her eyes.

"You are perfect, my love. Trust your heart and know—" Her throat clogs with emotion. "Know that we will always love and support you no matter where that heart takes you, for however long. There is nothing you can do that will change that." She sighs at the blisters on my hand. "Will you let me heal that?"

I sniff and then nod. She takes my hand, and cool relief washes over my raw skin, healing the burns until I can move my fingers like before. But for some reason, I can't let her erase the small acid wounds on my face. If they're gone, it feels like Tinger is gone, too. I'm not ready for that.

As if sensing my thoughts, she places her palm over my sternum and the vial containing Tinger's manabee. "Cherish his memory, and he'll live in you forever."

# CHAPTER
# FOUR
## WILLOW

Leaning against my closed bedroom door, I survey the clutter. Every nook and cranny is filled with objects I value.

*"Worse than a crow's nest,"* my mother once said, attempting to clean it up.

I'd bared my teeth and forced her to drop the driftwood. It wasn't much to her, but it was from the shore of the ceremonial lake when I first met Tinger and is shaped like an antler.

*"That's because it's not a nest,"* my father had proudly replied. *"It's a den."*

I take after him more than I like to admit; he collects little wooden carvings he's made. This nest, this den, is my haven. Whether the items have been stolen, given, or found, they all mean something to me. Piles of trinkets and books on adventurous escapades make me feel closer to Alfie, my dead human friend. Bottles of perfume on a dresser are my favorite scents. A whetstone and silver dagger that belonged to Rory. I'm not supposed to have that last one, considering it's contraband, but no one has confiscated it yet.

The window is open enough for a small wolpertinger to fit through. I stride across the room, slam the pane down, and close the curtains until I'm in complete darkness. I don't want light. I don't want to see the empty spaces he should fill.

Crawling onto my bed, I circle and pluck the blankets around me until I feel cocooned, then clutch the jade worry stone and rub my thumb over the groove. The rhythmic action takes me back to Crystal City. I would spend restless nights awake, stroking the stone and praying for rescue.

The taint on the Well blocked all communication from Elphyne in the latter years. I grew isolated from home. I relied more on Rory and Alfie to keep me sane amongst the never-ending murder lessons.

My sleepy thoughts turn to Alfie, and I smile. He was the same age as me, but with copper hair and freckles. He rose in the ranks of Nero's army to become an aviation captain. The night before the battle, he asked me to marry him. Apparently, Nero had already approved the union, so it felt like I had to say yes. But he didn't know I intended to escape to Elphyne. I sometimes wonder if things had worked out differently, would he have given up his captaincy to be with me? Would he have abandoned his beliefs so I could go home? He was my closest friend—I like to think yes. If not for his friendship, I'd have tried to escape Crystal City earlier.

My fingers wrap around the pendant on my chest, and my eyes drift closed. When I open them, I'm not in my bed. I'm not even in Elphyne.

I'm in a town square surrounded by dancing couples wearing luxurious, impeccable winter fashion. Flowing velvet dresses are variations of green and brown. Long hair is loose and adorned with sparkling gems or strings of pearls. Fur-lined ornamental capes fly as couples twirl. Males in tailored suits with ornate embroidery have their hair neatly styled. Above the heads of the crowd, I glimpse walkways high up in the trees. Buildings seamlessly blend with the branches until I'm not quite sure if they're real. Webs sparkling with jewels dangle between structures. Jovial music ebbs and flows from somewhere, carried on the wind. At my feet, cobblestones are interspersed with the same jade as my worry stone.

I also wear a flowing dress, and my feet are clad in glittering, soft, warm slippers. Couples glance at me and hurry away, never breaking the flow of their graceful dance. A space grows around me, and I feel exposed. Alone. Awkward.

"Where am I?" I whisper, turning in circles, feeling dizzier by the second.

Suddenly, I'm not alone, but in the arms of the rookie Guardian who approached me this morning. His blond hair is tied with a teal ribbon, the same color as his embroidered suit. He smiles down at me as though I'm his world, and I recoil, trying to pull away. He feels wrong. This all feels wrong. I break away but spin right into the arms of the crow shifter Guardian, who whispers something mockingly over my head. They pull me into a dance, twirling and spinning. The colors around me blur. Nausea rolls in my stomach.

I don't want this.

But my feet won't move. I can't escape. The toes of my leather slippers drag on cobblestones as I'm carried around, paraded before laughing faces. "You're not even fae anymore," says one.

"But you're not human either."

"You don't belong in any world."

"You'll never belong."

I try to scream, to resist, but nothing comes out. I'm paralyzed—whirled and twirled at their whims, blurring and flowing to someone else's dance. The music grows faster and faster, but then suddenly stops.

Storm clouds gather on the horizon. Shadows darken the streets. Ice-cold wind buffets my face. A deep, entrancing voice whispers, "There you are, our queen."

My mocking dance partners disappear. My feet touch solid ground. A ray of light breaks through the clouds to reveal six dark figures falling gracefully around me, their angelic owners twisting to kneel at my feet. They bow like knights, their wings spilling like silken shadows behind them. I am the center of their circle.

This feels familiar. Like I've been here before.

Their faces are beautiful carved renditions of perfection. Each more heart-stoppingly handsome than the next. The one with long dark hair has luminous skin like carved crystal. Sensuous lips curve at my surprise. He offers an elegant hand and murmurs in a voice oh so intimate, "Will you dance with us?"

Another says behind me, his fingers grazing my hips. "Will you be ours?"

My breath catches as I'm swept into arms, pulled into another's warm embrace. It's not like I imagined. Instead of cold fear, I feel safe and cherished. Accepted. Needed. Loved. A slow, tentative smile dares to touch my lips, and I start to float. Now I remember this feeling.

Five years ago, I connected with these six fallen angels on the battlefield. I found understanding, acceptance, need, and desire through one meeting of the eyes. They are beings trapped in the darkness.

*Yes, little wolf. It is not night when we see your face.*

My dance partner changes, his face morphing between the six, but he is always one in my arms. Always hauntingly beautiful. Their wings spread wide, flutter, and take us dancing above the square, spinning and spinning, laughing and singing. We are the envy of every beating heart. The females want to be me. The males want to be *with* me.

*This can't be real.*

Everyone should fear them. They should hate me.

*This must be a dream.*

The intrusive thought slams into me, and I fall. My angels tumble, too, swirling like autumn leaves in a tempest. They become devils, two with tails and horns. A glowing skull flickers beneath their skin. Sad wholly black eyes beseech me as if to say, "Don't leave."

"You're not our queen," the devil snarls in my ear.

Their words are lost in the musical wind. Rejection slams into my chest like a blade, cutting through my ribs and piercing the beating muscle beneath. It spasms. A scream erupts from somewhere deep within my lungs.

Jackknifing up, I wake in my bed, my blankets in disarray. As if I can stop my rapidly beating heart, I press my hand against my chest but feel Tinger's pendant. Exhaling, I close my eyes against my room's judgmental stare.

"It was a dream." A nightmare. That's all.

I felt sorry for myself before I fell asleep. I even thought of the Six then. In my dream, they looked different—almost human initially, but still monsters at the end.

I'd forgotten what they'd said to me five years ago . . . how, for a moment, I'd believed them. *It is not night when we see your face.* One had grabbed my ankle to stop me from fleeing up the airship's ladder with Rory. He must have expected the Well-blessed mating bond to trigger like it had with my parents, but he was dismayed when no twin marks appeared on our arms. Decades of machinating and manipulation to sculpt me into their perfect mate were wasted.

"*You're nothing,*" he spat at me, the battle still raging around us. His words hurt me so badly that I hurled my own back. *"You're monsters."*

I shiver and wrap my blankets around me.

"Just a weird dream," I scoff, shaking my head. "Ridiculous."

A foreign voice whispers through the shadows, "Yes, you are rather ridiculous."

I tense. "Who's there?"

The scent of lilacs and lichen increases.

"Titania, the Queen of Dreams. Who else?" A female emerges from the shadows. She is stunning, cut from the same luminous crystal as Legion was in my dream. Yet where his hair was a midnight waterfall, hers is rich brown and full of life. Inner warmth stains her cheeks with a blush. *She's flawless.* Her diaphanous dress is spun moonlight, adorned with intricate embroidery and gemstones. A fur stole draping her shoulders rustles in a breeze I can't feel. But it's her tiara that catches my attention. It's set with five types of gemstones. Oddly mismatched against her glowing, ethereal attire—a red stone, a milky stone, a dull granite, a black onyx, and—I gasp—a green marble. Irish Jade.

"How utterly subterranean of me..." She looms over my bed, lip curling with disgust as she grips my face between her forefinger and thumb. Pain slices into me like a hot blade. I try to move, but find my limbs are heavier than lead. Just like in my dream, I'm powerless. "... to think you, a mere mortal, as a rival to my radiance." She leans down and whispers, "Dear, are you even aware of the gift you gave me? You left those six precious jewels practically swaying in the cruelty you so carelessly cast. When hearts as beaten as theirs dare to rise on the wings of dreams, it merely requires a whisper, and their fragile hopes fall like autumn leaves. The last person they thought would be so heartless was their one true queen."

She shoves my head against the pillow, then she lets go. A

sardonic laugh peels from her throat. It cuts as deeply as her words. It says they were right. I am nothing. I am more monstrous than them. Eventually, she sighs and steps away.

"Now I am their beacon in the darkness," she declares, voice sweet and sour like rancid wine. "I am the answer to their deepest yearnings—a realm where no one looks upon them as nightmares, where they are venerated like radiant deities. I've witnessed your tragic dreams, dearest. They're ghastly and teeming with wild, violent tempests. You belong with the other nightmares. It's high time your realm acknowledges that, too. When you rise on the morrow, your visage will mirror the ugliness lurking within your heart." The sting of a thousand ants nips my skin, and I gasp, finally wrenching my gaze from her face. Her next words fade with her into the shadows. "Oh, and before I forget . . . your tongue shall be bound from revealing who cursed you and why. Relish the remainder of your fleeting dance beneath the sun, mortal child."

A RAY OF SUN SLICES ACROSS MY CLOSED EYES, AND I TURN AWAY FROM the window with a groan. I had so many nightmares last night. It feels like I never slept. They were so real. That moldy lilac smell still clings to my memory. I toss my blanket off and slide my legs over the edge of the bed, careful not to wake Tinger.

My breath catches.

The weight of the pendant grows heavy, dragging my neck and shoulders down. Suddenly, I can't breathe. I'm suffocating. Gasping. He's dead because of my negligence.

*Why can't you find something useful to do?*

Forcing air into my abused lungs, I lurch from the bed. But my stomach rolls like I'm riding on waves. I barely make it to the toilet in my ensuite before retching. Nothing comes out. Feeling hot and sweaty, I rest my cheek on the cool porcelain until the dizziness subsides. I don't want to get up.

I don't want to face another day feeling like I don't belong. Not without Tinger.

For too long, I stare at the walls of my bathroom. Not all homes in Elphyne have aqueducts and plumbing. The bathtub is heated with mana stones. After what happened to Rory, I can't stand being submerged in water. But right now, I need to feel something other than like a sinking stone. I need to prove I'm not the sum of my fears.

I drag myself to the empty tub and climb in but can't bring myself to turn on the faucet—another failure. Soon, even the hard walls of the tub feel stifling, so I climb back out. I wash my face in the basin, wincing as my fingers unwittingly hit the small acid scars on my left side. When I lift my gaze to check my reflection in the mirror, I scream.

# FIVE

## WILLOW

My reflection instills horror in my soul. Then disgust. Then shame.

*When you rise on the morrow, your visage will mirror the ugliness lurking within your heart.*

The voice from my nightmares was real.

Hardly able to breathe, I touch my face and test all the new ugly places that never existed before. I'm hideous. The scars are bigger, bulging, ropy and twisted. Everything is out of proportion and crooked.

Pounding at my bedroom door makes me jump. The mirror vibrates, and my horrible visage blurs like a disturbed reflection in a pond.

*"Willow?"* My father's voice booms from the other side. The doorknob rattles.

"Don't come in!" I shriek. "I'm naked!"

I'm ugly.

"Oh." His tone muffles. He probably cursed under his breath. *Not another drama from Willow*, I'm sure he's thinking. "I thought I heard a scream."

"I'm fine." My forced, cheerful tone makes me wince. A tiny shadow darts across the floor and disappears beneath my bed, giving me the perfect excuse. "It was just a spider."

"You want me to kill it?"

"I can kill my own bugs," I snap back, irritated despite my situation.

A stretch of silence follows. I sense him standing there but can't move my feet to find clothes. I can't let him see me like this.

"I know you can, Squirt." His deep voice is softer. "You were always better at that than me."

When I finally dare to walk to the door, he's gone. I lean back against the smooth surface and sink to the floor, my head in my hands. Is this misery my destiny? I was conceived when my father was cursed. Maybe I still am.

My tired gaze lands on a smooth green stone on the floor beside my bed. I keep returning to it. I'm drawn to it. Why?

The dream queen's crown had the stone set amongst others. Earlier in the dream, I'd danced on cobblestones made from something similar. It *was* a dream . . . wasn't it?

I gingerly touch my face, hopefully testing to see if my eyes deceived me, but when my fingertips graze over the old, fine scars on my left side, I find them thicker, knotty, and bulging. The shape of my face feels lopsided and warped.

The dream was real.

I crawl toward my bed and pick up the stone, turning it over in the shaft of sunlight. My mother wanted me to keep it. Did she know this would happen?

At the table, when Dad and I argued about the Six, she said they were gone. Not dead. I'd always wondered, but their disappearance had been so sudden and complete that everyone assumed they'd somehow died when Queen Maebh sent all the souls from the Wild Hunt into the undead so they could be killed.

My mother, the most powerful psychic in Elphyne, handed

me a portal stone to a place where the Six might be alive. And then she told me to follow my heart, to make my own mistakes. As soon as the realization hits, the tugging in my chest increases. I know it to be true. They're alive and on the other side of this green stone.

Movement at my side. The spider crawls out from beneath my bed. It doesn't run away. It scuttles toward me as though I'm its target. My fist comes down hard, squashing it.

Almost everything has been taken from me. The last thing I need is a poisonous bite to take my health. When I lift my hand, I marvel at the tiny black blob with enough poison to take me, a veritable giant, down. The spider knew the odds were stacked against it as it crawled toward me, yet it kept coming.

I'm envious of that courage. I have *six* giants of my own. They're beautiful, ancient soul-sucking beings who have a hive mind and are keepers of the Wild Hunt—the horde of wicked souls they punish. They're feared because killing them is nigh on impossible. They can only be tamed.

I dreamed the Six were normal—beautiful, revered, and admired by the crowd dancing around us. Titania claimed she made their deepest yearnings come true, to exist in a realm where they weren't looked upon as nightmares.

*Are you even aware of the gift you handed to me?*

I called them monsters, and she swooped in to claim them. I'll bet that vision was real. Her words were real. I'm sitting in ruin while they're with her, living like radiant kings . . . their dark hearts hidden behind whatever narrative she's spun.

Fuck them. Fuck all of them.

I might be small, mortal, and weak next to their might, but if a spider dares to face its foe head-on, then so can I. Crawling to my bedside table, I pull down Rory's silver-plated dagger. The hilt fits in my palm like it was made for me. Rory was like the spider. The mighty fae fist should have repeatedly squashed her, but she prevailed. She survived until she *chose* to stab Cloud's hand, forcing him to let go so that I could live.

She taught me everything she knew . . . and left me with this magic-cutting metal blade. I might not know much about the Sluagh, but I know plenty about Guardians. I know that even though they're blessed to hold metal and use magic at the same time, they can still die if the metal pierces their flesh. This dagger is my poison.

An hour later, I'm in my room packing my bag for a trip into the unknown. Without tears left to cry, rage has become my constant companion. It bubbles beneath my skin, making me aware of every horrible bulge and crooked feature.

The Six's obsession with me ruined my life. I hate them so much that I can't see straight. They can't get away with this. My plan to kill them depends on bringing Rory's dagger with me because there's no guarantee this new realm has steel blades. It could be confiscated, melted down at the forge, or locked away. This is why I broke into my mother's room after she left this morning. Perhaps the Well was shining down on me because my luck finally turned when I found a jar of Guardian manabeeze on her dresser—clearly labeled and ripe for the taking. They'll allow forbidden metal to pass through a portal.

My plan to track down the Six has never felt more right.

The rucksack weighs me down and rubs against my bone sword strapped between my shoulder blades, but I don't have another way to carry it. String secures a scarf over my face, hiding my ugly truth. I don't want to draw attention.

A bitter laugh puffs the silk at my mouth. No wonder the Six want me as their hive's queen. We have the same hideous, nightmarish insides.

There's only one thing left to collect. After we moved in here, I found a collection of charcoal portraits beneath a loose panel in the wall. I should have burned them, but something held me back. The artwork is stunning, and the artist took painstaking lengths to capture the personality of each subject. Each is labeled with a number and a name.

Knowing that one of the Six is psychic, I'm sure these were placed here on purpose. But I'm hijacking that purpose. I'm using these portraits to track them down, and when I find them . . . my thoughts trail off as I unfold the first sketch. That traitorous tug in my chest lurches at the sight of *him*.

"The First" is Legion. His long dark hair spills from a widow's peak, framing a hauntingly beautiful face. Even in black and white, he is arresting. His lips are full. His nose is aristocratic. At first glance, he's too pretty to exist. But something happens the longer I stare. Like a mirage, my perception changes. His beauty seems to harden into demanding lines and harsh angles. I see a ruthless leader who will stop at nothing to get what he wants.

"The Second" is Bodin. His skin is darker, his bone structure sharp and formidable, yet still so perfectly symmetrical. The sides of his head are shaved to reveal fae ears. Long dark hair is swept from his forehead in structured sections that might be braids or locks. Aunty Rory occasionally wrangled her afro into cornrows. Bodin's are tied in a knot at his crown. Something about his eyes makes me feel trapped, breathless. It's like he's there on the other side of the paper, promising dark things.

Shaking the feeling, I study the next and commit his features to memory.

"The Third" is Emrys. Close-cropped silver hair offsets dark eyebrows, both striking against pale skin. His fathomless black eyes instill fear into my soul, and I can't explain why he's more frightening than the others. Perhaps he was hewn from a different rock, carved with angry, hate-filled strokes. Black swirling tattoos strangle his neck but don't touch his face, as though the ink is too frightened to go there.

"The Fourth" is Varen. His angular, narrow eyes are framed with thick lashes. His cheekbones are high, and his jaw is square. The inches-long dark hair is swept from his forehead but shaved at the sides like Bodin's. His lips are tipped in a small half-smile as though the artist said something amusing. Each of the Six is achingly beautiful, but Varen seems almost feminine. Maybe delicate is a better word. It almost makes me feel at ease with him. I'll bet he's the worst.

"The Fifth" is Fox. The dimples throw me, and his short, curved horns almost seem cute. He feels like Legion's troublesome younger brother, despite them both carrying the ageless fae features. His short dark hair is ruffled around the horns. Mischief dances in his eyes. The longer I stare, the more dark hunger seeps through. This passionate, ruthless side of him screams so loudly that I almost drop the portrait, fearing it's enchanted.

Finally, "The Sixth" intrigues me the most. The name Spike has been scratched out and renamed Styx. Short conical spikes decorate the skin above his brows. Long, curved horns sweep back from his head, adding to his otherworldly appeal. It's impossible to tell the color of his skin in a charcoal sketch, but it's closer to the value of Bodin's. My vague memories give me hints of skin almost blue, but with a blush from blood—like the sky at dusk.

A flicker of doubt enters my mind. It's easy to think I am the spider . . . but I squashed that bug effortlessly with my fist. What if I'm making the wrong decision by going after them? What if they're truly unkillable?

I clutch Tinger's pendant and think about his life cut short because of my recklessness. If it weren't for the Six, I would never have been in that situation, hunting for purpose and respect. And Titania? My ugliness? She only attacked me out of spite— one last dig to drive the message home.

The veil over my face itches where the string is too tight. The acid burns are sore and will probably leave a mark. Hatred slams out my doubt. I'm left here looking hideous, and they're still so fucking perfect.

Fuck that.

I don't need to be good-looking to end their lives. I don't even need magic. It takes willpower to refrain from scratching out their eyes on the sketches. But I need the portraits if I'm to hunt them down, so I fold and tuck them neatly into the rucksack.

Then I sneak out my window. With my temper still spiking, I'm not careful. My fur cape catches on the latch, almost sending me toppling backward into my room. *Not a good start, Willow.*

I climb onto the gabled roof beneath my window without attracting attention. Twilight is a good time to move about unseen in Elphyne. Nocturnal fae are waking, and the others are usually winding down. No one notices me climbing down the trellis and creeping onto the lawn that doubles as the Cadre of Twelve training field.

I take one last look around campus, hear the distant sound of water trickling through culverts, and quickly pull out the portal stone. I never know how many manabeeze will be needed, but I think it has something to do with distance and the size of the stone. It ends up taking half a jar to activate, but that's okay. The rest will be enough to activate another portal stone for when I come home.

*If* I come home.

The stone heats in my hand to a scalding temperature, but I don't let go. I pray to the Well this is normal. The smell of ozone burns my nostrils, and a bright light explodes in my hand. I toss the stone into the air, where the light expands to a wide ring of crackling electricity. Shaking my burned palm, I watch as the landscape inside the circle comes into focus, and I gasp. It's green. Not endless white.

Holy shit. This is definitely real. Not a dream.

A dirt path leads into a forest stretching before me. A path means there are people. My heart leaps into my throat.

Guilt hits me hard. This feels like a momentous discovery. Peaches had the stone sitting on her workbench. If I don't tell someone about this now and can't return, they'll never know another place in this world is habitable. But if I do that, then I'm inviting questions and opinions.

A surge of bitter hatred pushes out my reason. No. This is my moment. My revenge. None of these people understand my pain. None were pawns and prisoners the way I was. If they were, and the opportunity to take revenge was given to them, I'm sure they'd take it. Cloud is still out there hunting down humans who robbed him of the chance to kill Rory himself. So, fuck it. If he can get revenge, so can I.

*I'll return*, I promise.

Clutching the half-filled jar of manabeeze, I stride through the portal. Little fire ants scuttle over my skin. Pressure pops in my ears. Light flares so brightly that I close my eyes and still feel like I'm staring at the sun. My palm burns, and I gasp again, sucking in a lungful of acrid portal air, but I keep walking. It's never taken this long to cross a portal. Maybe it's the stolen Guardian manabeeze—maybe the Well is punishing me again for defying the natural order of things.

The bright light fades, cold air bites my nose, and I dare to open my eyes. I'm here. The sky is gray and drizzling with rain. It smells magnificent—like dewy mountain air and blooming flowers. Birds sing melodious, happy tunes. Evergreen leaves on towering trees shiver in the frigid breeze. I drag my cape around my shoulders to fight the arctic temperature.

A grin splits my face as I glance up. The trees are enormous, bigger than I've seen in Elphyne.

"We made it," I tell Tinger, patting the pendant beneath my clothes.

Wait. My hands are empty. My jar of manabeeze is gone. Gasping, I whirl to face the portal, but it's closing. The electrical field grows smaller. I glimpse my mother's vibrant hair—her unreadable face as she taps her chest. Then she's gone, replaced by a tall handsome fae soldier wearing a green embroidered cape.

"You're late," he snarls.

LEGION
THE FIRST

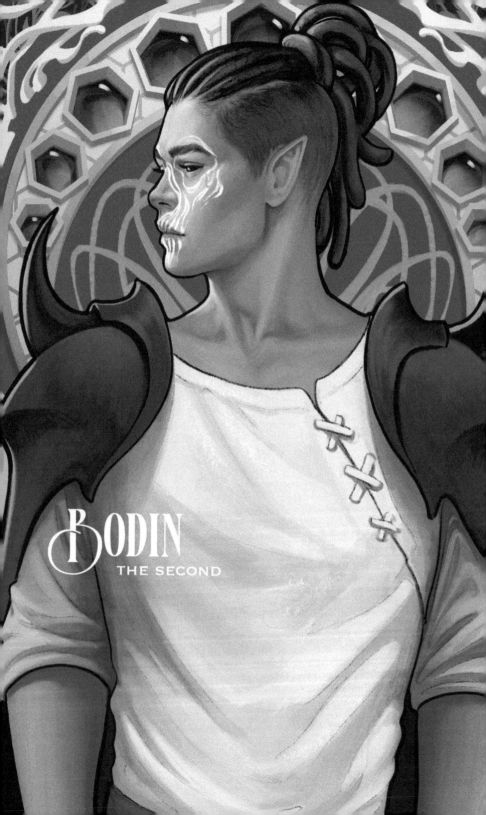

# BODIN
## THE SECOND

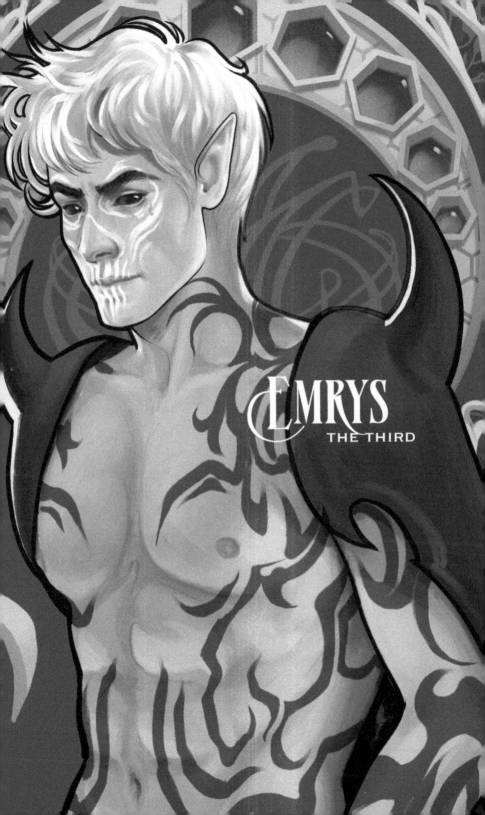

VAREN
THE FOURTH

FOX
THE FIFTH

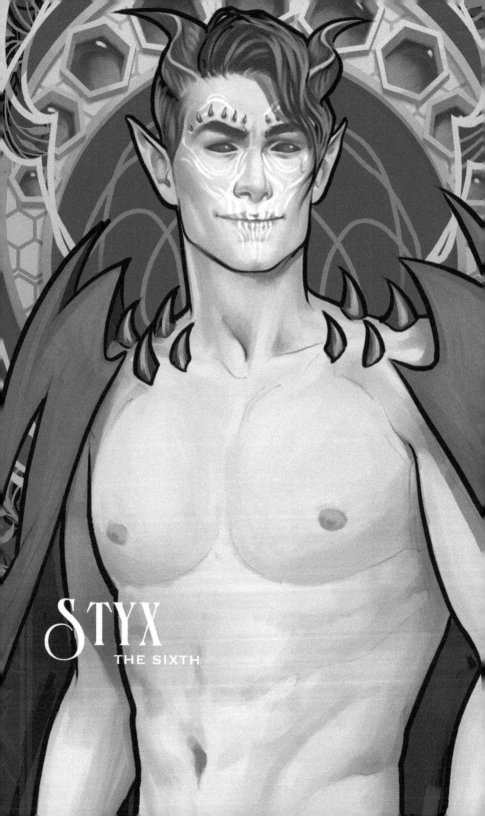

STYX

THE SIXTH

# PART TWO
## AVORLORNA

# CHAPTER

# SIX

## WILLOW

The soldier grabs me by the scruff and shoves me in the opposite direction. I stumble down the dirt path, numb with shock. It's not just a forest surrounding me, but a city built into the trees, like in my dream. The path leads to an arched gate woven from roots and branches. Guards wearing green and holding various weapons scrutinize the surroundings.

Another impatient shove against my rucksack makes me stumble on exposed roots. My hand hovers over the dagger hidden beneath my cape, ready to use it.

But then the soldier grumbles under his breath, "Dreams be damned. Puck will have my brows if more exhibitors arrive."

I don't think I'm in danger. Frowning, I glance at him, and he raises his brows. "Do not dally, mortal. Present your papers to the noble captain."

Papers? My eyes widen.

At the gatehouse, two more green-caped guards wait. One holds a clipboard and stares blankly as he takes in my face scarf. The cold has left its mark on all the guards, from rosy noses and cheeks to clouds blooming from breaths. Pointed elfin ears peek through the tied, russet hair. His brunette companion is equally impeccable. Their uniforms are starched and pressed. Embroidery on the deep-green vests and stiff collar emulates tree roots. Between the woven threads, little crystals and stones dangle. Some are polished to perfection. Others are uncut and raw.

Titania's crown had a mix of stones set in silver. These soldiers also have silver chains swinging from epaulets. If metal isn't outlawed, then I don't like my chances of it being a magic-cutting substance.

"Yet another exhibitor graces us with tardy arrival, Captain Sorrel." His lilting accent is a mix of lyrical and grump.

"Your name and region, traveler?" inquires the russet-haired captain.

The grump yanks off my rucksack. The brunette pats down my front. My first thought is to protect Tinger. My second is of all the weapons I'm hiding. And the third is the mask hiding my ugliness. I don't want them to remove it.

I shove them away. "Don't touch me."

"Now, now. There's no call for discourtesy." Sorrel's lips purse with impatience. "You're already late. Don't make it worse." He points to my veil. "Kindly remove that."

"No."

He blinks rapidly, astounded. "Unless it's donned as a penalty for violating the Old Code, I respectfully advise that you remove your coverings." When I don't move, he gestures with his pen at the brunette. "Briar, might you assist our guest in lifting her guise?"

My pulse quickens. Hiding my face is stupid when the alternative could be imprisonment or worse, but the instinct to protect myself from humiliation is strong. I'm out of my league.

Each guard patrolling the battlements has a wary glint in his eye. They think I'm here to sign up for an exhibition. Maybe I should roll with it.

The brunette stands before me, his astute gaze catching fear in my eyes. Strong hands land on my shoulders from behind. The guard behind me barks, "Now is the time to show your courtesy, traveler."

Still unable to unfreeze, I do nothing as Briar pulls out a knife and slices the string holding the veil around my face. With jerky, impatient tugs, it burns when he peels the silk from my skin. The pain seems to swell the surface of my skin, drawing awareness to every bulging feature and misshapen scar. My fingers fly to the ropy, knotted surface, and I cringe.

Their lips part. Their eyes widen. No one speaks. I want to sink into the ground, to hide beneath the rocks. Fuck the Six. Fuck that stupid queen. I'm going to kill them all. *I hate I hate I hate.*

"Unfortunate, indeed." The captain scribbles something down on his clipboard. "I see why you wish to win the blessing at the Solstice Exhibition."

A blessing? My fingers gravitate to my smarting skin, the knotted scars on the left, and the distorted features on the right. The acid wounds are pinpricks in size but radiate enough pain to fill my whole body. I lick my cracked lips and dare to ask, "What is the blessing?"

"Ah . . ." A wistful smile touches his lips. "We all pine for a dream turned into reality. Is this not true, my esteemed colleagues?"

They all nod and voice eager agreement.

"A dream turned into reality?" I repeat.

"I believe that's what I said." The captain turns back to me, and his tone becomes somber. "But the exhibition tournament is a blessing for mortals only. Even those—" He gestures around my face with barely veiled disgust, pausing as if trying to devise the right, inoffensive word. "Those with less pleasing appearances from the subterranean." He then hands me the fallen scrap of silk and lowers his voice. "Because that's where you'll be, mortal lass, if you don't win. But if you're strong enough to see the exhibition to the end of the Gentle Interlude, at least you'll be alive."

He doesn't seem too worried about my questions, so I ask another. "What's the Gentle Interlude?"

"The winter period where hostilities cease with Nocturna, the Subterranean of Nightmares. However, do not be fooled into believing the Old Code's mandates also cease. Outside the Interlude, those mortals who break the code—such as yourself—would be dealt death."

My gaze narrows. "Is refusing to take part in this Solstice Exhibition a violation?"

"Are you refusing to take part?" He levels his stare on me. "Why are you here, then?"

A shiver skates down my spine. I peer at the soldiers on the wall. They're all handsome, or at least without flaws. There's no way I'll get inside without being noticed.

"I'm here for the exhibition," I assure him.

The captain points to the silk in my hands. "Then this is your sole caution before crossing the threshold. You must not wear that again."

"Why not?"

"Because"—his eyes flash with a glimpse of that danger— "allowing criminals into our military base during wartime would be dimwitted, especially when the Gentle Interlude is on the cusp of beginning. So, if it pleases you, good traveler, the veil must remain off, or kindly do not register. Your choice."

Hardly a choice when the alternative means I'm a criminal.

"This exhibition is the only time we invite illegal immigrants through the gates." Briar gentles his tone and gestures at my face, confirming my suspicion I look like their enemy with this curse. "You'll miss the pageant if you don't arrive at the Nexus by midday. And should you aspire to draw favor from one of the radiant gentry, you must be clean, garbed in proper attire, and presented with flawless deportment, as per the illustrious laws."

"With a countenance such as hers," scoffs the grumpy guard, "the only attention she'll garner is that of chaos. I say we save our eyebrows and dispose of her now. Surely, a watergate is still open somewhere."

Briar's gaze narrows on my ears, and he points at them. "Her ears are of the Folk, not round like the mortals. The Old Code states once the Gentle Interlude begins, we cannot cast aside any of the Folk without a just hearing, even if they hail from the subterranean ranks. For if we do, we mirror their monstrous conduct."

"Unless they attack first." The captain's tone hints at trouble. "Then we're free to use any means necessary to eliminate the chaos."

"She cannot participate in the exhibition if she's one of us," the grump points out.

The captain squints at me. "Well, which is it?"

Confusion batters my mind, but I understand one thing well enough. Winning the prize in this tournament will allow me to kill the Six in one fell swoop . . . *if* I align myself with mortals.

"I have no magic," I reply vaguely, hoping that will be enough for them.

"How did you procure the means to step between the realms if you are mortal yet also of the Folk? Are you a changeling? Have blessings already been bequeathed by the noble gentry? Or are you playing the trickster with your clever countenance?" His eyes crinkle, and he waggles his finger at me. "That's it. Isn't it? You're a tricksy pixie to kick off the festivities. I must say, it's a remarkable mask then. Who sent you? Was it Glen? That scallywag."

My blank face causes his expression to drop with disappointment. I almost feel like I *should* be pranking him as an apology.

He clears his throat. "So then, what is your explanation?"

When conning a mark, my mother always told me that a version of the truth was the best lie. Not that she'd be happy I still use these lessons from my childhood. But she can't take them back.

"I used a magic stone," I answer.

His eyes narrow. "Show me."

"It's somewhere back there." I point to the spot down the path.

The grumpy guard hunts through the grass and finds the spent stone. He tosses it to the captain, who inspects it and says, "Ah. 'Tis an enchanted charm. So, you are a friend of the gentry?"

"Um . . ."

"A charmed protégé? A Shadow apprentice seeking fame and fortune?"

"Sure. Let's go with that."

"Tremendous news!" The captain's excitement sounds like I'm a riddle he's solved. His mood has set the other guards at ease. I guess I'm not enemy enough to worry about. He glances down at his clipboard and checks off a few boxes.

I ask, "Is the prize truly something I dream come true?"

He licks his thumb and peels away a flyer from his clipboard. He hands it to me and answers, "If your dream doesn't break the Old Code, then yes. Before arriving at the Nexus, please cast your eyes over that at your earliest convenience." He stares at me as if waiting for something else. When I remain silent, he sighs. "Fair traveler, what is your name?"

*Fair?* Now, I'm sure they're being patronizing. It leaves a bitter taste in my mouth. I briefly consider a pseudonym, but I'm not here to make friends.

"Willow O'Leary-Nightstalk."

The Six should know I'm coming for them. So be it if signing up for this tournament is the only way I can get through the

70

gates. I'll have more time to ponder the merits once I study this flyer.

He hums in acknowledgment as he notes my name, making eyes at Briar. "O'Leary is quite the mortal name."

"She's one of the *Folk*," Briar insists, gesturing at my ears again.

"Very well, good friend of the gentry, Willow O'Leary-Nightstalk. I assume your purpose is to enter the exhibition tournament?" His brows wing up.

I thought we just went through that. Is this a trick? "Um. Yes, that's right."

He scribbles something down and says, "Once the honorable Briar has inspected you and cleared your person of any objectionable items, you may proceed to enter. Hurry along to the gate platform and take the carriage along the Whispering Wind line. Briar, kindly accompany this fine guest so we may all begin our Gentle Interlude celebrations in earnest." He rubs his brows nervously. "None among us desires to bear Goodfellow's wrath for being a tardy heartbeat."

I allow him to pat me down while the other searches my rucksack. He finds my bone sword and dagger.

"For the tournament?" he confirms.

"Yes."

I hold my breath as the telltale prickle of magic crawls over my skin, then he hands them back to me with a warning. "Record their arrival during registration once you reach the Nexus. Your weapons will be rendered useless within the city gates if you fail to do so."

I give a curt nod and slot my sword into the sheath between my shoulder blades. The uneasy feeling in my stomach grows as I return my dagger to my belt. There's definitely something off with the whole metal thing. I'd assumed two realms on the same planet would live by the same rules set by the Well. This magic source is cosmic.

"What brought your misfortune?"

My eyes meet Briar's. He speaks softly enough that the captain and grump making a mess of my belongings don't notice. It's an odd question, considering people are born with all sorts of appearances. Does he somehow know I've been cursed? I open my mouth to explain, but nothing comes out. I try again, but all I manage is a squeak.

*You can't speak to anyone about your curse.*

A scoff of derision behind me draws my attention. The grumpy soldier found the portraits. Shaking his head with another mocking snort, he drops them and whispers something to the captain I can't catch. They both study me, but the captain shrugs and says, "Leave it."

The guard taps me mockingly. "It appears your earthly possessions are lying about with disregard. Perhaps you should gather them."

*No shit. Because you tossed them everywhere.*

Biting my tongue, I get on my hands and knees and repack my bag.

If I can't hide my unfortunate face, I'll have to deal with worse than this inside the gates. I may as well start steeling my spine now. It's not like I can run away and portal home without manabeeze. When I'm standing, the captain announces, "You're cleared for entry. Welcome to the Radiant City of Avorlorna, and remember to heed my warnings. Have a joyous Interlude."

He gestures at the gates, and the threads of webbed roots crawl away from the center, opening the passage.

"Come along," Briar says, waltzing inside. "I'll escort you to the platform."

It's hard not to look like a fool when I enter the city. A wild magic lives in the air. Branches, vines, creepers, and thorns have claimed the structures as their playthings. Instead of fighting it, the faerie architects have worked with it.

As we head toward the platform, I feel the weight of judgmental gazes on my face. My hands tremble on the flyer. I desperately want to touch the pendant, but force myself to relax with a slow exhale.

A woman cries out in pain. Rhythmic slaps and grunts echo in the street. My senses go on high alert as I scan the people around us. Every time the slap sounds, her cry jolts as though she's hit. A group of well-dressed people gather around a street corner, whispering and watching something beyond my view.

"Someone is being hurt." I frown in horror. "And no one is helping her."

Briar tries to stop me, but I hurry toward the commotion.

The crowd sees us coming, jolts in surprise, and then scatters to reveal a woman tossed over a low-hanging branch, her dress upturned, her buttocks raw. A male is behind her, wearing a pig's mask and nothing else. There's no doubt this is what's happening from the look on her face. I rest my hand on my dagger and step forward, but Briar stops me with a low warning: "Do not be foolish, Willow."

The use of my name stops me.

"She's being hurt!"

"'Tis a dream. No one is hurt in the waking world."

"What?"

"Look again." He gestures at the couple, but I don't know what he means until I see a flicker in their visage. They're not quite solid.

My heart still pounds. "Are you sure?"

"Avorlorna is the home of the Court of Dreams," he drawls as if it's obvious.

"But it looks so real."

"Admittedly, reveries are rare this time of day. But people

sleep at all hours." He softens his tone upon seeing my distress. "As a mortal, you might not discern it, but a distinct magical barrier exists around them. It is admirable that you wish to help, a quality not present in many subterraneans. Hold onto this during the exhibition, for it will serve well to remind your peers you are not truly one of them if not for your appearance. But if you intrude on another's dreamscape, the same wound will be reflected upon waking if you are injured there. Do you understand?"

I wince as the masked male renews his attention on the woman despite her tears. "Looks more like a nightmare to me."

"Dream or nightmare is a matter of perspective." He points to the man, whose grin is just visible beneath the pig mask. Briar ushers me back in the direction we originally headed. "You'll witness many wild dreams here. We attempt to capture or tame what we can, but the Interlude has not yet begun, and catcher reparations have stalled."

"Catchers?"

"The webs." He nods to an intricately woven cobweb dangling between two trees. The luminous silk must be as thick as my pinky finger. The entire structure is about fifteen feet wide. Gemstones and crystal ornaments dangle from intersections. I touch one and feel the tingle of magic. When Briar next glances away, I pluck it and slip it into my cape's pocket.

*Nothing to see here.*

As we continue walking, the hairs on the back of my neck lift as though someone is watching me, but when I scan for prying eyes, I find no one.

Turning back to our surroundings, I notice a wide variety of sizes and placement of webs. Some are beneath bridges between the trees, others are out in the open. The frequency increases when the number of residential buildings increases.

We arrive at the base of a particular tree with a red flag

beneath a six-foot dandelion. Briar plucks a large seed and hands it to me. It's feathery and hard to pin down as though an invisible hand tries to steal it. He squints up, shields his eyes, and points to a platform with a small group of waiting passengers.

"Catch the Dandelion Drift up. This flow line will take you directly to the palace and the Nexus. Stay on the carriage until the last stop a few beats away. Don't delay in registering when you get there."

With each passing second, the dandelion seed grows more willful. Briar places his hands on my shoulders to keep me from floating away. His eyes turn serious. His jaw clenches.

"If I can give you one piece of advice, it's to stay away from the House of Shadows."

"Who?"

"The portraits in your bag," he explains. "They're the Knights of the Queen's Hive. You must know they've never chosen a protégé. You're better off chasing nobles from another house."

He's talking about the Six.

"Anything else?" I ask, a desperate note in my voice. He's been unusually helpful and kind.

"Yes." His brows join in the middle. "It was indeed a pleasure to have made your acquaintance."

That sounds awfully ominous. He lets go of my shoulders, and I rise with the dandelion seed. The sudden weightlessness is disorienting, but at least it's not water. I can't help kicking my legs. My rucksack slides across my shoulders, shifting the weight. I almost swing the wrong way, but somehow, the seed knows where to go. It corrects its path and takes me to the platform, where I drop like a sack of stones.

I'm so loud that I draw attention from waiting passengers. They're all dressed and groomed with impeccable taste and care. Not a hair out of place. The males are clean-shaven. The females have faces painted with stunning colors and glittering highlights. Their clothes are shimmering embroidered gossamer contrasted with velvet and silk. Some don't bother looking at me, but those that do recoil in disgust.

I press my palm against Tinger's pendant beneath my shirt. Staring eyes drop to my hand and then they start whispering. The whispers turn into melodious laughter and grow louder by the second. I want to turn and see who mocks me, but it would only give them more fuel for gossip. The laughter abruptly dies when a carriage of delicate twisted branches and foliage arrives at the platform, floating on a cloud of mist and glowing balls of light. They look suspiciously like manabeeze, except they're too big. But I think the laughter came from them.

A door opens on the carriage, and out pours a group of well-dressed faerie citizens. There are at least twenty of them. And no one with a flaw or fae appendage other than smooth-arched elven ears. Not a single horn, furry dusting, or animal feature. I stand back until they're gone and am the last to enter the carriage. Sitting on one of the lush, upholstered seats, I feel like I'm soiling them.

It's hard to breathe, so I glance down at the flyer. The inscription says:

"*From the Good Folk to the Mortal, in shadows and light, comes the chance of a blessing in the radiant queen's gracious sight. No matter what you be, only one will emerge in victory to seize the prize of a dream turned to reality.*"

# CHAPTER
# SEVEN
## WILLOW

The balls of light driving the carriage are called will-o'-the-wisps and reflect conversations within as we glide around the city. The first sign that something is wrong is when their melodious laughter sounds more like sighing. Conversation inside the carriage has changed in tone. Faces look worried and pinched. Occasionally, I receive a stare, but they're not discussing me. I'm hiding in the back and doing my best to disappear.

Signs of the war are everywhere.

Damaged infrastructure is repaired hastily or covered with holly decorations for their winter festivities. Delicately woven bridges between trees are broken, leaving dwellers stranded or overflowing carriage platforms, as their usual route is blocked. Passengers complain about the Dandelion Drifts not growing fast enough to meet the rising demands.

Another passenger says that instead of spending winter playing war games and having parties to celebrate the Holly King's arrival, they should import food from the northern regions and stockpile for the resumption of war with the Oak King's return.

The pretty dream-catching webs continue into the city, but sometimes they're broken. Silk strings dangle, and their jeweled ornaments drift haphazardly. Buildings overflow with desperate and hungry-looking people. As with the trend I've noticed, they're clean and impeccably presented, but the quality of their clothes is diminished and threadbare. It reminds me of the humans in Sky Tower back in Crystal City. Because they were at war with the fae, they ran out of colorful resources to make dyes for their fabrics, and most fashions were affected. They'd also patched and recycled as much as possible.

I read more on the flyer. The Solstice Exhibition lasts for most of the Gentle Interlude, and exhibitors receive accommodation, meals, and training before a final tournament. There are parades, processions, and demonstrations of talents. There will be balls, feasts, and celebrations in the name of Titania's slumbering sacrifice. It sounds like she's asleep for the entire winter, which means she's not the priority. The Six are.

The forest and buildings eventually make way for green fields leading toward an ivory palace. Up close, it's majestic. Clouds swallow the tops of the spires. Winged stone statues stare at intruders from the turrets. All look fierce and dangerous, but still flawlessly symmetrical and pretty. As the carriage descends from the trees, we cross a bridge beside a deep chasm. The flow line tracks cross a rocky precipice to a moat far below. Oh, shit. Water.

I gasp and sit back in my seat, squeezing my eyes shut. *Don't think about the drop. Don't think about drowning.*

But try as I might, haunted memories return. Rory and I dangle over the airship's side—a glimmering lake beneath my kicking feet. She stabs Cloud's hand. He lets go, his face an agonized expression that echoes my own. Her open eyes as she falls, falls, falls. I replay that look and try to decipher the message in her gaze—if any.

The water sucks her into the deep and then she's gone.

The carriage suddenly stops, and my eyes flip open. Refusing to glance outside, I inhale deeply, then exhale slowly, and reach for the dagger at my belt.

All passengers except me disembark. Once they're out, I sit straighter and bravely look out the window. We're at a bridge platform, past the moat. It's only a few feet away, but it feels safer. Relief courses through me until I notice soldiers standing at the top of the ravine, their weapons trained down at the moat as though something will crawl out and bite them. The soldiers suddenly erupt into cheering and clap each other on the back when snowflakes fall in lazy whorls. Some tilt their faces to the sky and smile.

The Gentle Interlude—the cease in hostilities—must have begun. I'm fortunate to have arrived at this time. A week earlier, and I might have been shot on sight with this curse. The carriage lurches forward. Grateful to be alone, I sink into the plush velvet seat and hug my cape to warm myself. My breath leaves mist on the glass as we coast around the outskirts of the palace grounds. Curiously, a smaller, darker castle lurks in the shadows of the grand palace. I almost missed it. Black, angular turrets sit on top of its jagged towers. Wild briars, thorns, and creeping vines overrun the uneven stone.

The carriage jerks to a halt when an ear-splitting screech rends the atmosphere. I duck on instinct, fearing it might be a manticore or an equally dangerous monster, but I'm wrong. It's a dragon. I've only seen one other—only ever heard of one in existence—the Wild Hunt, the skull-headed death dragon who lived inside the bodies of the Six.

This dragon is smaller, has a muscular body of glittering rock, and its skull is on the inside where it belongs. Granite wings defy logic to carry that body as it swoops and lands on one of five towers within a forest on the other side of the moat.

Closer, just outside, is a plain building labeled *The Strategic Nexus of Avorlorna.*

I'm here.

I catch my reflection before the glass carriage door opens and wince at my ugliness. I quickly comb my silver hair to hide my face.

A guard takes me inside the plain building to a great hall that is empty except for a desk where a pretty female with coiffed pastel-blue hair listens to a male with short, slicked auburn hair. From her uneasy expression as he leans into her space, she doesn't welcome the attention.

I don't think this is another dream. No one is flickering. The male is dressed in tailored brown pants and a coat with intricate green embroidered foliage at the cuffs and collar. His outfit molds perfectly to a lithe, athletic frame. She glances at me, eyes widening.

He pushes off the desk and faces us with a scowl.

My body viscerally jolts at the impact of seeing his eyebrows have been shaved off. I try not to react. I know how much it hurts to see your face cause shock. But before I can offer a smile, his upper lip curls, and he strides past.

When the door slams shut behind him, the guard beside me exhales and says to the blue-haired female, "A latecomer, Peablossom—oh, dear love. What has he done?"

One of her eyebrows is missing. I was sure a moment ago she had both. The guard rushes to the desk and takes Peablossom's chin to inspect the damage.

"He said I was gossiping." Her soft voice is barely a whisper.

"Were you?"

She bites her lip and nods. "But it's the Pageant of Prowess today. How can we avoid discourse on the favored ones? It's so rare to have returning exhibitors, but this year, we have five. Can you believe it? It's simply the most—" She catches me watching and quickly deports herself with dignity.

He hums in agreement and steps back. "At least it's not a veil, Bloss."

"This is true." She plays with her hair, fixing strands that are perfectly in place.

"And it's only one brow," he reminds her.

"Also, a fair point." She sighs. "I just don't know how long I can take being ostracized. The other ladies-in-waiting have never been subjected to such prolonged punishment. And now this. I am positively grotesque." She absently touches her missing brow.

"Chin up, Bloss. At least yours will grow back. Goodfellow's won't."

For some reason, this brings a twinkle to her glistening eyes.

That name sounds familiar. I'm sure the captain at the gate mentioned something about eyebrows and Goodfellow. He must hold authority, even over the captain.

"Oh," says the guard, glancing at me briefly before returning to Peablossom. "City gates are now officially closed for the Gentle Interlude. The first snowflake has fallen."

"How delightful. Finally, good tidings." She claps her hands and then beckons me. "Let's make haste, sweetling, so that you can clean up before the pageant."

Taking out a piece of paper, she dabs the tip of a jeweled feather quill into ink and stares at me. "Your name, sweet cherub?"

"Willow O'Leary-Nightstalk."

She scribbles it down. "Which House are you affiliated with?"

"None."

"You'll room with the other unclaimed mortals, then. But don't fret, you'll have the company of others of your sort there."

She hands me a booklet. "Read the Old Code bylaws pertaining to the Gentle Interlude thoroughly. Some have changed since last year, especially for any mortal who . . ." Her voice trails off as she stares at my face and clears her throat. "Subterraneans, too, I suppose. Pay notable attention to the laws of Pristine Appearance, Conducted Conflict, and Radiant Sovereignty. Do you have weapons to check, my lovely?"

I nod and remove my rucksack so I can withdraw the bone sword. The blue, pulsing elven glyphs along the blade give my heart a homesick tug. I've only been gone for half a day but already miss familiar sights.

Peablossom recoils at the sword, picks it up with dainty fingers, and remarks, "One sword made of . . . bone?" Her complexion pales, and she dry retches. Then, she quickly places the weapon on her desk and magically adds some kind of tracking symbol. "Just a precaution," she notes. "In case we have any violations."

She gingerly slides the sword back, and I sheath it between my shoulder blades. A high-pitched giggle erupts from her lips and she fans her face.

"Phew. I'm delighted that's over. Kindly bear no offense, dearest confection. Now, where were we? Ah, yes, presentation." She squints at my figure. "Regarding your uniform, you appear to be of small size. I believe I have one remaining. Lucky you."

She retrieves a folded pile of gray garments from below her desk, hands them to me, and then adds a pair of black sturdy boots. I see no embroidery or fancy embellishments like the fashion in the city. The fabric is coarse to the touch and will likely irritate.

"Wear that garment daily, cleanse it, and suspend it to dry by your dormitory cot come dusk. You will indeed receive a stern reproach if you neglect to grace official events in your designated uniform. Rest assured, dearest, you will be given a fresh uniform if you are assigned to a House."

If?

"There's more to explain," she says, standing up quickly. "But if you don't tidy yourself before the pageant, it's my good nature on the line. And I don't fancy losing another eyebrow today. Quickly now. Embrace the flutter. Moments aplenty await."

With a clap of her hands, she leaves the sanctity of her desk and walks toward the same door Goodfellow went. I've never gushed over fashion before, but awe fills my soul when I take in her gown. The brocade corset is covered in gems and cinches a tiny waist. As she walks, the gem-encrusted skirt swishes and tinkles like bells. If the number of enchanted charms indicates status, Peablossom must be very important. She's covered in them.

Didn't she say she's a lady-in-waiting? Does that mean she works for the queen?

We enter a long hallway with lancet windows overlooking a stunning garden filled with blossoms, green foliage, and the forest I glimpsed while journeying. More snow has fallen, and now frost touches the windowpanes and tips of the leaves outside. Mist swirls down paths in the dense woods.

Peablossom waltzes gracefully down the hallway, a whimsical lightness to her delicate step. Her hands wave from side to side as though she conducts an invisible orchestra.

"And we are having fun," she sings, glancing through the frosted windows. Her smile seems forced as she continues. "And we are joyful." She pushes through another set of wooden doors. "Chin is *up*. All is *well*."

She faces me and broadens her fake grin, pointing to her appled cheeks. More singsong. "We are smiling, yes?"

"Sure," I intone.

My lack of interest doesn't bother her. She continues chanting platitudes about pleasantry and joyful manifestations. The next set of doors leads outside. The fresh air brings the scent of ice, pine, and moss. Even though she shivers in her gown, she pretends not to notice the cold and keeps her chin up. We head to another gray building at the end of a short, winding path.

"You will notice the fort on the right," she cheerfully says, tossing a graceful hand toward the woods.

I only glimpse two towers within the tall forest at this lower level, but I don't think they're what she's directing me to. One tower is a dark stone with red glowing veins. Air shimmers around the building like a mirage. Since snow avoids the area, I guess the air must be warm. The second tower is less visible but glimmers with green and turquoise adornments that might be seashell shaped.

She briefly turns and sings through chattering teeth, "There is a map in your registration leaflet. House of Embers." She points to the red-veined tower. "House of Tides." To the greenish one. She groans and then forces her smile back. "Yes, we are smiling. Hurry along. Embrace the flutter."

The most surprising part about this journey is that I *feel* the Six here somewhere. The awareness is in every fiber of my being, like a tug from my center with an invisible string. Are we connected? What does that mean?

Jogging to keep up with her brisk steps, I look for signs of the them and hug the uniform closer to my chest. Not because I am afraid, but because I just realized I never offered her my dagger after she checked my sword.

And I won't.

When Peablossom leads me into the dormitory commons, heads swivel our way. Long tables are filled with impeccably groomed people wearing gray uniforms—some smirk at me, some recoil, and some deadpan. Heat rises to my cheeks. I fight the urge to touch the ropy scars and misshapen angles. Instead, I touch Tinger's pendent and remember why I'm here, where I've come from, and who taught me.

Nero might have pushed me to kill, but Rory taught me how to do it well.

*Always have an escape plan.*

I survey the room and check for exits and threats. Two doors in the vast room lead out—one to the woods and one somewhere else. The raked ceiling is braced with wooden beams. Windows overlook the same manicured garden and dense woods. An open window to the kitchen emits steam and the scent of mouthwatering food. That's about as far as my survey goes because my stomach rumbles. I can't remember the last time I ate.

Peablossom whirls to face me and bunches her left shoulder

toward her ear. I realize she's guarding the side of her face missing an eyebrow.

"Dormitory sleeping quarters are through the back door," she says in a rush. "You're in the Malachite suite, bunk twenty-three. Toiletries and washcloths will be on your bed. Ablutions are clearly labeled."

"You won't take me there?"

Her pleasant tone evaporates. "I must freshen up, too, dearest confection. The pageant starts in—oh, I almost forgot. Here is your resonance stone. Always keep it on you." She digs into a skirt pocket and drops a smooth, round pebble into my palm. It's warm to the touch and feels like a mana stone. "When the call of your name echoes from the stone, do ensure you are impeccably presented according to the code and take your place in line at the fort's east entrance."

She catches herself frowning and refits her joy-filled mask before swiftly exiting. Her "We Are Smiling" song fades after the door closes. Conversations come into focus. My ears twitch as I pick up familiar words.

"When I win, I'm asking for a cheeseburger," jokes a woman.

A man responds, "Nah, I want my PlayStation back."

"I suppose we should do the right thing and dream for the dickhead who bombed the world to die."

"But first, make it so the bombs never dropped."

"I wonder if that's in the queen's power to give?"

My mother used to complain about never tasting a cheeseburger again. These people must be from the old world. Anyone awakened in Elphyne came with a tremendous capacity for holding mana. I might find valuable allies if I can locate these humans.

I can't imagine they'd be happy with how things are run here. They might even look past my face and see an ally, too.

86

My feet won't move. What if they laugh at me? It almost physically hurts to push past the fear, but I stroll toward the rear dormitory exit and scan the tables for signs of the old-worlders. Ranging in various sizes from tall to short, muscular to frail, humanity is evident by the shape of their round ears. Chewing my lip, I walk up to the table occupants still discussing their wishes.

"Hello," I greet. "You're from the old world?"

Everyone stills. A few nervous glances flick my way, but no one answers. After a prolonged awkward moment, it's clear they're ignoring me.

They're all glaringly attractive. My chest tightens, and it feels like the walls are closing in. Out of anyone who might have treated me kindly, I thought it would be them.

Behind me, a dry voice retorts, "You won't get anything from the Nevers."

I twist and spot a table across the aisle. These humans aren't perfectly flawless like the majority. A middle-aged curvy woman with short brown hair holds a walking stick and rubs her thigh with gnarled fingers as though it pains her. A man with gray whiskers squints as though he can't see correctly. A younger woman with curly black hair pulled into a neat bun has burn scars on one side of her face and neck. The man opposite her is balding but seems younger than the first woman. Possibly in his thirties.

The scarred woman meets my gaze and explains, "They're too chicken-shit to speak to a Nothing."

Laughter erupts behind me, but still, they don't engage. I don't have time to waste on people who don't have time for me, so I cross to the new table and offer a tentative smile.

"Hi, I'm Willow."

"I'm Geraldine," the black-haired woman replies. "I like long walks on the beach, drinking cocoa by the fire, and reading books about alien abduction." She then points across the table. "This dude here is Max. Say hello, Max."

"Hello, Max." The balding man waves. He has kind brown eyes. I immediately like him.

Geraldine stares at him, but when he says nothing else, she tells me, "He likes reading comics, doing arithmetic, and picking his nose."

"I do not!"

"Just kidding on that last one." She laughs and then uses her thumb to point at the older man. "That's Bob. Conspiracy theorist and classical pianist." He dips his head in acknowledgment, then does something weird with his fingers along the table.

"And this is Peggy." Geraldine claps Peggy's leg beside her. "Loves knitting, baking pumpkin pies, and . . ."

Peggy raises a sardonic brow at Geraldine, then smiles at me. "Honey, I'm none of those things. I used to be a corgi breeder before all this. But I am glad to meet you." She uses her walking stick to point at a vacant spot on the opposite side of Geraldine. "Take a seat."

"Nice to meet you." I wave, feeling a rush of endorphins at their friendly introductions. I plonk myself down and try to think of an interesting response. "Um . . . I guess I'm new here. I like collecting things, and by collecting, I mean stealing." I laugh nervously. "But your items are safe from me."

I cringe at my attempt to joke. Max, the Well-send, gives me a little chuckle.

Geraldine's gaze drops to my face, and I tense, waiting for the inevitable questions. But she skips across to my ears and notes, "You're not like us. But I thought only mortals could enter the exhibition."

"My mother is from your time."

She pushes a bowl of nuts toward me. "Help yourself to a pre-pageant snack."

"I'm so hungry." I toss as many into my mouth as possible, not caring how impolite I must look. Too hungry to worry about etiquette.

The others give me empathic looks, and Max pours me a drink from the pitcher. Peggy slides over a bowl of something white and gunky. My nose picks up spices, milk, and wheat. I smile gratefully but leave the bowl where it sits before Geraldine. I probably shouldn't take everything at once. I'll get to that next.

"So," I start, "how long have you all been awake in this time?"

"A few months," Geraldine replies. "I'm sorry, did you say mother before?"

"Yes. She woke in Elphyne about twenty years ago."

"Elphyne?"

"It's oceans away." I scowl at the room. "And nothing like this. Well, that's not exactly true. There's a war there, too. And I guess it's not so great inside Crystal City where humanity has been banished, but out in Elphyne, everyone can do what they want."

They look at me like I'm speaking another language.

"But humans are banished?" Geraldine asks.

"It's complicated. Direct fallout descendants of the quarantined believe fae are warped, tainted animals. They'd rather stay in their city than follow the same rules the Well sets for everyone else."

"Rules?" Max blinks.

I blink back. Is this land truly so different than mine?

"What's the Well?" Geraldine adds.

"Um. It's the source of all mana—magic—and life force. It's what's kept you preserved for all these years in the ground. The Well gives fae magic and immortality. In return for this gift, we must protect the earth. That means no use of forbidden substances like metal and plastic."

Even though I'm breaking one of those rules right now through the dagger at my belt. And even though everyone around here continues to use metal. It's odd.

"I could get on board with that." Max nods emphatically.

"Can we go there?" Bob blurts. His voice is raspy with age. "Can they make spectacles so I can see again?" He gasps. "Do they have pianos?"

My heart squeezes.

"To be honest, I'm not sure about the pianos. As for your sight, they might be able to heal it completely," I offer. I'll need to find manabeeze to activate the portal stone home first, but I know my parents will do everything they can to help.

"Like laser surgery?" He scratches his head.

"Um . . . I don't know what that is, but a healer in Elphyne uses magic to fix you." I gesture at the left side of my face where my acid wounds still smart. "Before you ask, my wounds are here intentionally. I don't want . . ." Tinger's little face hits my mind, and I shake my head, unable to voice anymore.

"You don't need to explain." Geraldine's eyes fill with empathy.

An awkward silence stretches until Max says, "Only Radiants can heal to that extent here. But none of them would help a *Nothing* for free."

Geraldine nods her agreement. "Some Chasers have earned the ability to heal or glamour. But again, no one does anything for free."

"What exactly are Chasers, Nevers, and Nothings?" I ask, taking another nut and popping it into my mouth.

Geraldine chuckles and shakes her head. "You truly are from out of town."

"Yep." Another nut goes in.

"Okay, so here—take a look." She points to the group of

humans I tried to speak with first. "The Nevers are pretty humans, or mortals, as the faerie call them."

"Ahem." Max raises his brows at her.

"My bad. Faeries is an offensive term for them."

"What do I call them, fae?"

"Good Folk, Fair Folk, the Good People." She rolls her eyes. "Talk about propaganda. I would totally respect their request if they called us mortals nice names. Anyway, despite the Nevers' perfect faces, they're unlikely to ever fall into favor with the Radiants"—she shudders—"who are the powerful noble gentry."

"Why won't Nevers be favored?"

Her eyes turn downcast, and she shrugs. "That's the secret we'd all like to know."

"The war?"

Another shrug. "The Folk are secretive. But Bob thinks it's concerning the ability to use charms." She points to a group of people with stones swinging from chains on their uniforms. "Chasers are wannabes—the holiest of suck-ups. Like, if they were asked to polish the turds of Radiants, they'd turn them into diamonds. Some Chasers are less powerful Folk, some are mortal."

Peablossom had many gemstones. She must be one of the less powerful faerie.

Max giggle-snorts and says, "We call their enchanted stones Lucky Charms."

Peggy laughs. Bill cackles, then covers his mouth. I don't understand the joke but return their smile.

Geraldine lowers her voice in warning. "Please don't repeat this to anyone unless you want to be punished for gossiping. I'm serious."

"Understood." I make a show of pretending to lock my lips and throw away the key.

Her eyes land on my fae ears. "So, you're mortal, right? Born like that?"

I open my mouth, but nothing comes out. It's not the curse, I don't think, but the shame that comes with knowing why I lost all my magic. Emotion threatens to pour from my eyes, and I dip my head, fingers fluttering to my bulging cheekbone.

"That's okay, hun," Peggy whispers, leaning past Geraldine to pat my arm. She almost knocks the bowl of goop. "Remember, you don't have to tell us a thing you don't want."

My throat thickens at her kindness, and I nod gratefully before changing the subject. "So, none of you were born with magic?"

They all appear baffled as if the thought of humans with magic is unheard of. But all who woke from the old world, like my mother, were gifted with immense power.

"How did humans from the old world get here?" I ask, frowning. "I'm assuming you were all frozen like my mother was. She washed up in a lake."

A haunted look crosses Max's face, and he glances at Geraldine, who gives him a nod of encouragement.

"As far as I know," he answers, "most of us crawled out of the dirt."

"Zombie apocalypse," Bob interjects. "I tell you, that's what happened, not a nuclear winter."

The others scoff and tell him he's dreaming, but the blood rushes in my ears as I recall the undead I brought to life five years ago. One of my aunts called them zombies.

At first, it was only the recently killed soldiers my magic targeted. But then, as the urge to kill the Unseelie Queen grew impossibly powerful, I reached into the dark place I pretended never existed and pulled out more magic than I ever thought possible. I felt it call to the stars, the darkness, and beyond.

Felt something ancient answer.

"If you're wondering where we fit into this menagerie of madness," Geraldine says, glaring at the tables around us, "we're the Nothings."

My heart kicks in my chest at that word. "What does that mean?"

Max replies with a bitter tone, "The Court of Nightmares is in the Subterranean of Nocturna. Any mortal like us, physically flawed or weak, is deported there. We're a blight on this perfect, dreamy society. All because we don't fit their idea of pretty."

"It's so fucked up." Geraldine toys with the spoon in the bowl and stares into the white globs. "First, the world is bombed, then we die during the fallout. But at least I was with my family. I don't know where I'd be if it weren't for this bunch of losers over the past few months."

She looks at her friends with an affection they each return.

"Ditto," Max mumbles, squeezing her hand.

The pressure on my heart increases. "How many are here like you?"

"Here for the exhibition?" Geraldine asks. "Or humans here in Avorlorna?"

"Here, anywhere."

"Thousands in the subterranean." Max's complexion pales. "I only counted about eight Nothings here at the tournament. But as you can see, there's over a hundred exhibitors."

I gulp. "Thousands in the subterranean?"

He nods. "We've seen them tossed down into the watergates. Entry to the subterranean is always through water."

My pulse quickens. Just another reason for me to stay away from water. "That's so many."

"Some Chasers and Nevers have been here since the start—five years ago. Both faerie and mortals awoke simultaneously, each as confused as the other." Max's gaze turns inward. "Do you think they call us Nothings because we're at the bottom of the food chain when sent down there? Or worse . . . if we cease to exist?"

His words make me feel sick.

*Five years ago.*

*Five years ago.*

They all woke at the same time.

"Best not to think about it, hun," Peggy tells Max.

"What's the war about?" I rasp, pulse racing.

"Who knows?" Max shrugs. "But Bob has a theory. Tell her, Bob."

The older man nods. "I saw one of them beasties attack a Radiant while living in Adularia. The nightmare had her pinned and begging for mercy." His eyes widen at what must be a dreadful memory. His tone becomes quiet, ominous. "She called it a *Devil*. It crawled out of the subterranean from a *puddle*. It looked as pretty as the Radiant . . . but had horns and claws. Maybe it's hell down there."

"What's your theory, Bob?" Max prompts.

"Oh yeah. I heard it say, 'Thief, thief. Return what you stole' repeatedly." He shivers.

Scandalized, Geraldine whispers, "But the queen claims the war is because the subterraneans want Avorlorna's land for themselves."

"Lies," I mutter.

"Agreed." Max gives my face a harrowing stare. "But for the record, the Folk are more likely to dispatch the weak, wounded, or disabled before those like you. With your ears, you might be able to find a Radiant who will enchant a stone to hide your . . . you know, visual shortcomings."

"Hun, they're just jealous," Peggy declares. "Self-confidence in people like us frightens them."

"Shh," Bob hushes. "You're getting too loud. Gossip will get us killed."

"What are they going to do?" She raises her voice. "We're dead anyway if we don't win."

Geraldine lifts the goop on a spoon, then watches it fall with unfocused eyes. "Is it bad that I still want to try winning, though?"

I take stock of the room. They're just mortals with enchanted stones. "We can take them."

No one seems convinced, and it cuts me to the core. I notice again that Geraldine's taken great care to maintain her pristine appearance. Her curly hair is plastered down with something slick. Her uniform is without wrinkles. She smells like rose petals.

My skin itches to hear more about the exhibition training and tournament. I'm fairly certain none of my companions have combat skills. I assume since I need weapons, that's what we have to do. Some other exhibitors are well-muscled, fit, and wear the same predatory look as my father and brother.

They're wolves amongst a flock of sheep, and they know it.

Peablossom said there were repeat exhibitors. Perhaps even those who have fought in the war. That makes them brutal competition.

A sudden buzz swarms across the room. People jolt and pull out their resonance stones. Peablossom's disembodied lyrical voice echoes as the first lot of names is called out. Along with personal resonance stones, her voice transmits from a large, carved owl in the rafters.

"I'd better get cleaned up." I suddenly feel motivated to win this thing.

When I stand, Geraldine's name is called at the same time. She jerks upright and accidentally knocks the bowl. White goop spills over her dark uniform. The bowl rolls loudly on the floor and eventually comes to a stop.

"Oh no," she gasps as it drips down her front. "I'm soiled."

"No use crying over spilled goop," I offer, trying to lighten the mood, but no one laughs. I use the corner of my cape to wipe her mess. Everyone is as silent as death's whisper.

Snickers echo from another table. Concerned, I look to Max for guidance.

His eyes fill with sorrow as he gestures around the room. "Some have been training and earning charms for years. I once saw a Chaser who could summon lightning in his hands. A Nothing's only hope of surviving is to be sponsored by a Radiant."

I sit down, remove the boots from my folded uniform pile, and hand her the clean shirt. "Take mine."

"What?" Geraldine's eyes fill with tears. "I can't. You need it."

"I'll go to the pageant in what I'm wearing."

"But you'll be punished."

"I don't care if they take my eyebrows." I shrug. "Can't make me look any worse."

"No." She shakes her head, spilling a few tears.

"Please." I shove it at her. "I know how to take care of myself. Trust me."

"You'd better hurry, love. Your name was already called." Peggy begins to unbutton my uniform shirt with her gnarled fingers and fumbles but then manages to open it all the way. Geraldine gives me one last agonized look, then strips right there —despite the gasps of shock. Getting half-naked in the commons probably isn't on the list of accepted behaviors. She must be desperate. Max comes around the table, licks his palm, and flattens her flyaway strands of hair as she tucks in her new shirt tails.

"Do I look okay?" she asks breathlessly.

"Perfect," I smile confidently, hoping it rubs off.

"Not quite," she shoots back. "But it's a start. I don't know how I can ever repay you."

"You already did by being kind."

She hugs me and whispers, "You're a special person, Willow. Thank you."

Then she rushes out the doors leading to the woods. The imprint of her words remains long after she's walked out. I don't feel special, but maybe there's hope for me.

I inspect the dirty shirt she left. It's honestly not that bad if I wash it in the bathroom. It might even dry before my name is called. There are close to two hundred people here. I have time.

I collect my rucksack but don't leave because my resonance stone vibrates, and Peablossom's loud, sing-song voice clearly announces my name.

*Oh, shit.*

Max and Peggy give me a petrified look. Bob's shoulders sag.

"It's only a pageant," I assure them. "How bad can it be?"

*"Willow?"*

The familiar voice tugs at my heart—the hairs on the back of my neck prickle—and the floor shifts. For a moment, I thought I heard a ghost call my name. I shake my head to clear the cobwebs and turn, ready to head toward the pageant with my rucksack, dirty clothes, and ugly face.

But I smack headfirst into a man. Two strong hands grip my shoulders, steadying my balance. I lift my gaze to the freckled face of an extremely handsome green-eyed ghost.

"Alfie?" I whisper.

# CHAPTER
# NINE
## WILLOW

The last time I saw Alfie, the undead were dragging him away. But here he stands, styled to perfection. His ginger hair is trimmed and combed with a side part. His gray uniform is more tailored than Geraldine's or Max's, and a string of charms dangle on a fine silver chain across the breadth of his chest.

He's a Chaser.

Breathless, I step back to get a better look and ensure I'm not dreaming again. He's bulked up with hard slabs of muscle. The past five years have sharpened all the soft lines of youth. I don't remember him being this good-looking and . . . virile.

Alfie inspects my face with abject horror. I recoil at his reaction and try to pull away, but his grip tightens on my shoulders. Green eyes flash with emotion, then promptly harden. He doesn't ask me for an explanation, and I'm not in the mood to offer one.

"We'll make you beautiful again," he promises.

I try not to show his words affected me, but my fingers are on my face before I can stop them. Clenching them, I drop my arms to my sides.

"I'm surprised you recognize me."

"I didn't at first. You're the last person I expected to see here, but it's you. It's really you." His gaze darts over my face, winces, and drops. "Your golden eyes and silver hair are unmistakable beneath all that . . ."

He glances at a group of Chasers talking at another table, then at my table. A muscle in his jaw feathers, and he hurries me toward the dorm exit with brisk, rough strides. I try to stop, ask him questions, or hug him, but a stone statue would have more reactions than him.

Outside, he pushes us into a jog down a long hallway. Seconds later, we're in a dormitory room with six single bunks. He crosses to a wooden chest against a wall, lifts the heavy lid like a feather, then rifles through it to find a clean uniform shirt.

"Put that on."

I catch it when he throws it to me. "Can we take a moment and—"

"No," he clips and faces windows overlooking more woods. "Be quick."

"Alfie, I'm still trying to process that you're *alive.*"

"Process later," he grumbles. "It's clear you know nothing about the Old Code, so you'll have to take my lead. Your name has been called. You need to hurry."

The authority in his tone is so foreign that it spurs me into action. But I trust him with my life. He already gave it once to protect me. I undress, shove on the uniform shirt and trousers, then drop onto the bunk to slide on the boots. He must hear the bed creak and glances at me. With a disapproving click of his tongue, he leaves the room.

I'm almost done tying my boots when he returns with a washcloth, drops to his knees, and wipes my face like I do for my twin sisters. His motions are abrupt and irritated until he reaches my acid wounds. The pity in his eyes withers my soul.

"What have they done to you?" he murmurs. His thumb grazes my right cheek. I know it's the unscarred, unwounded side, but it feels bulky and wrong beneath his touch. It takes all my willpower to avoid crumbling into an emotional heap. He gives me a hard look. "We'll find a way to fix it, I promise."

I flinch away and feel myself detach. "I'm fine."

"You're not fine." He stands, fixes his shirt, and clenches his jaw. "You will be, though. First, we get you to the pageant, away from the Nothings and at least grouped with the Nevers. For now. I already have half a plan forming to hook you up with some charms."

I shake my head. "They were nice to me. I won't ignore them."

His expression shutters. "Nice? Christ, Willow. I always knew you were a bleeding heart, but surely you know that fraternizing with them will get you killed. It's bad enough you were about to waltz over to the pageant looking like that. I've seen people get turned into *toads* for nothing but bad manners. Comb your hair and make it look presentable while you walk. With any luck, they're disorganized like last year."

His words are a slap to my face. But I trust him. Of course, I trust him. He's just being rude because we're out of time. So I comb my knotty hair but pause at something he said. "Wait. You were here last year, too?"

Of course, he was. It's been five years. He has at least twenty enchanted charms on his Chaser uniform. Alfie always had a knack for fitting in.

Chagrined at my progress, he takes over my hair. Not just fixing it, I realize, but braiding. His fingers fly about my scalp, weaving with deft skill, making me wonder whose long hair he's so familiar with. A beat of *something* squirms in my gut, but I stop my derailing mood with one thought. Alfie is *alive*.

"I thought you were dead," I whisper.

His hands still. His tone softens. "Me too. I mean, I thought you were. Dead, that is."

His sudden blustering reminds me of my old friend. The one who played with me in the bunker museum. The one who blushed every time he talked to me after hitting puberty. He stole a rose from the secret garden's hedges, carried it in his pocket all day, then gifted it to me, not realizing it had wilted.

"How . . . ?"

"Did I get here?" His charms tinkle. "I don't know. Just woke up here. You?"

My hair feels secure, so I face him. Pain is etched all over his features. He slams on his mask of pleasantry, reminding me of Peablossom's forced good moods.

I tap one of his charms and answer, "I found a portal stone."

His eyes widen. "Do you have one to return?"

"Yes. But no manabeeze to power it."

His shoulders drop. "You won't find any here."

"What do you mean?"

Another name being called echoes down the hall. He takes my hand and pulls me out of the dormitory, looking straight ahead as we jog.

"Whatever you do," he warns, "don't look them in the eyes. Don't draw their attention. Blend in. This isn't the first tournament I've survived, and it won't be my last. We'll talk more after the procession."

"Don't look who in the eyes?"

"The Gentry." At my confusion, he adds, "The Radiants."

Before he opens the door to the commons, he pauses and gives me a sideways look. The impact of his change hits me in the heart. *Look at him.* He's so handsome and strong now. So grown up. There's no sign of the gangly teenager while I'm here looking like dishwater.

He asks quietly, "I'm guessing you wouldn't be here if you had magic, right?"

Biting my lip, I shake my head.

His gaze returns to the door, and he swallows. "I still hear your screams in my sleep. I tried to come to you, but . . ."

My breath catches as all the loneliness and confusion I've felt since we were last together wells in my chest. I wrap my arms around him and squeeze. At first, he stiffens. He smells the same, like linen, soap, and something peppery.

"Willow . . ." His protest dies, but I squeeze him harder, bury my face into his neck deeper.

"I'm so happy you're alive, Alfie. I missed you so much."

He cups the back of my head. His muscles relax beneath my cheek.

"I missed you too." He tenses again. "Remember, don't draw their attention."

I pull back and realize something. I don't think he knows what the Six did to me. They were responsible for sending me to Crystal City. Whether directly or indirectly, everything bad that happened to me was because of their manipulations—the war, me being trained as a weapon, the undead I summoned, the people I killed.

"Rory is dead," I blurt.

"What?" His eyes widen.

Shame heats my cheeks. I try to shrink away.

"I'm sorry," he says, voice tight. "She was an excellent Reaper who taught you well. Which is why I know you'll survive the exhibition. We need to go."

He extricates himself from my embrace and opens the door. When I look affronted at his cold demeanor, he quickly closes it and says, "It's not personal, Willow. But your face makes you a

Nothing—a Nightmare. It's better if we don't appear as allies for now. I'll find you after the pageant. You trust me, don't you?"

Whether there's anything of the young man I used to know, I can't tell anymore. We used to play games under the tables in the grand dining hall. We used to dig up worms in the garden. He valiantly came to my rescue whenever humanity made fun of my ears. He stole away with me to the bunker, where we became lost in the memorabilia, especially the ancient pirate lore. We even started a secret explorer's club and vowed that one day, we'd break out of our tower prison, sail the seven seas, and claim all the treasure.

But that Alfie is gone.

At my hesitation, he tugs my braid. "I have a good chance of being sponsored this year. When I do, I'll have an in with one of the Radiants. But if they see me colluding with a Nightmare, we're both screwed."

It hurts that he keeps calling me that. "That makes sense."

"Come on," he croons. "What did we always say in the Gilded Buccaneers?"

He remembers—my heart flutters.

"For the Gold," I whisper.

A smirk touches his lips, and I am again struck by how handsome he's become. He grips my hand, then prompts me to finish our secret handshake with a back-handed slap and a tweak of our pinky fingers. He returns my whisper with a glint in his eye, "For the Gold."

I laugh. It's stupid. We're both adults, but those three childish words make me feel less alone. I hang back when he enters the hall to give him space. He's probably right. I just arrived in Avorlorna. I know nothing about how this civilization works or why the Well flows differently for them. I'm bound to fuck things up eventually. Pressing my hand against Tinger's pendant, I push into the room.

His strong, determined steps cut a line through the room like a shark. His magnetic command me with pride. He grins easily at a table of Chasers, clapping a few on their backs, tinkling their charms. Some glance at me curiously. Others with scorn when they take in my face. Alfie says something that makes them laugh, and a traitorous urge to retreat washes through me.

I'm sure he wasn't talking about me. He wouldn't do that.

Peggy and Bob are gone. Half the room has cleared out. Everyone left in the hall wears silver chains and charms. They're my real competition. I'll ask more questions about this exhibition when I see Alfie again tonight.

As I walk through the room, I notice alliances are already formed.

I'm reminded this is a return attempt for Alfie. No wonder he has friends. Bonds would strengthen during the war in warmer months. That kind of friendship is like steel.

My palm hits the wooden exit door, and it swings open. A chilly breeze bathes me with the smell of pine and ice. I follow other exhibitors down a winding pathway leading deeper into the woods. The music starts softly at first—a rhythmic beating of drums, delicate lyrical bells, then the hollow haunt of a flute.

After a few minutes, we arrive at a large, round stone structure built into more tall, dense trees. This must be the fort. It's multiple stories high and curves away until it disappears into the mist and shadows of the surrounding forest. Arched windows repeat irregularly around the curved wall. The music and revelry are inside. It's impossible to distinguish individual voices. My goodness, how big is the gathering crowd?

When I enter the building through a large open arch, I'm yanked to the side of the hallway by a dainty hand.

"I feared you'd vanished like a pooka in the night," Peablossom admonishes.

Somehow, she managed a complete outfit change. Her

powder-blue hair is now coiffed into a French knot featuring strings of pearls and artfully twisted holly.

Her dress is tailored and serious. No gauzy fabric or tinkling charms. The gray-and-black brocade is thick, with holly leaves embroidered on the sleeves and hem. She's the epitome of class.

Except for that one painted eyebrow.

She flicks lint from my shoulders. Her brows pucker, and she lifts the too-big sleeves from my shoulders and drops them with disdain. "This is not the size I gave you, my sweet."

"I—"

"Tut-tut." She smooshes a finger to my lips. "Mortals wrap themselves in excuses as if donning armor against consequence. Such armor only exists in dreams, does it not?"

She gives me a warning look, then lowers her finger.

"It won't happen again," I apologize.

"Finally. Some sense. At the very least, your tresses are arranged with some semblance of grace. Your ears will confuse the gentry, but nothing can be done for that." She casts a nervous glance over her shoulder. "As long as you're here and clothed in appropriate attire, my amendments are finished. Puck cannot complain I've failed my duty."

Puck? When she absently touches her painted brow, I understand. Fear of further punishment by Goodfellow is why she waited.

"And here I thought you were worried about me," I tease.

Her lips curve in a way I think she's amused, not mocking. But she says nothing. I follow her gaze and finally allow myself to soak up the atmosphere.

The corridor we're in surrounds the main arena. Through the archway, glimpses of stone and wooden architecture continue. Murals depicting romantic, majestical celebrations and adventures seamlessly blend between pillars. Our ceiling is low, but the brighter arena makes me think it's open air. Or perhaps there are more windows. I can't see much beyond the exhibitors forming units.

"You're too tardy to fall in line with the Nothings," she muses, gesturing at the arena. "So you'll need to look like a Never."

A decision weighs in Peablossom's eyes, then she grits her teeth and removes her tailored leather gloves. She cups my face, and little ants scurry over my skin.

I jerk back. "What are you doing?"

Surprise splashes over her delicate features. "You sensed that?"

"Yes."

"I thought you were mortal?" A flicker of fear enters her eyes. "Or are you one of Oberon's folk, artfully weaving your tapestry of deception while our guards are down?"

Oberon? Is he their enemy? "I don't know what you're talking about."

"Notably, with that face, you simply cannot belong to the Radiant Titania—even in the shadows."

*She did this to me!* I want to shout. *Your benevolent queen made me look like this.*

"Trust me," I counter dryly. "If I had magic, I wouldn't look like this."

She gives me a once-over as if assessing my truth by appearance. "I suppose that sounds logical enough. After all, who would willingly traverse beneath the stars with such an unfortunate visage?"

"People here are so nice." My smile doesn't reach my eyes.

"Precisely." She misses my sarcasm. "So accept this gift from me and joyously celebrate as one of Titania's flock. We'll both win."

I touch my face and feel the ugliness. My dried, sore wounds are also still there. "I don't feel different."

"It's a temporary glamour. Only the Radiants may offer something permanent."

"Won't they know after the glamour reverts?"

"What fools mortals are," she mumbles, slipping her gloves back on. "I simply require the Pageant of Prowess to pass without a hitch."

I tense. "Is the queen here?"

"No. The first snowflake has fallen. She sleeps so that her dream magic freezes the watergates, and the Gentle Interlude is blessed upon us. But that does not mean you can be tardy. Good-fellow resides in her stead. She will return for the final trial before Imbolc. Remember your manners, oh curious one, and all is well." At my confusion, she widens her gorgeous lips into a smile and points at her cheeks, singing merrily, "We are smiling. We are joyful."

The whites of her eyes show, and she nods eagerly for me to mimic her expression. I force my lips to stretch. She rolls her eyes at my attempt, then sashays away with a hasty gesture for me to get in line.

I scurry into the arena and slip into the last line of Never troops. I'm so distracted by Peablossom's words, it takes me a moment to look up. When I do, my soul swells with awe. The fort is magnificent. Multiple stories of botanical balconies and alcoves are filled with faeries of different kinds, all impeccably presented in their finest attire. Hats and horns entwine. Gossamer wings sparkle with added shine. Petite and tall, earthly and heavenly. Here is the diversity the city lacked. There, it was all humanoid fae or mortals with perfect, flawless appearances. I wonder if these wild faeries are disallowed in the city, or rather, they're shy and prefer not to be seen.

Rustling leaves draw my attention higher to where the boughs of abnormally tall Hawthorn trees are shaped into decorative columns rising into an open, overcast sky. Snow has stopped but will likely return. I still smell it in the air. The branches sway gently, reminding me of fingers flexing, eagerly wanting to close and shelter us from the elements. Perhaps that's what happens if the weather gets bad.

Multiple arched buttresses support the wall around the arena. Dragons occupy four, each on its own. The stony dragon watches troops like a hawk. A long-spined dragon with shimmering turquoise scales has wrapped its tail around its flying buttress. The third dragon is made of dark, smoldering scales that gleam with pulsing lava in the cracks. The fourth is a luminous, shimmering, ethereal creature with fragile gossamer wings that seem too delicate to fly. Then again, I find it hard to believe the stone dragon can fly, so those gossamer wings work just fine.

Above each buttress in the first tier of stands, a decorative private box contains a lavishly fashioned aristocrat—must be the radiant gentry they speak of. Their skin is luminous with the beauty of eternal youth, yet they emit an ancient otherworldliness. Judgment oozes from their watchful gazes. Carved signs below each loge announce the noble family within: Court of Dreams, House of Stone, House of Tides, House of Embers, House of Moonlight, and—my breath catches—House of Shadow.

Their private box is empty.

"I heard sometimes they don't even show," mumbles the entrant to my left.

I turn and realize the blonde's not speaking to me but to a man beside her.

"Lies," he replies, keeping his face forward. "They're always here. Somewhere. At least for the pageant."

"I also heard they don't sponsor a protégé because their dragon is dead."

"Who knows? I'm still convinced this is all a dream, and I'll wake up in my Soho apartment covered in biscuits. God, I miss the jam my aunt made."

"Shh," someone ahead hisses.

I return to studying the aristocracy, particularly Goodfellow, as he presides over this event from the queen's royal loge. But instead of his strange, eyebrowless face, I'm drawn to another's beside him. His beauty is a masterpiece of contradiction. Cruel, handsome lines mix with lush features. Devilish yet angelic. Short, white hair offsets his black, angular brows. His porcelain skin appears carved from marble, yet his rosy, wide lips look soft. *Emrys.* A jolt of recognition slices through me.

His portrait sketch is an accurate representation. Fiery menace bleeds from his pores, infecting his black coat with an edge of danger. The mandarin collar is cut extra sharp, and the military tailoring is harsh against his athletic physique. It's hard to see his tattoos behind all that pretty fabric and gloves, but they must be there. Apart from his lips and eyes, the only other color daring to touch him is the blue glowing Guardian teardrop beneath his left eye.

He's staring at me. Wait. Does he recognize me?

I briefly touch my face. The knotted scars and knobby bulges are still there.

He lends an ear to Goodfellow, who also looks at me. This can't be good. I thought Emrys was menacing, but the seething disgust in Goodfellow's gaze makes my hand drop to my dagger.

My fingers graze my beltless hip. I left my dagger in Alfie's room. *Fuck.* His warning comes back to me—don't look them in the eyes. Heart racing, I quickly glance down and count to three.

The gathering crowd is becoming impatient. Their conversations grow louder, eclipsing the music. The higher up the tiers, the less adorned and more wild looking. I'm sure some smaller faeries are playing a ball game with what might be another faerie as the ball. Green-cloaked guards bark orders to ensure everyone behaves.

Casting a glance over my shoulder, I search for Alfie. His

ginger hair is a flag I immediately lock onto. He sends me a reproachful glare, then faces to the front of the procession.

*Pay attention. Don't mess up. Do something useful with yourself.*

But my heart pounds horridly in my chest. Sweat prickles under my arms. My face burns as though someone is staring at me, cataloging every ugly mistake I make.

What am I doing here?

I should be home, in my room, organizing a funeral for Tinger.

I place my palm over the pendant's bulk beneath my shirt. The action grounds me, calms my heart, and centers my soul. Like me, he was a victim of High Fae whims. He was overlooked, unheard, and misjudged. But he was loved, and he loved in return. He was brave, he fought, he sacrificed.

He was the spider.

I refuse to spend the brief days of my new mortal life waiting to be taken seriously, only to have it cut short through someone else's mistake. My throat closes as guilt threatens to suffocate me, but I use my anger to push it back down.

Steeling my spine, I glance at the Court of Dreams loge, but Emrys is gone, and Goodfellow now speaks with a female dressed like Peablossom but with powder-pink hair.

"This is taking forever," the woman beside me whines.

Her companion replies, "Be grateful the march isn't through the city. I heard they did that one year."

She groans. "Fuck me."

"Stop cussing. You'll get us in trouble," another complains from the front of our unit.

A whiff of tobacco, absinthe, and something heady filters in on a breeze. The woman beside me freezes, her eyes widening at something over my shoulder. She curtseys and drops her gaze to the ground. "Knight Inquisitor, please forgive me."

# CHAPTER
# TEN
## WILLOW

"You will address your sovereigns with groveling respect." A smokey male voice drips with disdain. "Or forfeit the tongue that sputtered offense."

It must be Emrys. The tugging in my chest has become a vibration at his proximity, making me feel breathless. My shoulders bunch. I swallow the urge to scrape my nails across his pretty, porcelain skin. A million scenarios run through my mind. Run? Kill him now? With what? I have no weapons, no escape plan, no excuse.

Vaguely, I register her profuse apologies, but everything falls away as that feeling inside me thrums like the buzzing of wings. The sound grows to a roar in my head, ventilates my lungs with his scent, and curls something hot around my heart. It's like every cell in my body is drawn to him.

*Turn around.*

*Turn around.*

I turn and gasp as Emrys's eyes snap down to mine. The moment we connect, the restless thrumming in my chest calms. His eyes aren't wholly black like the portrait. The cruel twist of his angelic features slackens in surprise . . . *surprise*, not disgust. The longer we stare at each other, the more his eyes bore into me. His irises are a ring of rusty red surrounded by black. Like dried blood.

It should frighten me, but instead, I think about the crayons I used as a child. I was too scared to use the bright, angry red and would pick the subtler one between. Poppies, persimmon, sunsets, and my mother's hair. The association unsettles me, because it's a far cry from the dried blood of my first impression.

*Study your targets*, Rory would say during our lessons. *Know them intimately—their habits, routines, strengths, and weaknesses. Find the clues on their bodies, beneath their nails, and on their skin.*

Emrys's taloned, draconic wings are missing. The tattered silken membranes should be draped from his shoulders like a dark, regal mantle, but he wears a black cape over his military dress suit.

Something lurks in his eyes as his features harden again. For a moment, I think he recognizes me. Alfie did earlier, so I must look similar enough even with Peablossom's glamour.

His long lashes sweep lower with barely veiled frustration. He prompts, "Name?"

He doesn't remember.

"What is your name, mortal?" he snaps impatiently. Not a single drop of etiquette exists in his body.

"Willow," I answer, studying his reaction. "Willow O'Leary-Nightstalk."

Not even a twitch in his jaw.

My vision blurs. Blood roars in my ears. The fucking bastard doesn't remember my name. It's a punch to the gut I should have seen coming. Titania said she made them forget, but I honestly expected *something*.

They ruined my life. Hatred has consumed my every waking hour since I learned of the lengths of their manipulation.

"A private word, Exhibitor O'Leary-Nightstalk." He gestures toward one of the archways leading outside.

Lost memories of the battle bubble to the forefront of my mind, flashing images in my mind's eye.

*Darkness enshrouds me. Screams. Cries. Snarls. I try to lever off the corpse to stand, but my arms tremble, and I slip on bloody flesh.*

*Featherlight pressure surrounds my limbs. My stomach drops as ghostly hands lift me upright. For a horrifying moment, I am weightless, powerless. And then my feet touch the ground. Confused, I look around as the darkness clears and six sets of tattered wings swoop, their owners twisting to kneel around me in a circle. The fallen angels bow like knights before a queen, their wings like veils spilling behind them to cover the gore and death.*

That was the moment Legion touched my ankle, gasped in horror, and said I was not their queen. They were wrong. I'm nothing.

I almost pull that dagger from Emrys's belt and stab his eye, but something doesn't feel right. The Sluagh are telepathic and can reach into anyone's mind uninvited, but he asked for my name. If he has no wings, normal-ish eyes, and no telepathy . . . then maybe his wraith form doesn't leave his body either. Maybe he's not as powerful as before, just as I'm not. One thing is for sure: I need more information before launching an attack. I'll have to play the game.

As we step outside, the bone-deep cold seeps through every hole in my clothes. I look for a ray of sunlight and find a brave shaft punching through the trees. Considering the bleak weather, it will have to do.

"Here is good enough," he says, but I take three more steps until the sun lands on my cheek and face him with my chin held high.

*Look what your queen did to me, I scream in my mind. Come closer and see.*

I fold my arms and return his glare as he meets me under the waning sunlight. A feral edge laces his movements, but no signs of discomfort from the sun. He should be burning, but he doesn't even flinch—no perspiration beads across his brow or upper lip. The only sign of movement is his shadow writhing on the ground from dappled light cast through rustling leaves.

If he's not affected by the sun, then everything I knew about their weaknesses in Elphyne could be wrong. Desperately gathering my wits, I remember why he brought me here. Goodfellow didn't like me staring at them.

"For the record," I drawl. "Refusing to let anyone look you in the eye is just plain stupid."

Pure scorn fills his gaze. "Are you a simpleton or a fool?"

"Apparently, I'm nothing."

My insolence flicks a switch in him, but not the kind that triggers a rage. He swings the opposite way and falls so still that I hear birds hopping between branches. His next words are spoken in a tone so soft it sends a shiver down my spine.

"Did your upbringing omit protocols surrounding appropriate address?" He takes a threatening step toward me. Something cracks—his knuckles at his sides. "Do you require education?"

The predatory thrill in his eyes prevents me from answering. For the Knight Inquisitor, I can only imagine what "education" means. Interestingly, he doesn't seem bound by the same rules of pleasant vocabulary etiquette as everyone else. I suppose a dog like him would have a looser leash.

"How did you do it?" he asks abruptly, surprising me.

"Do what?"

Faster than I can blink, he fists my shirt at the collar and wrenches me closer. My boots scrape along the ground as he moves me with the ease of a doll. His breath heats my face—

Absinthe, tobacco, something heady and sweet. The raspy note in his voice must come from smoking.

If I only had my dagger, I would sink it beneath his ribs and pierce that black, withered heart. But again, I want to test his limits. Need to.

How far has Titania clipped his wings?

Surprise flickers in his eyes at my lack of reaction. He glances down at his fist—Tinger's pendant. My sharp intake of breath betrays my panic. If he's broken it, I'll murder him.

He lowers me to the ground and bites the gloves from his fingers. Wary, I watch him like a hawk. Peablossom removed her gloves before glamouring me. In Elphyne, we don't need to touch someone to cast spells, but maybe it's different here.

A flash of blue in my peripheral draws my eye to the faerie in question, watching from the wings of an archway. Dread dawns on her face as Emrys's surprisingly graceful fingers delve inside my collar and pluck out my pendant—Tinger's singular manabee sparkles proudly inside the tiny glass vial. Relief courses through my body. He's safe.

But then rage slams into me. He had no right to fish into my clothes.

"Give it back." My fingers clench into a fist. The pendant is still attached to my neck by a cord. The last thing I want to do is snatch it and break it.

"Where did you find this, little moth?" Emrys's husky murmur is hard to distinguish as he stares intently at the vial.

His quietness alarms me the most. Nero was like that. The worst killers, the most practiced of them, don't allow emotion when it's time to work. Maybe they have none to begin with. A Knight Inquisitor sounds like someone who would go quiet a lot.

I try to answer, but my words catch in my throat. He has no right to Tinger's final moments. That private pain is mine alone.

When Emrys' long lashes lift, something unsettling flickers

in his eyes. It's not the promise of death like I expected. But I don't know what it is.

At my continued silence, his tone becomes impatient.

"Puck said you are a Nightmare, that your face was as putrid as the shit he scrapes from beneath his boots. Did you harness this to glamour your face?" He holds out Tinger's manabee.

"I..."

Peablossom's missing eyebrow, her forced bravado, and the memory of how she wilted under Puck's dominance when I first arrived flash in my mind. She was petrified of the consequences of my tardiness. If anyone should receive a punishment for my behavior, it's me.

"Did you steal it?" he presses. "Are you a thief?"

"Yes," I reply. That excuse will do. It's not exactly a lie. In fact, I stole the glass vial he holds.

"And so you traded a wisp for a glamour?" He watches me expectantly.

A wisp? They must call manabeeze wisps here.

"I used a charmed stone. I did it myself."

He tucks it back into my shirt and then puts his gloves back on while studying me with unnerving scrutiny. He takes my upper arm in a punishing grip. Bruising pain crushes me, but I refuse to show I'm affected. With rough, unceremonious steps, he hauls me back to the arena. We pass Peablossom. Her shaky "Is all well?" falls on deaf ears.

I feel like I'm seven and back in Crystal City, dragged through the dining room filled with the elite oligarchs who mocked and humiliated me when I ate with my fingers at the table. My parents showed me manners, but my wolfish part always won.

Ants crawl over my face. Alarm zips through my veins. Has Emrys done something worse to me? But the moment fear hits, I remember I'm already ugly.

He can do his worst. It won't change a thing. It won't bring

Tinger or Rory back. It won't make me feel any worse for spending half my life at the whims of other people. When he places me in the first unit of Nothings, I briefly lock eyes with Geraldine two rows back.

The tall, silver-haired devil towers over me, blocking out the sight of anything else. For a moment, that surprise flickers in his gaze again as he takes in my face.

*I'm going to kill you,* I promise in my mind.

He strolls away and casually slips his hands into his coat pockets. I touch the pendant. At least he didn't steal it.

A musical trumpet echoes through the vast arena. The turquoise dragon yawns. Another growls. I brave a glance at Geraldine. She's within hearing distance.

"What did he do to me?" I ask, gesturing at my face.

Pity enters her eyes. "You look the same as you did before."

He stripped me of Peablossom's glamour. He wants me to be ugly.

Heat flames my cheeks. Hate is too little a word to describe my feelings for them. I want them dead. I want them obliterated from the face of this earth.

# CHAPTER
# ELEVEN
## FOX

Varen was right. Our queen has come for us.

From the darkest recess of our private box, I tap my foot, my stomach knotting as I wait for Emrys to return.

It's her.

It has to be.

Her unmistakable scent carried across the wind the instant she arrived in Avorlorna. I followed it and found her stealing a stone from a dream web in the city. It's taken every ounce of self-control not to go down there, sink my fingers into her hair, and breathe her scent in deep. I want it inside me, want it curling around my organs until she is the sole reason for my existence.

Traitorous hope rises in my chest, soaring on the wings of that scent. I could spend all day pulling apart the bouquet, splitting the whole until each note has a name. She is the woods. She is the sweet willow tree. She is a tiara of flowers—lily and lavender. I close my eyes and inhale, taking her into my lungs. I've suffered in this existence for five years, alone in my knowledge of hers.

And now she is here, and we are not ready.

*"Wait for her,"* Varen urged. *"Wait and prepare. She will come."*

*"Our fated queen hates us,"* I replied. *"She called us monsters. What if Emrys is right, and she's no better than the others?"*

*"She doesn't know us."*

He blinked at me in that knowing way.

*"When she comes,"* he murmured softly into my mind. *"When her heart opens to ours, we will walk in the sun for eternity. For this, I make the sacrifice."*

Wait.

Easier said than done when none from my hive remember her. None have been tasked with preparing for her arrival, dreaming of her sweet scent filling our lives.

Time has been torture.

Another whiff of her natural perfume pumps into my lungs. Fuck. My eyes flutter. My cock grows uncomfortably hard, demanding her fingers wrap around it, stroke it, make it hers. I pick up a note of heady, feminine musk and almost groan with anticipation. Will she smell like that everywhere? Will she taste like that?

As I exhale, I lose the battle with my voice. The agonized groan slips out. Legion glances at me, confused. His thoughts run circles of concern around me. He thinks I'm too distracted. He thinks only of rescuing Styx and finding a way to heal Varen.

If only they could remember her, it wouldn't be like this. But I've learned my lesson in trying to force the memories on them. It doesn't work. Titania's spell is too strong, and with the Keeper's seals holding their true selves at bay, they're losing their minds and wasting away.

Legion's hand lashes out to hold my bouncing knee. "Enough."

I still.

He eases back to his seat with a warning look. I don't like this version of him. I don't like any of them. I want my old hive back, but that will never happen. Even without Titania's spell, we are changed. From the moment Legion touched Willow on that battlefield, the final stage of our metamorphosis from death to life was complete.

"Fox was right." Emrys's raspy voice is unmistakable as he stalks into the loge, the curtain falling closed behind him.

Bodin bursts through the curtains next, his chest heaving as if he ran the entire way from the keep. That distance would take seconds if I could unlock their true selves. He is dressed for work in a shirt and plain breeches. He smells like the stables.

Nostrils flaring, his eyes dart to Emrys. "Have I missed it? What did you find out?"

The others stand to meet him in the eyes, but I remain down, hesitant.

"She wears a wisp within a vial around her neck," Emrys explains. "She admitted to stealing it."

Bodin folds his arms, expression pensive as he catches his breath. "And she is mortal, despite those ears?"

"Correct." Emrys's lips flatten before adding, "The blue-haired one glamoured her face to hide the scars. Puck requested I remove the deception. She is a Nothing, through and through. She belongs with the Nightmares, not with us."

Such vitriol in his voice. Has he spent too much time as Titania's lap dog to remember his roots?

"And so do we, brother." Bodin's lips curve wickedly. "Perhaps a nightmare is exactly what we need."

Emrys cracks his knuckles, his blood-red gaze turning inward, no doubt recalling his interaction with her. For this, I am the epitome of envy . . . he touched her. I scent the evidence on his hands hiding beneath the gloves. That alone is proof she's ours—can they not see?

Normally, the only touch he allows on his body is pain.

"I suppose she will not be needed for long," Emrys sneers. "I will endure it. For the hive."

I turn to Legion, for it is his decision we wait for. He already studies me with unwavering eyes.

He might not remember his true self, but he is no fool. He knows I am the only one keeping them all alive, separating dreams from reality, sustaining them with my own feeding, and defying the death sentence trying to smother us.

"Have you discerned the truth from her mind?" he asks me.

"No." And I never will unless she permits me.

"How will we know she is the one?" Legion asks.

My face slackens, and I let the glamour holding my true self at bay slip. The quick image of my true self is a trigger. Something innate inside them recognizes the monster within, and parts of that true identity return. They remember Legion is only the First because of Varen's sacrifice. But I must remind them daily because they forget every night.

As I stand, Emrys takes my arm. "Are you sure?"

I stare at his gloved fingers wrapping around my sleeve.

"She is a thief by her own words," I point out, "and a good one to hold a wisp on her person. She claimed to use a charm to improve her status, proving her resourcefulness." I know it's a lie, but they don't. And I'm prepared to do anything to bring her to our castle, where she's safe. Restoring their memories can wait. Until then, it's sometimes easier for me to follow the rules of Titania's spell—fit the narrative of this ridiculous place. "She has been trained in combat—you can see it in how she moves. And look—" I point down to where she strolls with her arm out, helping a flawed mortal to walk. "She is unafraid to break the rules. What more do we need?"

His gaze narrows on me with distrust. Legion may know how to read people, but Emrys knows lies, and they roll off my tongue like honey. Willow did not steal that wisp, but somehow, she is here in Avorlorna when we are most desperate for help. I never wholly believed Varen's prediction that she would come until now, so I followed their plan to free Styx.

But now she is here. This changes everything.

"You're hiding something," Emrys snarls.

I shake him off. "Doubt me again, I dare you."

He lets go but warns, "Once the djinn is out of the bottle, it will not go gently back in."

Bodin adds, "As soon as Puck knows, Titania will too. The clock will be ticking on Styx's demise."

"Don't you think I know this?" I hiss back. "He is as much a part of me as you."

I'll figure out how to save him, but it won't involve risking our queen. If I can't even get her to Shadowfall Keep, then she is dead anyway.

Emrys asks, "So why do you look at her with stars in your eyes?"

I step into his personal space and double down on my lies. "I will not sacrifice Styx's life for hers. The hive comes first."

"Good." Legion's voice is flat as he watches the mortal wolfling. "Because this plan falls to pieces without you holding us together. You must not waver."

I hate that he is right. For a moment, doubt flickers in my heart. Should I be risking everything when Willow casually walks side-by-side with another mortal, oblivious to the sleeping queen mere miles away? If she was ours, wouldn't she be overcome with the desire to kill our current slaver queen?

Only one can exist in the same place at the same time. It is the reason we had Willow sent to Crystal City as a child. The desecrated place blocked her blooming scent as she matured. Maebh was oblivious until Willow landed in the center of that battle with the humans.

Whether she is our queen or not, we still need a mortal to save Styx. This will still work.

"You have nothing to worry about," I reply curtly.

"Very well." He sighs and turns to the arena. "Then you know who to call."

# CHAPTER
# TWELVE
## WILLOW

The Pageant of Prowess is anticlimactic. It takes half an hour to march around the outskirts of the arena. *Oohs* and *ahhs* ripple through the crowd as we pass the buttress of each House. The Radiants cast their judgmental gazes on us, but the dragons unsettle me more. We don't have them in Elphyne. We have monsters.

Monsters are generally mindless. The dragons have clever eyes.

The burning one hisses smoke at my troop. The unit breaks formation, crying out in fear. Snickers and squeals of excitement erupt as our humiliation entertains. The dragon twists on its perch, keeping a smoldering gaze locked on us like we're tasty slabs of meat. I dart a look at my new friends. Peggy isn't doing too well. Without her walking stick, she favors one leg heavily but shakes her head when she sees me slowing. She gives Bob a pointed look instead. He keeps stumbling because he can't see well.

"Trade places," I mumble to the man in the row behind me.

Before he can protest, I grab him and twist our positions. I do the same with another until I fall into step beside Bob. I stretch my arm and murmur, "Take my elbow."

Chagrin crosses his expression, but it's not directed at me. I expect he's used to being independent. This whole situation would suck for him.

"No one will notice I'm helping," I insist. "I'm walking too closely."

His hand lifts, fumbles, then finds my elbow. "I used to be better than this. But now the shadows are darker. All I see are blobs of light and dark."

Spectator squeals clash with a dragon's growl on the other side of the arena. Is this pageant just an excuse to mock us as we run from magical predators ten times our size? I shouldn't be surprised. It feels exactly like the sort of thing done here.

"Wish I could see it all," Bob mumbles.

"The arena floor is dirt," I relay, "and a few patches of grass. We're surrounded by three tiers holding spectators amongst the trees around us. The architecture is truly interesting, completely blending nature and stone buildings. Reminds me of Delphinium back home. The elves there love working with wood. Although I haven't been there since I was little." I frown, annoyed that I'm rambling. "Anyway, the sky is still gray and dismal. Getting close to dark soon."

He doesn't respond, and I'm not sure I'm helping, so I fall silent. A few minutes later, he asks, "What else do you see?"

"On the second level, each fae House has a private box where their Radiants sit. Some of the fashion is ridiculous, if you ask me."

"How so?" he asks with a chuckle.

"I swear a lady wears a mushroom hat, but all I see is a penis."

Bob chokes as he holds back laughter.

"Sorry," I mumble. "Don't want to get you in trouble. I seem to be doing that a lot here."

"It's fine." His volume drops. "You know, I've been thinking about this exhibition, and I have some theories. It's odd that they suddenly allow mortals they usually banish. What if we're all just being fattened up so they can eat us?"

It's my turn to chuckle, but I see he's serious and remember Geraldine said he liked conspiracies. "You're probably not far from the truth," I tease. "At least, I think they're just using you all as fodder in their war."

He grunts and nods his head. "Hmm. I still think it's cannibalism. Or maybe they're monsters in disguise."

I pat his hand. "You should write all your theories down. I'm sure they'd make for interesting reads."

"Good idea. Maybe Peg can help me."

We continue marching. With so much to look at, I almost miss the three new arrivals to the House of Shadow's box.

This time, I'm prepared for the impact of their striking appearances. They're every bit the fallen angels my dream made them out to be. Long, silken black hair flows from a widow's peak as Legion braces the rail with graceful fingers. His pale skin is so perfectly proportioned it seems carved from crystal. He was labeled "The First." My snort of derision slips out. He carries the arrogance of someone who believes he's the first, too.

Bodin is a stoic statue beside him. Soft twilight hues paint his brown skin with a meticulous hand, highlighting the strong angles. His head is shaved around the base, from ears to back. As in the portrait, black braids sweep from his forehead to knot at the crown.

Unlike Legion, whose coat is unadorned and tailored to fit his body, Bodin wears a black casual shirt. The sleeves are rolled to the elbow. The laces are untied at the neck. His broad chest heaves as though he's run to get here. He also watches me with curiosity, judging me among the contenders. Not recognition.

Bitter disappointment sinks in my stomach. This revenge plan of mine is only sweet if they remember what they've done. A flash of white in the shadows reveals Emrys up there. He's probably told them about our interaction.

Alarm prickles my skin, and on reflex, I check the arena for exits in case I need to make a speedy escape. When I glance back at the box, another face appears in the shadows. Pale and with short, messy black hair. Fox has the kind of pretty-boy looks that can charm a siren into giving up her voice.

If he hears my musings, he doesn't reveal anything when he joins the others at the railing. He mutters something to Bodin and Legion, who both react with surprise. I don't waste another second of my time on them. The longer I do, the greater my need to stab something. I wish this stupid procession was over.

The melodious trumpet stops. A hush falls over the crowd. I glance at my fellow Nothings, but they're all the epitome of pristine behavior. Eyes forward. Backs straight. Hands by their sides. The pageant participants number in the hundreds. All desperate for something. All are willing to face death to get it.

Goodfellow swaggers toward the arena's center. Shortly after, the roar of four dragons heralds the arrival of aristocrats from the Houses, each escorted by an anonymous druid-type in a brown robe. A carved wooden mask hides their face beneath a hood. Each carries a flat bowl in their hands.

Someone nearby prays under their breath to be chosen. Another chants, "Pick me. Pick me."

Ahh. This must be the part where each House selects their protégé. Thank fuck it's almost over. My legs ache. I can only imagine how uncomfortable Peggy is.

The House of Tides is headed by an ethereal beauty in a long, shimmering dress the same color as her serpentine dragon.

Strings of pearls loop in her dark tresses, but she wears no other obvious adornment.

Next, a stocky male with sun-kissed, tawny skin leads the House of Stone. With that solid frame and rolling gait, I wouldn't be surprised if he knows his way around the battlefield—particularly with an ax. His fashion is no-nonsense and reminiscent of our dull-gray uniforms.

The House of Moonlight's aristocrat is a female with long silver hair. But that's where our similarities end. Her dress is of the finest pale tartan. She is tall, slim, and frail-looking. But I don't think she's weak. The moon shines from her pores, clashing with the dark heat from the House of Embers male beside her.

His black embroidered coat is trimmed with red, orange, and yellow flames that sparkle. With a hawkish nose and combed black hair, he walks with smug self-assurance.

Once the gentry and druids gather with Goodfellow at the center, each dragon slips down from their buttress and takes a position beside their leader. One by one, in perfect formation, the nobles march in a procession around the arena, as perfectly timed and executed as ours. No, that's a lie. They're far better. Each hand swings in the same direction at the same time. Left foot first. Right foot second.

They honestly take this nonsense seriously. I can't wait to talk to Alfie about it; I'm sure he finds it as ridiculous as me. It's absurd they can identify someone's worthiness simply by walking past them.

Unless there's magic involved. Okay, maybe not so ridiculous.

The heads of Houses don't stop at our troop. It's to be expected, but still, the disappointment in the eyes of my companions is heartbreaking.

Once the Radiants have completed a pass, they return to the center and wait beside the druids.

A loud, feminine, ceremonious voice announces from somewhere, "The Hollow Hunt and Her Radiance, Duchess Selene of Adularia from the House of Moonlight, will choose their favored Shadow first."

Commotion rustles through the tiers as the iridescent moonlit dragon takes an interest in a skinny man on the east wing. He looks like the whispering wind could blow him over, but he stands strong under the gale force breath exhaled from the dragon. Going by his unadorned uniform, he is a Never. The duchess beckons him forward with a serene smile plastered on her face. The druid beside her lifts their flat bowl, and she removes a long white shimmering scarf. The duchess takes her Never's hand and wraps both their wrists so they are bound.

Cheers erupt in the stands until the announcer speaks again.

"The Fever Hunt and the Marquess of Wulfenite, Lord Ignarius of the House of Embers, will choose their favored Shadow next."

The dragon with pulsing veins oozes smoke from cracks between its dark scales. Air shimmers from the heat. Nervous eyes widen amongst the contenders as the beast lumbers along, its tall suave leader strolling beside it. The Fever Hunt pauses, sniffs the air, and suddenly rounds on a troop of Chasers. It puffs smoke over them, obscuring them from view. Coughs and splutters can be heard from within. Lord Ignarius enters the plume and returns with a stunning raven-haired woman. The smirk on her plump lips as she's bound makes me think she expected this. And when Ignarius feasts on her with his eyes, I'm sure he expected it, too. This probably isn't the first time he's tied her up.

"The Dread Hunt and Marchioness of Connemara, Lady Nivene of the House of Tides, will choose their favored Shadow next."

The serpentine dragon sticks out its long, wet tongue, then licks an ethereal beauty from her chin to forehead. I didn't think Radiants could enter this tournament, but the similarities between her and the Lady are remarkable. Both have skin the color of sunburned sand. Their long, flowing bleached hair is a mirror image of the other. After they're bound and retreat to the arena's center, their gaits match. Their footsteps flow with liquid grace.

"The Baleful Hunt and the Earl of Heliodor, the Honorable Lord Sylvanar of the House of Stone, will choose their favored Shadow next."

The great stone dragon roars so loudly that the closest troop ducks in fear. All except one. A tall, muscular man who looks like he could eat Well Hounds for breakfast. He is a warrior through and through. Having spent half my life surrounded by Guardians, I recognize the sort.

The fierce roar must have been a test of fortitude, and he passed. The first dragon breathed on their chosen, another licked, and the fire dragon enveloped their troop with smoke. Were they all tests of some sort? The stocky House of Stone Radiant beckons his warrior with a stalwart flourish.

There are only four dragons. My stomach sinks for Alfie. He'd been so hopeful. I don't want to buy into this stupid tournament bullshit, and I hate that I'm disappointed for him. I just got him back. If he dies, I won't forgive myself.

Goodfellow gives a very un-noble-like shrill whistle, and everyone falls silent. I thought the sound was to gain our attention, but when a fluffy white cloud descends from the sky, I realize he called another dragon.

# CHAPTER
# THIRTEEN
## WILLOW

A cloud hits the ground at the center of the arena and unfurls in spools, revealing four legs, a long tail, incorporeal wings, and a dragon's head hanging heavy with lethargy. It's barely a part of existence with all the moving air and pale prismatic swirls rolling inside its body. *Fascinating*. I wonder if it solidifies.

During the battle in Elphyne, the Wild Hunt burst from the chests of each Sluagh and took shape as a swarming, dark shadow. It coalesced into an enormous storm cloud and morphed into a solid black dragon with a horned skull on the outside of its head.

The announcer's sweet voice echoes in the arena. "The Weaving Hunt and Chief Advisor to the Queen, Ser Robin Goodfellow, will choose their favored Shadow as representative for Her Royal Highness, Queen Titania of the Court of Dreams, Her Radiant Majesty of the Commonwealth of Avorlorna."

Goodfellow gestures toward the Weaving Hunt, and they begin their judgment walk. He takes his time inspecting each troop, but it feels more like he's paying lip service to the customs rather than truly searching for a worthy protégé. The dragon lumbers beside him, barely lifting its nose to sniff or waft a tendril until they arrive at a unit where a wisp unfurls to kiss Alfie on the cheek.

The Weaving Hunt sits on its haunches. Clouds puff from his rear end. Goodfellow sidesteps them, takes a scarf from the bowl of the Keeper following him, and binds his left hand to Alfie's. The druid nods and then returns to the others.

Alfie found the patronage he so desperately wanted, but it's from the Court of Dreams. It's with a mentor who makes my skin crawl.

Could be worse. Could be the House of Shadow. I glance at their box and startle when I find it empty. People kept saying they've never picked a protégé, so they've probably left early.

Typical.

Just like them to leave without an explanation.

The House representatives stroll the arena outskirts beside their Shadows, waving regally to the crowd in the tiers, then veer back to the center while their dragons are dismissed. It's all very civil. The Weaving Hunt returns to cloud form and wafts away while the others perch on their buttress of choice.

Some exhibitors sob quietly. I'm guessing this was their last chance. Goodfellow twirls his finger in the air to signal for the event to wrap up. The druids leave in single file, their flat bowls dangling at their sides. On the backs of their robes is an embroidered cauldron.

What does that represent?

The announcer reveals herself as she walks onto the arena floor—a lady-in-waiting with yellow hair. A bright smile stretches her ageless face as she speaks into a palm-sized stone. Her voice echoes across the fort from owl statues strategically placed about.

"In all my timeless existence, I've never beheld Shadows

shimmering with such potential. Congratulations to all. As usual, we shall draw the curtain on this evening's splendid spectacle—"

A high-pitched screech rends the air. Hands cover ears. People duck, both on the ground and up high. The light dims as though a cloud blocks the sun. Warning growls rumble from the throats of dragons as though they sense another predator encroaching on their territory. I sniff to see if I can catch something, but I can't distinguish anything new. Scales shimmer and muscles coil with tension. Smoke hisses from the Fever Hunt's veins. They glance up to where a small dark shadow spirals downward from the canopy like a vulture circling dying prey.

My gaze narrows. It's too small for a dragon. Is it a bird?

Darkness briefly consumes the light, and it has nothing to do with a cloud and everything to do with the four devilish fae prowling into the arena, commanding attention from the air itself. Legion, Bodin, Emrys, and Fox stir up a frenzy that borders on chaos. Green-cloaked guards flurry about, reminding the crowd of common courtesies.

"We are smiling!" a male guard shouts.

I almost burst out laughing. No one else does, making me worry there's something wrong with my sense of humor.

Two masked druids return to the arena through a gloomy archway, watching warily from the wings. Light returns as the four Sluagh arrive at the center. Radiants, I correct myself. To everyone else here, they're Radiants. Not soul-sucking bastards who eat anything and ruin lives.

Their fellow nobility aren't pleased. The announcer's smile is frozen stiff. She darts a nervous glance at Goodfellow, who smirks at Legion and says, "The Old Code states only ancient houses with an exalted High Dragon may choose to sponsor a Shadow for their protégé during the exhibition."

Gasps rocket around the crowd. Dread sinks in my stomach as the dark bird circles lower. It has a white head . . . and horns.

Legion's cultured voice pulls me back. "Does it now?"

The queen's advisor glances at his fellow Radiants for mutual support of his incredulity and then faces Legion again. "And we all know I, Robin Goodfellow, have been appointed the queen's regent in her absence."

"Sounds incredibly taxing."

Goodfellow's eyes flash, his anger palpable. Beneath his breath, he mumbles loud enough for my shifter ears, "You could have done this any year. Why now?"

Fox gives a nonchalant half shrug. "Because we can."

Bodin's nostrils flare as if he's tired of the theatrics, and then he points out, "We have a dragon."

Goodfellow forces a smile. Something is being said between the lines that I can't read. But before I examine them further, every head in the arena swivels as the small beast lands in a flap of wings and wobbly feet. It's a baby Wild Hunt.

I'm not the only one in shock, yet I wonder if I'm the only one who knows what this creature truly is—a prison for wicked souls, a terror of the living, a servant of darkness. They seem more surprised to see the Wild Hunt exists at all.

"What's happening?" Bob whispers to me.

"That screech was a baby dragon," I reply.

"What?"

"It's the Wild Hunt."

"My god. It's meant to be the most terrifying of them all. Wait. Did you say, baby? What does it look like?" His voice is filled with awe.

Fully grown, it should be at least twice as long and bigger than all the others. But it's tiny now—the size of a wolpertinger.

"I suppose it's cute if you like black glossy scales that catch colors in the light. His skull is on the outside of his head . . . or at least the top half of it. The lower jaw is black and scaled . . . except for the teeth. His wings' membranes are transparent with a reddish hue and veiny, but the talons at the ends are black and lethal."

"I'll bet they can stab through flesh like hot pokers," Bob breathes.

The Wild Hunt becomes a streak of black as it scampers toward the Sluagh, runs circles around each of their legs, then settles at Legion's feet with a little whine and a yip. A long, pink tongue lolls through its fangs, dripping saliva. Its long, spiked tail thumps on the ground like an overexcited wolf pup. Black liquid eyes beneath the bone impossibly widen with barely contained eagerness.

How can this tiny thing be the same Wild Hunt that swarmed from the Six's bodies during the battle in Elphyne? A shiver runs down my spine as I recall the ghostly faces of the damned pressing against the dragon's scales—peering out from the inside. The Horde of the Unforgiven Dead. The Wild Hunt. The Host. The ferocious, vicious, insatiable beast powered by death itself.

Legion's nervous glance at his hive is unmistakable.

The dragon's tail thumps harder. It gives a little restless shuffle and eagerly licks his lips. Only the hive's queen can call the Hunt from where it lives within the Sluagh. This is why they need a queen in the first place. She holds them together, somehow keeping them from descending into chaos.

*You are our skin,* their voice whispers from my memories.

I shove it deep down and hide it beneath my hatred. Who gives a fuck what they think of me?

Without permission, the Wild Hunt circles the group of Radiants and Shadows as though trying to round them up like cattle.

"Control your dragon," Lord Ignarius growls when it nips his ankles. The Fever Hunt hisses smoke in a warning.

The Sluagh ignore their tiny terror and stare at Goodfellow, waiting.

"Very well," he grinds out. "Choose your Shadow. But this will have consequences when she wakes, mark my words. The Keepers of the Cauldron have borne witness."

The druids waiting in the wings disappear except for one, who strides back in with a bowl and hurries to the House of Shadow's side.

"Hunt." Legion's bark of demand startles me.

The Wild Hunt skids to a stop, kicking up dirt. He glances at Legion, head pricking up.

"Let's go," Legion says, walking in my direction with the others.

Bodin wears the same curiosity I'd glimpsed before. Emrys still looks at me with seething hatred. As Fox draws near, I find an echo of something I've been searching for—recognition. The Wild Hunt must decide it's more interesting this way because he starts racing after them to nip at the heels of the Keeper with the bowl.

As the group approaches, the others in my troop stir. Some in fear, some in excitement. But the House of Shadow is interested in the one who doesn't move. The one who is as quiet as them.

Me.

# CHAPTER
# FOURTEEN
## WILLOW

The baby dragon races toward me, eyes wide, tongue flapping beside its fangs from the speed. I brace as it leaps. Pain peppers my body as tiny talons pierce my clothes. It scurries up my front to climb onto my head, circles, and plucks my hair, reminding me of how I prepare my bed. Just as I'm about to stop it from making my head a nest, a scratch on my cheek gets licked, and then it races down my front, takes a running leap from the ground, and launches back into the sky, flapping its wings.

Tiny things are capable of great catastrophe. The Wild Hunt terrorizes the crowd, triggering a stampede. Ignoring the chaos, Legion, Bodin, and Emrys stop a few yards from me and watch Fox continue alone.

He arrives at my side with a broad, heart-stopping smile, yet his murmur is for my ears only. "Hello, our queen. We've been waiting for you."

I am swept up in an escort toward the center of the arena. Blood drips down the inside of my pants from the Wild Hunt's talons, but I refuse to wince in pain. Legion and Bodin flank my front, Emrys and Fox at my rear. They don't speak. Their cool, stoic façade remains frozen on their faces.

My eyes scream for rescue at every person I pass, but I dare not raise my voice. The troops look on with jealous eyes, half the crowd is in bedlam, and the Radiants are poised and follow protocol. Yet their pleasantry hangs on by a thread.

I have no allies here. None, except Alfie, and he has just taken his vow to follow the Old Code articles relating to the exhibition. I'm suddenly struck with the notion that I could be crawling to him on my knees, bloody entrails dragging behind me, and he'd be as composed as the Radiants, a horrific smile plastered on his face.

The five mortal protégés appear dull next to the radiant faerie gentry. We are their shadows because we cannot be anything else.

Legion pins me with his unwavering gaze and removes a black satin scarf from his trouser pocket, snubbing the Keeper. He could be plotting my doom or dancing a jig in his mind. He is impossible to read. But when his fingers brush my inner wrist, a familiar tug at my chest threatens to ignite my blood. His hitched intake of breath is audible.

Does he feel something, too?

His elegant fingers are hypnotic as he expertly wraps the silk around our wrists, using a figure-eight motion to lock us together. Once. Twice. Three times is all it takes, and I am manacled. His fingers interlace with mine, and he lifts our hands above our heads as if we've already won—something the others didn't do with their Shadows.

The ego of that action vibrates outward, hitting each spectator with a different result. The Sluagh give slow, self-satisfied smiles while the Radiants lose their battle to remain pleasant. Steam emits from Ignarius. Sylvanar grinds his teeth. The ladies purse their lips.

Disappointment, envy, and bitter hatred are splashed across the faces of every unchosen, watching from their troop. But the chosen Shadows, the protégés . . . we stare at each other like enemies.

I can no longer slip through this Gentle Interlude unnoticed. Everyone will have their eyes on me, which means it's not a game anymore. This is reality.

I'm still unsure exactly what this exhibition entails, but I sense it will come down to us Shadows in the end. I feel it in my bones.

The best warriors study their enemies *before* engaging in battle, and I am acutely aware that I'm late to the party. The final tournament isn't for a few turns of the moon, but it's clear by the competitive expressions of my peers that the battle has already begun.

The lyrical announcer continues speaking, but her words are drowned out by the roaring of my pulse and the heat of Legion's fingers. He clings to me through the ensuing madness. The Wild Hunt screeches again, causing more pandemonium.

Troops return to the dorms in a rushed, barely coordinated march. The tiers above us empty at an alarming rate. From the twitch lifting the corner of Bodin's lips, I can't help but think this was all part of their plan.

The problem is, these people think the Sluagh are faerie gentry—the Good Folk, the People of *Peace*. But I know the depth of depravity in their chaotic souls. They're the pretty devils who ruined my life.

Goodfellow's unimpressed mood remains as he stares for a long, hard minute before reluctantly turning to address the circle of the elite.

"Shadows, you must now embody the pinnacle of decorum that your newfound station commands. Confrontations that might soil the Radiants' refined image are strictly prohibited. We do not escalate into disorder. We are not savage Nightmares. Understood?"

"Yes, Your Radiance," they respond in unison.

I neglect to answer out of ignorance, yet I catch Fox's dimples flashing as though he's proud of my perceived ill manners.

"You are now subject to the same Old Code accords as your fellow Radiants, and thus, you will also be subjected to a similar fate if you break them. If you feel the subterranean desire to sow chaos, exhibitors may flex their newly acquired warrior's skills strictly within these Nexus walls." He pauses for effect. "I will not warn you twice. If you're caught violating the code, you will be punished."

The Baleful Hunt gives a ground-trembling roar that spills tiny rocks from his body like an avalanche. My heart clenches. I'm guessing the penalties aren't as benign as missing eyebrows.

Goodfellow continues, "Upon arrival at the welcoming dormitories, you will gather your personal effects and transition into the Shadow's dwelling within your House's tower. The remaining regional aspirants will honorably delay their relocation until your task is complete. Training commences with the morrow's dawn. You are dismissed."

Each coupling unwinds its bindings, and then the House Radiant steps back, tilts their face to the sky, and opens their arms. One by one, each dragon bursts into their elemental substance and streams into their Radiant's chest. Afterward, Ignarius snorts a puff of smoke and then cracks his neck as though he's re-acclimatizing himself to the containment of his Hunt. Lady Nivene inhales a watery breath before righting herself. Lord Sylvanar appears to have indigestion, and Lady Selene's glowing skin fades with each passing second.

A few murmured words are passed between mentor and protégé, but most disperse immediately. Lord Ignarius gives

Legion a scathing look. But the others are hurried or less disgruntled about the disruption.

Legion does not uncouple us. He gestures to the three, and then we move toward the dormitory.

"Why are you *all* escorting her?" Goodfellow's sickly sweet voice trails us. "Why are any of you going at all?"

None of the other Radiants have accompanied theirs. Legion stops and glances over his shoulder. He does nothing to veil his disdain. "We will collect our Shadow's personal effects."

"Transporting a Nothing's belongings is beneath the station of a Radiant." The word *Nothing* sounds bitter in Goodfellow's mouth.

Contempt is echoed across the faces of all four Sluagh. They really don't give a shit about being poised and pleasant. The only time I saw them smile was . . . when they chose me.

"Do not presume to order us, Puck," Legion says.

Bodin adds, "*We* are above *your* station."

"I serve no master except Pain," Emrys rasps darkly.

Goodfellow's expression deadpans, and he steps back. I don't blame him. Something about Emrys feels like phantom nails scraping down my spine.

"Control your Hunt." Venom spills from Goodfellow's lips. He strides up and narrows his emerald gaze at Legion. "Or the Keepers of the Cauldron will do it for you."

"My, my." Fox feigns alarm. "Whatever will we do?"

"Knight Inquisitor?" Goodfellow turns his attention to Emrys with forced bravado. "You have unfinished work at the palace."

Emrys stands firm. "She is to remain at the Keep for the duration of the Gentle Interlude."

"Absolutely not. This is a code violation!" Outrage flares in Goodfellow's eyes. The Wild Hunt suddenly swoops, nipping at his auburn hair. He swats it away with increasing frustration, his faerie decorum melting by the second. "Shadows *must* relocate to their respective House Tower."

Emrys takes a menacing step forward, but Legion lifts an elegant hand, and he halts.

"That's right," Goodfellow retorts. "Keep your dog on his chain."

"Careful, Puck," Legion intones. "You know the punishment for spreading lies."

"My mistake." His eyes crinkle. "We all know it's the queen who holds the leash."

Bodin spits on the floor. "You think we *choose* to live in close quarters with a Nothing?"

"We would rather burn," Fox purrs, smirking at my surprise.

For a moment, I'd forgotten they were my enemy. What a fool.

Their vitriol placates Goodfellow enough to wipe his hand through his hair and straighten his vest. "Nevertheless," he says, "the move is against the code. You break it for the enemy, no doubt. One would almost wonder where your allegiances lie."

Legion's patience evaporates. He moves in the blink of an eye to face the auburn-haired advisor and bares his teeth. "You dare question our motivations when we are the sole receivers of the Cauldron's supreme blessing?! Avorlorna would fall to Oberon's whims tomorrow without the House of Shadow. The Nothing comes with us because she will be exposed to military secrets during our patronage, and we would rather our sovereign queen's decorum remain untainted by our . . . unique methods of discipline to keep those secrets where they belong."

His words make complete sense. Even the eyebrowless jerk submits.

"Why do you sponsor her if you're so repulsed?" he tests.

"Simple," Emrys purrs.

"We want to win," Bodin finishes, his dark eyes flashing.

Goodfellow's need to peel back my skin and learn what makes me tick is a palpable heat on my cheeks. My fingers twitch to test the bulges, cringe, and hide from scrutiny. But he settles for, "Four are not needed for the task."

Legion mutters something I can't hear through the ringing in my ears, then unwinds the binding and tucks it inside Fox's embroidered coat pocket. No words pass between them, yet somehow, everyone knows what to do next. Bodin and Legion leave together. The Wild Hunt whimpers when he's called, but a ribbon of shadow shoots from Bodin's hand and lassos around the baby dragon like a leash. Emrys leaves with Goodfellow.

It looks like a surrender, but it's not. When I turn, Fox is already walking toward the exit. He arrives at the archway and flicks me a disinterested glance. I can't tell what's an act and what's real.

"I'm going to kill you for what you did to me," I declare.

As if my words are imagined, Fox casually checks his nails.

"Hurry along now, little wolf," he says. "My attentions are in high demand elsewhere."

# CHAPTER
# FIFTEEN
## FOX

I am drunk on her scent. I thought I wanted to be closer to Willow, but now I can't think straight. We had to put on a show for that insufferable nuisance, Puck, and now she thinks we despise her.

*I'm going to kill you.*

Her words pierce my heart in more ways than she can imagine.

She still thinks we're monsters.

She hates us. She hates us. Varen was wrong.

And I don't know what to do, so I walk toward the dormitories where she left her belongings. I keep playing the disinterested fool, hoping the lies stop me from doing something that cannot be taken back.

I need time to *think*.

Need to clear my mind of her intoxicating presence. So I hurry along the winding path in the woods, eager for the fresh air to push her existence from my lungs. But she scurries after me, refusing to be ignored. I am a fool to think I can outrun her sweet poison. A dark part of me laughs at how perfectly savage she is. Even now, she fires off accusations and questions, refusing to be brushed aside. But the other part of me, the newer part made from glass, already cracks under the pressure of her opinion.

What if it's too late to change it?

"First," she promises, panting behind me, "I'm going to study you."

We duck past a low-hanging branch. I keep walking, my hands in my pockets.

"Then—ow, fuck. Stupid tree." Scurrying footsteps. "Where was I? Oh, yes. *Then*, I will find your weaknesses and come at you when you least expect it."

Revealing a plan to murder us might seem amateur to anyone else, but we know her. Not because we've watched her live a thousand lives through Varen's psychic visions, but because she is just like us. A natural-born predator.

"I've already learned a lot. For example, you remember me. The others don't."

In every version of her future, she was miserable unless she could dominate, kill, and control. She is a predator, but not like us. We have done it for the joy, the thrill, and nothing else except we can.

She will do it to protect, to save, and to serve. But to feel safe enough to fulfill this ideal version of herself, she needs us. And we need her.

But her sultry voice is utterly vexing. Her scent drives me insane. My body is not my own around her and I have no one to talk to about it. My brothers are blind.

"And you know what? I don't give a shit that you're different here. It doesn't excuse what you've done. You ruined my life, and I'm here to make you pay."

I frown, pause, and spin around. She bowls into me. I catch her by the shoulders and hold her at arm's length. For a moment,

I'm struck by the blush in her cheeks, the brightness in her eyes, the starlight shining from her soul.

"Get off me." She slaps me away, carelessly announcing to the creatures in the woods she cares little for the rules of the Old Code. Open conflict is a no-no. She is our Shadow and must only flex her fierce claws on other exhibitors within the Nexus grounds. We are nowhere near the privacy of our keep. Any minute, the pathways will fill with those traversing to their new homes.

"Careful, little wolf," I warn, my breath clouding in the cold.

Her golden eyes fill with rage. "You're dead. You're all dead."

A shiver of undeniable attraction runs down my spine. Such fire. Such hate.

But for what . . . because she thinks we ruined her life? She, who stands here, flesh and blood, smelling like the goddess of starlight and darkness all at once.

A knot forms around my heart. This isn't going to work. There is too much she doesn't know. Too much to explain.

*Wait. Wait and prepare to catch a falling star.*

Easier said than done when I'm alone.

And falling, too.

# CHAPTER
# SIXTEEN
## WILLOW

I'm left at Fox's mercy as we journey through the halls toward Alfie's room.

The fucker has all but ignored every threat I've sent his way. For a moment there, he rounded on me, and I thought he would acknowledge everything.

Nothing.

Zip.

Nada.

He carried on pretending he doesn't know me.

I'm not a short person. My father was well over six feet tall. He could rest his chin on top of my head without bending over. Fox's height is between my father's and mine, yet I feel like a mouse scurrying behind him.

As we navigate the corridors, exhibitors wait in their rooms for permission to begin relocation. Shadows come first. Behind Fox's back, a Chaser drags his finger across his neck as he meets my eyes. Another sticks his finger down his throat in a gagging motion.

Goodfellow mentioned something about keeping conflict on

Nexus grounds. I'm guessing these death threats aren't empty, but it's not me I'm worried about. As we walk, I peek inside rooms and search for Geraldine and the others but don't see them. I hope they're together. Safety in numbers will protect them.

As if he's walked these halls nightly in his dreams, Fox takes all the right turns until we arrive at Alfie's shared room. A bunk beside his is now empty. Must have been another Shadow if they've already left. Alfie is packed but sits at the edge of his bed, brooding over my rucksack in his lap. Panic flutters in my stomach. Did he go through my things?

Did he steal my dagger?

He glances up, relieved, until he notices Fox.

"Your Radiance." Alfie stands to attention, the charms on his chain tinkling. My rucksack falls to the floor.

If the Six expect me to gush over them every time they enter the room, they'll be disappointed.

"What a decadent dance of obedience, Shadow." Fox gives him a patronizing pat on the head, a sour glance at the other exhibitors waiting, then a look at me as if to say, *See? That's how you should address me.*

Then, he leans against the wall and gestures at my things expectantly.

What a dick.

As Alfie bends to retrieve my rucksack, I catch the way his mask of respect drops. When he straightens, he hands me the bag. His eyes say he wants to talk.

*Later,* I promise with mine. *Find me later.*

He gives a curt nod, and I exhale. Even though Alfie and the Six were present at the same battle five years ago, I don't think they recognize each other. Something tells me that Alfie wouldn't be standing there if they did.

When he hands me my cape, his eyes catch on the bloody stains spotting my trousers. "Willow!"

He reaches for my thighs to inspect, but Fox's snarled warning freezes him. "Do *not* touch what is ours."

Alfie slowly draws his hand back. He looks at Fox with a ruthless confidence I've never seen before. Again, I mark his changes—the hardness—and wonder about the lived experience that must have shaped his new, stronger body.

Fox sees it, too. He pushes off the wall and comes to my side, where he flicks a charm on Alfie's chain. "How quaint Puck thinks his trinkets will keep his secrets from me."

Alfie reverently lowers his gaze. "I would never think to hide anything from you, Knight Spymaster."

My brows raise. *Interesting.*

I chalk that tidbit up in the pros column regarding Fox retaining all his deadly Sluagh skills. The ability to ransack minds would be the perfect skill for a spymaster. Having an invisible wraith form to spy on conversations would be even better.

Fox asks, "Do you have something on your mind, Shadow?"

"I simply wish to tend to her injuries."

A film of darkness swims across Fox's expression. It's so brief I think it's imagined. He deadpans when he glances down at my legs. "You are wounded."

"You afraid of blood or something?" I return.

Fox's gaze lifts to mine, holds, and his wicked gleam returns. "Or something."

THE KEEP IS THE SMALLER, BLACK-STONED CASTLE IN THE SHADOWS OF the grand Ivory Palace. It sits about half a mile from the Nexus, and the journey through the woods will be cold. The chill drills down to my bones.

When I stop in the middle of the woods to put my cape on, Fox irritably stands to the side with his arms folded. He glares at the leaves swaying in the trees as if they hold the world's secrets. While he's distracted, I deftly search my rucksack and locate my dagger.

Two things in Avorlorna I prize more than my life: Tinger's pendant and Rory's dagger.

She shoved this blade into the Guardian Cloud's hand as he fought us on the airship, trying to stop us from escaping. Rory and I accidentally tumbled overboard. Cloud was torn over who to save—me, his friend's daughter or the ex-lover he'd plotted vengeance on for decades. He wanted Rory dead, but he wanted to make her suffer first. She knew anyone filled with that much hate would let me go first. So she stabbed him. She chose me. Then she fell.

I learned two valuable lessons that day.

Love sucks. And once metal pierces a Guardian's skin, they're cut from the Well just like everyone else.

Done with my adjustments, I refit my rucksack and continue down the forest path. Dream catcher webs glimmer between the trees. While Fox is distracted by his thoughts, I secretly squirrel away another gemstone without breaking my step.

Eventually, we arrive at a rickety rope bridge crossing a ravine. On the other side, the Keep looms behind a black stone wall overgrown with briars and vines. In the silence after a raven's caw, the unmistakable sound of trickling water instills fear into my mind.

The ravine is a moat.

I could drown in a moat.

My lungs seize. My steps falter.

Already halfway across the swaying bridge, Fox turns back. I pretend to be in awe of the Ivory Palace brightening the night sky, but really, I'm calculating how to escape without him hunting me.

When they chose me as their Shadow, I was shocked. Afterward, I thought *great*. They've invited a wolf into the sheep's pen. Killing them will be so much easier. The instant he called me his queen, I knew their obsession still rang true. They'll underestimate me at every turn.

But now, as the rushing water drowns out the rapid pulsing of my heart, I'm not thinking at all.

I'm terrified.

"What's the holdup?" Fox stalks back to me.

Does he not see the bridge swinging in the breeze? Hear those creaking ropes? The wooden slats click like decking on the airship.

Water is not my friend.

Water killed Rory.

What if the wind gusts and the bridge upturns . . . with me on it?

"We don't have all day." Fox clicks his fingers before my face. "Let's go."

*"Let me go," Rory rasps, smacking Cloud's tattooed hand gripping her throat.*

*Her body hangs at an odd angle, her legs flailing against the airship's hull. When we went overboard, he grabbed anything to stop us from falling. His other hand latched around my wrist, my dead weight almost yanking my arm from my socket. Black feathered wings beat frantically behind him, blocking the sky and gusting wind against our faces.*

*"No!" My shriek becomes a wail. "Not her! Me!"*

*"You know it should be me," Rory hisses, taunting him. "Kill me."*

*We're both about to die, dangling hundreds of feet over a lake, and she refuses to look at me.*

*Dread unfurls in my stomach. I know what this means.*

*No personal connections, she always taught me. Emotions cloud judgment. Avoid forming personal attachments that could compromise your mission.*

*She's distancing herself.*

*I see it. Cloud sees it.*

*The force of our weight mottles his face. Veins bulge in his temples. Dark, curly hair flicks in his eyes, but it can't hide his fear of the inevitable—one more breath and he will slip.*

*"Maybe we'll land in the water," I shout at Rory, tears streaming down my face. At least we'll fall together.*

*The hopeless look in Cloud's eyes tells me everything. Even if we survive the impact, something lurks in the depths of this lake, something horrifying no one wants to face. If we fall, we die.*

*Rory suffered too much. I would never have survived Nero's deadly games without her. Would never have grown into the warrior I am. When no one else could, she sacrificed everything to help me escape.*

*Desperate whimpers erupt from my lips. I try to pry Cloud's fingers from my wrists, to kick against the ship's hull, but Rory sees what I'm doing.*

*"If you hate me, then kill me!" Her voice is a choking gurgle, her throat collapsing under his desperate grip.*

*He roars his anguish in her face. It's so powerful, so deep-seated with rage that it vibrates the air. But he doesn't let go. His black feathered wings continued to flap. He continues to hold us both, paralyzed by indecision.*

*The airship jerks to the side as it's boarded. Cloud's grip slips. I drop an inch. My scream dies in my throat when he tightens, catching me again. My socket pops, blinding me with pain.*

*Warning shouts from the deck behind him—the metallic click of mechanical guns. Nero is here. To take us back. To make us pay for our betrayal. How dare we escape him? How dare I fail and cause so much death.*

*Cloud's mistake is looking over his shoulder. He should have been watching the woman he held by the throat. She grips his forearms and hoists herself with the same impossible strength a mother summons to protect her child. The action yanks him down. His head lowers for her to whisper something in his ear. Their gazes clash. His flares wide, lips part, and then she plunges her dagger into his tattooed hand.*

*Agony crumples his face as she falls, dark hair streaming like ribbons. But she doesn't flail. She doesn't scream. She holds his gaze until the deep-blue water swallows her whole and my heart is ripped to shreds.*

*She didn't look at me.*

*I am nothing.*

I am jerked from my nightmare when Fox tosses me over his shoulder and walks toward the rickety bridge.

# CHAPTER
# SEVENTEEN
## WILLOW

We're two steps across the bridge when I come to my senses.

"Put me down!" I shriek, loathing the fear cracking my voice.

Did he read my thoughts? Does he know my weakness? Mortified, I pound his back, but the rucksack tips, sliding over my head, tangling my arms against his body, and threatening to throw us off balance. Before I know it, I'm roughly deposited on solid ground and scramble to my feet.

"You're welcome," he mumbles, cheeks bright from exertion.

I am speechless, still mortified, disorientated, so I'm unprepared for his silent shove between my shoulder blades, urging me toward the keep's open gate—a dark stone archway between two smaller towers.

It takes a hot minute to right my pack. Somewhere along the way, the tie holding my braid fell out. Wind blasts my long hair in my eyes, but I stumble through the gate. Once inside, he waves his hand. Thorny vines weave a thick web between the archway, blocking me from the outside world. I'll have to climb thirty feet of granite wall to escape.

And cross a moat.

I'm fucked.

Hugging my cape to my trembling body, I face the keep.

Fox storms away, directly over a grass courtyard big enough to train a small army. Smaller outbuildings are to the left and right of the three-story castle. More dead trees surround the field, gnarled branches creaking in the quickening breeze. I shudder. A storm is coming.

Another two smaller towers punctuate the boundary wall further down, but none are as high as the tower at the main residence. It must be at least seven stories high. The gathering wind makes window shutters bang against the granite. Cracks in glass panes are a common sight. Paint peels from the wooden lattice. The climbing rose on the façade is dead.

Six people wait ominously on the porch landing, but only three are Sluagh—Legion, Bodin, and Varen. I set my eyes on the latter with curious suspicion. He is the spitting image of his portrait—pale skin, arresting eyes, high cheekbones. Two dimensions fail to convey his chameleon beauty. Depending on his angle, his features are sometimes hard, sometimes soft. His jaw is unshaven. Cool lantern light paints a blue, sometimes purple, sheen on his dark hair. Something vital is missing from his haunted eyes.

Disturbed, I move my focus to the pretty brunette beside him. Her fists bunch over a white apron, catching her dress skirt. She's either excited or angry. Her neighbor, a tall, lanky man, clasps his white-gloved hands. His stained work shirt and messy tawny hair don't match his suspenders and bowtie. It's like he woke up this morning and couldn't decide whether to be the gardener or the butler.

One Sluagh left unaccounted —Styx.

Fox strides up the steps and barges through the door without acknowledging the others. Legion arches his brow at Bodin. A second later, Fox returns and murmurs something to the woman that the wind steals from my ears. Then he's gone, the big carved door slamming behind him.

Movement two levels up. A curtain twitches in one of the many windows. Some are dark, and others are candlelit from within. But whatever was there, isn't now. Oh, wait. *There.* A long pink tongue finds a gap between the curtains and licks the paned glass. I glimpse white bone and flatten my lips to stifle a laugh. The baby Wild Hunt probably wants to be out here but isn't allowed. Like my sisters, he's probably making a mess in that room in retaliation.

*This place is falling apart.*

Good.

As I cross the lawn toward them, Legion descends the steps and stops halfway. "Welcome to Shadowfall Keep."

As I climb, he studies me from head to toe. Probably wondering why I'm not running in the other direction at all the creepy things I've already seen. But I recall their house in Elphyne before we moved in. Weirdly, it was in a state like this. They had no idea how to maintain a house—were lazy, or were too busy spying and scheming.

His gaze lingers on the dark patches of my trousers. He gestures at the gardening butler and says, "Finch will take your luggage to your room. Cricket will see to your orientation. Note that any goings on within these walls shall remain inside. Understood?"

He pauses. Our gazes collide, and I hold my breath. Is he going to acknowledge who I am? Or has he paused because he's horrified by the sight of my cringe-worthy face? It was easy to forget about the curse during the procession—too many distractions. But now the excitement's over, and I'm surrounded by the most beautiful creatures ever to exist, I feel my ugliness like a brand on my forehead.

He stares for longer than appropriate. The urge to shrink is overwhelming.

"We haven't formally been introduced," he eventually says, voice a velvet purr. "I am Lord Legion, sworn Knight Commander of Avorlorna and the First of the House of Shadow. You may address me as sir or my lord."

"I know who you are," I reply curtly.

His brows knit as if he doesn't understand my abrasive tone. "And you are Willow O'Leary-Nightstalk, correct?"

Sigh. "Yes."

"This is Lord Bodin, Knight Marshal and our Second. Address him as sir or my lord. And this is . . . this is our Varen."

Just Varen? My gaze swings to him. Why the pause?

Bodin gently takes Varen's arm, saying to Legion, "Perhaps, brother, formal introductions should be in the privacy of the keep."

Varen's brow furrows. "But the queen kicks the drones out of the hive during the winter. Keeping her warm is up to the rest of the hive."

I blink.

Bodin darts a nervous glance at me, then whispers to Varen, "We can talk about the bees later, Ren. Inside now."

"Yes." Legion rubs his temples. "Do go inside. Willow, it was not a lie when I told Puck having you here means we wish to keep an eye on you. That also means you are gaining access to a place no other in Avorlorna has been. I need your sworn oath not to tell anyone what you witness here."

His cultured drawl ends with a sharpness rivaling my dagger. I take a moment to soak in all that is Legion—the First, the Knight Commander, the Lord. He is the driving force of Avorlorna's military in a time of war, yet wrinkles dare not appear on his impeccably tailored suit. Knots fear to disrupt the silken strands framing his face. Even the light hides from the depths of his eyes.

"I don't have a choice, do I?" I shoot back.

Wrong thing to say.

His carefully presented stoicism implodes.

"Sleep outside if you are fishing for choice." His booming voice echoes against the walls. "But inside this castle, *all* of our choices exist purely to serve the queen. Now, I do not wish to repeat myself. Hold your tongue about what you witness here. Am I understood?"

"Fine." My voice is quiet.

His brow arches, unsatisfied.

I avert my gaze and hide my face with my long hair. "I mean, yes, sir."

Here, they're the saviors of the realm, but back home, they were villains. How is any of this fair?

Legion is the one to watch—the one to fear. Beneath that stoic exterior is a cold, calculating beast, which he showed as a warning. I doubt he warns twice.

"It's been a busy day, my lords." Cricket's deep, throaty voice isn't what I expect to come from her delicate lips. "Why don't you all go in and sit by the fire? I'll take care of the Lady Willow from here."

Legion starts up the steps, his boots dragging. He faces me just before entering and calmly says, "It's clear you do not wish to be here, but necessity forces our hand. We must all live with the arrangement."

"You chose me, not the other way around."

"We chose a Nothing who wears a stolen wisp around her neck. Hardly trustworthy behavior, but a deception we can use to our advantage." The effort to restrain his temper is a visible tremble as he rubs his temples. When he speaks again, his cool sophistication is back. "Your company is required for the Holly King's feast on Feyday evening. Ensure you are punctual."

He waits for me to respond with a "Yes, sir" and then enters the keep behind Bodin and Varen.

Glass breaking upstairs makes Finch cringe. "I'd best be off to deal with the wee wildling."

"Alright, love." Cricket gives him an affectionate smile. "You go do that. I'll take care of the lady."

He turns to me and lifts his chin. "Very nice to meet you, Lady Willow."

Most strangers cannot hide their shock at my face, but these two don't look twice.

"Not a lady." I return his smile. "Willow is fine."

"Don't mind the First. He's not himself lately. None of them are. But we're over the moon to finally have a guest in the castle."

I don't know what else to say, so I nod.

He gives a formal, sweeping bow and then collects my rucksack. *Mine.* Startled, I tug it back. The guards spilled the contents out, and I'm done with my things being meddled with.

"It's alright, love," Cricket says. "He'll just take it to your room. Promise."

Logic says they won't disrespect my things. I reluctantly let go.

"I'll deliver this to your room before seeing to the wildling." He gives Cricket a quick kiss on the forehead. "Wish me luck, my strumpet."

They act like an old couple in love but appear youthful like every other faerie in this place. No charms tinkle on chains, and I couldn't make out the shape of their ears. My gut says they're human.

After he leaves, Cricket says, "Come now, milady. We have much castle to get through before we arrive at your wing."

"Wing?"

"Usually, you'll sleep in the west wing. The masters are usually in the east. The clock tower is strictly forbidden. It will be hard to resist at first. And the castle will give you a little nudge now and then, but mark my words, you do *not* want to go in."

"Why?"

"No one comes out. As to the rest, you'll get used to the castle butting its nose where it doesn't belong. Servants are housed—oh, apologies, milady. We're not supposed to call ourselves servants here. The masters don't like it."

"Why not?" I ask.

"Don't know, to be honest." She scratches her chin. "They don't like us doing much at all. Drives us a little barmy, especially with how this place is falling apart. But we do what we can. It makes us feel like we earn our keep."

"You're boarders?"

"You could say that. We were here when they moved in, and instead of kicking us out, they let us stay. At first, they didn't want us anywhere near them, but Finch and I like to think we've warmed the cockles of their hearts with our cheerful dispositions. Shall we go inside?" Cricket watches me intently.

I crane my neck from the porch and look again at the neglected exterior. I came to Avorlorna to make them suffer, but I still haven't heard of Styx's whereabouts. Varen has lost his marbles. Their almighty death dragon is a wildling baby. I suspect none have the same indomitable power as in Elphyne, except maybe Fox. He remembers me, I'm sure of it.

Something is wrong.

I feel it in my bones.

It makes my skin crawl to have my choices made for me again, but something Legion said makes me think: "Inside, *all* of our choices belong to the queen."

They have no freedom either.

# EIGHTEEN

## FOX

Willow's nightmare screams in my mind as I storm into Varen's room. I promised myself I would never listen to her thoughts, but they were so loud. So distraught. I had no choice but to experience them with her.

Varen's chambers are known as the Hive Room, not because we often gather here, but because of what he's done to it. The peacock-blue papered walls are covered in charcoal sketches of honeycombs, scribbled nonsense about bees, and gibberish in a fictional language. As far as the eye can see, he's depicted a vast network of hexagons interlinked over peeling paper. The furniture's gold filigree is tarnished, the fireplace is dormant, and the air is frigid.

Fresh charcoal marks etch the wall beside the fireplace. For the millionth time, I touch the lines and try to decode the ramblings of madness.

Frustrated, I head to the hearth and use a poker to clear old logs before tossing in a fresh one. Gone are the days when a family of fire sprites would gladly warm the house in return for shelter. Gone are the days I'd eat the family who used to live in their house.

The sprites in Elphyne followed us from our prison in the Winter Palace, where Queen Maebh held us in a chokehold. Were they still there to warm Willow in our stead, to provide comfort as she cried herself to sleep?

There are no sprites in Avorlorna.

Flashes of her nightmare shove into my thoughts, and I toss another log on the hearth, then set it ablaze with my power, wishing to incinerate her pain with it.

The door opens, and Varen strolls in. He heads to the wall beside me, taps a section, cocks his head, then mumbles something about the honeycomb cells not being in the right place. Dark circles shadow his eyes. He needs a shave, and his hair is messy, no doubt from running his hands through it on the walk up from the porch.

He throws his charcoal stick at the fire, slams his fist into a honeycomb cell, and shouts, "Queen bees aren't supposed to be the rulers."

Dropping his head to his hands, he keeps mumbling nonsense, exasperated. The only way to calm him down from this state is to go along with it, to humor his whims.

"Why don't you take a seat," I suggest, dragging over an antique armchair. "Tell me about the bees while I clean you up."

He looks dubious as I guide him onto the seat.

"The worker bees control the hive," he tells me.

"Of course," I mutter and go to the dresser, fill a bowl with water from the pitcher, and locate his shaving kit. When he doesn't answer, I prompt, "Go on."

"Important decisions are made when the colony votes through collective behavior."

When I return, I notice Bodin and Legion at the doorway.

They know the routine. Bodin brings another chair to the

fireplace while Legion pulls over a side table for my bowl. As I sit and prepare the shaving cream, Bodin undresses Varen, careful not to use harsh movements, or he'll send our fourth into a fit of panic. Legion leans against the wall and pins me with all-knowing eyes.

"What was that?" he asks softly.

"I don't know what you're talking about." My knuckles whiten on the badger brush.

"Come now, Fox. Your foul mood was palpable, as was hers."

Swallowing, I whip the cream into a frenzy and refuse to meet his stare. "She is vexing. That is all."

I already attempted to tell them she is our queen today. It didn't stick. But they believed me when I said she was imperative to our plan to free Styx.

"Well, she is here now," Bodin points out as he slips off Varen's shirt, folds it, and places it on the settee by the windows. "As Emrys would say, the djinn is out of the bottle."

As if summoned by his words, the Wild Hunt scampers into the room and crawls beneath Varen's bed. Sounds of destruction filter out. He's found something to chew. Bodin sighs as he walks into the bathroom. He returns with a cloth and wets it in the bowl. "The pest is not my responsibility tonight."

Legion's jaw clenches. "I have reports."

"You always have reports."

"Because I am the Knight Commander."

Bodin sighs. "Fine. Then you take over here."

He hands the wet cloth to Legion with a dark look, and then leaves with the wildling. He is the only one of the Six whom Legion occasionally submits to. For millennia, I took offense—as did the rest of us. But now, all I want is for them to remember who we are to each other without having to remind them daily.

I shift my chair to face Varen. Firelight creates hollows in his cheeks and shadows over his naked, thin body.

I am no longer envious of Bodin's influence on Legion, for now I understand it is a burden. Legion takes the weight of responsibility into his soul. Bodin is his balance, ensuring he is not consumed by duty. Legion has borne that weight since the Morrigan spilled her seven first sons from the Cauldron's Wellspring eons ago. The goddess created us from chaos, but she is only one of eight manifestations of the Cauldron, or the Well, as Willow calls it.

A brief smile touches my lips when I think of her. But then I recall how she has been used by the deities too. A war as long as time itself has raged between the them. In the beginning, the Morrigan used us to tip the balance of power in her favor . . . Then, the war spilled from the Cauldron and into this world.

We are the battleground.

Through countless shackling queens, Legion has only lost one of our hive—the Seventh. But his loss was not in vain. We used it to break away from Maebh's iron fist, enough to make our own bargain with the gods.

Dabbing the brush into the cream, I raise it to Varen's jaw.

"Not yet." Legion's commanding tone stops me.

He drops to his knees, soiling his crisp suit, and wipes Varen's face with slow, gentle strokes from forehead to jaw. Our fourth sits through it all, eyes unfocused as he watches the fire dance. Legion rinses and cleans his body, meticulously washing every inch of skin. He pauses over the chipped and dirty fingernails. I ache to know what he's thinking. I ache to be one with all of them, but the seals veil access to our innermost selves. They close the doors on the mindscape we have shared for eternity. When we speak mind-to-mind, it is all through me.

*"What is it?"* I send.

He glances at me and replies, *"He wastes away."*

*"I know."*

*"If he refuses to feed again, you must force it down his throat."*

My eyes widen. They call me Fox because I am cunning, but Legion is deceptively devious behind that stalwart façade. He resumes cleaning, then stands and gestures for me to begin. I take Varen's jaw and dab cream onto it.

"Increase your expeditions," Legion instructs as he wipes his hands. "Nightly."

I tense. "That will rouse suspicion."

"Not if you stick to the usual haunt."

"But I can't take my fill there."

"Hence the augmented frequency. Small snacks will not be noticed if you continue with your charade."

My stomach churns at the thought of feeding this way. They don't remember much, but the seals can't hide our baser instincts. We are ravenous for sustenance. My thoughts inevitably turn to Willow, to her unique scent still clinging to my clothes. I bunch my shoulder, press my nose against the fabric, and inhale. Remnants of her remain and tug longing from deep within my soul.

*Go to her.*

*Catch her.*

*Give her your heart.*

Never have I felt desire so intense.

*You're dead. You're all dead.*

Sighing, I pick up the razor and press the blade to Varen's jaw. Metal gleams gold in the firelight, reminding me of another unfulfilled promise. At some point, I should probably start policing forbidden substances so the Wellspring can flow freely once more. After all, the abundance of this contraband is why no sprites exist in Avorlorna. The original faerie are growing weak, and Titania is too self-involved to learn why.

I find myself slow to rouse on the subject.

Whatever hold Titania and the Keepers have on us is a patch

job. And if there's one thing we Sluagh are good at, it's waiting. She will eventually summon her own doom.

"Fox," Legion prompts. "Am I understood?"

"Fine," I grit out, then scrape the razor down. "I will resume my midnight adventures."

"Good."

I feel his eyes on me. "Spit it out."

"Do not get attached to her."

"We are all attached." I wash the razor's blade, wipe it, and take a second pass at Varen's jaw. "She is our queen."

"Do not be facetious." He looms over me. "You are forbidden to take her as a lover, a plaything, or whatever it is you call your conquests these days."

Conquests. If he only remembered. My amused snort accidentally nicks Varen's skin. He barely registers the pain. When I remove the blade, a thin line of blood wells from the cut. Legion nudges my hand away and swipes the wound, testing the flesh— more blood wells.

"He is not healing as we do," he notes gravely. "How long has it been like this?"

I shrug. "A few turns of the moon."

"And you didn't think to mention it before?"

"You have a war to worry about."

His sigh ruffles my hair, and I close my eyes against the sensation. I miss the oneness, the openness with them all. Before, it was so easy to share. Now, we are an afterthought.

"Fox—"

"I know."

I hear his intake of breath, the parting of his lips to lecture over who comes first—us or her.

"*I know!*" I bark.

My eyes remain closed until Legion's footsteps recede, and I am alone with Varen.

In my mind, I see the face of the black-haired Guardian who caused Willow so much pain. The agony in his blue-eyed gaze reflects my own, but I shut my heart to it. If I were in Elphyne, I would track this feathered menace down and feast on his soul until his body is a dried husk.

And then I would eat his heart, enslaving him to the Wild Hunt.

But I am not in Elphyne. I am here, the Wellspring grows dry, and I do not care. Not when I have Styx and the rest of the hive to worry about. Not when Willow's scent drives me to distraction.

How can she smell so divine when she has no magic with which to claim us?

Legion is right to worry—the sooner I accept she can't be our queen, the easier it will be to betray her.

# CHAPTER
# NINETEEN
### WILLOW

The inside of the castle is as neglected as the outside. We enter a great hall with dust-laden decorative furniture. I don't believe anyone has sat on the brocade seats. Along the filigree-paneled walls is a collection of framed oil-painted portraits, one for each of the six Sluagh. Others feature faces I've never seen before. The last is of the queen who cursed me.

Titania.

She is prim, proper, and carries an air of wistful decorum. Foliage and flowers are the backdrop. Her dark hair is intricately styled in loops and braids. The only ornament on her body is the tiara. The rest of her radiance comes from her natural faerie beauty.

I hate her.

I want to slash the canvas across her face. See how she likes being ugly.

She's next on my revenge list.

"The dining room is in there this week." Cricket points to a doorway near the front of the hall. "Dinner is done," she says.

"Breakfast is at sunrise. If you're hungry, the kitch is down at the cellar level. Help yourself to anything in the stores. Mind the chatty gossip. She's a handful, and don't take anything she says to heart. She enjoys pushing buttons. Alright, moving on. This way."

Another staff member? Possibly the cook.

I remain bitter from seeing the queen's face as I follow Cricket through another doorway.

"No grand staircases in this castle, I'm afraid," she explains as we climb granite stairs. "They're at the ends of each wing and cold as a witch's tit. At least that's one place that never changes."

We arrive on the third-floor landing and head directly down a corridor.

Never changes? And earlier, she mentioned the dining room was there for "this week." Didn't she say something about the wings moving, too? Before I can query this, we pass an enormous library with rows of cedar shelves filled from floor to ceiling. I stop at the doorway, my lips parting in awe. Lush navy carpet sprawls across the floor. A grand fireplace is dormant across the way. The room smells like orange oil, candle wax, and ink. Chairs, sofas, and tables scattered around are occupied with historical artifacts and gadgets. It reminds me of the museum bunker in Crystal City. Alfie and I spent hours studying the history of a world long gone—the one my mother came from.

Dust and disorder are nowhere to be seen here. Cricket arrives at my side and proudly declares, "This is one room the castle won't touch."

"You've said some strange things about this castle. What do you mean?"

"You'll see after the clock tower chimes. Before that happens, best be getting to your room, safe and sound."

I refuse to move. "Why won't you just tell me?"

She laughs. "You're a direct one, aren't you, poppet? I hope you don't lose that here. The masters seem to be slipping more into the way of the Folk every day. So sad."

I open my mouth to question more, but she interrupts me.

"Seeing is believing. Hurry up, now."

She picks up speed, and her sense of urgency infects me. We take a turn down a narrow hallway and stop at a nondescript door. She sighs with relief after opening it.

"As tidy as I left it," she says. "And I see Finch has already delivered your bag and stoked the fire. Good man. He'll keep, that's for sure."

She steps back to give me room to enter. The chamber is small but neat and in good repair. Fire crackles, taking the chill from the air. A dressing table with a mirror sits against one damask-papered wall. Facing the dresser is a bed with decadent covers and pillows. A small bedside table holds a candle. The room is far more appealing than I'd accounted for. A yawn slips out of my mouth before I can stop it.

Cricket gives me a pitiful look. "Early start tomorrow. You get your rest, alright?"

"Rest doesn't sound too bad." I check behind the door and find a bolt. Reassurance washes through me. There are no other doors, only a window overlooking the gusting courtyard outside. I should be safe sleeping here tonight.

"If you're looking for the ablutions, try across the hall. The masters sleep in the east wing tonight, and the clock tower is beyond that. As I said, stay away from it, especially when it chimes."

I'm on the same floor as the Sluagh. My frown goes unnoticed. She says goodbye and closes the door.

I pluck out Tinger's pendant. The manabee glows nice and strong.

"Can you believe it?" I tell him. "This house is enormous. All this time, I was stewing over what they did to me, and they've been here, living like this." He doesn't talk back, of course. I carry on as usual and walk around the room. "I can't say I'm surprised at the dust and neglect. We know they weren't very good at that sort of thing."

I move items about the room, lift candlesticks, and check inside drawers. I place the stolen dreamcatcher stones beside the candlestick, admiring how the gems catch the firelight. My father said my rearranging habit is nesting. I think it's making myself at home. Glancing outside the window, I'm reminded of the grand scope of this castle. It might be run down, but it's huge. The wind howls through the gaps in the glass.

A strange feeling tightens my chest. I turn it over in my mind, trying to understand what it is. The more I see how life has moved on here, the more I feel . . . Angry. Sad? Resentful?

That's it. Resentful.

"It's weird, right, Ting?" I ask, pressing my forehead to the icy pane. "I mean, I know Titania said they were here, living their best lives . . . or something like that. But I wasn't prepared for how much it hurts to see how little I mean to them, how quickly they moved on from their obsession with me." I turn from the window and start plucking the bed covers, fluffing them up. "Not that I want them to continue their obsession, but . . . it's just . . ."

My bottom lip trembles. I can't voice my thoughts. It's difficult to acknowledge how fleeting my life was to them. They've completely forgotten I exist.

Once, before Nero kidnapped me, I chased butterflies in our old garden. I was so excited when I caught one. The wings were beautiful. The tiny insect was like nothing I'd ever seen in my life. I wanted to hold it forever, so I trapped it in a jar. My mother made me release it, saying it wouldn't survive inside the glass. Its beauty isn't for my admiration, but to help it survive against predators in the wild. Made no sense to me. I thought beauty was an attraction.

Mom told me the butterfly's life span isn't as long as ours, so five minutes in a jar could feel like an eternity to them. Reluctantly, I had let it go. But the temporary heat I'd subjected it to caused its death anyway. I cried and cried, but after my father gave me a sweet stick, I promptly forgot about the precious thing I'd accidentally killed.

That's what this feels like—the Sluagh are immortal, ancient beings while I'm just a butterfly they forgot they ruined.

I flop down on the bed and pluck the covers again. I miss my claws. Shifting them out at bedtime made preparing my covers so much easier.

My gaze lifts to my reflection in the dresser mirror. The small acid wounds have dried to discolored scabs. They'll be gone in a week, but they make the ugliness so much worse. How could I have forgotten how horrid my warped face is?

Warily touching my flaming, misshapen cheeks and then nose, I think about my interactions today. Disgust flickered in so many eyes as they gazed upon me. Puck's disdain—his instructions to remove the glamour, making me appear normal. Emrys's close and personal inspection. Walking before a tiered arena filled to the brim with judgmental, perfect, pretty eyes I'll never have again. And Alfie . . .

*We'll find a way to make you beautiful again.*

Tears sting. I blink rapidly. Why did I think I could do this alone? Why did my mother let me go? And my father? I was so unfair to him, so rude and mean. Our last conversation was an argument, and it was all my fault.

I'm a grown-ass woman. I should be able to handle these things, but I keep fucking up.

The Sluagh don't even remember me, and I'm here, risking my life for revenge. Homesickness hits me like a tidal wave. Tears spill out, hot and salty. I grow uglier as my face turns blotchy.

A knock comes at the door, and I jump up, gasping.

"Love." Cricket's voice filters through the cracks. "I forgot to tend to your wounds. May I come in and see?"

"No!" I shout, trying to hide my state. Realizing I've snapped at her, I exhale and force my tone to something more this side of polite. "I'm fine, thank you."

A pause. "The master insisted I help. I brought a warm bowl of water to clean you."

"Leave it on the floor. Please." I hold my breath and cover my face with my hands.

*Go away. Go away.* I forgot to bolt the door.

A muffled thud outside sounds like she put the bowl down. I hear breathing, and then she leaves. Trembling relief courses through me. I wait for a long minute before opening the door. A wash bowl is there beside a plate of cheese and crackers.

Her kindness spills more tears from my eyes. Sniffing, I collect the items and head back inside.

This time, I bolt the door, close the curtains, and toss my cape over the mirror to hide my face. Then I undress and check my wounds. The baby Wild Hunt left shallow gouges over my legs. I need to be careful with wounds now that I'm mortal.

After cleaning, I nibble the food and rifle through my bag for something clean to wear but realize I don't have spare pants. These leather fighting breeches won't be comfortable for sleep.

I empty the contents of my bag, taking stock. The portal stone from Elphyne is still there. Even though I have no manabeeze to activate it, simply knowing the stone is here feels like a safety net.

The portraits and dagger go on the bedside table. I toss a spare shirt and panties on the dresser, then return the salted meat rations to the bag and some smaller survival items. The last thing I pull from the pack is the Nexus pamphlet, revealing a piece of folded paper I don't remember putting there.

Unfolding it, I'm surprised to see Alfie's familiar hand-writing.

*Burn After Reading.*
*Midnight, alone tomorrow. I'll make good on my promise.*
*For the Gold.*
*A*

I DON'T UNDERSTAND. WE USED TO PASS SECRET MESSAGES WITH nonsense about treasure and then burn the paper so "marauding pirates" couldn't catch us. Does he want to play one of our old games? That's a bit awkward at our age.

No words are on the other side of the letter. I'll have to ask him tomorrow, but before I forget, I toss it in the fireplace and watch it burn. It's not until the flames die completely that I pull back the bed's plucked covers and slip in naked.

My shifter side of the family is nude half the day due to their frequent changes from wolf to fae form. I don't shift similarly, but I picked up habits like big puppy piles to sleep in, cuddling, nesting, and occasionally marking my territory. The twins often climbed into my bed and shifted out claws long enough to pluck my covers and nest with me.

The only wolfish part of me I hate is the fever heat that grips me when my cycle hits. For a few days, I'm tingling like a tinger in mating season and impossible to live with. My father was horrified when he found out I'd gone through my first heat in Crystal City—alone and away from any wolf shifter community that would explain I'm not a freak for my natural desires. But by that time, the taint on the Well prevented us from communicating through water. Rory had me assessed by the human physician, but they couldn't help.

Which made me feel more like a freak. No human wanted to mate with me. Alfie was stubbornly traditional and wanted to wait until marriage to have sex. I was left bursting with painfully unfulfilled needs. Seeing to my own desire never worked. It's like my body knew I was cheating.

All I could do to ease the suffering was fill a tub with iced water. I would soak for hours a day until the heat passed. But now, since Rory died, I refuse to soak in a tub. It's so stupid. I know I can't drown, but my nightmares don't care.

Swallowing my self-pity, I roll around and pluck some more until I'm settled in a comfortable arrangement, then close my eyes with a sigh. It smells like lavender. Clean and warm.

As my exhaustion catches up, a clock chimes somewhere in the castle, and then I fall asleep.

# CHAPTER
# TWENTY

## WILLOW

A weight lands on my chest. I jolt awake and reach for my dagger, but something wet drags up my face. My eyes ping open to see a horned dragon skull—the wet *something* dangling from his panting mouth and dripping saliva.

"Baby Hunt?" I squeak, blinking through the haze of sleep. Pre-dawn light sneaks through the gaps in the curtains.

He wiggles on my chest, squashing my lungs. *Oof.* Another lick and then his tongue lolls. His tail thumps on my stomach.

"Your breath smells like sour meat." I avert my face. Gross.

The wildling takes that as a sign to lick my other cheek like it's the tastiest meal. I pick him up. At least, I think he's a he. I check beneath his belly. Oh, yes. No mistaking that dangling appendage.

Moving him to the floor, I toss the covers and rub my eyes. The tiny terror starts running laps of my small room, tearing up the rug with his vicious claws. I grin at his excited black eyes. It's so strange how the skull sockets don't move, but I can still sense the change in his mood beyond the body language changes.

"You're happy I'm awake?" I chuckle. But then I notice the

destruction he made while I slept. "Oh no! You naughty little dragon. What have you done?"

He stops running and cants his head as if it's unconscionable I'm upset with him. But all my dried meat rations have been hunted from my bag and eaten. The portrait sketches are ripped and half-eaten. A trail of soggy paper leads to a wet patch that smells like puke. Coal and debris from the fireplace are all over the carpet. It's so Well-damn cold!

Shivering, I pluck my uniform shirt from the ground and notice it's covered in sooty paw prints. I think he tried to lick the white goop stain. *Crimson save me*, he got into everything. A quick check reveals the portal stone is still here, and I'm wearing Tinger's pendant. Another rifle through my clothes gives me the worst news of all.

"You ate my panties!"

I pick them up and hold them to the window. A giant hole exists where the crotch used to be. This was exactly what Tinger did. It's so gross, but an ache in my chest squeezes hard. I miss that little fucker.

"No." I waggle my finger at Baby Hunt. "Do you hear me? Do *not* touch my things again."

He lowers in submission and crawls toward me. His black eyes become glossy. A high-pitched whimper shoots from his throat.

"Stop being so dramatic." I scowl, tugging the dirty shirt over my head. "You ate my salted meat. It's my favorite snack. *My* yum-yums! And I'm *not* happy."

He hiccups, and a black cloud puffs from his fanged mouth.

"Great. You burp shadows." I shake my head and tap my nose. "I can smell the meat on your breath, Baby Hunt, so I know you did it. If I catch you in my things again, there will be consequences."

My disapproving tone keeps him crawling toward me until

he bumps his horns beneath my hand. My heart softens. He's covered in soot.

"Look at you." I clean smudges from his skull with my shirt, then can't resist those pleading puppy eyes. I deposit him on my lap. His body is so warm and vital. It feels good to touch, to cuddle.

"I can't stay angry at you."

He snuffles into me and licks my hand. When I stop scratching the soft part where his skull meets his neck, he impatiently nudges me until I start again. A vibrating purr in his throat reminds me of swarming bees. The Sluagh's wings made this sound on the battlefield.

I freeze, my fingers on Baby Hunt's body.

What am I doing?

Before I can put him down, his head pricks up as though he hears something. He rockets from my lap and scampers up the chimney, releasing a tumble of soot. Sighing, I clean what I can, then decide heading to the bathroom at this early hour would be best. I don't fancy bumping into anyone. But when I open the door, another bedroom greets me.

What the fuck?

I close the door and check there's no other door. Nope. Just this one. I reopen it.

The bedroom is large, decadent in black, and very messy. A ruffled bed covered with pillows and dark satin sheets is pushed against a wall with a dream web tapestry. I've never seen one like this. Black, pearlescent strands lace with intricate delicacy. Sporadic gemstones are darker than usual but glimmer like a starry night, casting reflections around the room. My fingers twitch with the urge to pluck one and add it to my collection, but I force myself to continue assessing the room for danger first. An ornate settee by the arched window is strewn with clothes.

Maybe I'm dreaming. That would make better sense. I pinch myself and yelp.

This is real.

The room smells masculine, sweet, mossy, and woodsy . . . like Fox.

As soon as I recognize the scent, I notice more signs this is his room. The clothes he wore yesterday are part of the collection on the settee. His shoes are on the floor.

I step inside and crane my neck to look for an exit door, but I only find an archway leading to a bathing suite. I take another step for a better view, but rustling in the sheets halts me. My gaze whips to the bed.

Fox.

Fox asleep, half-naked, and artfully tangled in sheets.

Beauty is too fragile a word to describe him. His hand rests behind his head, his face in profile as he breathes evenly, oblivious to my presence. The pose draws attention to the swell of his biceps and defined abdomen. He is the picture of masculinity, yet the blush of sleep gives him the innocence of youth. His lips are pursed enough to appear unhappy with his dream . . . and reveal dimples.

Something hot clenches low in me, spreading warmth through my body. *Shit.* I am *not* supposed to be perving on my enemy. And I'm certainly not supposed to be imagining running my tongue down the dips between stacked muscles. He is completely hairless except for the ruffled short black locks on top . . . and the dusting of darkness trailing down to his—

*Dagger.* Get the dagger and stab him in the heart.

As quiet as a mouse, I tiptoe back into my room and close the door. Then I sit on the edge of my bed and stare, my heart racing, my cheeks flaming. My fingers press against the angles and ridges of my jaw. I trace the ropy, knotty scars on the left and test the sore little wounds.

*Kill him.*

That's what I need to do. That's what I'm here for. But something about seeing him vulnerable has thrown me. He looked so innocent and not at all like an ancient being born of chaos . . . which is exactly why he's been crafted that way. He is the furthest thing from vulnerable, and he still ruined my life. He doesn't deserve my empathy.

When I pick up the dagger, the sharp blade scrapes the wood. It reminds me of my claws—how I scratched them on surfaces with satisfying purpose. I'll never do that again because of Fox and his five Sluagh brothers.

Rising to my feet, I steel my spine. I have no idea how our rooms moved during the night, but I won't look a gift faerie in the mouth. Attacking him while he's out will give me the best chance of succeeding. When the others discover his corpse, I'll lie.

When I push the door, it swings inward faster than I intended. I collide with Fox—my soot-stained shirt against his torso—*hot, hard, naked male torso.*

Embarrassment scalds my cheeks. His fresh scent invades my senses, and I stumble. He latches onto my hips, but he's too late. We fall together and land with a bone-jarring thud.

My traitorous dagger skitters away, twirling across the wooden floorboards and thudding against the edge of the rug. We both look at the weapon and then our eyes meet. His turn wholly black as he summons his dark side.

*Oh no.* I scramble toward the magic cutting blade. He lunges after me, so close that I feel his fingers graze my toes. My palm hits the hilt. I roll with a triumphant snarl, ready to—

Fox is a frozen statue, hand hovering in the air, reaching for me, lips parted. He looks so bewildered, like he's seen a ghost. What could possibly shock this ancient monster? His gaze lifts to mine, and his cheeks turn beet red.

"You . . ." he blusters, clears his throat, then quickly walks to the settee by the window and gives me his back.

I glance down. The shirt . . . it's to my thighs. I'm not wearing panties. He would have seen everything when I crawled away from him.

"I hope you got a good look," I snarl, brandishing my blade and striding toward him. "Because it will be the last thing you see."

He clears his throat and scrapes his fingers through his hair, still refusing to look at me. Does he not care I'm about to stab him? He exhales suddenly, dips his shaking head, and braces his hands on the filigree backrest. Is he *laughing* at me?

"I'm going to kill you," I warn, unable to stop myself.

"As stunning as you are down there, I assure you, my heart can take more than one look."

Is he talking about my . . . I tug the shirt down and growl, "I'm being serious."

"Then you'll have to try harder, little wolf."

My grip tightens on the dagger. I'm almost within reaching distance, and he still hasn't faced me. Tightly coiled muscles roll beneath the broad expanse of skin covering his back. My eyes lower appreciatively down his tapered waist to the breeches hugging his narrow hips and the curved outline of his buttocks.

I growl at my wayward attention. What in the Well's name is wrong with me? It's like I'm in heat. My eyes widen and I take a moment to assess myself for signs of fever, but I'm fine. I have no excuse for checking him out. Admiring his physique is *not* on my to-do list for the day.

*"Keep telling yourself that,"* his amused voice slides into my mind like spiced wine, curling heat through my body.

"Get out of my head!" Violent rage consumes me. This is exactly the twisted, morally depraved shit the Six are known for. I lunge, aiming to pierce the soft spot beneath his ribs.

"It's hardly my fault when you shout thoughts at me." The bastard pivots out of range and finally shows me his face.

"You don't get to play the victim. Not after—" My pain chokes me. *Tinger. Rory.* All the people I killed. I scream so loudly that my eyes water.

His perplexed expression deepens.

"I hate you," I croak. *You ruined my life.* "I know all the sick things you did. They told me you planned to claim me as your queen since before my conception. You tried to groom me into a queen who wouldn't treat you like slaves."

"Why is that so bad?" He cocks his head, genuinely confused.

"Because you *made* it that way. You manipulated the old Prime, teaching her how to curse my father so he was alone for fifty years—never caring how much it hurt him to be separated from my brother after he was born. Then you orchestrated events so my parents conceived me during a curse! Then you had me kidnapped by the enemy so I could learn to be as morally depraved as you. I could go on and on! What kind of sick bastards bargain with the Well for a child to mold into the perfect queen? Do you have any idea how wrong that is?"

He blinks at me, taking it all in. But I've been waiting to say these things for years. I don't hold back.

"And then you pretend to forget what you've done and make all these people think you're actually the Good Folk! You're the bad ones. The monsters. You belong in the subterranean with the other nightmares."

Hurt flashes in his black soulless eyes.

The imprint of his skull illuminates beneath his skin. A whoosh of air brushes my face, and then the flicker of his skull is gone. Fear strikes into my heart. I unwittingly back up, looking for impossible signs of an invisible attack.

"*They've* forgotten," he corrects. "But I remember everything."

His upper lip curls enough for me to glimpse monstrous fangs that weren't there before.

My back hits a wall as he slams his palm beside my head, rattling the picture frame above. Unseen pressure locks around my wrist, forcing my dagger to pin to my side. I struggle, but it's like fighting a boulder. In this form, he's two people at once. The wraith and the nightmare made flesh. He hasn't even revealed his wings or horns.

His face is inches from mine. I see every tiny pore on his porcelain skin, every perfect feature. His intake of breath is guttural and pained.

"We bargained for a queen who was our equal," he whispers hoarsely. "For an end to our eternal suffering." His second palm slams on the other side of my head, and I wince. "We wanted a *queen*, and they gave us a *child*."

"You can't blame this on anyone else. *YOU did this.*"

He scoffs, "You don't even know who 'anyone else' is."

My mind stutters to a halt. Is he talking about Titania?

His expression deadpans, and his taloned hands slide down the wall, scraping like nails on a chalkboard. His skull flickers, and his wraith form returns to his body. He is once again pretty and a devil, all rolled into one. Except now his eyes are sad, and he's at a loss for words.

"Who do you think gave us these secrets in the first place?"

I shrug. "Varen is psychic. You're old enough to know the difference between right and wrong. The blessing proves you do."

A cruel laugh spills from his lips. "The so-called blessing changed us into something new. We were children in the eyes of the light. Fish out of water, breathing air for the first time." He gestures hastily to his blue Guardian teardrop. "It took us *years* before we understood the intricacies of shame. Why do you think we sent you away? The only way to protect you from

Maebh's urge to kill you was if you remained with us. But a child?"

He's making too much sense. "You all whispered stories into my mind—preparing me with tales of knights and dragons."

"We distracted you from Nero's abuse the only way we knew how."

My mind races back in time, trying to relive those moments so I can prove him wrong. But all I can pull from my foggy memory is the first time I sat in Nero's secret garden, playing with a little bird, and he clouded my mind with his stolen powers of persuasion. He walked over to the bird, said something about lessons, and— *"Close your eyes," my secret friend's words cut through the wool in my mind. "You don't need to see this part."*

None of this matters. My life is still ruined. Rory is gone. Tinger is gone. I was rude to my family. Disrespectful to everyone.

"You claim I was your queen, but you abandoned me."

The crack in my voice reveals more of that pain I uncovered last night.

I can no longer deny it. For a moment on that battlefield, when our eyes had connected, time stopped, and there was no death, no life, just us—connecting over our shared sufferings. We were all prisoners, all used for our power, all wanting to be free but not knowing where to run to.

"You left me," I accuse. "And I continued to suffer."

His eyes glimmer in an all too human way that leaves me unnerved. "We never wanted you to suffer."

"I fought for you. I sacrificed my immortality and my magic, and I *trusted* you. I did what you asked of me on that battlefield, but you *left* me," I scream in his face. "I want you dead!"

His hand drops to mine, and he guides the dagger to his ribs.

"Do it," he begs. "Finish what they couldn't."

He lets go, leaving the final act to me, so there's no mistaking whose choice this is. I push into his soft flesh. His pupils contract to pinpricks in a storm of gray. I witness his pain and burrow for his heart, thinking it's poetic I learned to kill because of them.

His lips part when the hilt meets his skin. Warm liquid oozes over my fist, and still, we gaze into each other's eyes. He seems as lost as I feel. No amount of searching will fill the void in our hearts, and we're tired . . . so tired of swimming upstream. Maybe this feeling is why Rory never swam.

Fox inhales slowly through his nose as if my scent will summon the answer, and then a sly half-smile touches his lips.

"Happy now?" he murmurs, deep voice oh so intimate. "You've killed me."

I pull the dagger out and slam back in. He jolts, his head bows as if the pain is too much, but he does not fall. He does not die. "Finished?"

"NO. *Never.*"

"Then keep killing me softly, little wolf." He looks up from beneath his lashes. "If it makes you feel better."

Blood oozes down his front, staining his breeches.

"You can't want this," I cry. "You don't get to *allow* this."

"Oblivion was all we ever desired until you." He pauses, holding something back. "We deserve nothing less."

Feeling my control unravel, I stab him again. And again. But nothing helps. He's not dying.

"Why aren't you dead?"

He pulls the blade from his midsection and drops it at my feet, then strolls to his settee, dripping blood on the floor without a care. It's slower and darker than normal, but he still bleeds.

"I honestly thought if you ever turned up . . ." His eyes briefly light up, then empty. "Doesn't matter."

Facing away, his breeches come off, and he cleans blood from his torso with rough, jerky swipes. He slips on another pair of pants and then laces up. When he faces me again, he's already buttoning his shirt, but I see enough to know the stab wounds are gone.

"You're pretending to be good," I accuse.

"But we're monsters, right?" He gives my ugly face a pointed look to call out the one who is truly the beast. "You, of all people, should know there's always someone else pulling the strings. The worst part is that you don't realize we've sacrificed the only card up our sleeve to bring you into our home. You think you know moral depravity, pet. You haven't even touched its sides."

# CHAPTER
# TWENTY-ONE
## WILLOW

When Fox *flickers* and disappears, there's no doubt in my mind he's in full possession of all his powers. He can transport anywhere when he *flickers*, including through walls.

His door led to mine. How am I supposed to get out? I bang on the wall with my fist, shouting for help—hoping Cricket or Finch will hear me. I try shouting up my chimney for Baby Hunt. Nothing.

Releasing a strangled scream of frustration, I pace between our rooms and tug on Tinger's pendant around my neck.

"How dare he!" I hiss. "Like, what the fuck was all that?"

Was anything he said true? Even if it wasn't, I can't kill them. The blade doesn't work, which could be for several reasons.

"Maybe the Well flows differently here," I tell Tinger. "Or maybe we've assumed the wrong things about the Sluagh. The Six are the last of the Sluagh. Maybe that makes them more powerful, I don't know."

My brows furrow as I stop before Fox's bed, realizing he made it while I was in my room before our altercation. Did he know I watched him sleeping? Sheets and covers are now carefully draped over the mattress. He stacked pillows against the bedhead. It's the only section of his room that's in order.

I have a mind to mess it up again.

So I do. I jump on it, kick the blankets around, and when I'm out of breath and a little hungry, I flop down and stare upward, puffing a lock of hair from my face.

Scratches mark the ceiling. Gouges in groups, tallying something just like in our house in Elphyne. He waited for something here, too.

*You don't realize we've sacrificed the only card left up our sleeve.*

His words echo in my mind.

*You think you know moral depravity, pet. You haven't even touched its sides.*

Does he mean Titania, his latest queen and captor? Or them?

My stomach rumbles. I need to eat. I need to . . . I don't know, get back to the Nexus and ask around. Someone must know more about these creepy, beautiful monsters.

*But we're monsters, right?*

Gah. With a huff, I sit up and glare at his room. It's much nicer than mine. Full of nice clothes, even if half are on the floor. Sliding off his bed, I pad around and inspect his things. Crystals and gemstones—which I pilfer. Cologne—I spray it on myself and hate how yummy it smells. A book with strange runes on it and illegible text inside. *Interesting.* I flick through the pages, then rip a random one out. A packet of playing cards. Antique brass spectacles—I saw these contraptions in Crystal City. Eyesight often fails as mortals grow old. Bob wanted glasses. I wonder if these will help.

I hold them to the window and tilt, but no reflection glimmers in the lens. I poke my finger straight through the frame. No glass. Weird. Discarding them, I move my inspection to the bathroom and gasp when I enter.

The room is fit for kings. Black porcelain tiles cover the walls. A free-standing tub is constructed from natural stone and big enough to lie flat in, flap my arms, and still not touch the sides. Cautiously, I peer over the edge and smell minerals on the dry stone. No faucets. The water must be plumbed like the ones back home. Natural springs are a source of power for fae, a place to refill their inner well with mana rapidly.

I'm too cowardly to sit in the bath, but I'll happily strip, use the toilet, and clean myself with a washcloth. If only a shower were here, I'd be better. I particularly enjoy covering his sweet, woodsy-scented soap with the blood splashed on my body.

*Oblivion was all we ever desired until you.*

There's more than one way to get revenge, and if I can't kill them, I'll ruin their lives, too.

I dress in Fox's clothes instead of the uniform. I'm sure there will be consequences for that. As long as I cause embarrassment to the House of Shadow, I'm here for it. Afterward, as I brush my hair, a knock at the window startles me.

"Yoo-hoo, love."

I run to the window and release the latch. A flurry of snow drifts in. Finch dangles by a rope from a harness. He must have rappelled down from the castle roof.

"I'm so happy you came," I gush and hug him through the small opening. "I hope you're not freezing on my account."

"No problem at all." He valiantly pretends he's not shivering and hands me another harness. "When Master Fox walked past in a huff, we had an inkling the castle had fun with your rooms last night. Put the harness on if it pleases you."

"Oh yes, it pleases."

He smirks. "I'll go on up and drop the rope down again."

I touch my fingers to my mouth and push them down toward him in the Elphyne hand sign for gratitude.

He gives me an odd look. "You're not from around here, are you?"

"Um. No."

"I'd love to hear about it all. So would Cricket. And the chatty gossip in the kitch too. If you hurry, you'll make it in time for breakfast in the dining hall." He tugs on his rope, and someone slowly pulls him up.

I quickly put on my boots. The dagger fits on my belt beneath Fox's loose-fitted black shirt. It might not have worked on him, but it's still a weapon. Maybe it works on others.

His shirt has pretty lace detail down the buttons, cuffs, and collar. I smell like him. Frowning, I take my cape from the mirror and check my reflection to ensure Tinger's pendant isn't glimmering through the shirt, but the thick fabric hides everything.

My face is still an unavoidable disaster, but for some reason, the ugliness seems a little less severe today. Inadvertently, my thoughts shift to Fox's eyes as he caged me against the wall. Gray, forlorn, and hurt. And that one moment, that flicker of desire when he told me to keep killing him softly.

What did he mean? Frowning, I run my fingers down his shirt.

"I have to admit. These Sluagh have nice taste in clothes."

By the time Finch tosses his rope back down, I'm already in the harness and with one foot out the window. He pulls me up two levels with surprising strength for a thin man. Cricket is waiting at the top with a smile, puffed and bright-eyed from heaving Finch up earlier.

"Well, you survived the first night." She clasps her hands excitedly. "And I heard the wildling made a mess of your room. Don't worry, I'll get in as soon as possible to tidy up."

"How did you know?"

"Finch peeked through your window."

"Oh. Of course." When he was searching for me. "But don't worry about tidying. I can do that myself later."

"Not you too," she groans. "You need to let us do our job."

"But you said—"

Finch mutters to me, "Let her have what she wants. Happy wife, happy life."

"Well, in that case, I'd appreciate it. Wait. You're married?" My gaze darts between the two of them. "As in the human bonding ritual?"

I almost miss their wide eyes, and then Cricket starts rambling about breakfast and something else the chatty gossip said in the kitch that morning. It's a diversion, which is weird. Why would she be ashamed of being married? They're Nevers— mortals. Why hide it?

"Let's get down to the dining room," she says, ushering me across the roof. "The masters waited for you."

"All of them?"

"Except Master Fox." She frowns and fists her dress. "He left rather out of sorts."

"He'll be fine," Finch placates Cricket.

"He'll get himself into trouble, that one." She shakes her head. "You know he doesn't think when he gets like this."

"Like what?" I ask, feeling an echo of her worry.

"Like he thinks he's in this alone."

"He gets reckless," Finch adds, then opens the hatch door leading to a stairwell down. "But he's a grown man. He can take care of himself. Come on, love. Let's get the girl some food."

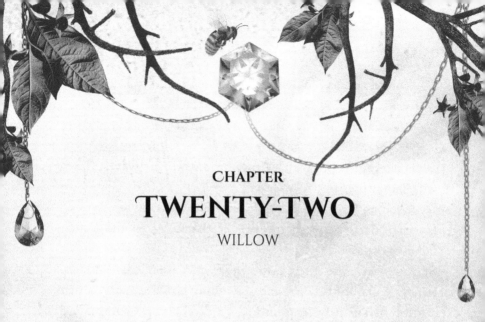

# CHAPTER
# TWENTY-TWO
## WILLOW

Legion, Bodin, and Varen sit at one end of a ridiculously long mahogany dining table. Their plates of food are untouched. Each is impeccably dressed for the day. Bodin and Legion wear military-style coats—black with furred collars. Legion reads from a stack of papers. He hands one to Bodin, who makes a deep, rumbling comment of some sort. While they converse, Varen moves his crockery carefully, mumbling when one piece isn't in the right place, then adjusting it again.

When they notice me, all three stand.

*Awkward.*

But also . . . respectful.

Bodin's gaze lingers on my attire—Fox's shirt. Legion notices the same thing. While they give each other a curious glance, I quickly drag more of my hair to shield my face.

Varen disrupts the room by swiping his hand, destroying his neatly arranged crockery. He shakes his head, eyes darting to and fro as if trying to recall something.

"To ventilate the nest," he says to himself, tapping the table, "groups of honeybees fan their wings near the entrance, thus pulling air from the nest." He swipes his finger two feet and taps. "But they *must* alternate. They're not alternating, and the nest is becoming hot."

He slams his fist down, frustrated.

"That's enough," Legion says quietly. "No more beeisms at the table, Varen. You'll frighten our first Shadow."

They honestly don't remember me.

And Varen has really lost his mind. Guilt punches me in the gut, and I don't know why. It's not my fault they're in this mess. I didn't do this.

I take a seat as Bodin tries to clean up Varen's mess, and the guilt morphs into something different—sympathy. Their sparkling, radiant life isn't so attractive up close. It's a little sad.

Cricket deposits a plate of steaming food before me. Mouth-watering vegetables, meat, and toasted muffins with jam. She returns a short while later with juice, water, and something hot that's both bitter and sweet smelling.

"It's called hot cocoa," she explains.

"It's delicious." I burn my tongue when I drink too fast. Geraldine said she liked hot cocoa, didn't she? It must be an old-world drink. I'll have to ask Cricket if I can bring some with me into the Nexus.

I dig into the food, ravenous, and smile gratefully through a mouthful. Her cheeks go bright red, and she grins, but then glares at Bodin and Legion before hurrying out.

They still haven't touched their meals. Why would Cricket be angry at them for not eating? Don't they feed on souls? Unless they've forgotten how to do that, too. The Wild Hunt also lives off the souls. Is it so small because they're not feeding it? Because they can't?

Was Fox's card up their sleeve something to do with the baby Wild Hunt?

Swallowing, I turn to the three Sluagh and say, "I can't help thinking the Wild Hunt is in danger because of me."

Bodin flicks Legion a glance, then clears his throat. His voice is so much deeper than the others. It rumbles like thunder.

"Did Fox confess this," he asks, "when you were . . . intimate with him?"

"Intimate?"

A flash of Fox's blood covering my hand enters my mind. "Why would you say that?"

"You wear his clothes."

Legion gives him a trying look. "He was specifically forbidden to take her as a lover."

My jaw drops. Sputtering, I don't even know where to begin explaining.

"I only took his clothes because our rooms moved during the night, and the exit doors opened to each other. He could *flicker* out. He left me alone, and with no clean clothes to wear for the day, I had access to his."

"You stole his clothes." His eyebrow twitches.

Bodin sips his drink and mumbles into the cup, "Fox was right."

"You know I can hear you, right?" I gesture at my ears. "I might be mortal now, but my shifter senses work just fine."

Legion clears his throat. "Regarding your earlier inquiry, an infantile dragon is a target. There are those at court who would just as soon kill him to eradicate our position altogether. The dragon-bonded draw power from their beast. By revealing ours is so small, we've announced our weakness."

Fox didn't look weak . . . but I suppose the rest of them do. They've lost their memories, don't seem to eat actual food, and I haven't seen them use magic except for that little display of shadow power at the fort. "You're *all* in danger?"

Why does my tone sound concerned?

He stares at me, eyes sharp and scrutinizing. The attention makes me squirm, and when he idly taps his finger on his stack of papers, I know he's thinking about me—things I want to know.

"Why did you do it then?" I ask. "Why put everyone at risk to bring me here? I'm a Nothing, right? I'll weigh you down and cause delays."

He grunts in agreement. "This is a fact. However, you carry a trapped wisp around your neck. Are you aware they're sacrilegious to keep?"

I'm starting to realize how adept these Sluagh are at avoiding questions.

Put aside the fact it's Tinger's, they should be able to harvest wisps—manabeeze—from every living Well-connected fae in this place. Even from the monsters they fight during the war against the subterranean. "I call wisps manabeeze. Where I'm from, they erupt from bodies at the moment of death. Don't they do that here?"

Bodin's astute gaze narrows. "Where are you from?"

I groan. This is going to be weird.

"I'm from Elphyne." *The same place as you.*

"Where is that?" he asks.

"Across the oceans." *We know each other.*

"Another realm?" Legion's eyebrows lift. "How did you cross oceans when they're fraught with sea monsters neither Dream nor Nightmare? Too many unattended watergates in the deep block free passage between the realms. The Mer Folk refuse help to the Folk of the air and land. Only the Tidal Hunt can ensure safe passage across the sea. Since Lady Nivene does not know who you are, I ask again—how did you get here?"

"You don't use portal stones here?"

Bodin whispers something to Legion, who turns to me and

says, "The city guard mentioned you arrived through a burning circle of light. Was that created by the stone you speak of?"

"Yes."

"Like a flowstone or an enchanted charm." He taps his finger. "How did you make it?"

"I didn't. I stole it too."

Amusement flickers in his eyes. "Can you procure more?"

I think about the portal stone in my room.

"None of this is relevant," I return. "You Sluagh can *flicker* anywhere you want."

"Flicker?"

"Like Fox did earlier when he abandoned me in our rooms."

A deathly chill enters the air. Legion's stoic features grow stormy.

"He left you in his room knowing there was no way out?"

"As if you care. Why are you acting weird about this?" I shovel a forkful of spinach into my mouth, then mumble through a mouthful, "Finch and Cricket figured I was trapped."

I stop chewing when Legion abruptly gets to his feet and buttons his coat.

"You're late for training." He scowls. "And you have terrible table manners."

Then he walks out.

Bodin sighs heavily and sinks in his chair, sprawling long, powerful legs beneath the table. His eyes close as if trying to be patient, but then he collects the piles of paper and stands.

"Don't forget the Holly King's feast on Feyday eve," he grumbles. "We'll arrange for more fitting attire."

"Good," I shoot back, surprising him. "Your baby dragon ate my panties. I'll need more of those too."

It's the least they can do.

At Bodin's silence, I lift my gaze, expecting him to be a bewildered fool at my crudeness, just as Fox was after glimpsing my naked rear end. The impact of his open desire knocks the breath from my lungs. Surely he's not . . . All I want to do is scrape my hair back over my face but resist the urge. Instead, I nervously lick my lips.

His gaze drops there, and a flutter low in my groin sparks more of that heat Fox had kindled earlier. It's impossible not to be attracted to him, to any of them. But Bodin is something else. His long dark lashes are so thick, I'm jealous. Worse, I want to feel them fluttering against my skin as he traces his lips along it. A shiver wracks my spine, giving me the strength to avert my gaze.

The weight of his attention lasts another torturous heartbeat, and then he stalks out, the papers crushed in his fists.

# TWENTY-THREE

WILLOW

When my father wished for me to find something useful to do, I thought of coming to Avorlorna and killing the Six. But everything is being turned upside down. Manabeeze are called wisps, and it's against the law to keep them. Baby Hunt is in danger. I live in a castle that changes structure nightly.

I stabbed Fox, and he welcomed it.

And Bodin. That heat.

I'm so filled with sexual confusion that I forget Varen is still here until his cutlery chinks as he moves a fork. His jaw and the sides of his head are freshly shaven. I can't imagine he'd have the wits to do it himself, which means one of the others did. My brow furrows at the thought of one of them carefully attending to him.

Varen's blue-black straight hair is swept from his forehead. His suit is casual yet elegant—black with blue embroidery and a skull emblem over his breast pocket. Our gazes clash. I almost think I see recognition, but he smiles tentatively and gestures to his untouched plate of food.

"Drone bees do not collect pollen or nectar from flowers," he announces. "Instead, they rely fully on worker bees to feed them."

"Um . . . okay." What is this? Does he want me to feed him?

His lips flatten at my perplexed expression, and tension creeps into his tone. "Bee bread is a mixture of pollen and honey. This is not bee bread."

I don't know what to say, so take another mouthful of food.

"Talk with him, love." Cricket bustles in and clicks her tongue at the full plates left by the others. "It seems to calm him down."

She collects the dishes and leaves us again. I squirm at the awkward silence, so say, "Bee bread sounds delicious."

And ridiculous. I'm imagining black-and-yellow striped furry baked goods. But his eyes light up at my response, and my heart melts a little. Re-enthused, he returns to arranging cutlery into hexagon shapes. He made a mess of it earlier. As I chew my next mouthful, I slide a butter knife from my side to his.

"Drone bees have a very large appetite." He positions the knife. "They eat about three times more food than worker bees."

"That's impressive." I slide a fork to him.

A smirk touches his lips as he takes it. He leans across the table to mischievously whisper, "This gives them plenty of energy to fly in search of virgin queens during mating flights."

I burst out laughing and cover my mouth.

He grins, eyes sparkling with mirth. There is no hate, no disgust, no ulterior motives in there. Just pure, genuine gratitude for the conversation. Maybe even affection. That tugging feeling in my chest begins again. When my hand flutters to my sternum, attempting to rub it away, he sits back and pensively stares at his cutlery.

"Drones are kicked out of the hive when food is scarce because they do not participate in building combs." His eyes dart to and fro, once again filling with anxiety. "How can they be expected to repair the hive if they don't know how to build the combs?"

Intuition prickles my skin. His gaze keeps flicking to me as if he's waiting for understanding to dawn on my face.

"Are you trying to tell me something, Varen?"

The moment passes, and he returns to his task, enthralled with making a pattern and mumbling more bee facts to himself. Disconcerted, I finish my meal in silence, and Cricket returns for my plate.

"Best be off, love. The snow has stopped."

The only way to the Nexus is over the moat, and I'm not in the mood for bravery. "I might just stay here and talk bees with Varen."

He looks at me, eyes hopeful. "A court of worker bees constantly attends to a queen. They feed and groom her."

"See?" I tell Cricket. "Varen wants me to stay. I'll even let him groom me if that's what he really wants."

"Nonsense." She taps me on the head. "The masters said you're late. You have classes, and I'm sure you have friends waiting for you."

Alfie. Geraldine, Max, Bob, and Peggy.

"Okay," I grumble. Maybe the moat is already frozen. No chance of drowning, then.

Appeased, Cricket leaves with the dishes. Varen has gone quiet and watches me stand with a pinched brow.

"Are you okay?" I ask, collecting my cape. "I was only kidding about the grooming. Obviously, you don't have to touch my face."

His frown turns into a scowl. Irritably, he walks me to the door and insists he tie the cape around my shoulders. I take in his uniquely calming scent—something sweet with jasmine. As he focuses on tying the laces, I take the opportunity to study him more closely. His angular eyes are a deep, warm brown. His cupid's bow lips are full yet still delicate on his face. It's strange how I don't feel on edge around him. My defense walls are down, and I can't say I hate it. In another world, another time, we could be friends.

After tying my laces, he won't let go.

"I have to leave," I whisper.

He gives a melancholic nod and steps back. I turn, but he takes my shoulder and warns, "The drone's sole purpose is to mate with a virgin queen bee, but very few succeed." His grip tightens until I wince. "Those that don't mate die quickly once cooler weather sets in."

What is he on about?

"You're weirding me out, Varen."

His eyes grow dull, and he returns to the table.

I'm not sure what disturbs me more, his words or the dismay that I couldn't help him. To avoid thinking about it, I read the exhibition pamphlet on the brisk walk to the Nexus. It's not like the Sluagh offered any advice on how to win. They've neglected to talk about it at all. For now, I'm all about the pamphlet.

The distraction tactic works so well that I manage to cross the rickety bridge without panicking. I barely even notice the sound of gushing water and cracking ice. Don't even think about getting stuck beneath it or freezing to death.

I lie.

The instant I'm over, I'm on my hands and knees, hyperventilating until I feel frostbitten.

The guide distracted me again afterward, keeping me engaged with words instead of my racing heart as I walked through the woods. The exhibition program involves classes leading up to a few celebrations, more classes, and a tournament at the end of winter. Both House of Embers and House of Shadows run combat skills, weapons techniques, and offensive strategies. Tactical warfare is a specialty of the House of Stone. The House of Moonlight teaches monstrous tactics and vulnerabilities. House of Shadows oversees combat, and stealth and infiltration. I scoff. Of course, they'd know all about being sneaky, wouldn't they? Magical defense seems to be about using charmed stones to counter enemy magic. Everyone pitches in for medical training.

This exhibition is a front for conscription—to train mortals as grateful fodder. It leaves a bitter taste in my mouth. The Good Folk are cowards. They have strict rules against gossiping, are obsessed with perfect appearances, and consider bad manners unacceptable.

As I near the main campus, Peablossom darts out from the shadows of a tree. Her dress is as luxurious as it was when we first met. Hundreds of gemstones and raw crystals twinkle on chains wrapped around her torso. Combined with her blue hair in a twist, she reminds me of a whirlwind.

"You're late!" she hisses, then shakes her head and smiles broadly. Her next words are joyously forced out through chattering teeth. "My sweet shadow cherub, you're the sole sponsored contender who missed orientation."

Who is she kidding with the false pleasantry? "I thought your job here was done."

"Indeed, it was . . . until the pandemonium you so graciously instigated during the pageant. Now, I find myself tasked with supervising the entirety of the exhibition."

"I didn't instigate anything. They chose me." Or rather, Baby Hunt did.

"Yes, well." Her lips purse, and she exhales. "Behold your schedule. You are most graciously welcome. I collected it for you."

"Thank you."

She hands me the weekly outline. As I scan it, her finger hooks on my cape. Her lips part as the front opens. "You're bedecked in Lord Fox's finery. The bold embroidered appliqué is unmistakably his."

"He shouldn't have left his clothes lying about," I grumble, reading.

"Cunning little mortal," she exclaims, delivering a playful swat to my shoulder. "You will, naturally, incur a uniform violation. But I suppose you knew the code amendments stipulate that a Shadow's discipline is in the hands of their Radiant. Rumor has it Lord Fox excels at . . . how shall I phrase this delicately . . . beguiling remorse from those who've erred."

"Yes." I deadpan. "That's exactly why I did this."

"I must say I am rather offended on your behalf that he's yet to rectify your countenance." She pouts and rearranges my hair, drawing strands to shroud my jawline further. "We all know your circumstances can be avoided with a quick sleight of hand."

I lower the pamphlet. "You mean like how your glamour hid my . . . flaws?"

Her lips purse again. "We really shouldn't discuss such matters openly, my dear. The ravens are ever attentive. But, I admit, we may never find a moment like this again, so here goes. Your mentors can rectify your appearance permanently. No illusions are required. Then you'll not be"—her nose twitches with disgust—"one of the Nightmares."

The paper crumples in my fist. Everywhere I go, people point out my face.

"Why did you lie on my behalf?" she asks quietly, fixing the other side of my hair.

"Because it's none of their business."

Her dainty arms drop to her sides. "Overseeing exhibitors is a gift compared to Puck's attention."

"What would he have done if he found out you helped me?"

"Choose your poison." She fidgets, and her voice turns shaky. "I could be stripped of charms or glamour, brow erasure, dream deprivation, turned into a statue of contemplation, banishment."

"For glamouring me?"

"For aiding and abetting the enemy."

Her words stab my heart. Geraldine and her friends are targets.

"Why are Nothings encouraged to enter the exhibition?"

She looks at me as though I'm daft. "You strike me as a clever cricket, Willow. I thought you read the Old Code?"

"Not all of it," I lie. I've read none.

She glances over her shoulder, then leans in. "You tread on treacherous ground. Make haste to read, study, and live by it for your own safeguarding. Be especially aware of article four, section three, where the Folk cannot engage in the brutish pastimes our subterranean kinsfolk enjoy. That is what mortals and dragons are for."

"So I was right," I murmur. "This exhibition is a trick. Service and potential death is expected for all who survive."

"Consider us on an equal par for favors yesterday rendered." She swipes her skirt, tinkling her charms. "Most who have graced this realm long enough to witness several Gentle Interludes are aware Nothings rarely endure until the end. In fact, it appears to be somewhat of an initiation rite for Shadows to dispatch them before the tournament. But that's mere whispers in the wind and certainly not idle gossip you acquired from me. Now, are you certain of your destination?"

My life is in danger. Not just mine, but Geraldine, Max, Peggy, and Bob. I glance down at the crushed timetable and force my hands to remain steady, but I can't focus. I keep seeing Bob holding my arm as we march in a straight line. How is he supposed to survive? How will any of them survive?

Peablossom points to the timetable and says, "That quaint depiction of a flame denotes the combat class is held in the House of Embers Tower. If you hurry, you'll arrive before they close the doors. Tardy souls are strictly forbidden to enter. Off you go, and remember," she points to her dimples and sings, "we are smiling, yes?"

It's an effort to return her smile, but she helped me. As far as the Good Folk go, she's not so bad. Satisfied, she hums in approval and sashays away.

ALFIE WAITS OUTSIDE THE LAVA-VEINED TOWER, ARMS FOLDED, LOOKING as virile as ever in his uniform. His biceps stretch the gray fabric of his shirt. Another new, twinkling red charm hangs from his chain. I break into a jog but stop short of hugging him.

"Did you get my note?" he whispers.

"Yes," I breathe. "I burned it too."

"So, we're good for tonight?"

Tonight? Does he really want to meet somewhere? Before I can ask for clarification, he gapes at my cape and pulls it further apart. "Why aren't you in uniform? And . . . what are you wearing? Wait. Is that your Radiant's clothes?"

I swat him away. Why does everyone think they have the right to peer beneath my cape? "My uniform was dirty, so I stole his."

"You can't wear their clothes instead." Panic tightens his voice. "They'll roast you alive when they find out."

I scoff. "What can they do without getting violent?"

Alfie's disparaging look reminds me of Peablossom's list of punishments, particularly the one about a statue.

"They can do plenty," he replies curtly. "Look, Willow, back home, you were President Nero's favorite pet. With Rory looking out for you, you got away with murder . . . literally. But here, you're on your own. Your Radiants haven't cared enough to fix your face. Doesn't that tell you something about their motivations?"

My arms wrap around my middle. When did he get so bossy? "You don't trust them?"

"I trust no one." His gaze softens. He touches my hair. "Except you. Just . . . don't sit in the first row. Don't volunteer for sparring until you learn about your competitor's weaknesses."

"I know how to fight, Alfie," I counter with a droll tone.

"Yeah, but you're charmless." He scrubs his face. "You're as mortal as me, so do me a favor and, for once, heed my warning. I've got something in the works to help you."

My brows knit together. "You sound like *them*."

"I've been here a long time." Ghosts flicker in his eyes as they search mine. "I'm so glad you're here. Have I mentioned that?"

"Yes." Warmth blooms in my chest. I step into him, and he doesn't push me away. "But you can say it again."

His head dips until I feel his heat. Wait. Is he going to kiss me? My heart jackhammers and I freeze, unsure what to do. He knew the real me before this curse warped my face. That should make me want to close the gap between our lips. Shouldn't it?

He quickly untangles us and glances over my shoulder.

When I turn, I catch Geraldine and Max hurrying away as though they were about to say hello, but changed their minds.

"Geraldine!" I shout. "I'll be right back, Alfie."

"Willow, you shouldn't be associating with—"

I don't hear the rest. I'm already halfway to Geraldine. She gives me a shy smile and backtracks from the entrance. Max tells her he'll save a seat.

"Ooh, me too, please." I stick up my hand.

"You'll sit with us?" His mouth gapes slightly.

"If that's okay with you."

"I mean, sure. We'd love you to sit with us."

"Great." Is it stupid that I can't stop the smile on my face? That I'm making friends here? I turn back to invite Alfie, but he's already left.

# CHAPTER
# TWENTY-FOUR
## WILLOW

"It's not a good look," Geraldine mumbles after Max heads in. "For you, I mean. You shouldn't sit with us."

"Why?"

"You're a Shadow now."

"Pah." I wave the notion off. "It's ridiculous they think you're the enemy. Not that I've actually seen the enemy, but I highly doubt you four are the epitome of Nightmares. I'm out of good looks, anyway. How are you? How's the dorm? Have you been treated fairly?"

Has anyone attempted to kill them?

"Same as usual."

But she avoids my gaze. Something happened overnight.

"Where's Peggy and Bob?"

"In a different class."

"Geraldine." I take her hand. "Is everything all right?"

She forces a smile that crinkles her burn scars. "We're good, I promise."

"Okay." I nod, wondering how much of what I learned from Peablossom to tell. I don't want to freak them out if it's not true.

But I also want to prepare them if it is. I feel sick from not knowing the best course of action. What if I make things worse? "Um. Geraldine, do you know about the mortality rate for Nothings in the tournament?"

"Well, I assume it's not good," she replies dryly. At my silence, her shoulders drop. "That bad, huh?"

"How many others are in your dorm?"

"Until last night, there were eight in total."

My blood runs cold. "What happened?"

"Apparently, she died in her sleep." Her eyes become empty. "We'd better go in. I don't want to be late."

She's right. It's one thing for me to ignore the rules in the name of revenge, but she can't afford to get in trouble.

"What's with the clothes?" She gives me a sideways glance as we walk, and Fox's trousers flash through the gap in my cape.

"One of my Radiants pissed me off."

"Oh my god, you have a death wish."

She's not joking. I breathe in and then exhale. "You're probably right."

The ground level inside the tower is an empty hall about forty feet wide. At the center of the room, a podium holds a map of the floor plans. The red pulsing veins in the walls radiate heat like the Fever Hunt, so it's much warmer inside, and we remove our outer layers. While I wait for Geraldine, I scan the map and learn a spiral staircase winds around the tower's internal wall. The next level up is the classroom, followed by a library on the next, then the house commons, dorms, the Shadow's private room, and temporary accommodations for the visiting noble. There's even space on the turret for a dragon's nest.

Done with her cape, Geraldine continues toward the staircase without checking the map. I jog after her. "How do you know where to go?"

Her cheeks flush. "As soon as I got the timetable, I visited

209

each location and timed how long it took to get from place to place."

"Smart."

A tight smile. "I need to be."

We emerge on the next level to a classroom with two rings of seats surrounding a round gym mat at the center. The room is filled to the brim with exhibitors. Max gingerly waves at us from seats he's saved across the floor.

Alfie is too busy chatting with the red-lipped, raven-haired Shadow to notice me. Two more Chasers listen intently to his story, their heads bowed as though it is riveting. Everyone is impeccably groomed in pressed, starched uniforms without a trace of dirt. Every fingernail is trimmed and polished.

I'm the only one with my hair out and wild.

My confidence evaporates as a thousand eyes turn my way. Conversations hush. Scandalized gazes rake down my stolen clothes and unkempt appearance. Unfortunately, Max saved seats in the front row. Geraldine walks over to sit beside him, stowing her cape beneath her seat. I sit next to her, do the same, then face forward, hugging my middle.

I force my hands to rest on my lap, but they fidget without my permission, so I retrieve my cape and use it to clench. Revenge sounds easier in my mind than in reality. The only person I'm hurting right now is myself. My disregard for the rules better reflect poorly on the House of Shadow, or I'll have to chalk it up as another stupid mistake.

A bell chimes in the distance. Any student left standing scurries to an empty seat and sits spine straight, hands in lap.

I'm chewing my nails again. It almost physically hurts to readjust, as though the action leaves me vulnerable to mockery. These people don't openly scorn, but do it in other, veiled ways. Take the Never sitting next to me. The moment I sat, he leaned away. The person on the other side told him to lean back, that sitting next to someone like me makes him look good.

Perfectly punctual, the House of Embers Radiant arrives and strolls to the center of the mat. The Marquess Lord Ignarius is the same suave sophisticate I remember from the pageant. His dark tailored suit is trimmed with flames—the fabric shimmers as though catching reflections from the simmering veins in the walls. A small lapel pin is the shape of a flame, like the icon on the timetable. His dark hair is greased back, and he smells like campfire smoke. It tingles my nose.

With his hands behind his back, he takes a turn of the room and studies us with haughty superiority.

"You are here as dream chasers," he announces solemnly, "in an exhibition showcasing cutthroat talents to the good people of Avorlorna. I shall refrain from insulting your intellect by teaching combat rudiments." He stops before a Never who has her ankles crossed. She quickly untangles, and he resumes his walk. "You are fragile sparks in the inferno of a war threatening to consume us all. Now, I claim no mastery"—a self-congratulatory smirk—"but unless fire has spontaneously learned to douse fire, divergent tactics must be deployed when facing an opponent who mirrors your form."

As he passes, his smokey scent tickles my nose to an eye-watering point. I scrunch to stop the sneeze, but it's making me squirm. Geraldine gives me a concerned side-eye as he continues.

"Today," he announces, "I bless you with knowledge revolving around this very—"

My sneeze echoes against the walls. He stops, twists, and stares at me.

"Sorry," I mumble, silently grateful I don't have to sign my apology in Avorlorna. I think my hand is covered in snot.

"Are you quite finished?" he intones.

I nod, tuck my hands beneath my cape, then hide them under my arms. Across the mat, the red-lipped House of Embers Shadow mimics me. I return my hands to my lap. She does the same.

What is her problem?

Ignarius's lips curve when he takes note, and he returns to the center of the mat.

"What better way," he announces with a flourish, "to demonstrate this lesson than to invite two exhibitors who, for all intents and purposes, *should* reflect each other's skills. House of Embers Shadow, Dahlia Vella, if it pleases you, take the mat." His smile turns smarmy as she sashays out with as much grace as a dancer—or a fighter—and looks at me.

My stomach hollows with dread. My gaze flicks to Alfie's alarmed eyes. He knows what's coming.

"And you, House of Shadow's Shadow." He snorts in an unbecoming way for a noble. "Indeed, that's quite the tongue twister. Perhaps they ought to have been more meticulous with the naming conventions." He stares at me. I don't want to move because my dagger is tucked into the back of my waistband. I was stupid to bring it. "Do you require a formal written invitation, my delicate subterranean bloom?"

A twitch forms beneath my eye as snickers break out in the room. Unable to think of an appropriate reply, I purposefully sneeze and spray. While everyone averts their gazes in repulsion, I simultaneously remove my cape from my lap, hide the dagger within the folds, and give the lot to Geraldine.

Distraction is the biggest tool in a thief's tool kit. I still remember the day my mother taught me that during our secret communications. She said, *Bump into them, and while they're thinking of the big knock, your nimble little fingers will be doing something magical they can't see.*

I join Dahlia at the center.

Ignarius stares at me again, this time with open distaste. I wipe my nose with the back of Fox's sleeve. The more disgusting they think I am, the more they'll underestimate me.

With a pompous flourish, he returns his attention to the class, signals vaguely in my direction, and says, "One can never predict the guise Nightmares adopt when they surface from the subterranean watergates. A Terror can materialize as your reflection, or they can assume the identity of your wildest fear."

"You never asked for my name," I interject.

"Nothings don't have names," he snaps, cold eyes spearing me for longer than appropriate. He turns to the class and continues. "Or so we've been told. They reject harmony and light. They are the dark blight tarnishing the pristine purity of the Cauldron's eternal Wellspring. They are the enemy, yet"—he dramatically lifts a finger—"one has somehow ensnared the attention of our esteemed military leaders. One might also postulate that, to receive such attention, these two Shadows stand on equal ground regarding refinement and grace." He pauses for effect. "Something doesn't quite add up, does it? One could also assume more lurks beneath the surface." He gives me a withering stare. I catch tears glimmering in Geraldine's eyes and remember I'm not the only one he's insulting here. "Is it enchantment? A beguiling trick? Are we peering into the murky eyes of a Terror in Radiant clothing right this minute?"

Gasps fraught with fear fill the air.

I should receive a medal for resisting an eye roll at his theatrics.

The Marquess continues, "Is she simply biding her time until we least expect an attack? Perhaps during a wander in the woods alone, a quick nap in her presence, or a daydream . . . and she will rip out your throats when you least expect it."

Hatred simmers hotter than the lava-like veins between granite. It's clear he's setting me up for humiliation, or at the very least, hopes I'll move up the list of Nothing targets for assassination. But do I dare take the bait? Will acting out serve my revenge purpose, or do the opposite? Maybe I should skip classes altogether. I might get at least two days of freedom before Peablossom tracks me down. Two days to explore the castle, cause some havoc, and maybe even figure out what in the Well's name is going on with the Sluagh.

"Now take Shadow Dahlia Villa, for instance," he drawls, eyes filling with desire as he takes his fill of her body. "What a stunning specimen of perfection. The complete opposite of the Nothing."

"Willow," I growl through clenched teeth. "My *name* is Willow, not the *Nothing*."

He ignores me and strides into Dahlia's personal space, inspecting her so closely that he probably sees down her open-collared shirt. She wears a size too small, so her breasts almost burst the buttons.

"One would assume Shadow Villa's charms draw her exquisite beauty directly from the Cauldron itself. Such flawlessness can't possibly be innate unless it belongs to a Radiant." He suddenly inhales, snapping out of his bewitched daze to continue. "And if her charms are harnessed for beauty, then it's safe to presume her paramount talent must reside in her martial prowess or mental acuity. The point is, my fledgling flames—" He yanks her Chaser chain from her uniform. Gemstones and crystals scatter to the mat. Gasping at the violation, her hand flutters to her chest as if he'd ripped off her shirt. But her appearance doesn't change, which I suspect must be common if some charms hold glamour.

Flow charms or stones, Wellsprings, wisps . . . the similarities are stronger now. We might have different words in Elphyne, but the theory behind our source of power is the same. Knowing this flips a switch inside me, instantly grounding me.

Ignarius murmurs to Dahlia, "You may retrieve your charms, darling."

He rattles on for another few minutes, delving into a fable about a snake who dares to believe a pretty bird isn't a bird or something. I wonder if we'll actually spar or if this male just loves the sound of his voice.

When silence becomes pronounced, I realize I've missed a cue. Everyone stares at me expectantly. I glance at Dahlia. Her charms are threaded back onto her chain, but it's now wrapped around her wrist like a bracelet.

"Give me your best shot, Nothing," she taunts.

"What?"

"You're the savage. You go first. Everyone knows Dreams don't start trouble."

"Oh, come on," I groan. "Give me a break from the righteous bullshit."

Hands fly to mouths as delicate sensibilities are bruised. How in the Well's name will any of these people survive a violent tournament, let alone a battlefield? But then I notice some Chasers aren't shocked—the ones who must have competed before and served time in the military. Hardness in their eyes separates them from the naivety of others. As most wear charms, I assume their battle scars are hidden. Some could have been permanently erased by their Radiants, just as my Aunt Ada heals a wound as if it never existed . . . if she gets to it on time.

Goodfellow's missing eyebrows come to mind, and I wonder if they're a battle scar. It occurs to me that as Dahlia's Radiant, Ignarius knows full well what her charms do. Didn't Fox say something about Alfie's newly gifted charms now that he is a Shadow? And now he watches me like a hawk.

Why do I feel like this is a trap?

# TWENTY-FIVE

## WILLOW

Tingling skin warns me to duck before Dahlia strikes with her fist. A breeze brushes past my hair as she misses. The close call sends my heart racing, pumping adrenaline into my veins. Wide awake now, I dance backward on light feet.

Her manicured brow raises, impressed at my maneuver. She quickly hides the reaction and circles me. Her legs snake in a way that draws attention to her womanly hips. It's almost like we're in another pageant. Scampering ants flare just before her boot hits my knee. Pain rips an ugly cry from my throat. I'd expected another punch. *Rusty*. Rory would be disappointed in me.

I drop to the mat, clutching my throbbing injury. I've had worse. It's not dislocated—I'd know. But I need a moment to collect my thoughts.

Alfie pushes to the first row of spectators, his eyes filled with apprehension. "This isn't a fair fight," he announces.

"The war isn't fair, Shadow Taylor."

"She hasn't even finished reading the registration pamphlet," he counters. "She doesn't know the Old Code rules of engagement for conflict resolution are void on Nexus soil for exhibitors so long as a Radiant isn't involved."

"She does now." Ignarius returns a tight, impatient smile. "Unless you wish to be collateral damage, step back."

A vague recollection of Goodfellow's warning at the pageant resurfaces. No rules. Got it. I shoot Alfie a wink in my mind. He returns to his group of Chaser friends and mumbles about this only ending in slaughter, but I know he means mine of her—not the other way around. I hope.

He mentioned something outside about underestimating my opponents. The thought spurs me to reassess Dahlia. She's fast, too fast for a human. Nothing visible on her changed when Ignarius ripped away her charms. One must be enchanted for speed, maybe even strength.

This lesson is about assumptions, so what do they assume about me?

That I've got a card up my sleeve—something big enough to warrant selection as a Shadow, despite having the face of the enemy. They *know* I have no charms making me pretty. The light from Tinger's pendant is hidden beneath Fox's black shirt. So they must assume that without a pretty face, all I have are my wits and fighting skills. Why else would the House of Shadows choose me?

I'm still wondering the same question because it's not to have me as their new queen, despite Varen's quirky words. I've been there and rejected that.

Apart from my ability to sense the flow of magic, I have no other advantages. Oh, wait. I have my halfling shifter traits— speed, smell, sight. Granted, I'm not as fast as Dahlia, but I can keep up. And I've killed.

Many, many times before.

For all her talk about not making the first move, she comes at me again with a quick one-two jab. I dance back, but my knee smarts, and I limp. Her next strike glances off my shoulder, and I fall into the first ring of spectators. Max tries to protect Geraldine, but we all clash and scramble awkwardly. This tower room isn't big enough for sparring.

"You hurt?" I ask. She took the brunt of my fall. I try to push myself off without making it worse. Max's gaze widens over my shoulder, tingles scorch my back, and a hard shove propels me forward. I headbutt Geraldine. Blood spurts from her nose. Pain radiates from mine.

"No!" I drop to my knees and use Fox's long shirt to stanch her bleeding. Geraldine's whimper is small, but the agony in her eyes is epic. Clenching my jaw, I take Max's hand and guide him to use my cape instead of my shirt. No one offers to help. Not even Alfie. It fills me with hot, itchy rage. I shoot daggers to where Dahlia smugly retreats, barely a hair out of place on her silken head.

When a rival wolf invades another's territory, there is no hesitation to defend the pack. In fact, the defender strikes first, and they keep attacking until the rival submits, flees, or is dead. Dahlia knew what she was doing, kicking me into these two. She saw me walk in with them, sitting and chatting, handing my cape to Geraldine for safekeeping. She thinks if she hurts them, she'll hurt me. What she doesn't realize is that she's now marked them as mine.

Straightening, I turn and give my knuckles a one-handed crack. While my arms dangle loosely, I stretch my neck and target her scent—cloying, floral, tart. She's no godlike crow shifter. No acid-dripping monster. I've faced down a two-thousand-year-old vampire Unseelie High Queen and lived. Dahlia is just a mortal relying on stones for an advantage.

To them, I have nothing. I *am* nothing. Which means I have nothing to lose and everything to gain, just like those charms wrapped around her wrist.

"You going to stand there all day and stare?" she taunts.

"You gonna stand there all day and let me?"

Her cockiness fades. My lips curve with an idea, and I limp closer.

"Cowardly shot," I say, "kicking someone while they're down."

She shrugs. "Normal rules of engagement are out."

"So no one will mind if I steal your pretty Chaser chain and use it to strangle you?"

Incredulous laughter erupts from her pouty lips. My smile becomes feral, wolfish. My canines aren't as big as they used to be when I shifted, but they're still extra sharp. Fear flashes in her eyes before she hides it with a snarl contorting her features into something as ugly as mine.

"You're such a pathetic, disgusting waste of space," she spits. "No class. No elegance. Why anyone wants someone grotesque like you is the greatest mystery in Avorlorna."

"Sounds like you're jealous."

If I could shift my claws out, I'd gouge her delicate throat. But instead, I shove down the emotion Rory hated so much and lean into their prejudiced opinion of me. At this point, it can't get any worse.

So, I spit in her face.

Horrified, she balks and reaches for her contaminated eye. She's so revolted she might puke. I'm not stupid enough to go straight for her wrist-chain. I lean a little further and tighten the noose. She wants inelegance? Fine.

I go wild, screeching, brawling, and scratching her flawless skin with intentionally clumsy movements. Consecutive hits to her vanity blind her to my nimble, pick-pocketing fingers. Her Chaser chain falls into my palm.

*For the Gold.*

Now it's time to teach this bitch a lesson. I wrap my legs

around her torso, twist until I'm at her back, and loop the chain around her throat. I hold Ignarius's coal-eyed stare as I choke his Shadow with her own damn charms—the ones he probably gifted her.

The silver cuts into my palms, burning enough to scar. My muscles scream in protest, tremble, and threaten to give up. But I lock them in place. I ignore the distant voice telling me everyone is right, that I'm not good enough. I'll lose. I don't know what I'm doing making these types of decisions for myself. It was better when I followed orders and did as I was told.

I shake under the strain and can't hold on much longer. I've neglected my strength training after Rory died. I was solo for too long and wandered aimlessly about the Order, wondering what my purpose was, stealing shit and getting into trouble with Tinger. Why did I waste so much time?

Dahlia taps me repetitively, begging me to stop, but I'm not looking at her. I'm still holding the dark gaze of her mentor. It's interesting how he tries to play chicken with me.

*"No, Willow,"* Nero's disapproving voice hits from the past. *"He wasn't dead."*

*My adult victim scrambles away on his knees. He stopped making sounds and went limp. I hold my trembling little girl's hands before my face. Not my blood. It's not my blood on my hands.*

*"I thought you taught her better than this?"* Uncle Nero is so *angry.*

*"She's a child."* Aunty Rory is angry, too.

*"Look at me, Willow."* Nero gestures after the crawling man. *"Kill him again. This time, don't stop until you see the life empty from his eyes."*

Lord Ignarius claps slowly, staring at me. An excruciating heartbeat later, he stands with a grandiose swirl and addresses the room.

"And *that* is exactly why we never assume, especially when a *Nothing* is concerned."

I let go of Dahlia and stand back, my lungs heaving, my hair falling over my face. My bloody palms are steady as I hold them before my face. I must look like a fright, like the very thing sneaking into their nightmares.

But for the first time since I was cursed, I don't feel so ugly. I feel victorious.

"My name is *Willow*." I toss the bloody chain on Dahlia's mottled, gasping face.

"You can keep the charms." Ignarius's dry proclamation offends Dahlia. "To the victor goes the spoils."

As if my triumph was part of his demonstration. What a joke.

"I don't want your trinkets," I scoff.

His goodwill evaporates. Steam curls from his skin as though he's just stepped out of the shower. "I don't want your trinkets, *my lord,*" he reminds. "I am your superior, and you will address me as such. For your uniform violation, report to the registration desk at noon and accept your punishment."

"No."

# CHAPTER
# TWENTY-SIX
## WILLOW

Ignarius chokes. "Excuse me?"

"You can take it up with my Radiants." I lift my chin. "The amendment to the Old Code for the Solstice Exhibition states that a Shadow is disciplined only by their respective Radiant."

*Thank you, Peablossom.*

"You'll come to regret this," he points out dryly.

The tower clock chimes, and he signals class is over. He turns his back on me as exhibitors file out, finally showering his Shadow with attention. "There, there, my precious wildflower. 'Tis naught but a scratch. Nothing your Radiant can't fix."

He waves his hand over her face, and the bleeding welts diminish. Not even a scar remains on her flawless skin. It's not a glamour, either. She breathes normally again.

Alfie's eyes meet mine from across the room. I start limping toward him, but he crouches to attend Dahlia. My behavior wasn't exactly ladylike, but his cold shoulder feels like a slap in the face. Ignoring my throat restricting, I face Geraldine and Max.

At least I've made anyone think twice about targeting them. But as we leave the room, we're hit with a mix of embittered and fearful glances. It's not the kind of fear that says they'll run. It's the kind that says they'll attack first. The kind that fills a wolf with a desperate need to protect its pack.

Dismay cramps my stomach. I've messed up again. People are afraid of what they don't understand.

*Freak. Even the boogeymen didn't want her.*

I wait until we exit the tower before speaking. "I shouldn't have done that."

"You were amazing." Geraldine's eyes still glisten, but her nose has stopped bleeding. When I shiver, she hands me my cape.

"I'm going to be honest and say a little scary too." Max offers a lopsided grin. "I've never seen a girl fight like that. No offense."

"None taken. But that wasn't a fight. That was me being reckless. I lost my temper."

He snorts. "I'm so out of my league if you don't call that a fight."

The gravity of his words dampens the mood. I can't imagine how it would feel to walk into a place like this, knowing it's your only chance of survival. I wanted to feel like I was the spider staring down the giant, but I'm not. These guys are.

I am privileged with my combat knowledge.

"I'll teach you," I suggest. "I'll give you all private lessons. I'll request to move back into your dorms."

"No!" Geraldine gasps loud enough that we receive dirty looks from passersby. "No," she repeats, lowering her voice. "We can't let you do that. You have an opportunity to learn from military leaders. Don't pass that up for us."

"They can't teach me anything I don't already know."

"Who *are* you?" Max's eyes widen in awe.

"Someone with a messed-up childhood." Because of those supposed military leaders.

Maybe.

Fuck, am I really questioning who's to blame for my life now? Max is right. Who *am* I?

Geraldine covers my hand where I still clutch the cape. "I'm so sorry. Were your parents horrid?"

"No." My smile is genuine as I think about my biological family. "They're pretty awesome. It's—" The words catch as Nero's soulless eyes enter my mind. Soulless, unless they were disappointed.

"Willow!" Geraldine turns my palm up. "You're bleeding."

I gently tug my hand from her grip. "It's more your blood than mine."

The reminder sharpens my gaze, and I scrutinize our surroundings for anyone looking too hard at us. I pick up ice in the air, but none of Dahlia's cloying scent. My hand slips inside the folds of my cape, hunting for the hardness of the dagger's hilt.

What I wouldn't give for proximity stones right now. I could set them up around the Nothing dorm room and keep the alarm stone at the castle. If someone tries to kill them in their sleep, I'll know about it. But from what Legion and Bodin said this morning, manabeeze aren't easy to come by.

Twinkling in the nearby woods draws my attention to a glittering dream web. There are plenty of stones knotted into the threads. It gets me thinking. Maybe there's a black market here, like at Cornucopia back home. Everyone wants something they don't have. It's a fact of life. It's also a fact that someone will try to make a quick coin over their misfortune.

Feeling a new purpose trickle into me, I nod toward the House of Stone tower.

"We have a class there next, right?" I ask.

Geraldine nods, wiping her nose. "We should get cleaned up first. A uniform violation for us is slightly different than for you."

I glance down at my blood-soaked shirt. It's black, but the stains are noticeable. A walk to the keep and back will make me late, so I'm damned no matter what I do. "No point in me changing. My exhibitor uniform is dirty, anyway."

"I'll take you to the registration desk," Geraldine offers.

"No." Max stops us. "You two head to the dorms, and I'll go to the desk. I'm sure Peablossom will understand."

She's stressed from having to manage this entire exhibition. Max's shirt is also blood-stained. "I'm already in trouble," I point out. "You two aren't. Why don't we all go to your dorm? Then, while you clean up, I can look around and ensure no one's tampered with things."

"You think someone is out to get us?" Max asks.

"Um." Why did I say that? Now they're worried. "Hey, random question. Have you ever heard of a Nothing winning this tournament? I'm curious about the previous winners."

They both avert their gaze and shrug.

"How did you hear about this exhibition?" I ask. "Were you staying with others like you outside the city?"

"I'm not supposed to talk about them." Geraldine bites her lip.

Max saves her from answering by offering his own brief story. "When I crawled out of the dirt, I thought I was in hell. I'm completely serious. Wait—do you know what hell is?"

"Oh yeah, sure. My mother's been in Elphyne for thirty years but still talks like an old-worlder."

"So weird—"

"And awesome," Geraldine adds.

Max agrees. "Yeah, and awesome to hear you say things like that. We don't feel so alone. Or that our life back then was just a random dream."

My smile hides another plan formulating in my head. I'll find some manabeeze to power my portal stone home and take these guys with me.

"It was so cold," Max continues. "I almost died from exposure, but then a villager took pity on me and fed me under the condition that I help on their farm over the summer. They seemed to have recently risen or awoken like us and needed help establishing things. The condition was that I turn myself in for the exhibition."

"So, you didn't have a choice?" I turn to Geraldine, but she looks to where four students pass, giving us a wide berth. Their scathing glares are pointed at me.

Word must be spreading like wildfire. I've drawn attention to Max and Geraldine through no fault of their own. Alfie's reasons for staying away from Nothings make complete sense now.

"You know what?" I channel Peablossom's bright smile. "Maybe it's better if I don't go with you to the dorms. At least until the heat cools off."

Concern flares in Geraldine's eyes. She's about to respond, but Max says they'll be late. We can talk about it later.

"I'll see you in the Tactical Warfare class." I'm about to wave them off when I finally find my dagger inside the cape. "Wait."

Geraldine stops. "You okay?"

Before I lose my nerve, I hand her Rory's dagger and help hide it beneath her shirt. "Look after it for me. Hide it under your pillow when you sleep."

I can tell she wants to say something—Max too. But I remind them they'll be late. She walks backward and suggests, "Maybe we can hang out tonight?"

"I'd love that."

The walk to the House of Stone tower is cold. I throw the cape around my shoulders to stop the wind from turning the wet, blood-stained fabric to ice against my skin.

I just handed over Rory's dagger.

Just . . . handed it over.

Fuck. Scrubbing my face, I try to shake off the nerves. For the millionth time, I consider skipping these stupid classes. These people aren't even hiding they are training mortals for the slaughter. I should focus on the Six or locating manabeeze, not taking classes.

Sighing, I drag my feet to the classroom. The teacher is a male noble with pointed ears and a rotund frame. He's almost identical to Lord Sylvanar but rounder in his flawless face. He is a Radiant, going by how he carries himself and his lack of charms. He frowns upon seeing my state, writes a note in his palm-sized book, and politely advises me that my infraction has been recorded. That's basically how my day goes.

I turn up to a class, I receive a violation, people stare, and I ignore it all. There's only so much hiding behind my hair I can handle.

The day's class highlight is *Monstrous Tactics and Vulnerabilities* with the House of Moonlight. Each exhibitor receives a copy of a codex outlining various breeds of subterranean nightmares. Interestingly, a few are similar to monsters in Elphyne. They have different names, but I recognize their appearances.

My trouble is following the text. Some ancient runes are a language I've never read before. The book is stamped as written by the "Keepers of the Cauldron." I sense we're missing vital information.

By the afternoon, my grand total of five uniform violations finds a friend with my new "failure to appear" violation delivered by a raven. The blackbird squawks and drops the folded parchment on my head.

Finally, by the early evening, I arrive at the House of Shadow tower itchy, still in blood-stained clothes, and exhausted. I'm also starving, so when I slam the double doors open and find the tower empty, I growl. I was sure the next two hours were meant for private tutelage time for Shadows.

Was the class canceled, and no one told me? Fine by me. I was going to spend the time being a royal pain in their butts, but at least now I can eat. I pivot but freeze when Ignarius walks in.

"Multiple code violations in one day, Nothing." His smug tone drills into my bones. "Not exactly the paragon of decorum, wouldn't you agree?"

Glancing around, stretching my senses, I don't hear another soul inside the tower. As he leans forward to inspect me, his hawkish nose is a direct line to his coal-like eyes.

"Yes," he mutters quietly, smoke blooming from his breath. "No one can deny the Morrigan has marked you with a face like that."

I track him as he strolls around me, examining me like a specimen in a jar.

"Have you naught to say regarding your flagrant disregard for the Old Code?"

"I've been busy."

His eyes flash at my lack of proper address.

"Indeed, therein lies the conundrum." He cants his head. "How serendipitous that your evening has opened after an attack at the gates monopolized the Knight Commander's attention."

"What?"

Voices outside elevate as people walk by, heading home for the evening.

"Hmm," he continues, glancing toward the closed door. "Without a class to attend, I suppose now you'll have to walk home with the rest of them. Public disgrace can hardly transpire when there is no public to bear witness, don't you think?"

# CHAPTER
# TWENTY-SEVEN
## WILLOW

"My punishment is my Radiants' responsibility," I remind Ignarius. "It should wait for them."

Not that I want that, either.

The Marquess steps further inside the shadowed room and waves his hand. One by one, each wall sconce ignites, illuminating the darkness. As if he owns this tower, he saunters around, wiping his finger to inspect for dust.

"Your superiors are also subject to the same laws of the code," he explains. "Yet, lamentably, none appeared sufficiently invested to grace the registration desk with their presence when they were called. The matter has now been handed to the court's official disciplinarian."

There's no way around this. I'll have to face the consequences, as stupid as they are.

"And I suppose that's you?"

He laughs. "I'm merely here to bear witness."

Goodfellow? Someone else?

"I wonder which mode of torture he'll decide to mete out?" His smarmy gaze drags down my body. "As is tradition, the penalty should mirror the offense. Disrespecting the uniform implies you traverse the streets naked. However, the queen's watchdog may harbor other, more imaginative propositions."

The carved wooden doors open, and Emrys prowls in.

Feral magnetism wraps around his athletic physique. His pale hair is disheveled, and his black military coat is crumpled as though he's come straight from a hard day's work. Dried blood is caught beneath his fingernails. He is death and life personified, the taker and the giver, and when he looks at me, I forget to breathe.

The fumes of torture are his drug of choice. But he's also my Radiant. Surely, he wouldn't be so cruel as to treat me like work, not when it could affect my chances of winning this tournament. Bodin said they chose me because they wanted to win.

"Ah, naïve bloom." Glee enters Ignarius's eyes when he notes my confusion. "The Knight Inquisitor isn't like everyone else. He cares little for the rules, just like you. Ironic if you think about it."

Emrys's lip twitches as he holds my gaze. I don't know what he sees, but he rounds on Ignarius and crowds him against the wall.

"You dare drag me from work for this?" Shadows seem to follow Emrys wherever he goes. "I do not answer to you."

A flash of dragon peers from Ignarius's eyes as he gestures my way. "You have responsibilities, Inquisitor. She has repeated uniform violations and flagrantly disregarded the call to atone."

Emrys steps back as though dark magics were uttered, but I fear it's much more sinister than that.

*Interest.*

Coppery-red eyes swing my way. He opens his palm to the Marquess, who hands him a folded paper. As Emrys reads, his black brow arches. His lips curve into a mortally wounding grin.

My heart races. I can't decide if his smile is insanely attractive or just plain insane. His gaze flicks down to my chest, then back up to my eyes.

"Careful, little moth," he utters, stepping forward on silent feet. "You wouldn't want me addicted to the song of your beating heart."

In all the opponents I've faced, never have I seen the look in his eyes. I've seen cruelty, emptiness, hatred, fear, regret. Emrys drinks me up with an unquenchable thirst. There's no doubt in my mind he revels in his job.

I back up, but there is nowhere to go except up the spiral staircase.

The door suddenly opens, and in walks a tired-looking Legion. He halts and calmly assesses the situation. Guilt flickers over Ignarius's face. He said this was about public humiliation, but there's no doubt Emrys is imagining how to bleed contrition from my skin. He barely blinks when Legion tugs the paper from his hand.

"I see calamity has been encouraged today." The subtle rasp in Legion's smooth voice hints at his restraint.

"It's not like I went looking for trouble," I hiss, but quickly add, "sir."

"Hush now," he clips, still reading. "The adults are talking."

My brows raise, but something tells me to do as I'm told. I can't explain it, but every cell in my body knows he won't throw me to the wolves. Maybe it's because they need me to win this tournament, maybe to heal Varen, or maybe to free them from Titania, who knows? But if I openly disrespect him, he'll have to discipline me.

Done reading, Legion folds the orders and stares at Ignarius. "Your ineptitude is truly enchanting."

"Pardon?" Ignarius blusters, his cheeks reddening.

"You heard me. No violation exists for which discipline is required." Legion glances at me, almost with boredom. "She

231

wears our House colors with permission and will do so from here on."

"She attempted to kill my Shadow."

"Upon your instructions."

"I never instructed her to kill."

"Yet you failed to forbid it." Dismissing the Marquess, Legion faces Emrys. "Unless you wish to be present when the ladies-in-waiting arrive, I suggest you leave."

Something like true fear flashes in Emrys's eyes. He shoves past the Marquess and exits with lightning speed.

"You cannot change the rules as you see fit." Steam wafts from Ignarius's skin. "The Queen—"

"Is slumbering," Legion finishes curtly. "Do not cause trifles of unrest when we are fighting a war."

"The Gentle Interlude is upon us."

"Come now, Ignarius. Do you need me to spoon-feed you the answers?"

"I do not care for your tone, Knight Commander."

"You know as well as I that the freeze does not erase danger to our citizens. Nightmares wreak havoc the instant we close our eyes."

"Speaking of which, shouldn't you be attending the attack?"

"The Knight Marshall is taking care of it." Patience wears thin on Legion's face. "I am yet to receive this week's regional report from you."

Silence.

Steam hisses from Ignarius's nose. Peablossom arrives with two giggling females carrying bolts of fabric and what appear to be dressmaking supplies. One lady has yellow hair, the other a fine weave of silver. Each is dressed in a tailored, flattering gown of glitzy organza. The tinkling of restless charms continues in their sudden quiet.

"Lady Peablossom." Legion regally inclines his head. "Ladies

Cobweb and Mustardseed. You have my eternal gratitude for my short notice."

They curtsey as best they can without dropping their loads.

"What's this?" Ignarius demands.

"Not your concern." Legion motions for the females to enter.

"I thought you canceled class for other matters."

"Perhaps you should heed your own lesson." Legion tucks the folded paper inside Ignarius's breast pocket. "One should never assume."

Oh, he definitely received word of the lesson. Probably from Peablossom going by the doe-eyed devotion she flutters his way. Something ugly twists in my gut, and I'm too damn stubborn to give it a name. Thankfully, she herds the ladies upstairs.

Ignarius glares at me. This matter is far from over, but he leaves without another word.

In two brisk strides, Legion invades my space, and the air flees to make way for his intoxicating leathery scent. His accusatory gaze strips me bare. Lying now would be futile.

"You sparred with his Shadow?"

"Yes." Why do I sound breathless?

"Yes, sir."

For the Well's sake. "Yes, sir," I repeat.

"And you triumphed."

"Yes, sir."

"Yet you wear no spoils of victory . . ." His lingering gaze trails heat down my body. "You claimed spoils from your tousle with Fox. Why not her?"

Does that mean he knows I stabbed Fox? Wait . . . he thinks I won? A goofy grin starts to form on my face, but I force it down. "If you want his clothes back—"

"We have neglected our duty to provide you with basic needs." His lips twist in self-disparagement, something I sense is a rare sight. "Which we will rectify now. But first, I must tend to your wounds. Show me."

*I don't need your help.*

My body goes rigid with denial, but the longer his eyes remain steady on me, the more that tension falls away. Eventually, I hold out my hands.

His tongue clicks with disapproval as he grazes his thumb along the welts.

"May I heal you?" It sounds like a request, but his tone is more of an order.

Still, the resistance within me is wilting. Today's events battered my self-esteem.

"Yes," I reply.

Ants scurry at his command, and my flesh knits together. No scars. Once satisfied with his work, his long lashes lift. He sees the gash left from headbutting Geraldine. He rubs his thumb over the bump.

"Are you hurt anywhere else?" His voice has become soft, intimate.

"Maybe my knee."

He kneels, crumpling his elegant suit. The fall of his long, silken tresses as he bows sends shivers down my spine.

*He bows like a knight before a queen, his wings spilling behind him, covering the ground as if to protect me from the gore and death.*

The battlefield memory is as crisp in my mind as it was five years ago.

His fingers trace up my leg, lifting Fox's trousers until he exposes my swollen knee and heals that, too. When he digs higher, I gasp. His touch brushes upward, tingling my thigh. My protest dies in my throat. Arousal spikes low in my belly, once again rising like the fever that usually doesn't grip me until my cycle.

When more tingling sensations pepper my leg, I realize he's

found Baby Hunt's claw marks from yesterday. I rub my sternum as he attends to my other leg.

Peablossom's sing-song voice carries from upstairs, "We are waiting, Good Folk of the twilight. Embrace the flutter, for the clock is ticking."

Legion sighs in chagrin and unfolds his body with feline grace. His unwavering attention remains on me, and for a heartbeat, I think he'll glamour away my curse. But he doesn't wince at the ugliness. His fingers brush the scarred side and linger over the acid wounds.

When the itchy tingling abates, he steps back and gestures for me to go upstairs. "The ladies will take your measurements and craft a wardrobe befitting someone of your station. The Holly King's feast requires a dress code, and it is mere days away."

The familiar stab of rejection hits me squarely in the chest. It's not that I'm ungrateful for the healing, but he had every chance to hide my ugliness. In a world where appearance is everything, he's just shown his heartless cards.

I ache to crawl beneath my covers, to hide until this feeling of inadequacy leaves, but now I must survive a fitting with three stunning females scrutinizing every inch of my body. Refusing to let my mood show on my face, I follow Legion up the staircase to the next level. The ladies have rearranged classroom furniture to provide space with a footstool at the center where I'm to be poked and prodded.

"Ladies, you have your instructions." He flicks through a few swatches, then heads back to the staircase. "I will leave you to your privacy."

"You're leaving so soon, my lord?" The yellow-haired Lady Mustardseed casts a nervous glance in my direction.

"I have much work to do," he replies.

"Oh."

"Do you require further clarification?"

"Sir, if it pleases you, we require guidance regarding one particular instruction."

Peablossom's brows lower. Mustardseed gestures to Cobweb, who quickly collects a long swathe of fabric and holds it lengthwise at the base of my throat. When the undead turned on me, they clawed my left side. The scars run from my cheek to my décolletage. Logically, I know they were only fine silver slivers after being healed, but this curse makes them bulbous, hot, pulsing ropes of regret throbbing for all to see.

"Here?" Cobweb's tinkling voice grates my nerves. She lifts the swathe higher, as if covering more skin is a blessing. "Or here?"

I jerk back as she knuckles my chin. Her shudder is unmistakable. My soul shrinks, and I want to crawl into the shadows.

"Lower," Legion clips, a note of displeasure in his tone.

Cobweb blinks, surprised. But she lowers the swathe—an inch. "Here?"

I'm about to shove her in the face when a growl rumbles through Legion's lips. "Peablossom."

"Never fear, my lord. I have everything noted." She pats a notebook to her breast.

Mustardseed laughs uneasily, glancing at Cobweb for assistance. The petite faerie is the very picture of her name—delicate, refined, and a pretty death trap. The sense of danger oozes from her porcelain pores as she sidles up to Legion, bats her lashes, and purrs, "My lord, surely you don't wish to place your tender subterranean blossom in such harsh light. Perhaps she would be more comfortable if we . . . draw less attention to the . . . features less admired by us Good Folk."

"You can't cover my face," I snap. "A veil is a punishment, isn't it?"

"Or a blessing," Mustardseed mumbles to Cobweb.

"The perception of lack-witted folk is not my concern." Legion's sharp tone seizes the air in my lungs. "She's perfectly suited to the light."

He blinks, seemingly bewildered at his own words. His mask slip is brief, and then the imperious Knight Commander returns.

Peablossom cuts in front of the other two, smiling broadly at Legion. "Your Radiance, I will see that your explicit instructions are followed to the last letter. Never fear. I know how to direct our precious bloom so that she is a ray of sun breaking through the shadows."

"Better." Legion starts down the stairs, stops, and then looks at me as he instructs the ladies, "Treat our Shadow as you would our queen."

# CHAPTER
# TWENTY-EIGHT
## WILLOW

"I feel ridiculous in this dress," I mumble, walking in silken slippers through a city street. At least it hasn't snowed for days now. My new, fur-lined cape keeps most of the cold from my body.

It's now the end of the week. I've hardly seen Legion, Bodin, Fox, or Emrys. Any time I inquired, Cricket gave a standard response about the war pulling them away, but not to worry, they would return for the Holly King's feast.

Without a target for revenge, I had no choice but to go about my days like every other exhibitor. Each was a copy of the first. I woke up, found my room somewhere it hadn't been the night before, ate breakfast while Varen and I conversed about bees, puked after crawling across the rickety bridge, and attended classes.

Alfie's Radiant kept him so busy that I hardly saw him either. At first, I thought he was avoiding me after what I did to Dahlia, but this morning, he pulled me aside on my way to a very boring Tactical Warfare class and asked me why I never showed up.

"What are you talking about?" I asked, but he only had time

238

to respond, "Midnight tonight, then. Burn After Reading. Don't tell anyone."

I'm still trying to decipher his words, but I hesitated to ask Cricket.

He's left me walking into this feast without a clue. Another custom of the Gentle Interlude is how nobility from each house must troop through the city, making a show of stability and pleasantry for the general public. I see it for what it truly is—a distraction, a faerie trick. It's a pretense that all is well despite the war bubbling beneath the surface.

Legion walks ahead of me, elegantly dressed in a black tailcoat, a vest, and pleated trousers. Moonlight catches his silken tresses with every step. I can't see his face, but I doubt he's smiling. His grueling pace is akin to a wolf on the hunt, as though this city is his next meal.

But if he thinks I can't keep up, he's mistaken. I can outlast anyone.

Bodin is a silent and steady presence at my back. His clothing allows quick movement, as though he expects danger to spring from behind each tree or structure. His decorative loose black shirt is laced at the neck, and his buckskin breeches are dyed similarly. Seemingly impervious to the cold, he wears no cape. No weapons are visible on his person, but only a fool would believe he's unarmed. His sharp gaze treats every flicker around us as a potential attack.

My voluminous skirt rustles more than once, and he pauses to listen for danger.

Black silk organza and gray lace surround my legs like a decadent storm. A tight bodice accentuates my waist. The V-neckline is exactly how Legion requested—plunging and wide. When I checked my reflection in the mirror, it didn't look too bad. I think the worst of my curse is in my face, yet even that seemed less hideous tonight. Maybe I'm getting used to it.

Over the past few days, I've stewed over his behavior at the dress fitting and have concluded he's setting me up for humiliation. How else can I explain that he had ample opportunity to hide my ugliness, but instead decided to display it?

*She's perfectly suited for the light.*

Except in this city, anything less than pretty is a nightmare.

With every step, the pillows of my breasts wobble and threaten to spill from the bodice. The ridges of my scars rub and irritate along my collarbone. I feel exposed with my silver hair pinned into an intricate knot at my nape. With nowhere to hide Tinger, I should have left him at the castle, which I suspect was Legion's plan. But if he thought he could steal the precious manabee, he would be sorely disappointed. I pat the bulk beneath the skirt at my hip. Tinger is with me now.

Wreaths of holly and berries decorate doors. Garlands entwined with otherworldly lights swing beneath the webs. I force myself to relax and appreciate the scenery. Children giggle and play in the twilight shadows, occasionally daring to dart from their homes to glimpse the valiant House of Shadow Radiants.

Once or twice, I catch Bodin teasing them with a spurt of shadow curling from his hand. They squeal and retreat to the safety of their home.

It is busy on the towering, tree-lined street. Buildings rise to multiple levels, with railings and walkways running between the establishments. Both faerie and mortals brave the low temperature to celebrate the rise of the Holly King with joyful flute music and whimsical dances.

I don't think he's a real king, but a representation of winter. People are dressed in their finest—glitter sparkles around their eyes like snow in the sun. I'm so enthralled with the magical sights that I almost step into a dreamscape.

Bodin yanks me back in time to avoid a dreamer's wild swing

as she takes an ax to a blob shaped like a man. She screams in bloody triumph, and then the tingling of ants recedes as the dream fades.

"Sorry," I mumble.

Bodin leaves his warm grip on my nape, guiding me gently forward until we arrive at a Dandelion Drift beside a building. The restaurant entrance is on the upper level. As we politely wait our turn on the muddy street, the occasional stare is cast our way. A satyr child with cute horns clip-clops up to Legion and offers him a handmade crown of twisted laurel and holly. He bows reverently for the crown to be placed, then straightens without a word. The little satyr fumbles a curtsey and skips off to her mother, cloven feet splashing on the muddy path with glee.

Legion purposefully walked us through the lower-class district even though it was colder, muddier, and messier than the walkways above. I wonder if these people see the Radiants as often as the upper levels do. When the Drift becomes free, only two seeds remain. Legion plucks them free and mutters something about a lack of supply.

"You take her." He hands a seed to Bodin.

"Naturally." Bodin slides his arm inside my cape, around my waist, and tugs me close. My hitched intake of air fills with his warm, woody scent. It is much deeper and headier than Fox's, yet still reminiscent.

My pulse quickens as he drops his gaze to my lips and asks, "Are you ready?"

"Yes," I breathe.

We become airborne together. It's hard not to feel protected inside the steel barricade of his arms, not to feel moved by his beating heart against my cheek. He holds me like something precious, not with the distance I'm accustomed to. Even Alfie's touch seems cold compared to this. The ride is only seconds, but

I'm still breathless when he deposits me on the tree-bough walkway.

I stumble. He grips my elbow, steadying me, and holds my gaze until I mumble, "I'm okay."

He hesitates to let me go but steps back for me to follow Legion toward the restaurant's holly-adorned doors. Inside the tree house, jovial accordion music is the backdrop against conversations. The architecture inside is more tree than manmade. Glass windows are manufactured between gaps in low-hanging branches pulled aside like curtains.

With a start, I realize we're inside an overgrown Weeping Willow—my namesake. It was unrecognizable from the ground level. Disturbingly, this seems to be a pattern in this city. Much of the architecture is artfully constructed so the upper levels have the prettiest views. I can't see the ground level through the windows. It's almost like the city street we walked through doesn't exist.

After closing the door against the cold, sycophantic attendants remove Legion's gifted wreath and our outer layers. They usher us up a staircase of artfully entwined roots. Our table is the only one on a mezzanine platform overlooking a beautiful half-frozen lake on one side and the main restaurant floor on the other. It is packed with reveling citizens dressed in their finest luxury, each with a smile beaming on their face.

Every so often, eyes turn our way. Some are interested in the striking males I accompany. Others are curious about the Nothing they brought.

My ears twitch when the waiter can't meet my eyes. He cringes as he deposits a napkin on my lap. A powerful, elegant hand whips out, latching onto the waiter's wrist.

"Do be careful with our Shadow." Legion raises an indignant eyebrow.

The waiter blusters, cheeks reddening.

"Groveling will redeem your foolishness." Legion eases back in his seat.

The waiter bows and apologizes profusely.

"Not me, fool. Her."

The waiter turns his attention to me, fawning and complimenting me to the point of embarrassment. The effect is the opposite of what I suspect Legion intended, or perhaps exactly what he intended. The waiter hurries around the table, lighting the centerpiece candle, then pouring a glass of mulled wine for us, including the fourth vacant setting.

"Leave us." Legion's short temper startles the waiter, who then scurries away.

"Somebody's hungry," I tease.

"You have no idea." His tone lowers to gravel as his hungry gaze lands on me.

Bodin exhales through his nose and asks, "Fox?"

"Your guess is as good as mine," Legion replies quietly.

"Did you read the report about the bodies?"

My ears prick up. Bodies?

Legion nods. "All male, pale, tattooed and with short black hair."

Why does that description sound familiar?

"Willow?" Bodin asks.

"Me? Why would I know anything about that?" I blurt.

Legion's lips flatten at my lack of an appropriate title, but before he can complain, Bodin sighs, "Spare the formalities tonight. It is just us."

We settle into an uncomfortable silence until Legion notes, "Our colors become you, Willow."

The compliment throws me. I tug at the neckline, irritating my scar. Fuck it. I'm just going to say it.

"Are you mocking me?"

"On the contrary. We are most fortunate you are our protégé." He sips his wine, eyes roaming the crowd below.

Bodin's eyes crinkle as he takes me in. "Tales of your calamity reached me in Heliodor." He seems almost proud, not pissed off like Emrys was.

"Calamity. You mean a few days ago with the Marquess?"

"I refer to the Shadow you sparred with." Bodin's brow furrows. He turns to Legion. "What happened with the Marquess?"

"More tedious posturing from the derelict," Legion grumbles. "Too busy minding others' business when he should concern himself with patrolling his region."

"Willow," Bodin says to me, his expression hardening. "You were victorious in the sparring match; however, wounding yourself was an unnecessary sacrifice. Private tutoring to hone your physique and combat efficiency will begin tomorrow."

"Agreed," Legion returns. "Endurance and strength. I want her as nimble as a fee-lion."

"Technique first," Bodin insists.

"Mental resilience is also imperative. This is a marathon, not a sprint."

"Um, hello." I wave. "I'm sitting right here."

Two sets of piercing dark eyes look my way. I should have kept my mouth shut because their combined attention consumes every ounce of air in my lungs.

Stomping up the private staircase announces Fox's arrival. I never thought I'd be relieved or grateful to see him, but at least it's not me being stared at now.

But then I take in his ruffled appearance. His eyes are puffy and glazed. His shirt is untucked, his buttons haphazardly joined. He reeks of spirits and looks like he's rolled out of a courtesan's bed. He laughs boisterously as he flops onto his chair and almost spills the wine.

Legion's glare could cut diamonds. "Where have you been?"

"Expending pent up—"

Bodin clears his throat and gives me a pointed look. Fox faces me and blinks, as if trying to pull me into focus.

"Well, well, if it isn't the bewitching little backstabber herself. Or should I say, front stabber?" He raises his glass in a toast toward me, spilling wine. "Finally wriggled free from the nest, I see."

"That was days ago," I shoot back. "And no thanks to you."

"Gratitude. Let's toast to that next." He leans in with a whispered snarl, "Or lack thereof when we literally bleed for you."

How dare he play the victim. "Aw, did I hurt the big bad boogeyman's feelings?"

Anger flashes in his eyes, but Legion speaks before he can retaliate. "Enough. We must display a united House. It's a miracle we've managed to keep the wildling hidden. We don't need more scrutiny."

"Who looks after him now?" I wonder aloud.

"Emrys," they all say.

My brows raise. Bodin explains, "He is averse to fanfare."

Fox slides down in his seat, sprawls his legs, and watches my reaction as his foot hits mine. My fingers curl around the dinner knife.

*"Quite happy to continue what I started,"* I think loudly, hoping he'll hear it in his mind.

His boot jabs my shin. I jolt, and my knee hits the table, spilling his wine onto his fingers.

"For *Nicnevin's* sake, Fox, clean it up," Legion says with a sigh, rubbing his temples.

Fox deliberately licks his fingers, rebellious eyes on his leader. Tension thickens the air. If Legion had full access to his power, I imagine he'd choke his Fifth with invisible ghost hands.

*"You'd love to watch that, wouldn't you, little wolf?"* Fox taunts

in my mind, still daring Legion with his licking. *"You'd have front-row seats, maybe even—"*

"Ow." He scowls as I kick him hard beneath the table.

"People are watching, *Fox*," I reprimand, fighting a smile.

"Mm, but that makes it even more arousing, *Willow*."

A blush creeps up my neck, tingling my ears to the point of twitching.

He notices. "Don't get shy on me now, love."

"Have some respect for your House," I shoot back. "This is an important appearance."

His gaze narrows. Silence at the table makes me realize I've just tried to protect their reputation.

"What happened that morning?" Legion asks, eyes darting between us. "Besides the exchange of tempers and . . . attires."

"Tell them," Fox dares me. "Tell them how you plunged your knife into my heart."

# CHAPTER
# TWENTY-NINE
## WILLOW

Hurt flashes in Fox's eyes, but then the rogue is back.

"Really?" My brow arches. *"I'm expected to explain why I stabbed you when they remember nothing of who you really are?"*

*"Try it."* He leans forward expectantly. *"Taste my suffering for the past five years."*

Gritting my teeth, I face Bodin and Legion and declare, "I'm going to kill you all for ruining my life."

They blink, astounded. For a moment, my hope soars, which is stupid. Even if they recall what they did, I still can't kill them. I don't know how.

Legion calmly answers, "Assassinating us for taking you in is a tad overdramatic."

Bodin folds his arms, grumbling, "And unladylike."

I flip up my middle finger at them. Bodin throws his head back and laughs, drawing the attention of everyone downstairs. And me.

I can't take my eyes off the thick column of his throat. What is it about a male when he puts his neck on display like that?

What exactly about it causes heat to bloom in my lower abdomen? The strength? The distended veins? The Adam's apple? I have to look away. But staring at Legion is no better. He hides his smirk behind another sip of wine.

They took my promise of death and fit it into Titania's narrative.

Fox sits back in his chair, cruel satisfaction twisting his pretty lips, then stares at Legion. Their prolonged silence makes me think they're conversing mind-to-mind.

"I'm hungry," I protest. And considerably outgunned.

Legion's gaze swings to me. He gestures for the waiter, who arrives promptly with steaming food I don't remember ordering. The plate is full of meat and delicious smells my wolfish side craves. The instant I dig into the food, Fox's antagonistic mood dampens.

The three talk quietly amongst themselves in a short, direct exchange. Legion mentions my drama with the House of Embers leader. Bodin mentions my near-death experience—or rather, Dahlia's experience—and Fox stares at me when they mention I've worn his clothing daily instead of the Nexus uniform.

Their conversation turns to the trouble brewing in the regions, and my ears prick up.

With all the dragon-bonded Radiants here for the Gentle Interlude, hidden Nightmares are coming out of the woodwork to wreak havoc around the Commonwealth. Apparently, it's standard behavior for this period and likely another reason why the House of Shadow has never participated in the Solstice exhibition. They're far too busy protecting the realm to play war games.

Legion again asks Fox to explain the trail of bodies with dark hair.

He replies offhandedly, "I didn't appreciate how the mortals looked at me."

Instead of another reprimand, Legion intones, "Keepers watch us from downstairs."

Where Legion and Bodin seem unruffled, Fox stills. He stares at a space above his glass for a beat, then turns around to look. Downstairs, two robed druids sit by the city-side window. Their hoods are up, concealing their faces, but I catch a hint of wooden mask. No plates or glasses are set before them. It's obvious they're not here for the revelry.

Fox explains to Legion, "I was . . . fractious. My hunt was purely for sport, no harvesting. They can't tie it to us."

"Regardless," Legion replies. "Such recklessness is courting the Cabinet. One of us there is enough."

"What's the Cabinet?" I ask, my voice raising unavoidably. "And what do you mean, hunting for sport?"

Fox claims they've changed since receiving those Guardian blessings, but if he was killing for sport, it's an obvious lie.

"This exhibition is a waste of time," Bodin quickly says, redirecting the conversation. "It teaches them nothing."

"Agreed," Legion returns.

Fox scoffs, "Half these primped and coddled mortals have no idea how to fight."

"Nothing but vapid sensibilities." Legion pushes his untouched plate away.

He seems a little disappointed. So does Bodin. They're trying to distract me, but I'm a hound once I scent blood written between the lines. The topic they're avoiding concerns the Keepers, who are still and attentive.

A party horn blares, startling me. People cheer. Accordion music picks up, and applause gathers as some take to dancing downstairs. Someone has taken a holly wreath and parades around pretending to be the Holly King.

Bodin pushes his untouched plate away, tension creeping into his posture.

"You're not eating, either?" I ask.

"The food here is not to our taste," he replies.

*This is not bee bread.*

I felt like Varen was trying to tell me something that morning. Maybe this is it. The Sluagh are not feeding on souls as they should, and someone—a worker bee—is supposed to collect the honey and nectar to make the bee bread. From the guilty look on Fox's face, he was meant to be doing just that these past days, but instead became distracted with hunting dark-haired, pale men. He left the day after I arrived at the castle, after he carried me across the bridge because I was too terrified to move.

Cloud is pale and dark-haired. He is the reason Rory drowned —the reason for my phobia. I accused Fox of leaving me, of causing my suffering . . . Surely, he didn't go on a rampage to express his frustration over not being there when I needed protection.

His quiet gaze clashes with mine.

"Fox . . ." The hint of a plea in Legion's voice steals his attention.

"Fine," he grinds out, flicking his napkin. "I suppose it's a beautiful night for such macabre delights."

"Don't make a show of it," Legion reminds him.

"Why not?" A note of bitterness turns Fox's tone to ice. He stands and fixes his shirt. "That's what I'm made for. Besides, no one will remember."

"But you will," Bodin warns.

A buzzing tingle erupts in the air, itching my inner ears.

"Something's wrong," I mutter.

"What are you talking about?" Fox flops back down, exhaling.

A stampede of invisible ants vibrate over my skin. This feels different than the usual sensation. It's grimy and gritty. It's like the ants crawl over sand, scraping my skin with tiny cuts.

Slowly, I push back my chair and walk to the window overlooking the half-frozen lake two levels below. Placing my hand on the cold pane, I scour the shadows around the mist.

"Willow?" Bodin asks.

I face the table, unsure how to explain what I'm sensing. Fox appears to be falling asleep, half drunk. Maybe I'm imagining this. But the itching of fire ants makes me scratch. It's getting worse. Bodin lifts half out of his seat. Legion's head tilts, listening to something far away.

"The Cauldron stirs," he warns.

Ants scuttle up my spine, lifting every tiny hair on my body.

"Something is coming," I whisper.

Something wicked. I blink, glance back at the mist, and the feeling goes.

"Must be imagining it," I mumble, my hand sliding down the pane. But as I turn, something moves at the edge of my sight. I startle and turn back. The lake is the same, still and misty. "I could have sworn I saw—"

"Move away from the window," Legion bellows.

An ear-piercing shriek shatters the window, pelting tiny glass fragments like a hailstorm. A rancid, moldy scent. A figure leaps toward me from outside. I glimpse spindly, disjointed limbs and a terrifying face with two holes for eyes, then shadows explode. Darkness consumes the restaurant. Screams unleash chaos and the sounds of destruction. Tables topple. Bodies clash. Electrical sparks flicker in the darkness like twinkling stars, and then I am pulled into a warm, safe embrace that smells faintly of wine and sweet mossy woods.

I am in Fox's arms.

When the shadows dissipate, his eyes are wholly black and directed at something behind me. Legion and Bodin are on the floor by the broken window, hands pinning a nightmare creature down. It thrashes and bucks, spits in their faces.

"Finish it," Legion orders.

"I see you, my prince," the creature cackles.

"I said *finish* it," Legion barks. I'm not sure who he directs, but then a whoosh of air rushes around me. Flesh-and-blood monsters, I can handle. Invisible nightmares?

I shield my face against Fox's body. He cups the back of my head, holding me to his chest. I'm not easily frightened. I've looked rotten corpses in the face and knew I was connected to them, made of the same stuff. But this . . . this is something else. When it's over, I pull away in time to witness Fox's skull illuminating beneath his skin, and then the black bleeds from his eyes.

All signs of his dark self are gone.

"Are you hurt?" he asks me through clenched teeth.

"I'm fine."

The creature's spindly body is a dried husk. Small, liquid blobs of an oily substance ooze from its corpse and drip up. Gravity is in reverse. They fall upward and splash on the ceiling, causing rot to form in the wood. But their path upward is slow. Lazy. Sort of like . . . I gasp. These aren't manabeeze. Not wisps.

"What are they?" I step closer for a better look.

Legion glares at Fox, who tugs me back to him.

"Don't let one touch you," he says quietly in my ear. "Blots are far worse than wisps if they hit your body."

Shade, a vampire Guardian in the Twelve has an old-world mate blessed with the power to rot anything she touches. She said it's a curse, her darkness. Her punishment for helping build the bombs that destroyed the old world. The way this wood rots reminds me of her power. But Shade taught her to see each power can be used in reverse. She eventually learned to help remove the taint on the Well.

While Bodin holds down the corpse, clearly concerned it might not truly be dead, Legion collects the candle from our table and drops it on the nightmare. Fire consumes the shape.

"I never knew shadow was so powerful." I am in awe of how they dispatched it within seconds.

"It's not the shadow," Fox murmurs against my ear. "But what we do inside them that counts."

Pieces of the puzzle fall into place. That whooshing air on my face—the sparks in the darkness. Fox's skull illuminating. His wraith form had caused the damage. They use shadows to hide the truth.

"You fed on it," I note.

"On that?" Fox balks. "It tastes horrid."

Okay, so maybe it was something else.

"We much prefer the juicy virginal types," he teases quietly, tightening his grip around my middle.

"You do not," I scoff, rolling my eyes. Or . . . wait. "Do you?"

"Hush now," Legion clips.

Fox's silent chuckle sends shivers down my spine. I should be afraid, should shove him away, but somehow, I still feel safe within his arms.

Thudding up the staircase announces the druids. Their eyes are visible through the ornate wooden masks. And they are *pissed*.

One whips out a hand. Water springs forth from their palm like a geyser to douse the flames. The other takes in the scene, studying everything from Fox's arm banded around my front to Bodin and Legion now casually standing by the balcony railing.

"Late as usual," Legion notes dryly.

While he debriefs the Keepers, Bodin comes over and quietly instructs Fox, "See our Shadow home safely. Ensure you remain with her until we return." He lowers his volume. "Legion was right. The Cauldron stirs."

Fox's arm tenses around me. "But there are . . . midnight adventures to be had."

"This takes priority." Bodin sighs, then pinches the bridge between his eyes.

"Hardly." Guilt flashes beneath Fox's scoff. "You can barely stand on your feet. I've delayed enough."

Bodin's warning growl reminds me he's the hive's Second. Where Legion commands with calm, dominating allure, Bodin is a strong and steady power. He is the stone relentlessly honing the blade.

"Fine," Fox grinds out. "I'll babysit."

I bristle at the insinuation and twist out of his arms. "I can take care of myself."

He is the picture of decorum as he offers me his hand. "Shall we?"

*"If you have any sense"*—his whisper caresses my mind—*"you'll do as you're told. We are watched."*

*"Why would I care if your secret gets out?"*

*"Because they work for the queen, someone who will want to kill you the moment she meets you."*

Or curse me, I want to say. But he might have a point.

While talking with Legion, the Keepers have their eyes on us. Something about their stare is more creepy than the Sluagh who just saved my life.

I take Fox's hand and head toward the staircase.

Downstairs, the revelers are almost all gone. Only a few drunkards are left. Tables are upturned. Decorations and food are spilled. Our waiter hands me my cape, and we leave the restaurant. It's not until we're a few steps along the bough's walkway that my mind clears, and I remember what the nightmare said to Legion.

*I see you, my prince.*

Two minutes down the muddy city street, I whirl on Fox. "What the fuck happened back there?" I ask and check to see if we're followed. The trees and buildings aren't as lit up as before. People must have heard about the attack. The denizens on this level are veterans of war. They know when to hide.

He ignores me and continues walking, his long legs eating up the distance faster than I can keep up. I break into a jog, hating my hindering stupid skirt.

"Fox."

"The sooner we get you home, the better." He glances at me over his shoulder. "It's a long walk, and I'm not supposed to *flicker* until we're out of sight."

I chase after him until the buildings lessen and the trees grow thicker. My feet are cold, and my ears are starting to ache, but I don't want to wait until we get to the keep.

"Stop." I pull his arm.

Exhaling, he faces me and raises his brows. What changed

with him? In the restaurant, he was joking one minute and irritable the next.

"What was that thing?" I whisper harshly. "And why did it call Legion prince? Was it there to hurt him?"

"So now you care about our welfare?" He steps toward me.

I step back, annoyed he might be right. "I care for the truth."

Nothing here is as it seems. My world is spinning, and I am at a loss for what to do. I think it's safe to say I'm no longer in the kill-zone part of my revenge plan. I'm not sure I want revenge at all. But I don't know what I feel except that I need answers. Any more secrets and I'll lose my mind.

"I've only given you the truth." He throws his hands in the air. "You don't want to believe it."

"What was that thing?"

He stares. "It was a Nightmare. A Terror called a Corner-twister, also known as The Thing in the Corner. It lurks at the edge of your vision, induces paranoia, and can turn a person insane."

I blink. Well, that certainly sounded like the truth. Who would make that up on the spot? My mind scrambles over the codex we've been given at the Nexus. "I've not learned about that one yet."

"You wouldn't. The Nexus only teaches what Titania and the Keepers want you to know."

"Why did you burn it then?" I accuse. "Because it called Legion—"

His hand covers my mouth. "Keep your voice down."

*"No one is here,"* I shout with my mind.

He pushes me back, keeping his hand over my mouth. My spine hits a smooth surface—the column of a tree trunk supporting a flow line track.

*"The streets are empty,"* he returns. *"But don't be fooled into thinking no one will hear or see us."*

*"What happened back there?"* I widen my eyes, but don't push him away. *"Why are you afraid of the Keepers?"*

*"Wait until we're at the keep."*

*"Tell me now, or I'll walk the other way."*

*"None but my hive and you know I can speak mind-to-mind. It will look suspicious if we stand here staring at each other for too long."*

I lick his hand, hoping he'll be grossed out and let go. He tightens his grip, so I shove him. He stumbles back, amused, as if this is a game. He even laughs and sways, as if he's drunk.

Darting my gaze, I see a few stragglers approaching us from the restaurant's direction. By the way they sing, and use each other to stay upright, they're intoxicated.

"I don't like being lied to," I say quietly, folding my arms to distance us. "I don't like being manipulated."

He stills, knowing exactly why. "I'll tell you at the keep."

"Don't you get it?" I hiss. "I don't trust you. Why would I return to the keep?"

I have Tinger. Rory's blade is with Geraldine. That's all I need.

"Fine." He shoves his hands in his pockets. "But we'll have to occupy our mouths to explain why they don't move as we stare longingly into each other's eyes for long minutes."

"Oh."

I start walking, hear his laughter, and stop as fumes shoot from my pores. I can't work out if this is another way to make fun of me or if he's serious.

They took me to a restaurant inside a Willow tree for a meal I adore. None of them ate. Fox was supposed to gather souls to sustain the others, but instead, he was on a murderous rampage . . . maybe because of something I said.

They all saved my life.

Half the time, they're looking out for me, the other half lying. I'm not sure I'll ever trust anyone again, but I expect direct answers if I ask a question. That's the only way forward. I blink into the darkness, realizing where my train of thought just took me.

I *want* to trust them. I don't want to murder them. What's wrong with me?

Alfie's face flashes in my mind. I grip the bulk of Tinger's pendant beneath my skirt and shake my head. I should forget about them and find Alfie. He has a plan. And I promised Geraldine and the others that I would spend the weekend with them. Taking an early night is the logical thing to do.

"I have plans, anyway."

Fox is suddenly inches away, breathtaking eyes narrowing. "What plans?"

"Plans," I return.

"You were just attacked," he reminds me. "It's not safe out here."

"A moment ago, you were willing to play Tickle My Tonsils, and now you want me off the street." So trustworthy.

I need to go. Need to see a friendly face.

"Willow," he warns, eyes a little too wild. "*What* plans, and with whom?"

"Jealous?"

"Do you want me to be?"

My back hits a wall, and I gasp.

"Answer me," he demands.

"It's none of your business."

"You are our queen," he declares. "You are my only business."

He braces an arm against the thick trunk behind me, leaning in. He is such a pretty thing. How can anyone say no to him?

"Why not just pillage it from my mind?" *Show me who you really are.* Let's be done with this game.

"I'll never do that."

"So then tell me the truth. What's going on? Why did that thing attack? Why were you gone for days, on a murd—"

His lips press against mine, halting my incriminating words as the drunken couple passes. I should be outraged. I should be choking him or kneeing him in the balls, but instead, I think, if he were the monster—wouldn't he have hurt me? Wouldn't he have taken me somewhere? Hit me? Imprisoned me or bent my mind to his will?

Desire scorches through my veins, yet I am frozen, caught in a paradox wrought by his cheeky, reverent mouth. The tug in my chest opens my lips, inviting him deeper into the kiss. Our tongues touch. His low, agonized groan skates shivers through me, shaking loose that feeling in my chest, awakening it, making it sing.

How can something wrong feel so right? Fox cups the back of my head, holds me firm, and sweeps his tongue against mine. He takes my mouth with hungry, demanding strokes. This time, it's me groaning, growing breathless, swooning, falling.

My hands are on his stomach, hunting through fabric for skin. His hip digs into mine, squashing Tinger's pendant. It's like a splash of cold water. No one sane would kiss someone who looks like me. He still hasn't told me the truth. I bite his plush lower lip and shove him away. He stumbles back, swipes his lower lip, and sees blood on his fingers.

Lifting smokey eyes to me, he purrs, "Pain is more Emrys's kink, but I'm willing to experiment if you are."

"What?" I blurt, taken aback. "I'm not . . . I . . . I . . . You had no right to do that. That's why I bit you."

His brows lift in the middle, looking far too innocent in his confusion.

"Stop it," I hiss and wave around his face. "Stop with the adorable cuteness. Stop pretending to want me. We're not fated anymore. You called me nothing and left me." I shake my head. Why did I say that? "I mean, you know what you all did."

*"Yes,"* he replies in my mind, lashes lowering. *"I'm well aware of what we did. I'm the only one who remembers the suffering we've caused."*

"So you're admitting it." I gape. "You're admitting to being a —" A monster.

His demeanor changes. Turns cold. I must have thought the word loud enough for him to hear.

"Careful, pet, or you'll end up without an escort home." A gust of wind ruffles his hair. It tinkles charms on a web above us. "The Court of Dreams is a dangerous place at night."

"Are you threatening me?"

"I'm telling you the truth. Isn't that what you so desperately want?"

I shake my head in disbelief. It didn't take long, but here he is, threatening and playing with my emotions. Yeah, it's dangerous on the streets. I could walk into someone's dream. A nightmare can attack. Who knows what else is out there? But to use that sense of danger to keep me in line is a low blow.

"I don't just want the truth," I murmur. "I want no more secrets."

"Fine. I'll tell you what you want to know." He grinds his teeth and glances around, checking to see if we're watched. Then his skull flashes beneath his skin. I don't know where his wraith form went, but it's not here. Probably keeping watch. "The truth is," he says, "the others chose you as our Shadow because it takes a mortal to break into Titania's Cabinet of Curiosities."

"Okay . . ."

That doesn't seem so bad. But his demeanor is still tense, still looking at me as though I'm going to bite his head off.

"What is it?" I hug myself. "What aren't you telling me?"

"Styx has been turned to stone. If we can't release him by the end of the Interlude, he could be that way permanently."

"Dead?"

"Trapped."

"I'm sorry. That must be hard on you all."

"Don't feel sorry for us." A pained look enters his eyes. "Not when they planned for you to take Styx's place."

I blink rapidly, trying to process his words because it sounded like he wants me to be a statue instead of Styx.

"They've forgotten you," he says, reaching for me, but I side-step, and his hand drops. "I'm trying everything I can to find another way. But Titania's damn binding seal keeps fucking with their minds."

The ground seems to shift beneath my feet. "I can't believe I almost . . . almost changed my mind about you."

"I'll never let it get that far. The tournament is months away."

Shaking my head, I stumble away from him. My world is spinning again. "I have to go."

"I'll take you home," he offers, his skull flickering as his wraith returns to his body.

I look at him directly and say, "I'd rather be stuck in someone else's dreamscape than with you."

He jolts as though hit by an arrow, then turns away. It shouldn't hurt this much to see his pain over my rejection. His back heaves with breath. Once. Twice. Three lungfuls of air. Then he turns his head, giving me his profile. "At least we can agree on one thing—reality is a disappointment."

His visage flickers, I blink, and he's gone.

A short, sharp, incredulous laugh bursts out of me. I grab Tinger's pendant to reassure myself.

"He just left," I tell my friend. "It's exactly what I expect from him. From all of them."

I kick the muddy dirt and growl. How could I be so stupid?

It takes me a moment to gather my composure. My body wants me to break down and cry, but I've survived too much trauma to let another bump in the road take me down now. I'll figure something out. I always do.

Hugging my cape, I start walking. I'll head to the Nexus and find Alfie. That's what I'll do. Midnight is an hour away. I might arrive before he heads out to wherever this secret meeting place is.

But after a few minutes, I realize this isn't our route to the restaurant. Instead of elegant multi-level architecture blended into the trees, the buildings now have only one story. Branches above bend and groan under the wind, looming like predators. Shadows shift in the dark.

I'm sure there was a flow line up there a moment ago.

A woman's wail drifts in on a breeze, and I quicken my pace. I'll end up at the Nexus if I keep in the same direction. But after half an hour of walking, the taller trees make way for smaller ones. It becomes less of a city and more like a forest, whispering warnings to turn back. I must have taken a wrong turn. No signs of the upper walkways anymore. No carriages or Dandelion Drifts. The streets are trodden paths, and the occasional person I glimpse is less interested in keeping up with pristine appearances. When they see me coming, dressed in finery, they hastily fix their clothes and hair as if expecting a reprimand and then disappear. Afraid.

Eyes follow me wherever I go.

*Fucking Fox.*

I scrub my lips with the back of my hand. Every time I think of his kiss, my stomach clenches. A part of me liked it. A part of me still craves it. I must be insane. He just admitted they're going to sacrifice me to save Styx.

But isn't that what I wanted? The truth?

Would my true enemy have confessed something like that?

The Six were beings of the dark for so long—pure chaos like that nightmare twisted corner thing. I'll bet those blots would have dripped upward from their corpses after death. But then they were blessed by the light and had to learn about life.

Maybe they're still learning.

Maybe I'm still learning.

If what Fox said is true, he's been stuck here alone, trying to find a way out of the frying pan without falling into the fire.

I kick the dirt again and stub my toe. Grumbling, I trudge onward, deeper down a path into the woods. Another five minutes gives me a glimpse of the moon between the leaves. It's high. Almost midnight. Shit. Where the fuck am I?

I turn down a forest path and halt at the sound of the ocean. Or is that the wind through the leaves? I'm so lost. Wherever I am, I doubt it's anywhere near this place Alfie wants to meet.

The sound of rhythmic drums and music filters in on a warm breeze, too warm for this time of year. It's odd. I tilt my head, and the music grows louder. A small white light flickers ahead—too big for a manabee. The fleeting light circles back to me, then glides away again, humming down a small path that wasn't there a moment ago.

"Hey," a deep voice calls.

I spin, cape flaring, hope rising, thinking it's Fox. But it's Alfie. What on earth is he doing in the middle of the woods?

"Didn't mean to sneak up on you," he laughs.

I launch at him, forcing him into a hug. I don't care what weirdness is between us. He's here, wherever this is, looking for me. Fuck Fox for abandoning me.

"You made it." Alfie's voice is soft as he cups my head.

"I'm so glad to see you."

"Me too." His hand slips down to my nape, and he pulls me in tighter, inhaling the scent of my hair. "God, you smell so good."

I hold him at arm's length. A suave, tight shirt accentuates all the new, buff parts of him. His Chaser chain drapes between his front and rear pockets, drawing attention to tightly packed assets. Thick thighs. Curved buttocks. I give a low whistle. "Alfie, you look kinda hot."

He glances away, blushing. "Stop it."

"I mean it." I touch his hard pec. "This could take my eye out."

He snorts, then runs a hand through his hair. "Need to dress to impress at this place."

"This place?" I frown.

He splits my cape to peek inside, then raises his brows. "Don't worry, you'll fit in just fine. And the lights are low there, so . . . um, the rest won't look as bad."

My fingers flutter to my face, feeling the ropy scars and angles. They're extra sharp now, extra pronounced.

"I was at a feast or something," I mutter. "Wait, who are you impressing? And what are you doing in the middle of the woods?"

How could he have known to look for me here?

"It's midnight," he says, as if it's obvious. "Wait, if you aren't here to meet me at Burn After Reading, what are *you* doing in the middle of the woods?"

The blood drains from my face. "Burn After Reading is a place?"

He lifts my chin, angling my face toward the glowing ball of light somehow still floating behind him, almost like it's waiting.

"You were so beautiful before." Disapproval creases his brow, shadowing his eyes, oddly reminding me of the holes the nightmare looked out of. "I can't believe they haven't fixed this for you."

"What do you mean?" I get it, he wants to help me, but saying shit like that does the opposite.

"The House of Shadow is known to shun favors for vain reasons. I rarely see them grant boons at all." His displeasure rolls off him in waves. "All they need to do is hide your flaws, and you're safe from banishment."

"To be fair, I haven't asked them."

He blinks. "Why not?"

Because the curse prevents me, I want to say. Because I don't trust them. But the truth is, I could have found a way. I'm too stubborn and proud to admit weakness around them.

"Don't worry. That's why we're here."

"Where's here exactly?"

He gestures down a dark path behind him. "I thought you figured it out."

My perplexed look spurs him on.

"It's a tavern run by a witch. She spells the entrance to move locations. Once inside, you can only leave after reading an enchantment that burns away memories gained while in there. All we're left with are the clues I gave you and the knowledge this place exists. Want it bad enough, and the location magically comes to you."

I want to say that I had no clue, but wouldn't that mean I never wanted to meet him badly enough? Maybe my stumbling into these woods *was* me wanting it bad enough. I clear my throat.

"So . . . burn after reading . . . so there's no evidence. Clever."

"Yep. Not even Radiants have the power to break the enchantment."

"Radiants come here?"

He snorts. "Even they can't stand the rigid rules of the Old Code. Come on. Seeing is believing."

He takes my hand, and the glowing orb hums along the path, lighting the way for us. Rhythmic music grows louder as we walk.

"If we can find a Radiant willing to exchange favors for a charm that makes you pretty again, we can keep you safe. At least until the tournament."

My free hand toys with my hair, pulling strands free to hide my face.

We stop at a thicket guarded by a horned howl who scrutinizes us from a high branch. It hoots twice, and then the thicket separates. Roots and branches break repetitively, creaking and cracking like breaking bones. A glittering tunnel opens, leading to a bonfire-lit space in the near distance.

The air thrums with primal drumbeats and feels infused with heavy magics. An alluring spice goes straight to my head, racing my heart. Alfie drags me through the tunnel, grinning from ear to ear. As we emerge on the other side, tingling fire ants burn through my body. The onslaught is dizzying. Almost as bad as crossing a portal.

"You'll get used to it," he says, a little distracted.

My breathing slows as I take in the scene. We've emerged into a glade surrounded by thick oak trees hiding secret, shadowy alcoves on every side except for one. Over the gathering crowd of revelers, a setting sun paints a turquoise thatched roof gold. Moments ago, it was midnight.

Brine in the balmy air belongs to a warmer climate by the ocean. I glimpse the furled sail of a ship over the thatched roof. I'm sure I heard waves from the forest. If this music was quieter, I'd probably hear the ocean now. But it's hard to focus when faeries, mortals, and everything in between drunkenly participate in a debauched free-for-all.

Alfie tosses an arm around my shoulder and guides me onto a lush, rose-scented lawn.

"They're wild tonight," he jokes.

"Um . . . you can say that again."

Scattered through the writhing masses are decadent settees and low tables bearing exotic fruits, elixirs, and flowers with burning petals. Smoke unfurls from the blooms, wafting the heady spice into the air. Could be dangerous if I breathe too much.

"You're not shocked?" he asks. "Not scandalized?"

I laugh. "I'm not seventeen anymore, Alfie."

I'm still a virgin, but that's by choice. I've fooled around, but my partners all looked at me and saw rumors, my traumatic history, or my heroic family. It was never just me.

"I know." Alfie pauses. "A lot can change in five years."

"This is true."

"You know, we're still technically engaged."

"What?"

Something hot and intense burns in his eyes. "There's been

no one else like you. There never will be. I want you to know that."

Does he still have feelings for me? I don't know what to say, but he doesn't wait for my reply. He returns to scanning the crowd.

"Everyone knows that what happens here stays in here, Willow. So, fair warning, it can get *very* wild."

"Okay."

Closer to the outskirts, natural grottos hang with gauzy drapes between the trees. Plush pillows, lounges, and lazy bodies are reclined in bliss as others tend them . . . some servants are mortals in collars and demeaning costumes. Other alcoves have the roles reversed. It's the fae tending to the whims of mortals.

A muscular man is strung between branches, squirming against his bonds but begging for more as delicate females flay strips from his flesh. It's almost like I've stepped into a dream where every carnal, violent delight is realized.

More beastly shapes prowl the shadows at the fringes. A horned one with swirling eyes crawls toward a couple fucking in the open. It's being beckoned, invited to join.

It strikes me that the beastly creatures might not be from Avorlorna. Burn After Reading could be neutral territory like Cornucopia—a place where both sides of the faerie coin put aside their differences in the name of revelry.

Weirdly, for the first time since arriving in this strange new land, I feel closer to home. Those with unique appearances and desires aren't met with scorn here. Instead, they're welcomed with open arms.

This is the resistance I've been hoping for. A sign that not everyone is happy with this regime. It's also proof that not all nightmares are banished to the subterranean. Legion said something to Ignarius earlier about the nightmares never leaving . . . I glance at the darker outskirts again, where the shadows play.

"This is wrong," I mumble. "Isn't it?"

"What?" Alfie glances down at me, still distracted as he searches the crowd.

"I mean—" I nod to the shadows where a hunched beast prowls on cloven feet. "Tell me that's not a subterranean."

"It probably is." He shrugs, but a muscle feathers in his jaw. "We can't do anything about it here. Just stay away from them, and you'll be fine."

"But isn't it wrong that no one remembers some subterraneans are just people like us?" They're certainly a far cry from the Cornertwister.

"I wouldn't call that a person, Willow."

"You're missing the point. Why are the weak, different, or flawed"—I swallow—"like me, banished? It makes no sense."

"It makes perfect sense when we're at war." He shakes his head. "We can't trust anything we see. You've only been here for days, but I've seen Terrors that make you believe you're going insane. Trust me. It's better this way."

*The Nexus only teaches what Titania wants you to know.*

"Anyway," he continues. "I told you I have a plan. Come on. I'll give you a quick tour, tell you who is who, and then you can ally with the *right* Radiants."

His derision is clearly aimed at the Six.

"How do you know who is right if you can't remember afterward?" I sidestep a naked leg kicking out from an alcove's diaphanous drapes.

"I forgot how many questions you ask." He grins. "When you leave here, you'll remember Cait's rules, fragments of feelings, and flashes of memory. It's not much, but we infer a lot after talking. It all adds up."

"So it's not as guilt-free as it seems." I raise my brows. "Not as anonymous."

"Cait says she lets the rules slip a little through the enchantment because they keep the Radiants accountable."

"Cait?"

His eyes flash with warning. "She's the witch who runs this place. If you see her, walk the other way. And whatever you do, don't—"

"Alfie, Alfie, Alfie." A feminine purr behind us. "I thought I told you to stop bringing in strays?"

He tenses. We turn and find a curvy woman with emerald feline eyes, smirking. Black pointy cat's ears twitch through her chin-length auburn hair. Her flowing cream top is cut low to reveal bountiful cleavage. Her bronze skin is marked with pale splotches of discoloration—a star at her breastbone and more on her hands that almost look like fingerless gloves. A delicate chain dangling from her left earlobe to nostril carries sparkling gemstones, and there are more gems on her choker. Something about them feels different from the usual Chaser charms. They glow with unearthly light.

"Last one, I promise," Alfie begs.

"Careful now, mortal." Her eyes twinkle. "Making promises like that is far too tempting to resist."

He shows his palms, eyes crinkling flirtatiously. "Okay, okay."

"Now, introduce me to your friend."

"Cait, this is Willow. She's from . . . the same place I am. Mortal, but . . . yeah. Wasn't always."

"Truly?" Cait's dark brows rise sky high. She touches my pointed ears. "You still reek of wolf . . . and, oh . . . *ooh*. I see." After scrutinizing my face, she winks. "I can reverse what she did if you like."

My heart stops. Does she mean Titania's curse? "You can?"

"Well, not all of it." Her manicured hand waves around my

face. "Just that part. Give me your cape, and I'll check it at the bar. You can collect it when you leave."

She's nice. I don't know why Alfie warned me away. I smile gratefully and undo the laces. It's so warm here that I'm sweating. As I pull it off, a loud burst of raucous laughter draws her attention, followed by the distinct sound of a fist meeting flesh.

"*Nicnevin,* save us," she mumbles, rolling her eyes.

"Who is Nicnevin?" I ask. "Legion said something like that too."

Her gaze snaps to me. She stares for so long that I start squirming. Alfie fidgets, and I fear my offense will have me turned into a toad. But then she relaxes and gives a shrug, answering, "Us oldies are a sentimental lot, praying to deities no one cares about anymore. Old habits die hard, I guess. The damned gentry are feral tonight. What's up with that?"

"Holly King's Feast?" I suggest.

"Hmm. Good point. Stifling traditions always lead to—hey! Fisticuffs in the ring only!" Her profile reveals a black, furry tail lashing with agitation. "Kai! Get your butt in there."

"Don't let us keep you," Alfie says to her.

"Fine. She can stay." She gives him the side-eye. "But no antics like last time, got it?"

"I don't know what you mean."

"Of course, you don't." Her grin reveals sharp teeth. "Just checking. And you—" She takes my cape and sniffs it. "Dogs and cats aren't meant to get along, but I like you. Find me later, and we'll talk. And if you don't, be sure to remind your tall drink of dark water I said my offer still stands. Welcome to Burn After Reading."

"Sure." However, I have no idea who she's referencing.

"Hey!" she barks at the brawling group, pushing up her sleeves. "What did I just say?"

She charges toward the tumultuous group, completely

unafraid of the brawny, muscular man exacting bloody retribution on someone unseen. Oh. Maybe that's Kai, the one she called for.

Alfie exhales. "That was close. She must like you."

"You weren't sure I'd be allowed in here?"

"Let's not dwell on that part."

"Who did she mean by *tall drink of dark water*?"

"Probably the Knight Commander." He glances down to where my breasts almost spill from the low-cut bodice, then takes my hand and guides me toward the thatched roof building. "Speaking of drinks, let's get one."

"You were telling me who to watch out for," I remind him.

"Oh, right. I'll point out a few Radiants who're benevolent enough to give you a charm."

"For what?"

He gawks at me. "For your survival. For your appearance."

"Alfie," I stop him. "No Radiant here will look at me twice. I have nothing to offer. Why would anyone think I have something to trade for a charm? I'm better off using this time to learn where I can buy or hunt down manabeeze."

"Wisps," he chides. "Stop using Elphyne words if you want to stay out of the dungeons. Or worse, they won't wait for the end of the exhibition—they'll banish you out of fear."

Embarrassment shoots heat up my neck.

"I might have bitten off more than I can chew coming here." I desperately wanted to go it alone, to be useful on my own, but remaining confident is harder by the day. "I should focus on finding *wisps*. Then I can activate the portal stone, and we can go home."

"That might be a while. I've never seen wisps here like the ones Nero harvested from the fae. The charms are always already enchanted. You should focus on them." He points at the ones on his hip chain. "This one keeps nightmares from infecting my mind. This one makes me silent on my feet. This helps me speak mind-to-mind with my Radiant. Look around, Willow—the rules help the privileged stay on top. If you hide your flaws and play the game, there are ways of getting ahead."

"Maybe I can steal a few." I frown, eying a few charms dangling from drunken patrons. "The other Nothings need charms too."

"You can't transfer their power. Doesn't work that way. Once a Radiant gifts it, it's yours." Annoyed, he looks away. "Just leave the Nothings alone. You can't save them."

How can he disregard them so easily when they're his people, too?

"You'll be surprised at how innocuous the favors can be," he says, pointing to a mortal youth dropping grapes into someone's mouth.

"He's a bit young, though, right?"

"Looks can be deceiving, especially in here." He pulls me past moaning grottos and alcoves overflowing with pillows and sparkling fluids I don't even want to think about.

"Don't bother with Lord Fox, though."

"What?" I tense, swinging back around.

He nods toward an alcove near the outskirts of trees. A group of well-dressed nobilities stand before a gauze curtain. They sip from glasses of glittering liquid, laughing at something in conversation. I recognize the scantily clad Lady Nivene from the House of Tides. Her sunburned Shadow wears a sheer gown, revealing her nakedness beneath. Her sparkling collar leads to a leash she flirtatiously taps against a bare, sculpted male torso. One I'm intimately familiar with after I made it bleed all over my hand, after I buried my hands beneath his shirt—the same shirt that is now carelessly unbuttoned.

Fine red welts run down Fox's abdomen. Scratches. From her nails.

A snarl catches in my throat.

Alfie scowls openly. "Irisa *knows* not to bother with them."

His voice warbles as I take in Fox's dark, almost maddened expression as he looks at her. But she eats it up, scrapes those dainty nails down his glistening abdomen. I swear the air around him grows darker, as though shadows are pulled from it.

*It's not the shadows, but what we do inside them.*

A twisted, ugly feeling knots in my stomach. I should look away, but Fox is magnetic. Every move he makes, every twitch draws attention. Whether it's a smile or a scowl, he is the center of the universe. He leans toward Irisa and whispers something that parts her lips.

What did he call it at the restaurant—Midnight adventures? Macabre delights?

Alfie and I stand transfixed as Fox takes the leash and jerks her after him. Lanterns nearby throw enough light to catch the raw hunger in his eyes before he sits, facing away from us on a gilt-edged ornate sofa. The backrest hides everything from his shoulders down, but by the movement of his arm, it's obvious he pats the empty seat beside him.

Instead of sitting where he instructed, Irisa hikes her dress and straddles his lap. Triumph flashes on her face as she flips her long, sandy hair to one side. That twisted knot in my gut tightens when Fox fails to push her away. He slides two fingers beneath her collar and tugs her lips to his, but halts at the last second to avoid clashing.

I swallow. All that control in two fingers.

For a moment, they don't move, but then they kiss. It starts slow, seductive. Her hands slide around his nape and burrow into his short hair. From the way she grinds against him, they may as well be fucking. My heart races. Maybe they are.

*This is why he left me?*

Anger boils my blood. My grip tightens on Alfie's hand. It

takes every ounce of self-control to stop from walking over there and punching him in the face. But it's not my business. We're not a couple. They want to fucking betray me. This is just more proof that his kissing me was all part of his act.

I rub my sternum and tell the defiant ache to shut up. I'm *not* their queen. I don't even know what that truly entails.

I want to leave, but something about the exchange mesmerizes me. It's every glimpse of her facial expression when he angles his head—a flash of bliss, a hint of agony, then back to ecstasy. Can it be like that? Can sex be a drug, an addiction, a pain you can't get enough of?

*Pain is more Emrys's kink, but I'm willing to experiment if you are.*

I thought he was being flippant when he said that to me, but he wasn't.

My rage morphs into something hotter as my curiosity deepens. Like gunpowder embracing a flame, Irisa sees her imminent doom fast approaching, yet she keeps chasing his lips. Faster and faster, she rides him. He still holds her lips to his with two fingers, a steady force, while she writhes and moans and comes undone. What would it feel like to be her, to be consumed with such need that I'd throw myself on fuel to attract the flame?

Fox suddenly rears back, face tilted to the night sky, his long arms spread lengthwise across the backrest. He looks done. Sated.

Now, nothing obstructs our view of Irisa's face. Her lower lip catches between her teeth, her brows lift in the middle, and a sheen of sweat glimmers over her skin as she chases that dagger's edge of ecstasy and agony. Her helpless whimpers quicken, as do my pulse and breath. Within seconds, she grips the backrest beside Fox's head and seizes. Her climax screams from somewhere so deep that it sounds like grief. And it goes on and on . . . so long that I start to worry if she's really hurt, but Fox whispers something, and her spine turns to jelly. Her head flops to the side, an exhausted smile touching her lips.

Everyone in a fifty-foot radius witnessed her earth-shattering orgasm. A few smirks are tossed her way, and a few give jealous scowls, but when her lashes finally flutter open, it's not Fox her gaze lands on.

"Alfie," she gasps.

Fox twists. His fathomless eyes lock with mine and widen.

*"This isn't what it looks like."* His panicked voice punches into my mind.

I am frozen. Rooted to the spot. Alfie seems just as shocked. His hand cripples mine in his grip. Maybe Irisa taught him how to braid hair. Maybe they dated. That's why he looks so crestfallen.

Fox's gaze darts to Alfie, then down to our hands. His expression switches to violent outrage. In the space between heartbeats, I glimpse the promise of murder.

He shoves Irisa. She flies backward off the sofa. Before she hits the ground, he vaults the backrest and comes at us so fast he must be *flickering.* I barely have time to breathe. He's almost here, eyes black as the night and skull illuminating beneath his skin.

"Stop!" I shout, stepping in front of Alfie.

Squeezing my eyes shut, I brace for impact. Nothing comes except a brush of air. I peel one eye open, then the other. Fox is inches away, heaving lungfuls of air like he's drowning. He glances down where I hold Alfie behind me, my hand touching his hip. Pain crumples his features, twisting them once again.

*"It's not what it looked like,"* he repeats in my mind.

*"None of my business,"* I return, hating how my instincts don't agree.

*"I didn't fuck her. I fed from her."* His brows lift in the middle, then slam back down as he retargets Alfie. *"If he doesn't remove his*

*hand from you within five seconds, I won't just sip on his soul like I did hers. I'll fucking consume it whole."*

I back up, pushing Alfie with me.

*"If you have any sense,"* I send, echoing his warning at the restaurant. *"You'll walk away right now."*

He blinks, suddenly realizing we're being watched by everyone, including Cait, who's pushed through the gathering crowd. She narrows her eyes in warning, but he bares razor-sharp fangs at Alfie. They're growing in number and size, just like all the horror stories I heard about the Sluagh. It's like he's possessed, crazed.

"Fox, stop." I push command into my tone. Black eyes hit mine, imploring me to listen to him. But this behavior is wrong. He can't do this.

*"I'm sorry I called you a monster,"* I send, genuinely meaning it. *"I was wrong to call you that. I was hurt, defensive. But if you kill Alfie —my friend—then a monster is what you'll be. And there's no coming back from that."*

His sadness is marked in the slump of his shoulders. After what I witnessed, how is it fair to feel like I've done something wrong? Fox doesn't speak. He just lets his eyes return to their normal shade.

*"I want you to trust me,"* he sends.

*"Then give me space."*

"Right," Cait's voice rings clear in the night. "Willow, Alfie, let me buy you both a round of drinks."

"Let's go," Alfie whispers harshly behind me. "The bar is this way."

# CHAPTER
# THIRTY-TWO
## WILLOW

I'm still frowning when Alfie guides me through the crowd, making a beeline for Cait's auburn hair ahead. Everyone has returned to whatever hedonistic entertainment occupied them before, but I can't forget the image of Fox standing there, forlorn, as I turned away.

A tornado lives inside my mind. Everything whirls and churns. Everything from my feelings, my arousal, jealousy, anger, then . . . was it relief when he explained he was only feeding from Irisa? Did *she* know that?

Logically, my eyes told a different story. She had a *very* good time on his lap. But his trousers were buttoned. When she climaxed, his head was back, staring at the sky, both his arms wide and resting on the sofa's backrest. He wasn't touching her.

Maybe that's how the Sluagh feed. Maybe supping on souls creates some kind of erotic reaction in their prey. In Elphyne, there were wild tales about willingly walking to your death in the arms of a Sluagh, smiling the whole way.

All I know is that I still have no answers. I'm still cursed—still a confused mess.

We follow Cait to the teal-thatched building. The atmosphere is tamer inside, and I suspect it's because this is the boss's domain. A long wooden bar lines the back wall. Bottles upon liquor bottles, elixirs, and tonics are displayed on shelves. That burning flower emits a heady scent here, too.

Bamboo-constructed booths with leather seats circle the outer walls. Open windows overlook cliffs and the ocean, all shadowy in the night. The music here is soft and melodic but easygoing. It suits the balmy air. Already, I feel calmer.

A stunning pale redhead in a tight green dress tends the bar. She doesn't notice us walk up. She's too busy leaning on the counter, flashing her ample bosom, and flirting with two males who lap up her attention like a dessert. With her chin in her hand, she flicks open the man's collar. He's too enchanted to care.

"Sorcha," Cait snaps, lifting the bar's hatch to enter. "What are you doing this side of the bar?"

She faces Cait with red, flashing eyes. "You're ruining my fun, kitty cat."

"Fun, or your next meal?" Cait continues along the bar to where we wait.

"Wh-what?" splutters one of the men. "Meal?"

Sorcha bares dainty vampiric fangs and then hisses. The males flee so fast that they leave their drinks. She turns to Cait, cocks her hip, and scowls. Her pose splits her dress, revealing a seductive thigh morphing into a furry deer's leg.

"You ruined my flow," Sorcha grumbles.

"Go and flow somewhere I can't see you." Cait rolls her eyes.

Alfie shoots me a wide-eyed stare, gives a shaky laugh, and rakes his hand through his hair. "Told you things would get wild."

I force a smile despite not feeling it. "You can say that again."

Sorcha walks away, all curves and seduction. With those legs and Cait's feline traits, I don't think they're Avorlornian natives. When I turn back to Cait, she watches me with emerald eyes.

Someone shouts Alfie's name from a booth. He glances over and grins. Patting me on the back, he says, "Get me whatever you're having, and then come and meet the crew."

"Sure."

He bounds to the booth, shakes a few hands, and slides into a seat. Along with two Chasers, two Shadows are there, including Dahlia. They all give a good-natured laugh. Dahlia looks at me, smiles genuinely, and waves before returning to the conversation.

What, so we're friends here?

Perplexed, I turn back to the bar and mumble, "He got over it fast."

Cait's lips curve. "It's amazing how resilient people are when they know they'll forget the trouble they cause . . . or the enemies who become friends, just for a night."

"Seems a little counterintuitive."

Her gaze softens on me. "You'll get used to it."

"I keep telling myself that, but things keep changing."

"I'll make you something special to cheer you up." She collects two bottles and two glasses. She keeps glancing at me from beneath her lashes as she prepares the drinks.

"Figure it out yet?" she asks. "Where I'm from?"

"Nocturna?" I guess, glancing at the redheaded vampire luring another man into a dark passageway. Interestingly, the big brute bouncer who broke up the fight is brooding as he regards her from a doorway. Kai, I think his name was.

Cait slides two glasses my way, each with a straw and a tiny umbrella.

"What's in the drink?" I narrow my eyes.

"Vodka and Orange juice. Mortals used to call it a Screwdriver in the old days."

I'm familiar with the ingredients from Crystal City. But Alfie warned against trusting Cait. I'm not sure how much of myself I should reveal.

"Nothing else in it? No surprise enchantments?"

"Just that." She salutes me. "Scout's honor."

"Who is Scout?" I put the straw to my lips and take a sip. It's nice. Sweet.

Cait laughs. "I thought you'd be all over the old-world lingo with who your mother is."

I tense. "Who told you about my mother?"

She leans against the counter. "I know plenty of things about you, Willow O'Leary-Nightstalk."

Taking another sip, I study her again. Is she psychic or something else? Our first conversation comes to mind.

"Fox told you." Another sip. "You're friends."

"Clever girl. What else have you deduced?"

I raise my brows at Sorcha, then glance at Cait's duo-tone skin and tail. "I don't think those would fit the Old Code's mandates about flawless appearance."

She flicks the gems dangling from her nose chain. "I help people fit the code in Avorlorna." She gestures around her face, and suddenly, her ears and tail disappear. The white patches on her skin become the same color as the rest of her.

"Your charms glamour away flaws?" I ask. Maybe I can buy or barter for some to help Geraldine and the others. "How much does it cost?"

"Only your eternal soul."

I blink. She doesn't.

"So . . . when you said you could help me with my . . . this." I gesture at my face. "The price is my soul?"

Her smile reveals the tip of her white canines. "But you won't need my help. Not yet, anyway." Before I can press the subject, her humor dissipates. She leans forward to speak in a hushed, warning tone. "I've never seen Fox so unhinged before. If he loses it like that in public, his little secret is not so secret anymore. Do you understand?"

My eyes widen. "His wings will be clipped like the others."

"Oh, much worse than that if *everyone* sees it. Titania hides their true identities for selfish purposes. But if her court finds out he's a Nightmare, the only way to wash her hands clean is to pretend they're all infiltrating on Oberon's behalf."

"She can't execute them. They don't die."

"Everyone dies at some point." Another feline grin. "You take care of my little creeps, okay?"

"Um. Sure."

"Good. Good." She eases back and glances down the bar as a tall, lanky man walks in. Must be the barman. She nods at him, then refills my glass—pouring from both bottles simultaneously. When she's done, she gives me a wink. "See you around, Your Majesty."

I stare in her direction long after she's gone.

"Willow!" Alfie startles me by grabbing my arm. "What's taking so long?"

"Um." I frown.

"You look like you've seen a ghost. You okay?" He takes the drink I offer.

"She just said something weird."

He grins. "Don't worry about it. You'll forget it the moment you leave here. Come on, meet the others."

Nervously, I allow him to guide me to his friends' U-shaped booth. I recognize most as the crew he was with on the first day in the commons. Dahlia's cheeks and eyes are bright, her red lipstick smudged. The man beside her is the Shadow who probably eats monsters for breakfast. The other two have charmed chains dangling from shoulder to shoulder. The woman is blond, round-faced, and seems out of breath. The man has a red headband on his long dark hair.

Alfie shuffles me forward and points to Dahlia. "You already know this nut job, but you might not know she's a Woodrunner, Unit Six-Oh-Four in the Avorlornian army. Lindon is the House of Stone Shadow and a Warden like me. Unit Six-Oh-Four represent." They all pound their fists together.

I smile around my straw, secretly thankful I have something to distract myself from Fox.

"These two Chasers are Guardsman Becky and Special Guardsman Ryder. Also in Six-Oh-Four." He slings his arm over my shoulder and grins. "Everyone, meet Willow, my fiancée."

I cough and pound my chest to cover my shock.

"Go down the wrong hole?" Alfie shoots me a concerned look, slapping my back. The rough action jerks me forward, and it feels like my breasts are about to burst from my top. Panicking, I fumble for my cleavage but end up spilling more drink.

"I'm good. I'm good." I quickly correct my glass, wipe my face, and smile at him.

A flicker of irritation flashes in his eyes, and then he pushes at Ryder. "Shove over for Willow, will you?"

I dart a glance around as if someone will save me. My skin prickles with unease. But I bunch my storm cloud skirt and slide in next to the big guy with the red headband. It smells coppery, like blood. And he breaths really loud.

Alfie squeezes in on the opposite side of the table and starts chatting with Lindon as if his declaration is old news.

Dahlia leans past Ryder and says to me, "Hey, no hard feelings here, alright?"

"Ah, sure."

"I mean, out there, we're rivals. But in here, we got each other's backs."

"Six-Oh-Four," Becky crows, and they fist-bump.

That will get real old if they don't stop soon.

Everyone at this table serves in the same military unit. That kind of bond is strong. Unbreakable. After a few awkward minutes of me sitting on the outskirts, with Ryder joining the same conversation as the other boys, Dahlia urges him to swap seats with me.

The queasiness in my stomach says I'd rather not, but I think the vodka is starting to get to me. I slide across so I'm beside the two women.

"Hey." Becky reaches across and squeezes my hand. "I'm sorry about your face."

"Me too," Dahlia breathes. "I mean, I'm sorry too. I can't imagine having to walk around looking like that. It must be horrible."

Yeah, this isn't making me feel better. It's none of their business, anyway.

"But don't worry." She bumps my shoulder with hers. "We'll teach you the ropes. We still have a few hours left tonight. We can get you hooked up with a Radiant to earn your first charm, and if things get a little crazy"—she nods at my drink—"at least it's a rest day tomorrow."

I glance at Alfie, who smiles back at me.

Dahlia swirls my straw. "I know you're probably thinking, why the fuck should I trust this bitch? But we're all here to let off steam and maybe, if we're lucky, find a benevolent Radiant."

Irisa sidles up to the table with a round of drinks on a tray. Her hair is still messy, but her sheer dress is straight and perfectly presentable again.

"Drink up," she says, distributing her load, not acknowledging me.

Rude.

Everyone cheers, happily taking another glass, except Alfie.

At first, I think he's taken a slight to her ignorance of me, but when he avoids her eyes, I realize it's about their shared history.

"Aw, come on." She slides him a drink. "You can hardly blame me, Alf. It's not like I'm going to marry him."

Alfie glances at me, takes his drink, and snarks, "I hope you got what you wanted, Irisa."

Her expression blanks. Then she laughs. "If you mean the best sex of my life, then hell, yes, I did." The girls whoop, and she high-fives them in succession. She pauses when she gets to me and smirks. "You know what I mean, right?"

She tries to high-five me, but I don't engage.

"Why would my fiancée know what he's like to fuck?" Alfie fires.

Irisa pauses, then glances at me before returning to him with an exaggerated sigh. "Oh, right. Her face. Sorry."

A nasty worm wriggles in my gut. I take another drink to wash it down, but my resentment rises to lift it back.

Dahlia tosses a straw at him. "Loosen the fuck up, Alfie. It's every man for himself here. You know that."

He shuffles over to make room for Irisa, but she scowls at him. "No thanks. You're bringing the vibe down. And look—your *fiancée* needs cheering up. You're not doing a very good job tending to her needs."

"I'm fine." I raise my palms. Please don't bring me into this.

"Actually," Dahlia blurts, trying to stand on the bench seat. Her shirt is on backward, and a part of her skirt is stuck in her panties. "Let's go and dance. I haven't scored a charm tonight, and Iggy isn't here, so I don't want to waste any more time."

I'm guessing Ignarius is Iggy. That none of the others blinked at her pet name probably means she's spoken about their relationship outside of this place.

When all the women climb out of the booth, I have no choice

but to go along. Before Alfie sits, he crowds over Irisa and says, "I'm going to marry her, so help her out. You owe me."

"I don't know why you bother." Irisa rolls her eyes.

"Because if she can pass as a Never, she won't get deported after the Gentle Interlude."

"Feeling sorry for her will get you killed."

He pokes her. "Out of anyone who will get killed, it won't be her."

Pride swells in my chest. I want to smile at his faith in me but settle for meeting Irisa's stare.

"Don't worry," she replies. "We'll show her the ropes."

"Let the girls help you get a charm," Alfie tells me, imploring me with his eyes. "You can trust them in here."

Something in the air doesn't feel right. "You know what? I think I'll head home, thanks."

Alfie takes me aside and whispers, "You need to start taking my lead, Willow. I've been here for five years. I know how things work."

"These women hate me out there, and I'm suddenly expected to trust them?"

"They don't hate you. It's the exhibition."

"Call me naïve, but I think people should be genuine the whole time."

I meant it sarcastically, but he levels his gaze on me. "You *are* naïve, Willow. You spent half your life as President Nero's princess in the Sky Tower. Everyone tripped over themselves to please you. And your parents in Elphyne . . . don't get me started. Both were one-of-a-kind, unique, *powerful* heroes. You're not better than everyone anymore. Now that you don't have magic, you need to learn how the rest of us survive. Can't you see that I'm trying to help you?"

His words cut me to the core. This is the second time he's

CASTLE OF NEVERS AND NIGHTMARES

mentioned me being sheltered by Nero. He obviously has a gripe about it. I guess the gloves are off in Burn After Reading.

"I'm telling you this for your own good," he continues. "You're not used to navigating the real world. You saw what Nero wanted you to see."

The more he talks, the more he makes sense. My mother said something similar, didn't she? That they've sheltered me too much. That I need to make my own mistakes so I can learn from them? The only problem is the thought frightens the Well out of me. Maybe that's why I pretend he hasn't just said the cruelest things.

"Fine," I agree.

"Thank god." Before he sits down, he whispers in my ear, "Do it for the Gold."

For fun.

For adventure.

Fuck it. I won't remember this tomorrow. If I can't make a few mistakes now, when can I?

# THIRTY-THREE

## WILLOW

Buzzed on Cait's Screwdrivers, I follow the girls out of the tavern and onto the scented lawn. In the time we were inside, behavior has grown rowdier, more loose and wild, more debauched. Lanterns blow in the balmy wind. Trash litters the floor, and lost clothes roll like tumbleweeds.

Trust them in here, Alfie said, but not out there?

Dahlia notices my frown and shrugs. "Look, we're all fucked up. But here we can pretend the fucking world didn't end, and we're just having fun. You should try it."

"Yeah, I get that," I return. "My mother and her friends were like you. I'm sorry for your loss." I rub my fist over my heart, accidentally reverting to the hand-signing tradition.

She stops. Sways. "Your mom is from our time?"

"Alfie never told you?"

"No." She pouts.

"He never said we're from Elphyne?"

"Where's that?"

Before I answer, Becky throws out her arms, pirouettes, and screams. When the others join in, going with the flow, I want to

288

follow. It's nice to be included and not always looking over my shoulder.

We receive dirty looks, and someone shouts for us to take it to the ring, but other than that, no one cares. At some point, another drink is shoved in my face. Then another. I can hardly walk straight by the time we stumble to where the primal drumming is loudest. I think there's a flute somewhere in the mix, but my mind could be making up things. Bright buzzing fireflies swarm overhead, lighting a path to where a small crowd jumps and dances.

Becky's round face appears before me, and she whines, "No offense, but Alfie won't shut up about you. Since you got picked by the House of Shadow, it's like Willow this, Willow that. Now we finally know why he's so obsessed. You guys are getting married."

"I don't know why he keeps saying that," I slur drunkenly. Maybe sway. Wait. Where are my shoes? Doesn't matter. "I mean, we *were* engaged. Five years ago."

"Don't worry." She laughs. "People say shit in here. They get it out of their system so that out there, it's easier to hide cos, I mean"—she scoffs and scrunches her nose—"he can't exactly declare he's going to marry a Nothing, right?"

"No need to be rude, bitch." Dahlia pokes Becky. To me, she adds, "I think what she means is that it's freeing to get shit off your chest. I fucking wanted to *kill* you for embarrassing me in that class. Wanted to peel the Nothing-skin right off your face. But then I was like, you know what? If this bitch gets through the exhibition, I want her in my unit, you know? I want a crazy bitch who knows how to fight."

"Yeah," Irisa adds, coming up to my right side. "And when Dahlia told me about you, I was thinking, *finally*, some competition."

Dahlia gapes at her. "What?"

Irisa's makeup-stained eyes crinkle. "Well, come on. Be honest. You're nowhere near as good as me."

"I think Iggy would say otherwise." Dahlia pushes Irisa, who looks down at her as if she's a child.

"Honey," she drawls. "The whole world just watched one of the most eligible Radiants fuck me. *Her* Radiant. I think I win."

"Maybe *she* wins," Dahlia sneers, "since she's obviously fucking them all."

My brows lift. They all stare at me and then burst out laughing.

"Nah," Becky says. "We know you can't be." She sobers. "But seriously. If you want to be, you gotta sort that face out."

Irisa's eyes flash. I blink, thinking I might detect a little jealousy, but she's the picture-perfect smiling sweet thing on the next blink.

"Your turn," she says. "Shout something you've been dying to let out. We can take it."

They look at me expectantly, but I freeze.

"First night jitters." Dahlia nods emphatically. "Don't worry, you'll eventually warm up. A dance will help." She scans the group of dancers, frowning. "I think Lord Sylvanar's son Milford is here. He's always good for an easy charm."

The drums quicken, but it feels like my heart is pounding inside my brain. The heady scent of burned petal spice is dizzying. A raucous cheer rings out. Then another. Coming from somewhere else. Turning, I feel disorientated.

"What's that?" I mumble, flaring my eyes to see better in the dark. But everything is starting to blur together. Dahlia tries to tug me away from the cheering, but I'm drawn to it.

"No, no." Dahlia tugs harder. "This is a waste of time."

"What is?"

"Just show her," Irisa grumbles. "Get it over with, then we can find Milford."

"As long as you don't do this every time." Dahlia waggles her finger at me. "Fine. We'll take you to see the Radiants blow off steam."

By letting off steam, she means no-holds-barred brawling. And by Radiants, she means Fox and Emrys, circling each other, fists bloody, grinning wildly. Both are shirtless, sweating, and dirty, as if they've been rolling on the ground.

"Holy shit," Irisa mutters, eyes wide.

"What?" Dahlia pushes to the front of the crowd. "No way."

Fox still holds that feral glint in his eyes. Emrys stalks him calmly, almost amused. His fists might be bloody, but his body is a pristine mix of pale skin and black, arcane tattoos. Barely a scratch on him. They don't move like normal people. Not even like animals.

I'm transfixed as Emrys taps his jaw, taunting Fox.

"Never seen two of them fight each other." Becky raises her brows.

"How would you fucking remember?" Dahlia scoffs.

"Oh yeah." Becky hands me another drink from somewhere. I blink into the cup. How are they finding drinks everywhere? What is in this? I sniff it, but my nose isn't working. It smells the same. Like alcohol. Oh well. Here's to making more mistakes. I toss it down the hatch. Bodies suddenly surge, applauding.

"Come on," Dahlia moans. "We don't have time to waste on these assholes. They don't care enough to hand out charms."

"You shouldn't say that," Becky mumbles, eyes glassy and distant. "They saved my life more than once."

The reminder of war is an iced bucket of water tossed on us. In their silence, the crack of bone blares as Emrys's fist connects with Fox's jaw, spurting dark blood. I wince, forgetting he can heal faster than anyone I've seen. But Fox smiles through bloody teeth, spits a wad, and asks for more. My jaw drops. He wants to be hurt, just like he wanted my dagger in his heart. This isn't a fight. It's a beating.

"Yeah, they've saved our lives," Dahlia agrees sardonically. "But charms can do that too."

"They put their bodies on the line." Becky shakes her head. "The others just keep sending us to the slaughter from a distance."

"I'd rather have something I can trust than wait for a hero." Dahlia looks at me. "So what's it going to be, Willow? You going to wait for a hero or save yourself?"

"What?" I blink, facing her.

Everything is spinning. Suddenly, I'm nowhere near the fighting. I don't think. I'm facing a portly man without a shirt on. His round belly is covered in sweat—or wine or something glittering. Gross. I try to keep my eyes open and clear. I think he's got arched fae ears, but then again, maybe I'm seeing double. His pants are loose and tied by a sash at the round waist. Dangling from the tie, positioned at the center of his crotch, is a small red gemstone sparkling under the nearby lantern light.

"This is Lord Milford," someone says beside me. They take my hand and plop it on his.

"Charmed to meet you, Willow." He bows and plants sloppy lips on the back of my hand.

I tug it back. "Sir."

"No need for formalities here. We're all friends."

"Sure."

Speaking of friends, where did the others go? I turn, but my head swims. I glimpse lights, dark shapes, and heads of a crowd. I think that's the ring—the cheering. How did I get this far?

"Oh, they've given us a little privacy. They know how this goes." He hands me another drink.

This one is filled with something glowing. "What is this?"

"Don't worry, dearie. They've all been here before. Even your redheaded Warden."

"Alfie?"

"Such a sweet boy." His eyes turn lecherous. "Such a sweet mouth."

"Wait. How do you remember? I thought everyone forgot?"

"I'll let you in on a little secret," he whispers in my ear. "There are ways to remember. Why else do you think this place exists? Take a look around and tell me what you see."

Swaying, I clutch the cup to keep from falling over. But I manage to stay upright, to hold my vision steady enough to catch a few things I didn't notice before. Amongst the grottos, alcoves, and secret sex nooks, sharp-eyed faeries make sinister deals, bargains, and alliances. Coins pass hands, charms, probably favors. Lady Nivene converses seriously with another Radiant who looks familiar, but I can't place them.

"Take her, for instance," Milford croons, pointing at the lady. "She's the only Radiant with a water dragon powerful enough to guard the seas for safe travel. She owns the waters. And here she makes sure it stays that way."

Lady Nivene's companion drops a bloated coin bag into her hand.

"Indeed." Milford swipes my hair from my neck. "You know, it's deplorable how they treat you."

"Who?"

"All of them, but especially your so-called mentors. It's so easy for them to gift you charms, to help you avoid deportation after this is all over. If you win, you'll have to waste your dream on that very wish. It makes you wonder why they chose you, doesn't it?"

293

I stare at the cup. The glowing liquid swirls like a whirlpool. My brain wants to do the same. I should go. I might be shit at making my own decisions and very drunk, but at least I know when something doesn't feel right. But he's also making sense.

"Why do you think they chose me?" I ask.

"Come, sit. Let's talk some more where it's quieter." He gestures to a vacant grouping of pillows beneath an oak tree. "Maybe we can make a deal of our own."

# CHAPTER
# THIRTY-FOUR

FOX

E mrys's fist connects with my nose, breaking cartilage and firing sweet pain into my brain. The crowd cheers, eating up the violence like candy.

Agony is bliss compared to the shame still coursing through my veins. I can't believe she saw me like that . . . I can't believe she thinks I would ever want another female touch me that way, that any of us would.

"Although this is incredibly satisfying," Emrys taunts. "You bore me, Fox."

Visions of Willow's wide eyes still pierce my heart. But then I remember her clutching the mortal's hand for support. *Him*. I know where it's been, what he does with those hands, who he touches, who he thinks he is to her, what his thoughts scream about her.

My sanity unravels. The Morrigan whispers in my ear tonight. The Cauldron stirs. I am too weak to deny her thirst for blood. But at least if it's mine, I am not the monster Willow runs from.

Emrys prowls around me with coiled, predatory energy, his muscles feathered to make another explosive strike. He stops, gives me a pitiful look, and then lashes out and resets my nose. *Crunch.*

Pain. Sweet pain. It blinds the heart, the mind, the memory.

I see why Emrys relishes it so much.

Pain obliterates.

"This ends now." He cracks his knuckles. "You're distracted well enough. You even failed to notice she watched you for the past five minutes. Go home and patch your bleeding heart before you embarrass yourself."

I glance around the ring, searching for her silver hair. Most spectators are now disbanding, disappointed we've stopped letting blood. When I locate a silver head receding into the darkness, my breathing becomes ragged, my heart erratic. Pent up, trembling energy fills within me again, building and begging for release.

"No," I tell Emrys. "We're not done. Hit me again."

"For what, the entertainment of bejeweled locusts?" His gesture is whip-hard in Willow's direction. "For another leash?"

Bitterness oozes from my every pore—and exhaustion. I'm tired of repeatedly explaining who she is to us. But I can't give up.

Emrys's rage drops to scorn. "We have more important things to worry about than a mortal needing an education in obedience. She lasted one night here, and already she prefers the company of insects."

I glance over, but she is gone. Only the mortals she kept company with remain. Their souls spill secrets to me, drunkenly sharing all the dark, nasty deeds they've filled their lives with. They fool no one. None of these people do. I see right through to their rotten cores.

Willow is the only bright spark among them.

The brunette female catches my eyes and smirks. I stalk over, ignoring Emrys's long-suffering sigh.

"Where is she?" I demand, still a slave to the darkness building inside. I could rip the answer from their minds, but I promised Cait I would behave. I have already broken her rules tonight. If this continues, she will not let me feed here freely.

Feeding out there will draw suspicion from the Keepers. They already suspect something is wrong.

"Who?" the brunette replies, tracing her finger down my torso.

I capture her hand and crunch. Her scream is the call of a siren to Emrys. I sense him turning from where he buttons his shirt. I shouldn't make a scene, but my hands are not my own. The taste of darkness erupts in my mouth, sowing shadow in the air.

I squeeze harder until her secret spills out. "She's getting from him what you failed to give."

"Who?" My vision turns red. I'm five seconds from pillaging her mind, and I've been trying *really* hard to respect boundaries.

"Let go of her." My recent meal shoves me.

I should have finished her soul and laid waste to them all.

"She's back there making a deal to fix her flaws. To help her fit in." Another mortal beside me. I cock my head, study her face. Round, plump cheeks. Her soul is not as dark as the others. My mouth waters for the taste, hungers for the fragility. But then she gives me a new target. "With Lord Milford."

A banshee shrieks in my mind.

Milford. Lord Sylvanar's son. The miscreant preys on vulnerable mortals, gives them a kind shoulder to lean on, and learns their vulnerabilities and fears. He promises help, fashions a charm to fit those fears, and then makes them remove it from his cock after he fucks their mouth.

Darkness explodes from me, ripping apart my being until I

am hunting through the night, barreling through air toward a serpent who whispers temptations to one already perfect.

I conquer, devour, and glut myself on his wickedness. My life becomes a sea of blood, viscera, and the liquid ecstasy of a soul. A groan of satisfaction leaves me as I sup on the sustenance I've denied.

Why did I wait so long to feed this way?

Blinking, I suddenly find myself elbow-deep in a chest cavity, ribs cracked open like the wings of an angel. My tattered ones are draped at my sides. My tail lashes behind me. I am both inside the corpse and outside. My wraith form fills every inch of my prey, relentlessly scraping each vestige of his soul.

Delicious.

*Thud thud. Thud thud. Thud thud.*

What is that?

*Thud thud. Thud thud.*

It is not my tail but a heartbeat. The cavity between the broken ribs is empty. Blood oozes down my chin. If I ate it, then why can I hear it beat? I glance up, horrified.

Willow.

She sees me in all my monstrous glory. Here I am, the wretched thing she despises, and I have no excuse. My every last shameful inch is on display.

"F-fox," she stammers. "What have you done?"

Sounds garble somewhere behind us . . . where are we? I didn't mean to lose control.

What have I done?

There is panic. Pandemonium. But I dare not break eye contact with Willow lest I knock loose her final straw. While my hands are inside a desiccated husk, I wait for judgment.

"Fuck you, Fox." Cait's angry shout from somewhere.

But it's Emrys who arrives to witness my destruction first. His boots stop at my side, and he sighs. "You left nothing for me."

Willow gapes at him. Sways.

"Quickly, now," Emrys warns me. "Put your shadows away. People come."

I tug my hands from the body and call my wraith home. It brings vitality and power, gallons of it filling me to the brim until my eyes water. My two halves unite, and I once again see in color. Milford's wicked soul is ours, rolling inside, a whole insect swarming against its temporary cage.

His screams of injustice rattle the bars, vibrating my spine.

*"Shh,"* I croon. *"Hush."*

*"Murderer!"*

I lick blood from my fangs. Feasting upon a heart is unnecessary to extract sustenance from a soul, but there is no honorable death for cruel cowards. His mortal victims would agree if they remembered the depths his depravity forced them into. He deserves eternity in the Wild Hunt's belly, tormented with endless expiation under the righteous will of our queen.

A fitting end for him, considering she was to be his next victim had I not come along.

I wait for her reaction of horror, for the inevitable disgust— that word I never want to hear again from her perfect lips. But what comes out is unexpected.

"Oh fuck," she garbles, covering her mouth. "I'm going to puke."

She launches into the shadows behind the tree, retching loudly.

"Emrys." Cait's husky voice is without reprimand, only exhaustion. "It's been a long night. Be a darling and help the boys get the patrons out. Fox and I will take care of this . . . situation."

He slides a withering glare her way, already plotting her destruction.

Cait is impervious to his moods. Always has been. Her emerald eyes flash, her tail lashes, and then she smirks.

"If you hurry," she teases, "you'll get there before they read the enchantment, and you know what that means."

He stares. Chews over her words in his mind. Stares some more. "Fine."

Dark circles shadow his eyes. Catering to Titania's whims takes more of a toll than it should. He must feed properly.

"Emrys," I say. "Return to the keep tonight."

He walks away, cracking his knuckles, pretending not to hear.

*"You fool no one,"* I whisper into his mind. *"We know you are at the palace, so we are not."*

He sends back, *"Give my share to the wildling."*

"Let him go," Cait grumbles. "Let him play with his toys. You have other problems to deal with."

She glances at the silhouette of Willow crouching, her head hanging low. I touch her mind with mine, checking her well-being. She is intoxicated and about to pass out. I should go to her.

"Fox." Cait stops me, a palm to my chest. She gives my bloody hands a pointed look. "This is the last time I cover for you."

"I know."

She drops her hand and glances to where Emrys stalks stragglers. Once he is out of earshot, she asks, "Do you have the payment?"

"Nowhere near five hundred." I think about the lives I took. I went as far as Wulfenite, and still, not a single body erupted with wisps at the time of death. "They are not abundant here like in Elphyne."

"Then perhaps you should return there."

"I can't." The hive suffers if we separate for long.

This is probably Titania's plan—anything to stop Oberon's reclamation of us.

"I've known you long," Cait says, "but I won't endanger my crew unless you pay us."

"I know."

"If you can't get it to me soon, you're out of options."

"*I know.*"

She sighs. "Fine. Then you know what to do. Take her memories."

The idea of violating Willow's mind sickens me. "No."

"Is this how you want her to remember you?" She gestures at my bloody body. "You were the one who sat in here, night after night, bemoaning how she rejected you with that word. And now you want her to remember it?"

I grind my teeth. It is the last thing I want. "I need her trust more."

"If you don't, I will," she warns.

"Touch her," I snarl, my voice turning guttural, "and our deal is off."

A hissing feline growl erupts from her throat. "This whole place hinges on that deal. The *resistance* hinges on that deal."

In return for letting me feed here, I allow her to tap my aura when I erase memories. She distills her memory-burning enchantment from this. If I have to give up my anonymity to protect Willow, I will.

I meet Cait's unwavering stare until she curses under her breath and jabs a finger at me. "This is the *last* time I clean up your mess."

I gather Willow into my arms. She stirs, furrowing her brow. *Flickering* might make her ill again, but I have no choice.

"Fox, a word of caution." Cait plucks a flow charm from

Milford's sash and puts it in Willow's pocket. "Go straight to the keep. Don't let anyone see you. The last thing you want is for Sylvanar to find out you killed his son."

"Understood."

Jostling wakes me. My stomach rolls. Drunkenly, I catch fireworks in the darkness of changing landscapes. Fox's sweet moss-and-woodsy scent. Blood. Ribs sticking out. His hunched, dark body feeding like a wild animal.

Vomit burns the back of my throat, and I scream, shoving him away from me. "Get off me!"

The flashing gets faster. We're moving at breakneck speed. But something is wrong. We pause, jolting to a stop, then surge forward again. I don't remember it being this bad. I can't hold it.

Nausea rises. I somehow push him and roll at the same time. We spill from the darkness. Icy air blasts my sweaty body, and then I hit the dirt hard. I tumble, and my stormy skirt catches and rips.

"Willow!" Footsteps thud closer.

I land on my stomach, groan, and breathe heavily to stop more puke pouring from my throat. How much did I drink? My head pounds. My mouth is somehow cardboard and wet at the same time.

"Are you okay?" A sticky, bloody hand reaches for me.

303

I shove him away. "Don't touch me."

"I'm sorry. Something is wrong with my *flickering*. It's not working as it should."

Where are we? I force my bleary eyes to look around, but I can't fight the pounding in my head.

"We're almost home," he whispers, reaching for me again. "Just let me get you inside before anyone sees."

"No." I push him away. All I see is the blood. One minute, the sweaty Radiant tugged me onto his lap. The next, he was on the ground being ripped apart and devoured. Wheezing, I stagger and rein in my vision to focus on the tall, dark-haired, fucking stunning male specimen before me. Even with all the blood dripping from his mouth and down his carved chest, coating his arms, he still looks perfect.

The blood isn't what horrifies me. I've ripped apart my opponents with fangs and claws. Nero wanted to eviscerate the poor souls. Wanted to see how far gone a body could be before I failed to return it to life.

The answer was far. Very far.

What horrifies me is how Fox lost control. He was a beast ruled by primal hunger. Milford was dead in seconds. There was no time to stop it. At that moment, I witnessed the birth of the horror stories, the real-life boogeyman. The reason humans fear to tread in fae territory. This is the side the Sluagh have been hiding from me.

"Why did you do it?" I can't breathe.

"He wasn't a good person." His eyes widen as I stumble back. "Please, Willow. Let's go inside. I'll tell you everything you want to know."

Turning, I realize we're outside Shadowfall Keep. Right before the rickety rope bridge.

Wait. How can I remember why Fox is covered in blood if we're out here?

It's hard to make my thoughts walk in a straight line, but I know I'm supposed to forget everything.

"You did something naughty to get me out," I ramble. "To let me keep my memories."

I stagger forward, eyes locked onto the ropy bridge as an anchor for my wandering balance.

He's at my side instantly. "Let me *flicker* us inside."

"I'm not going with you."

"You're being stubborn." He tries to take me, but we *flicker* two feet. I stumble, scream in frustration, and shove him away.

"I said I don't want you!"

Dismay crumples his expression. He shows his palms in surrender. What I meant to say is I don't want to *flicker*, but the path between my brain and tongue is disconnected. Now I feel shitty for hurting his feelings. This could all be another trick. Another manipulation.

I want to walk to the keep on my own two feet.

Somehow, that feels important.

Or hands and knees. That works, too.

"Just get inside," I tell myself, dropping. "We can get inside ourselves."

The impact jars through me. The ground is so cold. Stubbornly, I grip each wooden bridge plank and crawl, unsure if the swaying is in my mind or the wind. My skirt keeps catching, ripping, and tangling in my legs. I hate it. I want to rip it off.

"We don't need anyone to save us." Tears prickle my eyes.

A gust of wind hits me with the scent of ice and pungent moat water. It lifts my hair and whips it into my eyes. I shake my head to clear it, but my stomach revolts. I swallow it down. An icy coffin waits beneath the planks. I'm sure the moat wasn't this frozen when I last crossed.

Fox waits on the other side, worry etched into his handsome

features. *Stupid nice face.* He must have *flickered* to get there first, to get a good view of the dumb Nothing on her hands and knees.

"That's not fair." Tinger berates me. "He's never called you Nothing."

"Except five years ago," I counter.

"Maybe they called you *a* nothing. Not *nothing.*"

"Oh, so *now* you talk to me," I sob out. "When I'm drunk."

"Just focus on crossing. Don't look down. Eyes ahead."

At the thought of Tinger, nightmares join the whirling in my mind. Water. Rory falling. The empty look in her eyes. Tinger's little body, wheezing his last breath. My father's disappointment. My mother's apprehension. Dahlia's weird behavior—I thought maybe she was being a friend. Alfie said I could trust her there, but she pushed me toward Milford.

*Nothings don't have names.*

My limbs lock. My head hangs. My vision crowds and then panic hits. I reach into the skirt pocket, desperately fumbling for Tinger's pendant. What if I lost him? What if he's gone? What if he fell out during the *flickering*?

Relief courses through me as my fingers wrap around the glass. A sob bursts from my lips. Vaguely, I hear Fox ask if I'm okay. I clutch the pendant to my heart and rest my forehead on the cold wooden plank. It's okay. He's still here. He never left.

"We're okay," I mumble. "We're okay."

I imagine him puffing his furry chest and digging his broken antler into my ass, telling me to stop feeling sorry for myself, suck it up, and get going. Taking a deep breath, I lift my head and tuck the pendant into my skirt just as a gust of wind knocks me to the side. The pendant slips.

"No!" I reach, fumble, lurch. My fingertips slip over glass vial, and we both tip sideways.

I face the starry sky in freefall, surrounded by hair and a stormy skirt—my mind empties. I'm in shock. Is this why Rory looked dead as she watched Cloud's face grow smaller? A wall of icy concrete slams into my spine. The wind knocks out of me. I can't breathe.

But I'm not dead.

I'm not drowning.

Trembling, I try to sit but swoon. Fox bellows in panic, scrambling down the bank from the bridge. He looks weird. He *flickers* and stumbles. It's like his brain is disconnected, too. Doesn't his magic work?

"I'm okay." My breath leaves a white cloud. I glance around, hunting for Tinger's pendant.

It's only five feet away. Triumph fills me so violently that my eyes burn. "I'm coming, Tinger."

*I'll save you this time.*

"Stop, Willow!"

"It's okay," I blurt, feeling better than I have in a while.

Adrenaline clears my head. I didn't drown. Tinger is okay. I scramble on my hands and knees. All this time, I was worried about drowning, but I'm here. Sore, cold, but alive. Ice cuts my fingers as I slide my palm across the frozen moat, reaching for the leather cord.

"Got you," I breathe, tugging him back to me.

*Crack!*

My heart seizes. I glance down at the breaking ice. *Crack. Crack.* My eyes clash with Fox's.

And then I plunge.

# THIRTY-SIX

FOX

I thought I knew death.

Eons of draining life, consuming it, watching eyes empty, hoarding wicked souls for eternity, watching them suffer for their sins was death.

I lived and breathed it, dealt and took it. I've seen it all.

But when Willow's eyes collide with mine, time stops. No wind rustles the leaves. No birds chirp, nor insects crawl. There is only the vacuum of my heart, the black hole growing deeper as she is ripped from her place within it.

She is gone in seconds, falling beneath the ice, and my body will not listen to me.

"Willow!" I howl, stumbling down the bank to get to her and *flicker* simultaneously.

One second, it works. The next, I run. Stumble. Then I'm sliding across the ice, attacked by a thousand tiny cuts, and plunging into the moat's cold embrace. The wisp is a lure sinking in one direction. But her silver hair is in another, almost swallowed by the darkness. I try everything in my arsenal to get to her. I shoot shadow to catch her, *flicker* to her, and send my wraith out. It all fractures as though she holds a charm to block my power.

Somehow, I have her. I'm gathering her in my arms and squeezing tight, willing my magic to obey. *Save our queen.*

In a flash, we're on the rocky shore, gasping for breath. She chokes, coughs, vomits water, and gulps for air.

"Oh no," she wails, scrambling to the frozen moat. "I lost him."

I've never seen her so distraught. Her pain bleeds into mine. Her mind screams as she battles me to let her go. *"I need him I need him without him I'm nothing."*

"Willow, stop."

Grief crumples her face. Her lips are blue, her teeth chattering. "Please please please."

"If you need him." I cup her wet face between my hands. "I'll get him. Stay here."

Setting my jaw, I dive back in. This time, my body listens. My power is my own again. I *flicker* around the expanse of arctic water and fight the undercurrent for a single, shining star. It only takes me a couple of seconds, and then I am back on the shore, handing her the dangling pendant and watching the starlight transfer to her face.

I thought I knew life.

I thought the blessing gifted us that joy.

But as she takes her precious cargo, cradles it to her chest, and looks at me with glimmering gratitude, I realize I have only begun to understand it.

I am still the darkness, through and through. Yet, she is the light guiding us home. Her numb lips try to form words, but the cold seizes her frail, mortal body and tries to steal that light from me. Her lashes droop. Her shivering stops. The pendant slips from her fingers.

Gathering her and her precious cargo into my arms, I

attempt to *flicker* her inside but go nowhere.

"FUCK!" My bellow echoes against the keep's walls. What is wrong with me?

With a fire lit in my soul, I stagger up the bank and try everything to warm her. The shadows won't touch her. The air won't heat around her. Her heart is slowing, and I don't know what to do.

Somehow, I get through the gate and shoulder through the castle's front doors, leaving wet tracks behind. Never in my life have I asked for help, but I scream for it now until my throat is hoarse.

"Help! Someone help us!"

I'm already down the hall and halfway up the stairs when Finch shouts from somewhere below, "Master Fox?"

"She fell into the moat," I croak, my feet still climbing the stairs. I don't know why. I don't know if I should turn back and take her somewhere else.

"The bath!" Cricket shouts. "Warm her up."

Yes. The bath. The eternal Wellspring fills the tub. I am jogging with her now, navigating the hallways in a panic. It's after midnight. The castle has changed. Rooms are not where they were. Bodin appears like an apparition from the shadows, sleepy-eyed and dressed in loose night pants.

"I need—"

"There." He points across the hall. "You're in there."

I barge through the door, enter the bathroom, and climb into the always-filled tub. Warm water overflows as we sit, her in my lap, my arms around her cold, unmoving body. Her fingers are pale claws gripping the little star. She feels like a corpse.

"What now?" My gaze darts to Bodin as he hurries in.

Legion and Varen are behind, similarly dressed, shirtless, and in loose pants.

"Massage her heart," Legion orders. "With your wraith's hands."

The sluggish sound of it beating is the nightmare on my shoulder, the thing in the corner whispering in my ear. *She's going to die.*

"I can't," I choke out, frowning. "My magic won't work around her. I don't know what's happening."

"Excuse me, coming through." Cricket pushes past the others, eyes wild and hair a mess from sleep. She looks at Willow's limp form, drops to her knees, and presses her fingers beneath her jaw. Cricket stares into the distance and counts quietly.

"What are you doing?" I ask.

"Shh." She scowls, then returns to staring into space. Her hands drop. "Her pulse is weak, but she's alive."

"I could have told you that," I snap. "I hear her heart as if it's my own."

"Don't you take that tone with me, Master Fox." She waggles her finger in my face. "I'll be damned if this nonsense wasn't something you cooked up with the way you've behaved lately. And is that blood in your nails?"

Guilt slams into me.

This is my fault. Everything tonight is my fault.

My eyes widen. From the first time we met Cricket and Finch squatting in our castle, she saw straight through me. Both flawless in appearance, they were Nevers herded up as part of Titania's new regime. She conquered this newly awoken realm like a Lion conquers mice. So much magic had been drained from the land to build this empire. Cricket and Finch were ordered to work in the Ivory Palace, separated after a decade of marriage. We should have turned them in, but I saw the first wrinkles of age dawning at the edges of their mortal eyes. It was only a matter of time before Titania changed their status from Never to Nothing and banished them to the subterranean.

So I changed their appearances, hiding their fate, and lied to the hive about what I'd done. They would never have understood without memories of what we learned in Elphyne. That was when Cricket figured out I was not like the others.

But she's kept my secret. She's swept my lies under the rug and never asks questions. She cleans up after my messes.

I lost control of myself in Burn After Reading. It is like Willow said. I'm ruining her.

She stirs, and my heart soars.

"Tinger," she slurs.

I cover her hand with mine, remind her it's there. "You have him."

She blinks. "Where am I?"

"In my tub."

Her body turns to stone in my arms. Her lips try to form words, her eyes dart. "No," she whispers. "Water."

"I've got you." I tighten my arms around her. "Feel that? It's real. My arms are real."

She violently twists in my arms, splashes, and pierces me with frightened golden eyes. So afraid she can't speak. Her free hand claws at me, trying to climb out *over* me.

"I'm here," I clamp down and squeeze, trying to blanket her body with my arms. It's a stupid notion. But I want to cocoon her with me, not with water. I hold her gaze and murmur, "I'm not leaving. I'm here."

I feel the moment she decides to trust me. It's a click against my soul. A burning between the ribs.

"You won't leave?" she chokes.

"Never."

"Won't let go?"

"Not while we're in here."

Sighing, she sinks into me and mumbles something delirious about her warm blanket.

The silence in the bathroom is deafening. I know they're all watching me, wondering who the fuck I am to behave like this.

"She'll live," Cricket says, dusting her nightgown. "When her color returns, put her in your bed all snug. I'll bring warm cocoa."

"Whiskey," Finch grunts.

"I think she's had enough grog, love." Cricket pats his chest. "But we can have it on standby."

After the mortals leave, I want to bask in the warmth, my arms around Willow, and listen to her pulse grow strong. Legion sours the mood when he perches on the tub's stone edge, long graceful legs dominating the space. Bodin rests against the wall, folds his muscular arms, and stares at me. Varen remains in the doorway. They are half-starved, and here I am, filled to the brim with sustenance, soaking in the tub.

"What happened?" Legion's demand is curt and sharp.

"Has Emrys arrived?" I return, finding myself too cowardly to relay the night's events alone.

"Not yet," he replies. "Does he need to be?"

Willow knows about Styx, I want to say. But what comes out is, "I have fed."

Their eyes widen. Hunger peers out.

As if knowing his fate, the soul inside me stirs and buzzes against his cage. Legion's head cants, almost as if he hears. I watch him, waiting to see if he recognizes or feels what I do. But our hive state is nowhere to be found. Just another whisper on the wind of time.

I thought if anything were to push through that barrier, it would be the soul swarming inside me. The Wild Hunt can grow enormous because of our hive's joint custody of the horde. Other dragon-bonded are mere echoes of us, inferior copies they created after our unit grew too powerful to tame. To avoid making the same mistake, they distributed power among many.

*Divide and conquer* is Titania's favorite motto.

"Who?" Legion asks.

"All of Milford . . . and a mortal snack."

He stands, schools his face to something unreadable, and nods toward Varen. "Give him the snack and the complete soul to the wildling."

I sigh. "Emrys said the same thing, but we cannot retain sustenance from the Wild Hunt until he can live inside us."

For that, we need the hive state.

"Then we are in agreement." Legion gestures at Bodin. "Let's go."

"That's not what I meant," I growl. "I can split the soul— carve him up for each of you. Denying your hunger isn't helping." I squeeze Willow, then sigh as the truth dawns on me. In my shame, I've tried to ignore our baser instincts. I've kept my feeding to tiny morsels, thinking that made me less of a monster. But my brothers need more. "Midnight adventures are no longer tenable. Tomorrow, I will embrace the hunt."

"No," Legion replies, eyes hardening. "Your meal already puts Styx in danger. If more High Fae disappear, the Keepers will know it's us. To gain this much power from mortal souls, you will leave a trail of unexplained disappearances and husks. We have enough to worry about with the Wild Hunt being exposed."

Bodin adds, "They already fabricate disasters so we must leave the keep. It won't be long before they're foolish enough to infiltrate and kill the wildling."

I clench my jaw, silently defying them.

"Fox." The authority in his tone draws my gaze. "You are the Fifth."

"Fuck you."

"Do as you're told." Legion storms out.

"I'll find the wildling," Bodin sighs, then leaves too.

I glance at Varen, who stares at Willow snoozing softly in my arms. One look at her and every ounce of unease melts away.

"Moisture is bad for bees," he mumbles.

"Water is okay for Willow," I reply. "Cricket says she needs the warmth."

He stares at me. "On severely wet or cold days, bees form a dense cluster around their queen to keep her warm. She can't have her wings wet."

"Willow is not a bee, Varen." It's hard to hide my impatience. I feel my body tensing, already anticipating his rage. Occasionally, I think he's trying to tell us something but can't form the right words and lashes out. But when I listen in on his thoughts, it's nonsense.

He needs another shave, and I know the others are right. Varen should be fed first. The hungrier he is, the less he makes sense, and the more volatile he is. He scrubs his hand through his hair, a wildness filling his eyes as he stares at the tub water.

"Bees can't be *wet*," he insists. "They go *cold* and *numb* and can't do anything until they dry and get warm." He starts pacing, now arguing with himself. "But they can't shiver their wings to generate heat if wet, so how can they grow warm?"

"Varen," I grumble. "She's not a bee. It's okay if she's wet. I'm not going to let her drown."

He strides beside the tub, mumbling facts like a puzzling equation. He won't calm down at this rate. I glance at Willow and see more color in her cheeks. Her pulse is stronger.

Varen faces me and opens his mouth, but I speak first. "Fine, we'll get out."

His jaw clicks shut.

"But first let me feed you."

He steps back. I don't know why he constantly resists sustenance, but tonight, he glances at Willow and shuffles closer again. He kneels and grips the tub with white knuckles, then closes his eyes and mumbles, "Adult drones don't feed themselves but depend on nurse bees to feed them."

"So I'm a nurse now, am I?" Great. Readjusting Willow to one arm, I slide my hand around his nape. "Give me your mouth."

He flattens his lips, refusing.

"Varen," I warn. "It won't hurt. It will feel good. You need to be healthy to look after our queen."

Anguish wrinkles his face. He holds his eyes shut, but nods. "A well-reared, healthy drone can produce 5–10 million sperm."

I laugh. Whatever. I seal my lips over his, and for once, he opens. I release the lid holding the morsels of soul at bay. Varen's skin warms as he takes what I give. The tension leaves his neck.

I don't give him everything, despite what the others said. Fuck them. I'll force it down their throats too. When I'm done, I let go of Varen, and he opens his drunken eyes. Color has returned to his cheeks.

"You good?" I ask.

He shudders, confused, then starts mentioning more facts about wet bee wings.

"Okay, fine. Let's get her out."

Together, we lift Willow out of the bath. She whimpers, but Varen is right. She can't sit in water all night. She rouses enough to hear me ask if she's okay letting us help her dry and dress.

At first, she stubbornly tries to do it herself, but after she almost slips, she admits she needs help. We peel her out of her wet clothes. I must be a saint, not a devil, because my eyes remain on her face the entire time. I tug a clean, soft shirt from my closet over her head. She only lets go of her pendant so I can secure it around her neck.

While gently drying her hair, I notice a bump on her head and frown. She must have hit it during her fall. I glance at Varen, who looks on with concern. Did he know about this? Is that why he wanted her out of the bath?

I move to heal her, but his fingers lock around my wrist. "She has a stinger, but it's only to kill rival burgundy queens."

"You're killing *me*, Varen."

Willow rouses at my impatient tone. "What are you doing?"

"Can I heal you?" I ask softly.

She nods and sinks against my chest, burrowing her arms around me. My heart stops. Before it stays that way, I quickly heal the bump. Oddly, my powers listen to me.

After I help her crawl under the covers on my bed, I try to tuck her tight like Cricket said. But then Varen yanks the quilt from my hands, slides in behind her, and wraps her in his arms.

"Um . . . Varen." My thumb points away from the bed. "Out."

Annoyed, he mumbles something about a queen's pheromones, making me more uncomfortable. But then, "She lets the hive know she is well through her pheromones."

"It's okay," Willow mumbles, patting his hand over her heart. "He's just happy you got him bee bread."

An amused snort slips out of me before I can stop it. She sounds delirious; I shouldn't find that funny.

"I'll take him to his room," I offer.

Her lashes lift halfway, still drunk. "Maybe he's right. Maybe you need to listen to him more."

He said bees form a dense cluster around their queen to keep her warm.

"Fine." I slip under the covers and get as close to her as I can, shaking my head. "I'm fucking clustering, but I draw the line at vibrating my wings, Varen. Happy?"

He scowls as if it's not enough.

Her breathy sigh of contentment tickles my neck, but then her brows pucker.

"Willow," I whisper. "Do you want us to leave?"

Her eyes squeeze shut. "Why won't you ... glamour me?"

My heart clenches. I hunt for damage but find nothing new. "What do you mean?"

Her lips part. She tries to say something but coughs as if her words hurt. "Never mind."

Her silence extends, but that crease remains. I try to smooth it with my thumb, but the stubborn little wolf holds her tension. I don't want to argue, so let my hand trail down her cheek. When I reach her old scars, I linger. And linger. And linger.

I brush my thumb over them, savoring the sensation. When she tries to pull away, I won't let her.

"Are these what you mean?" I ask.

Her breath hitches. "Sort of."

"Willow . . ." I lick my lips, trying to find the right words.

Finally, after her breathing evens out, I confess the truth. "I'm a selfish bastard. I don't want your scars gone." Another attempt. "The berserker rage between queens might be uncontrollable, but you gave everything you had to win." No, that's fucking wrong too. "Queens have gone insane with fear when they from learning what they inherited in us, but I see your scars and know . . ." Another failed attempt. I graze the tiny scars on her cheek. "I see these, and I am filled with pride that you fought for us." That sounds even worse. I scrub my face. "Fuck it. I'm messing this up. What I'm trying to say, Willow, is that your scars are what make you beautiful. Hiding them is hiding history, and I refuse to erase a single moment of you from our lives."

I press my forehead to hers and pray she's asleep, but I'm too cowardly to check her mind. She's breathing so quietly. Shit. She heard. I've offended her.

I brace for the disgust, the hate . . . but she tangles her legs around mine, her soft body arches into me, and she exhales. A small smile touches her lips. I breathe her air until it steadies.

Before I lose my nerve, I drop my nose to her neck and inhale her intoxicating scent deep into my lungs. Every cell in my body groans as she infuses me with an overwhelming urge to . . . to I don't know what. It's more than arousal, more than attraction or the need to claim her. This is a bone-deep desire to keep her here forever, protect, feed, hold, and comfort her. It is the same bouquet as before, yet it feels so much stronger. I know, logically, she has no magic. She cannot complete the ritual to bond with us. Yet there is no better scent in the world than her lily, lavender, musk, and—my eyes flip open.

"I smell Titania," I snarl, shocked. "I smell a curse."

# THIRTY-SEVEN

### WILLOW

I wake to a familiar weight on my chest and smile at the baby Wild Hunt's snoring lullaby. I'm warm and cozy and almost want to return to sleep, but I force my lashes to lift. Repetitive gouge marks on the ceiling let me know where I am. I count Fox's tally. He's added a few more marks. *Interesting.* Maybe he wasn't counting the days until they met me.

The baby dragon's horn is perilously close to stabbing me. His head is twice the size as before. Black eyelids cover the eyes beneath the bone sockets. Little cute lashes fan the space beneath. Black shimmering scales ripple as he moves and huffs. I crane further and see that he's bigger everywhere. Once the size of Tinger, he has doubled overnight.

*Tinger.*

My hand slaps over the pendant. He's here. Thank the Well.

Last night's events crash into me. The feast, the Corner-twister, Fox kissing me, ditching me, the Burn After Reading shenanigans. My stomach flutters when I recall Fox feeding on Irisa, but then I scowl when I remember Alfie and his friends—I gasp and sit up, disturbing the wildling.

320

That Radiant, that *fae-fucker,* had pulled me onto his lap and told me to play hide and seek for a charm in his pants. Those bitches fed me to him. And Alfie—a ball gets lodged in my throat —he said I could trust them.

I could barely walk straight from all the booze they plied me with. Fox had unleashed on the Radiant. He consumed every last vital cell in his body. Then he *flickered* me home, but something went wrong with his magic. My mind scrambles to piece together more. He tried to help me across the bridge, but I refused. I fell. He dove in after me. *Saved* me. Then went back for Tinger. Afterward, I think a warm bath was involved, and now I'm in his bed, in his shirt. Was Varen here, too? Cricket?

Or was it all a dream?

"Get off, sleepy head." I push the heavy skull from my legs.

One black eye opens. He has the decency to look guilty, then scrambles away and settles on Fox's pillow with a snort of shadow.

I toss the covers, go to the toilet, and wash my face in the basin. So much has happened in the space of a few days I'm reeling. But most of all, I feel less alone this morning—more at peace.

Braving a look in the mirror, shock barrels through me. Am I still dreaming, or is my ugliness less . . . ugly today? The scars are smaller, closer toward their old silvery lines. The bulges and malformed angles are less . . . I poke and prod . . . less obvious.

Why?

Alarmed at the difference, I rest my hips on the basin and contemplate the floor. Something monumental shifted last night. Between the feast, Fox's kiss, Alfie and his friends, and almost losing Tinger, almost drowning. I rub that tight spot in my chest—I *need* to understand it.

Pushing off the basin, I pad through Fox's room but find no sign of him. A glance outside the window reveals I've slept most of the day. Shit. I promised Geraldine and the others I'd spend time with them this weekend. I'd better hurry and find Fox, then.

His bedroom door leads to the hallway, not another room. A few steps down the corridor, the cold temperature seeps into my system. I should have brought a blanket, but when the scent of burning wood lures me into the library, I linger in the warmer air. The fireplace simmers with old logs and dying embers. It's been on for a while.

Tugging the shirt down my thighs, I search the long, shelved room and find Fox hunched over a table, sleeping on an open book. A dark blanket covers his shoulders, but his feet are bare and sticking out at an odd angle.

The round spectacles from his room are beside him, still without glass lenses.

As I approach, I realize the blanket is actually his draconic wings. They drape majestically down his spine in a silken, tattered waterfall. Two curved, stubby horns protrude from short, disheveled hair. His wings hug him because he's only wearing cotton drawstring pants.

Biting my lip, I remember something else from last night.

I shouldn't be able to recall what happened at Burn After Reading last night. But here I am, staring at Fox's fully dark Sluagh form, and I'm not afraid.

After he consumed Milford, I vomited from that sparkling drink they gave me. To be honest, I vomited other drinks too. Better out than in, though.

I was close to passing out but still conscious when I heard Fox speaking with Cait. She warned him that if he didn't erase my memories, I'd always see him as a monster from witnessing his feeding of Milford. But he refused to tamper with my mind. He said, "I need her trust more."

The fluttering in my stomach intensifies. The unexplained ache in my chest vibrates, urging me to go to him.

*Touch him.*

I shouldn't.

*Do it. Just see what he feels like.*

Curious, I slide my finger along his horn. It's rougher than it looks but also oddly smooth around the inward curve. A shiver wracks his body. I jolt backward, afraid I've woken him, but he remains asleep. My gaze continues down to his forehead, smooth skin, and lands on the glowing teardrop twinkling beneath his long-lashed eye.

He's so innocent like this, so vulnerable and trusting. How can he be my enemy? If he said receiving the Guardian's blessing changed their entire perspective, it must have been a horrible, confusing, and self-flagellating time. From being the hand of death for eons to suddenly understanding why their victims screamed in horror, what being called a monster actually meant . . . I bite my lip, hating how many times I tossed that word so carelessly.

Maybe they made mistakes while they figured things out.

I know I did.

He wakes with a sharp inhale through the nose, startling me.

"Willow." His voice is husky from sleep. "What are you doing here?"

"Um, I—"

Shit. Caught red-handed. His eyes flare at his wings. His otherness is gone in a flash. Now he can't look at me. He shifts around the items on the table, organizing them into useless piles.

He's embarrassed. Ashamed.

"Hey." I perch on the table's edge, stretch my legs, and cross my ankles. "You don't need to hide yourself from me."

His gaze snags on my bare thigh, then darts to the open book. He clears his throat and turns a page, but I'm sitting on it. I tilt my hips so he can slide the book out, but his cheeks flush bright red.

I fluster him. *Me.*

My fingers test the skin around my scars, reminding myself it's not as bad as I thought. *I'm* not so bad.

"What are you reading?" I ask.

"Nothing. Everything. All of it."

A nervous laugh. "Okay."

Agitated, he stares hard at his book for a few heartbeats, clenching his jaw. Finally, he lifts his gaze to mine and asks, "Do you still think I'm a monster?"

Silence.

Guilt stabs my heart.

"You saved my life, Fox," I whisper. "You stopped me from drowning. I don't think a monster is capable of that, do you?"

Gray eyes harden to steel as he declares, "I would drink every drop of water in existence if it meant saving you from drowning."

It's hard to breathe. I believe him. Fuck. What does that mean? More nervous laughter bubbles out of me. "Let's hope it will never get to that."

"So . . ." His lashes lower, all shy again. "Even after seeing me . . . you know, with the heart and the teeth and the, you know . . . and the—" He mimes some kind of action with clawed hands I can't understand. "You know. That."

My brows lift. "Are you talking about what you did to Milford?"

"He deserved it." His mood darkens to dangerous levels. "Some of the shit I've seen him do in there is deplorable. Unforgivable. His existence has eaten at me for years. So I'm not sorry."

He stares at me, waiting for something. A reprimand? A fight? Disgust?

"Milford wasn't a good person, Fox." My lips curve slightly at his obvious relief. "I'm not saying it's okay to run around

CASTLE OF NEVERS AND NIGHTMARES

murdering anyone who pisses you off, but you wouldn't have been in that position if it wasn't for me."

Anyone who takes advantage of drunk, vulnerable people is an asshole of the worst kind.

He plucks the edges of the book. "So . . . I shouldn't go around murdering people who piss me off."

I try not to laugh. He's serious. As he contemplates the book like it holds the answers to life, I remember why I came here.

"Fox. Can I ask you a question?"

"Anything." Hopeful eyes swing my way. "Whatever you need."

How can he be so perfect? It's confusing the shit out of me.

"Actually, I have a few. Why did you leave Elphyne?" A wave of panic rolls through me. I've made guesses, and they all involve Titania, but I need to hear it from his lips. "If I was to be some kind of fated queen to end all queens for you, why leave me?"

"Not *was*, Willow," he reminds. "You *are* our fated queen. Present tense."

"You know what I mean."

He considers something, then sits back on his seat, sprawling his legs, gifting me with the perfect pose accentuating his magnificently sculpted body. His thoughts seem far away, so I don't think he notices the way my heart rate spikes.

"It's a long story," he eventually says. "But you need to hear it."

All I can manage is a nod.

"Wait here." He leaves me to wander the shelves and search the books. Every so often, he pulls one out, opens it, then closes it. When he returns, he sits and places an old hand-illustrated manuscript down before him. He finds a page with three females and taps them. "In the beginning, the Morrigan arose as one of the primeval triple war goddess representations of the Cauldron —the eternal Wellspring."

"The Well."

"Same thing." He nods, then flips the page. Ravens and shadows surround a dark, hooded female. "About 2500 BC, her popularity with warring humanity rose to such significance that she had the power to birth seven original demigod offspring." He flips the page. Seven darkly hideous creatures stand side by side —the Sluagh.

"They look nothing like you," I gasp.

He shoots me a crooked smile. "Our hotness came later. But thanks for noticing."

I snort. "My apologies, oh radiant demigod of sexiness. Do continue."

"That's better, pet," he jokes, stares intensely at me, then returns to the book. "As I was saying . . . what was I saying? Oh, yes." He clears his throat. "Other Sluagh were eventually created after us, but none were as potent as the first seven. They terrorized the world unchecked and became too wild to contain, each soul consumed helping them grow in power . . . even to the point they rivaled the Morrigan herself."

Shit. I move to stand behind his seated form, and lean over his shoulder to read the book, now completely riveted. "What happened?"

He tenses when the length of my body presses against his arm. I didn't mean to get so close.

*Don't move,* that nagging inner voice urges me. *Press closer.*

Fox flips the page to an image of a cauldron tipping, and seven figures fall out of its dark liquid.

"The Cauldron was out of balance," he explains, voice somewhat rough. "So it formed more deities."

I lean into his space and turn the page. Ten deities are lined up, each with a name. Five are light. Five are dark.

"Danu, Dagda, Brighid, Rhiannon, Aine," I mumble. "They're

the light. And so the Morrigan, Cernunnos, Arawn, Nicnevin, and Caber are the dark. This is fascinating. Do they still exist?"

"Oh, yes." His lips flatten. "And they're still at war."

I open my mouth to ask more, but he shuts me down.

"You wanted to know why we left you," he points out, face angling toward me. "The reason why starts here."

"Sorry. Go on." The next page reveals the same symbol on the Keepers of the Cauldron. "They were formed to control you?"

"In a way," he replies. "Druidic worship allowed communication between the deities and the beings of this realm. The seven original sons were too powerful and destructive, so the Keepers and the light deities banded together and bound us for long hibernation. The Morrigan was furious. To avoid more imbalance, they appeased her by allowing us periods of controlled release where the souls we fed on were trapped in a ghostly parade called the Wild Hunt. Unable to survive without these souls, the Sluagh had to remain close to the parade. Thus, their reign of unchecked terror ended."

Fox's gaze grows unfocused. He no longer turns pages but instead seems to be reliving the events he relays.

"Each time they hibernated, they grew closer in the confines. A hive mentality started to form. This was the Morrigan fighting against their containment. They became stronger together, indestructible. Then, with the Morrigan's help, a young, ambitious Unseelie noble seized control of their hibernation seals from the druids. For a time, he could summon them at will and use them any way he wanted. He even learned to distill aphrodisiac philters and elixirs from the byproduct of their feedings."

He stops speaking altogether.

"Fox?"

He shudders, shakes his head, and clears his throat. "Long story short, the other dark deities and the Keepers worked together to tame the Wild Hunt. This resulted in queens collaring them, starting with Titania."

He sits back. Tension rides every ounce of his body. His hands clench, his jaw works, and his muscles are rock hard. He never once said "us" or "we" but it's clear those first seven were Fox and his hive. I've known for a while that Maebh killed their seventh a long time ago in Elphyne. But his reaction when speaking about the Unseelie noble feels like a horrific memory.

"Titania summoned you?" I ask. "That's why you suddenly left me in Elphyne?"

A quiet nod is my answer. More clenching of the fists. "She'd slumbered for thousands of years, but the queen link passed down from queen to queen. With each reign, we changed." He gestures at his face. "We took something from each and became what they desired. But we never understood why they wanted us to look this way until . . . we understood disgust and shame."

I can't help myself. I touch the blue, glowing Guardian teardrop beneath his eye. "How did this happen?"

"When Maebh killed our seventh," he continues, still staring into space, "the Morrigan wept for the loss of her son. And we were tired, so tired of our endless cycle of suffering. So, while her back was turned, we wished for oblivion. Instead, the other deities made us an offer. If we accepted their blessing while the Morrigan's back was turned, then they would give us a new queen who would treat us as equals. They never explained how the blessing would change us."

"They tricked you?"

He shrugs. "It didn't stop us from yearning for freedom."

"Independence from needing a queen." I nod solemnly.

"That's not true freedom for us now, and I think that's the rub. With our blessing, we understand how dangerous it is for us to roam free. We might have a tiny drop of goodness in us, Willow, but there's far more of the dark." He goes quiet. "You saw what I did to Milford. Imagine six of us losing control, acting with one mind, using the Wild Hunt to sate our hunger."

My heart aches for them.

"So what is it, then?" I ask. "What is true freedom for you?"

His sad eyes collide with mine. "Unconditional love."

# CHAPTER
# THIRTY-EIGHT
## WILLOW

The yearning in Fox's eyes forces me back. I can't be this person for him. I'm the wrong woman. He misunderstands my retreat. His expression drops, as it always does when I call him a monster.

"I can't be your queen," I insist. "I can't be the one to magically rein you in when I have no magic."

"Then why do I feel like this?" he asks, rounding on me. "Why do you?"

"I don't know." I rub my sternum.

"You have to be," he insists, taking my hands. "You're the one. I know it."

"How?"

"You're here," he points out. "You traveled all this way alone, and you're *here*."

"But I came for revenge."

"You don't want that now, right?"

A sigh leaves my lips. "I don't know. That's not—"

"She's cursed you." Danger flares in his eyes. "I can smell it on you."

330

The air solidifies in my lungs. He knows?

"You probably can't talk about it," he murmurs thoughtfully, running his gaze over my body, marking every pore and freckle like a constellation in the night sky. "She's probably forbidden you to speak about it, but I know it's here somewhere. I scented her magic on you last night. I can't for my life find signs of what the curse does to you."

How can he not see it all over my face?

"Wh-what do you think I look like?"

"Beautiful." His answer is immediate. Definitive. Unwavering. "Like our always queen."

I avert my gaze and shake my head, but he lifts my chin.

"Willow. That she's cursed you means you're still a threat to her. With or without your power, she's terrified of you." His apprehensive eyes dart between mine. "Can't you see what that means?"

"Maybe she's just a petty bitch."

He laughs. "Oh, she's petty, alright. But only for those who threaten her power."

"She found me because I dreamed of you, that's all."

"You did?"

"It was just dancing. But I remember the city was much like this one. Are you telling me it was probably a public dreamscape?"

"It makes sense. Dancing with us undermined her authority. You might have dreamed secrets that shouldn't have been revealed. Like our wings or—"

"I did. I dreamed you all had wings, and we danced above everyone else."

His lips curve. "Is that something you want? To dance with us in the clouds?"

"That's not the point."

"You're right. The point is, if you didn't dream of us, she

would have carried on, never caring about your existence. But for your dreamscape to travel here from Elphyne . . . that's . . . that's something."

"That's embarrassing."

"My magic has been erratic around you lately. Until now, I never understood why." He looks at his hands wrapping mine. "I think we've already started bonding with you."

"What?" I step back, my pulse racing.

He moves forward, refusing to allow me space. My back hits the table, jostling the contents on top.

"After Legion touched you on that battlefield, we developed the ability to shift and to walk under the sun."

"From me?"

"We echo our queen so we can protect her best. When she orders us," he explains, "we must obey. Our nature is to revere and submit to her. So when you refused my help last night, my magic wouldn't work properly. But when you were drowning, and I needed to *flicker* to save your life, it suddenly worked again." His expression becomes serious. "Willow, you belong to us."

"Fox . . ."

"Deny it. Try." He cages me in with his hands.

My mouth opens and closes. Nothing comes out. I don't know how to answer. I'm just confused.

"Being our queen means you're ours, but we're also yours." His tone lowers as he inhales my scent, eyes fluttering as if I'm a drug. "*All* of us. I just need to make the others remember somehow."

"All of you . . ." I repeat. *At once?*

"We'll bow to you, obey, worship, pleasure, feed, and protect you with our eternal lives. We'll exist for you and only for you because you are our skin. Without you, we fall apart."

Worship . . . pleasure . . . an image flashes in my mind—me, surrounded by all of them. Hot, naked, sweaty. Arousal vibrates down to my core, spreading hot, prickly, uncontrollable need. It's so sudden and violent I fear my heat has unexpectedly come on, even though I'm not due for a month. The only other time a shifter feels like this is when they meet their mate.

"I need time to think, Fox." My body tells me one thing, but my head whispers another. Half a lifetime of hatred for them is not so easily erased.

He eases back, sits on his chair, and spears fingers through his hair. "Of course."

Those two little words do more for me than anything else. He'll wait for me. This demigod of darkness will wait until I tell him I'm ready.

I could walk out right now, and despite everything he's confessed, there's no doubt in my mind that he'll let me go. But if he thinks I'm in an ounce of danger, he'll find me.

*Go to him.*

That damn ache in my chest is back, making demands.

*Touch him. Be one with him.*

Maybe he's right. Maybe we are fated.

*Yes. This is what you're made for.*

My parents hated each other, but look how they turned out. They're still hopelessly in love.

"Okay, maybe I have one other question," I blurt, needing to change the subject. My thoughts flit to the gouge marks on his ceiling. I perch on the table, stretching my legs again beside his chair.

His gaze lingers on my bare legs. "Anything."

"What were you counting? I've seen the tally marks."

A bashful blush stains his cheeks.

"Oh, now I have to know." A teasing smile tugs at my lips. "You said *anything*."

"You'll laugh."

"Promise. I won't."

His lips press together, and he shakes his head.

"Fox," I warn. "Tell me."

He covers his face with his hands.

"Seriously? You want to play coy?" An indignant laugh chuffs out of me. "You don't know me well if you think I'll give up." I grit my teeth and yank on his hands. He holds them firm on his face. "Grr. *Fox.*" Another tug. He giggles. *Well-damn* giggles. Competitive outrage fills me. "Oh, game on."

I launch off the table and onto his lap, using every ounce of my strength to wrestle his hands from his face. Each time he thwarts me, our hysterics increase. He's too damn strong to beat in a tug-of-war, and I almost give up, but then my elbow slips and digs into his ribs. His giggles intensify.

"Ticklish," I gush. "Ooh, you're ticklish!"

Unluckily for him, I have two sisters who are the same. I terrorize his vulnerable torso with my fingers, digging and stabbing all the soft spots until he's a squealing ball of giggling nerves. "Stop, stop!"

"Never," I declare, and increase my efforts. "Unless you tell me what I want to know."

With his hands on his face, his armpits are exposed. I'm not a squeamish girl. I don't give a shit about hair or male sweat. My lips curve, and I go for them. He throws his head back, roaring and half squeaking with laughter.

"You're a little mouse!" I tease, tickling. "Squeak squeak."

His grin deepens his dimples and lights up a face that looked so forlorn and dejected moments ago. His joy is an arrow to my heart, burrowing deep, hooking its barbed head into the core. He takes advantage of my pause and bands steel arms around me, pinning my arms to my sides. He presses our bodies together hard, enforcing the friction where I straddle him.

We don't need to break eye contact to know we're both

extremely aroused. I have no underwear on, and his thin cotton pants rapidly dampen where his erection presses against me. He flexes. I gasp. A thousand sparks shoot fire around my body. Within seconds, I am breathless and prickly with desire.

Fox's long, shuddering groan blooms against my lips.

"You're wet for me," he murmurs.

He sounds surprised, almost awed, as if my desire is a gift he never expected, not the other way around. I squirm, and he bands his arms harder with another lust-filled groan. I shouldn't be doing this. But *this* feels so good, so much better than the fever heat.

Here, I am in control. Here, I'm not a slave to my wolfish biology, not afraid of it. Not afraid of him mistreating me, using me, or taking something precious I'm not ready to give.

"You don't know how many nights I've dreamed of this," Fox whispers hoarsely, gaze dipping between us. Except he can't see where we join. We're squashed too tightly.

I remember his bashfulness when I accidentally flashed him in his room.

"A couple of days?"

Hot, reproachful eyes collide with mine.

"Try *thousands*," he grinds out, jaw flexing. "Five thousand, nine hundred and eighty-eight, to be exact."

The tally. "*This* is what you're counting?"

"You promised you wouldn't laugh," Fox breathes.

"I'm not. I'm just . . ." I do the math. "How could it have been that long? I was only a child."

"I didn't mean—*fuck.* It wasn't your actual . . ." He releases me and sits back, covering his face again. But this time, he confesses everything in a rush, his voice muffled behind his hands. "We didn't understand what was happening to our bodies. We weren't attracted to *you* as a child, but the idea of you as our queen. Previously, queens came to us as adults. That's all we understood. Varen's visions were always of you like this, an adult, our equal. When the old-world females mated with the Guardians in Elphyne, we started to . . . *banshee's balls,* this is so hard to say."

"I'm right here, Fox." I rest my hand on his forearm.

He refuses to drop his hands, takes a deep breath, and clears his throat. "We awoke . . . desires we never knew existed. We saw things were different between them. We learned how it was meant to be between lovers through watching them and learning. We started hoping . . . dreaming we could have that too." He trails off.

I feel bad. What if something bad happened to him while he was with the other queens? "You don't have to tell me. I get it."

His hands slide down his face, but he's not embarrassed. The heat is back, a thousand times more intense than before.

"While we waited for you," he says, tone deepening, sliding his hands attentively up my thighs. "We wanted to learn how to pleasure you, how to keep you satisfied. One of us had the bright idea to see a courtesan. I was the most eager, so I volunteered while the others watched the lesson from my mind." His gaze runs a path down my front, lowering to where his shirt barely covers the apex of my thighs. He cants his head as if he's imagining me there. "It was so arousing to have her react to my tongue that way, and yet, I kept thinking . . . what if it was *our* queen? What would she taste like? Would she make those little moaning sounds or something else? The idea of your pussy on my lips was so fucking irresistible that I—" He swallows, looks up at me. "I, ah, finished in my pants."

My cheeks heat.

I don't have enough experience, personally, but I've heard stories. My aunts are very loud sometimes with their girl talk. They gather regularly for what my Aunt Laurel calls cock-tales. It's weird they named a drink after gossiping about their partner's penises, but whatever. They all thought it was sexy when their male was so turned on by them they couldn't contain themselves.

"Um. I think finishing like that is normal. Sometimes. I hear."

Fox shoots me a wry look. "*Once*. It happened once. But it was enough for me to realize how special that feeling was. How personal. It was wrong to give it to anyone else, so when I returned home, I forbade the others from experiencing that

337

sensation with anyone else but you. And then I found an hour-glass, sat at the kitchen table, and started counting."

I bite my lower lip. "So you haven't since . . . I mean, that's a lot of . . ."

"A lot of planning." Gray eyes darken. "Fantasizing." He eases off his chair and crowds me, forcing me to lean back on the table. "Thinking of your taste." He swipes the books from beneath me, clearing the surface. "Imagining all the ways to pleasure you. Coming up with special moves." He lowers me the rest of the way. "Learning how to make you scream." He nips my jaw. His voice deepens. "Just say when, little wolf, and I'll make a meal out of you."

Warm breath tickles my lips as he waits for permission. No longer bashful, no longer hesitant, he is the picture of control, strong arms locked at my side, hips nestled between my thighs. Unmoving. Barely breathing. Waiting for me to tell him I want this.

I've never been so aroused in my life. My skin feels too tight for my body. My nipples are hard peaks. I ache from the brutal press of his erection against my pussy. I'm drenching his pants, but he doesn't care. He watches my lips like they're the starting line holding him back. My galloping heart is the ticking clock. A bead of sweat forms on his brow, sliding down his temple.

So many reasons to walk away flood my mind. Someone could walk in. This is crossing a line. Maybe I care. Maybe I don't. I don't know everything about them yet, but will I ever? If we do this, what will *this* mean? But even as the thoughts fire in my mind, my body language is louder. My hips roll into his, chasing friction. I whimper, needing, begging.

But he waits. He stares at my lips.

So I say the word he's waiting to hear. "When."

He explodes into action, ripping open my shirt and planting kisses on my neck, devouring every inch of my skin. I suck in a hissing breath. *Hot, greedy mouth.* More. I need more. He breaks away to capture my mouth, to kiss me with fast, brutal demand. He steals my breath and then returns to my body, ravenously making his way south. I know where he's going—it's inevitable. It shouldn't feel so damn incendiary, but I yearn for him to get there. I'm an impatient bitch who's spent half her life dreaming of this moment, too.

I just never knew it was with him. Them. Him. Fuck, I don't know, just that I need him there—easing the sweet ache with his tongue. Glancing down, I growl, "Horns. Give them to me."

They erupt from his head at my command. I use them to push him down, fitting his lips where they belong. The moment his tongue connects with my clit, I cry out and arch into him. He smiles against my intimate flesh, a deep chuckle in his throat. I snarl at his slowed pace, give his horns a warning tug, and then he spears his tongue into my entrance. He drives in deep, licks the seam between my folds, showers my pussy with attention.

So good it hurts.

When he stops, I moan, "Again."

He humors my whims. Panders to my desires.

"Fox!" I cry out, quivering into him when he hits a sensitive spot. "There!"

His long, savoring groan is my answer. His tongue lashes my clit, tasting me everywhere. With each expert move, I submit to the rising bliss. My grip slackens around his horns, and I melt against the table. It might be frozen outside, but it's an inferno in here.

"You taste so good," he murmurs between licks. "So fucking good."

Faster and faster, he works me, shooting my pleasure point into the sky. Everything tightens. Coils. I'm a gasping mess, whimpering, moaning. I don't know how much more of this I can take. It's too much.

"Fox," I plead, not quite knowing what I need.

"I've got you, love." He pushes a finger into my tight entrance as he flicks his tongue. He explores my inner walls, and then pumps in and out. My eyes roll. So good—so right. The combination of his fluttering tongue and punishing finger is a dynamic rhythm of contrasts.

For someone who's only done this once, he is a master. Pleasure intensifies, threatening to consume me. A keening wail slips from my lips. I bite my lip to stop it. My head thrashes, but I'm so tight, so wound up, so close to something big. I whimper. Pant. Beg for more.

"Come for me, my queen," he groans, sliding my wetness over my seam. "Yes," he moans, gliding his fingers from clit to ass. His hair tickles my thighs as he pulls back enough to indulge in viewing what his fingers do to me. "You love this, don't you?"

"Yes." My deep-throated moan urges him to spread my pussy lips.

"Your cunt is so fucking beautiful, Willow. Just like the rest of you." His groan is almost a growl as he pushes a second finger inside, stretching my inner walls. "You belong with us."

He drops to my clit, sucks hard, and my orgasm breaks with the force of a hurricane, ripping apart my being. Stars. Fire. Lightning. It all shatters inside me and I scream, thighs clenching around his head, spine arching off the table. He laps at me, seeing me through wave after wave of ecstasy until the storm ebbs from my body, and I collapse in the aftermath.

I cover my eyes with my forearm and try to catch my breath, try to pull my thoughts into some kind of order.

"That was . . ." I whimper when his tongue flicks me again, sparking aftershocks of pleasure. When they die, and he eases off, I push up on trembling elbows to look down the length of my torso. He reclines with a lazy grin. His mouth and nose glisten with my arousal. Bone-deep satisfaction is written over his face.

Wholly black eyes meet mine as he licks around his lips, continuing to relish what he can. Then he tosses his head back and releases a long, shuddering sigh at the ceiling.

"Fuck," he groans. "You are . . ." Another deep breath. "I lied to you."

"What?" I tense.

Black eyes level on me. "I lied when I said reality was a disappointment. You're so much better than I ever dreamed."

"But I didn't do anything."

He rocks back on his chair's hind legs, one hand dangling at his side, the other idly swiping his lower lip. Another long exhale as he contemplates the ceiling. Is he . . . reliving the experience? Committing it to memory? Savoring?

I can't see his eyes at this angle, just the dark lashes fanning his cheeks, the thick column of his neck, the bobbing Adam's apple as he swallows. But his body is perfectly built for the pleasure of the female gaze.

He acts like going down on me is enough, that his dream has come true. But he's never had the experience of a woman go down on him. Something animal has awakened in me. Something possessive. I need to be the first one with my lips around his cock. I quietly slide off the table and lower to my knees. When I place my hands on his thighs, he startles. Tenses. Sucks in a breath. His chair crashes onto all fours.

"What are you doing?" he whispers.

I tug at the drawstring of his pants, and then ease the waistband down his narrow hips, freeing the length of his erection. Holy mother of . . . my mouth salivates at the sight of him. As with the rest of his body, his cock is crafted to perfection. Just long enough, just thick enough, just veiny enough. His musky scent blooms and unfurls in my lungs, coaxing a moan of appreciation from my throat.

I pump his length and guide the tip to my mouth, but pause.

My shuddering breath draws a glistening bead of cum at the slit of his crown. I dart my tongue out to claim it. He curses one of his gods repetitively under his breath.

Then I afford him the same respect he gave me. "Just say when, little Fox, and I'll—"

"When." He flexes his hips, bringing his tip to my lips. "When when when."

# CHAPTER
# FORTY
## FOX

Willow's plush lips part to receive my cock. But just as my fingers knot in her silken hair, and I prepare to fuck her perfect mouth, I sense someone coming.

"Stop." The word hurts to whisper when my body begs for me to continue.

Her brows pucker. She looks up at me like an innocent angel, her soul burning brightly beneath her skin. Her hair is silk spun on the moon. She glows like the stars she's crafted from. It fills every dark corner inside me, banishing the anguish from this moment.

*"Someone is coming,"* I warn her, mind-to-mind.

Golden eyes widen. *"Who?"*

I let my mind wander and feel the familiar touch of Bodin's mental fortitude. I relay who it is, and she gives my cock a forlorn look. She strokes it once, hard and impetuously, annoyed she's being interrupted. Pleasure burns up my spine, and I gasp. Footsteps grow louder. Dark desire flashes in her eyes. It's like she's considering continuing to suck me off, to let him walk in on us like this. Maybe watch us. Ah, fuck. Another drop of tingling cum beads at the tip of my cock. But then she nods and stands, buttons her shirt—*my* shirt. A few buttons are gone, so she folds her arms.

I quickly tuck my cock into my pants, but I'm not disappointed. Not in the least. Our queen isn't quite ready, but one day, she will be. One day, she'll be ready for all of us. Until then, I'll prove Varen's faith in me was right. I'll fix this mess we've found ourselves in. I'll keep her safe. Somehow.

Bodin stalks into the library, locks eyes with me, and scowls. I bite my lip to hide my smirk and pick up the fallen books. Willow drops to a crouch, suddenly the picture of innocence as she helps me.

*"You're going to be trouble for me, aren't you, little wolf?"* I tease, shooting her a private wink. *"One minute looking at my cock like you want to devour it, the next pretending you know nothing about such sordid acts."*

The coy glance she returns says it all. I grow impossibly harder, and wince at the ache. This is torture. I slam the books on the table and take a deep, controlling breath before facing Bodin. His astute gaze drops to my mouth. He walks toward me until he's a few feet away, then inhales.

*"Your breath smells like her pussy,"* he sends me.

*"So?"*

*"You were explicitly forbidden to take her as a lover."*

Eyes mockingly wide, I shrug. *"Oops."*

"Secret talking is rude," she grumbles, dropping another book on the table.

I love her. Fuck it, I love her.

That must be what this is, this burning ache in my chest, swelling, and making me insane with need for her. Bodin's mood darkens. His gaze narrows on Willow.

"Your training starts tomorrow morning," he grumbles.

I step up to him. "She almost died last night."

"And she had the day to rest." He sweeps the mess with a disparaging glance. "Or whatever the fuck this was."

*"Mm, fuck,"* I send him, making a show of licking my lips. They still taste like her and I want more. *"Fucking. That's next on my to-do list with her."*

He glares at me, then snaps at Willow, "Be dressed in training gear by the stables ten minutes after dawn."

She thinks, *"I'm in trouble."*

*"No,"* I return. *"He's jealous, and he doesn't understand why."*

Or he's pissed because I'm getting in the way of their plan to use her to free Styx. A queasy feeling rolls in my gut. I glance at the spectacles I've been trying to enchant. They're my backup plan, but I'm failing at that, too.

Bodin folds his arms and stares at her.

"Okay, then," she mumbles and awkwardly points to the door. "I'll just . . . yeah. Get some food, I guess, and . . . yeah. Do some stuff. Maybe even head into the Nexus."

"No," Bodin and I both clip. Our eyes clash. At least on this, we're on the same page. She must be protected at all costs. We don't want to draw attention after Milford's disappearance.

I gentle my tone. "You had a harrowing experience yesterday. You should rest."

"Fine."

*"Call for me if you need me,"* I send her. *"And Willow, I'm going to fix everything. Trust me."*

She gifts me with a shy smile and then quickly walks out. When my gaze swings back to Bodin, he still stares at the space she vacated.

"That was rude," I drawl, raising my brows. "Next time, just ask to join in. No need for the theatrics."

His dark brows slam down, and he shakes his head. "That's not why I'm here."

Dark circles beneath his eyes remind me that he, Legion, and

345

Emrys refused to take sustenance. A thrill flutters through me at a mischievous idea. I close the gap between us until we're toe to boot. If all goes well, and Varen's long-awaited predictions of our happily ever after with our queen come true, then I'll never have this power over Bodin again. He'll always be the Second. Always be stronger, bulkier, a hammer to my wing.

*"You may be the Fifth, Fox, but you were the first to understand true freedom."* Varen's voice bubbles from my memory. *"Catch our falling star, give her your heart, and she will guide us home."*

For years, I ransacked my brain, trying to understand why Varen thought I understood true freedom.

We need love.

Unconditional love.

We need someone who accepts us, fangs, chaos, and all. She might not love us yet, but she will. I just need to keep my arms open, keep waiting for her bright light to fall into them.

"Time to feed, Bodin," I state.

Before he can pull back, I grip the knot of his braids and tug his mouth against mine, making sure to smear the last remnants of our queen's desire over his lips.

He stills. Gasps. But draws more of her scent into his lungs. His mouth opens enough for me to spill more sustenance. It only takes seconds, and then his wits return. He palms my chest hard, sending me sprawling backward.

"The fuck?" he growls, dark eyes flashing. He might have his wings clipped, but he'll gladly try to beat me to a pulp. I'm not in the mood to burst his little bubble.

I'm not sorry and shrug to show him. "Legion said to force it down your throat if you refuse."

*"Varen's* throat," he grumbles. "Not mine. I want nothing to do with her unless it's to help us save Styx."

"Oh yeah?" My brow arches, and I look at his tongue slowly sweeping his lips. "Then why are you savoring her taste?"

His lips part, then press together in a flat line. I've never seen him so flustered. Normally, he's the first to lash out with violence, to crush his opponents in one fell swoop. It's Emrys who likes to make the torture last. But Bodin's fists flex at his side. Tension pulls his broad shoulders taut. He gives me a hard *don't fuck with me* glare, and then he storms out.

My amusement dies the instant he's gone. This isn't right. He shouldn't be running from her taste. He should be begging for it. I close my eyes and trace my lips while mentally replaying every last glorious second of that act. I hope the more I do, the more I'll commit it to memory. Because if I can't figure out how to stop them using her to save Styx, it won't happen again.

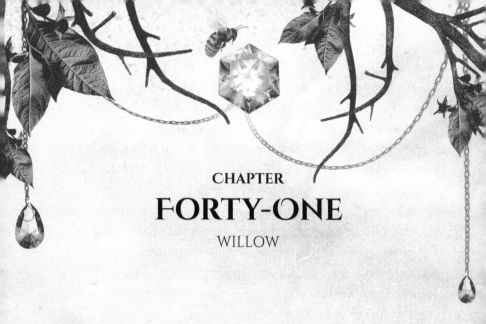

The next morning, Bodin unleashes a new nightmare on my body: running laps of the frosted grass courtyard behind the keep. Snow comes in sparse, random spurts over the day. It's not enough to make training out here difficult.

Any time I pause for a breath or a drink, my sweat turns to ice down my spine. My hands are strapped to protect them from frostbite, but apparently, it's not too cold to be out. My woolen trousers, cream tunic, and leather vest are useless protection against the elements. But at least my breasts are pinned. I'm on my fourth lap, and they remain under control. Peablossom got that part right when she designed the outfit.

Or was it Legion who gave her the notes? He seems the type to notice details and direct everything down to the cotton used in hemming.

I can't complain. Bodin wears a thin linen work shirt, the laces untied. He's impervious to the cold. Must have blood made from ice. He's no seven-foot vampire Haze, but he's thicker and taller than the other Sluagh. Fox is lither with tightly coiled whip-sharp strength. Once I start the comparisons, I can't stop.

Fox has woken a hunger in me. Last night, I tossed and turned, unable to get him out of my head. His expert fingers. His complete, utter devotion to making me feel good. With his tongue.

The wolf in me is restless and eager to return to him, but I need more time to build trust.

"Enough." Bodin's deep voice cuts through the crisp air. He leans an elbow on a wooden fence by the stables, scrutinizing me from afar.

"Thank fuck," I mumble and stop, bending at the waist to wheeze and pant. "I'm definitely out of shape."

Fox's confession about their past makes sense. He even had a damn history book to back him up. It changes everything. Or, at the very least, forces me to rethink my perspective. One that has nothing to do with his tongue.

Or his lips.

Or his—

"Choose a weapon," Bodin grunts out as he strolls onto the grass and pivots to watch me.

Weapon? I scan the ground and find a collection before a rosebush. Nothing too lethal. I skip the wooden practice swords and go straight for the steel dagger, spinning it in my palm to test the weight.

"Metal," I note, then point it at Bodin's Guardian teardrop. "What's the deal with it here in Avorlorna?"

"What do you mean?"

"You're a Guardian. Shouldn't you police forbidden substances so mana can flow from the Well properly?"

"The Wellspring?" He scratches his jaw, confused.

My blade lowers. Titania's spell makes him forget his basic Guardian duties. I try a different tactic. "What would you do if you learned metal and plastics blocked the flow of magic from the Well . . . spring. Wellspring?"

"What is plastic?"

I sigh.

"Never mind." I circle him. There's no point explaining an old-world product if he can't remember the condition of his blessing in the first place. "Have you heard other Radiants complain about their magic not working or for it to hurt when they touch metal?"

Recognition flashes in his eyes, but then it's gone. "Enough talking. Show me your so-called calamity."

We go two fast rounds of me trying and failing to stab him before he orders me to choose another weapon. The Knight Marshal is light on his feet. It's much of the same for the next hour. No conversation, just testing, watching, and judging.

"Return the sword." The stalwart grump is a male of few words today.

I bite my retort and do as I'm told. The faster I get this over with, the better.

"Willow."

"Yes, Bodin?" I spin to face him.

His eyes narrow as he reminds, "Sir."

"Sir."

A muscle ticks in his jaw. His gaze flicks to my lips, then back up.

"Why are you less recalcitrant?" he asks.

"What do you mean?"

"You are amenable to training and addressing your superiors correctly." He gestures at my attire. "You wear appropriate clothing."

I shrug. "I need to train. I'm rusty."

"So this is self-serving?"

"Does it matter? You want me to win, right?"

A breathy grunt of agreement. "On that note, you must

understand your ability to sense the flow of magic. It will be crucial to passing all three trials in the final tournament."

My ears prick up. This is the first I've learned of the exhibition tournament. The pamphlet was vague. "What are they?"

"First, you must escape a nightmare dreamscape. Second, you will battle a nightmare in the flesh. And the third is a heist—infiltration of the subterranean."

My skin prickles with unease. "How is that an exhibition when no one can witness it? I assume the rest of Avorlorna isn't going to come with us into the subterranean?"

He gives me a flat look. "What was the lesson you learned on day one?"

"Never assume." I sigh, shaking my head.

"There are charms that relay images," he offers. "Similar to the resonance stone."

A charm that relays images? Aunt Peaches would love to know about that. I'll have to bring one home to her. The thought of returning to Elphyne constricts my chest. Procuring manabeeze should be at the top of my to-do list. If that fails, winning this tournament is still my best bet for returning home.

"Does everyone else know the trial details?" I ask.

"The repeat exhibitors do. But your competition is not your concern. No charm can sense the flow of magic as you do. Since Terrors prey on your fears and weaknesses, then turn them against you—knowing what is reality will give you the path to domination." His wide lips flatten. "We must strengthen that ability."

He lashes out to grip my wrist, spins me, and shoves me face-first to the ground. Adding insult to injury, he presses a knee to my spine and growls into my ear, "I'm starting to think rumors of your calamity were falsified."

Fucker.

He shoves off, leaving me in a pool of hot, prickly embarrassment.

"You took me by surprise," I return, climbing to my feet.

I glance down to dust myself. My attention wavers for a blink. An instant. But he's on me in a snap, trapping my face with his large hand, voice guttural as he snarls, "Distractions will get you killed."

He has my lips smooshed like a pancake, forcing my eyes to his—my heart races. There's something about how he is stoic one moment but switches to primal and dominant the next. Part of me wants to stab him still, but the animal part Fox awoke is vibrating.

I can't start feeling all swoony over him, too. Can't breathe in his leather-and-spice scent and like it. But the kernel of attraction started days ago when he carried me on a drift. This only adds fuel to the fire.

"You seem a little tense, sir," I mumble through squashed lips.

His biting pressure almost bruises me, but I'm not afraid.

I've been studying him as he studies me. His fighting style is blunt, with no frills. Fast and arrogant. It's the kind of style belonging to apex predators who've been on top of the food chain forever.

He lets go and steps back with a grunt.

As we circle each other, I work my jaw to test for damage. It's just an ache. He knows exactly how much force to exert without causing lasting harm. I wonder who he practices on.

His next strike comes with the prickle of fire ants over my left side. Shadow rises to hide his swing, but I block left and send a right hook into his ribs. My fist glances off.

Oh, that hurt. I shake my smarting hand. "Are you made of stone?"

Suddenly, I'm tossed off my feet, sailing through the air and landing with a spine-jarring thud. His unyielding weight pins me. His teeth clamp hard on my neck, shooting needles of pain and lust into my body. I bite back a moan. Does he not know this is how wolves mate? They pin their female down, bite her, then rut. Every ounce of my blood begs me to submit to Bodin, to invite his leathery scent in deep.

But his coiled tension stills me. I must have said something wrong. He has me in his teeth, and my insides are in a frenzy. I squirm, and he bites down harder, knee pushing between my legs. I gasp as his thigh hits my apex, tingling every nerve ending Fox left begging for more.

"Keep squirming like that and see what happens," he mumbles against my flesh, no longer biting.

I didn't realize I still was.

*Fight back.*

*Do something.*

But my brain has left the building. I wriggle, chasing sensation. My throaty whimper of need surprises us both. He rears back to look into my eyes. Two powerfully built arms brace on either side of my head. Long braids trail down his shoulder and tickle my cheek. I bite my bottom lip to stifle another stupid, girly sound. Wrong thing to do. Whatever obsession he has with my lips is sexual. His volcanic gaze drops to my mouth.

"Distractions will get you killed," he murmurs, now as breathless as me.

Scratching and knocking precede Cricket's loud string of curse words and what sounds like the baby Wild Hunt escaping the conservatory. I would look, but Bodin has me pinned.

Cricket curses again, then shouts, "Last chance for a meal before the kitch closes for lunch."

I raise my brows at Bodin.

"Fine," he grinds out, still staring darkly at my lips. "Eat."

But he fails to move, even when galloping paws rapidly

approach. The cocky bastard thinks he's invincible, but not from two of us attacking at once. The wildling's collision jolts him to the side. I fist his shirt, hook my leg around his waist, and use the momentum to roll us. Within seconds, I'm on top, straddling him and pressing a dagger against his carotid.

"That enough calamity for you?" I ask.

"You were told to return that weapon."

My lips curve. "Never assume."

Our eyes lock. A bolt of heat pulses my pussy. His pupils dilate, and suddenly, our mouths clash, our tongues duel. The unyielding stone beneath me softens with a breathy groan. His hands slide across my hips to squeeze my rear end. I rock into the hard length pressing between my thighs. Our kiss lasts five delicious seconds, and then my brain screams a timely reminder. *He wants to sacrifice you.*

I try to break away, but his hands trap my head. He holds me still to continue his ravaging kiss. He's so punishing that, at first, I think he's using this to reassert his dominance. But then he flexes his hips, and his erection digs into me with hungry jabs. It feels so good that I almost submit.

*You don't trust him!*

Don't I?

*No. You don't. Unlike Fox, he hasn't proven any kind of loyalty.* I press the blade against his neck until I draw blood. His lips stop moving. He waits a moment, then drops his hands.

He grumbles, "I warned you not to squirm."

"Right, so this is my fault." My body is a bag of trembling fury, adrenaline, and lust. I don't know what else to say now except, "I'm hungry."

"You're always hungry." His tone is distracted, and his hands return to my hips, idly massaging my aching muscles in circles. "You need to eat more."

Stop it. Stop trying to make it sound like you care. I push off him and wipe the blade on my trousers. I'm attracted to him, to them, but that doesn't mean they're good for me.

I walk toward the conservatory glass door. Rustling at the stables stops me. Nose deep in the bottom of a rose bush, the baby dragon sniffs a trail toward the horses kept within. Bodin's eyes widen. He maneuvers off the ground but doesn't run after the beast. He steps back, away from it.

It's almost laughable how the big protector, whose word sways even the likes of Legion, is terrified of corralling a tiny dragon. I put two fingers between my lips and let loose a shrill whistle. Baby Hunt scrambles out of the bushes and lifts his head in my direction.

"You want some yum-yums?" I shout.

He perks up, but then glances at the stables when a horse whinnies. I pat my thigh and call him again. This time, he runs toward me like a streak of black lightning, his wings tucked back for aerodynamics. When I open the door, he races inside the conservatory, and I leave Bodin alone with his gobsmacked expression.

# CHAPTER
# FORTY-TWO
## PUCK

"This is unacceptable, Goodfellow." Lord Sylvanar storms into the dining hall and slams his fist on the table, jostling the fine porcelain crockery.

While I finish my mouthful, I give his dull, flat attire a scornful look. Why he demands to wear such dreary colors is beyond me. I wipe my mouth with a napkin. "And what, pray tell, is it this time?"

"My son has not returned from Burn After Reading. You have been warned about the repercussions of allowing this perverted establishment to continue operating."

"You mean your queen, your *queen* has been warned. I merely serve as her proxy during her sacrificial slumber. As to your claims over the nature of the establishment, she allows it because it affords her most loyal Radiants the freedom of coloring outside the lines of the Old Code while the rest of Avorlorna is beholden to it. You cannot deny you have benefited from this arrangement." He opens his mouth to retort, but I hold up a polite finger to shush him and continue. "As one of her original subjects in this new commonwealth of hers, you were consulted upon waking from your ancient slumber. Do you wish for me to tell your sovereign that you are reneging on your word?"

His eyes stir with the unmistakable otherness of the Baleful Hunt. Fury bubbles in my blood so swiftly that I can barely contain it. The fool is not worthy of the dragon-bonded blessing. He has been a thorn in my side, in Titania's side, since the Awakening. I've been waiting for an excuse to cut him down a notch, and here it is.

"Return your dragon to his post immediately." I force a pleasant smile.

"I will return him once my son has been found, no sooner."

"You are courting treason, Sylvanar," I warn. "How many times must I warn you that due caution must be taken to secure the Cabinet of Curiosities."

He scoffs and prowls to the tall, open windows overlooking the crystalline landscape beyond. Artful statues, dream webs, water features, and architecture are bedecked in prismatic ivory, sparkling like a rainbow.

"Two years ago," Sylvanar sneers, "you were among the exhibitors, mortal scum beneath our boots."

"But I'm not mortal now." My forced smile stretches. "Am I?"

I'd wished to be Titania's most trusted Radiant, and here I am, chained to her will. But I am not disappointed. She is the sugar in the lemon juice of my existence. I only regret that I failed to include my recently burned eyebrows in the wish's wording. How was I supposed to know my appearance would freeze from that day onward?

"What will you have me do?" I give an exaggerated sigh.

He turns to me, baleful gaze still that of his dragon. He could petrify me where I sit if he wanted. The fact he has not taken Avorlorna for himself is a mystery that plagues me. It is an unwanted threat in our lives—a lemon souring the sugar.

He barks an order. "Send the Knight Inquisitor to visit the witch who runs the establishment."

"No," I reply. "He was seen entering it last night."

Indignation flashes in his stony eyes. "Then the entire House of Shadow must be investigated. A commotion outside Shadow-fall Keep was reported by the ravens last night. What if it had something to do with my son?"

He steps perilously close to the Crown's single most valuable secret. I lift a goblet of bubbling elixir to my lips to hide my tension. But I can use this to our advantage.

Reclining in the chair, I intone, "Accusing the house in charge of the commonwealth's safety is a dangerous play. If you are wrong, there will be grave consequences against your house."

"The queen *must* take action." He slams his fist on the dining table. Stone cracks into existence, spidering from his fist to petrify the tabletop.

I wince and remove my hands before the stone reaches me. "Because you are a father in dire straits, I will allow your discourse to slide. However, if you continue to make demands of your sovereign while she sacrifices herself for the good of a realm, you will be punished."

"Do not play me for a fool, boy." His upper lip curls. "We all know you commune with her in this state. If I do not receive an answer by midnight, I will take matters into my own hands."

The audacious prick walks away from me.

"Lord Sylvanar," I call, knowing he hears despite continuing his trajectory. "It will be considered treason if you do not return your Hunt to its post."

The Cabinet must be protected at all costs.

Finally, the Earl has the sense to say, "I will uphold my end of the bargain so long as she upholds hers. Keep me apprised, Lord Goodfellow."

"If you return your Hunt to his post, you have permission to question anyone suspected of attending Burn After Reading last night."

"Questioning is useless if they cannot remember what happened inside."

He cannot possibly be this dimwitted, can he?

"Tell me, Lord Sylvanar, how is it exactly Radiants can conduct business here from within an establishment where no one remembers proceedings?"

His dull-witted confusion is why his son was nominated as the House of Stone representative for such political endeavors.

"Inanimate objects hold no memory," I explain dryly. "Objects, clothing, or, perhaps, something as innocuous as a flow charm can leave the establishment intact. It is well known your son Milford extorted new exhibitors through his charms. If I were you, I would begin my search with any mortal who has suddenly gained a new House of Stone charm." I pause. "And Sylvanar, remember to smile."

"WE HAVE A PROBLEM," I TELL THE TWO KEEPERS OF THE CAULDRON standing guard outside the queen's royal chambers. "I must speak with Her Majesty immediately."

One carved wooden mask faces me. "Disturbing her in this state will have a toll, Robin Goodfellow."

"I understand." I bow reverently. "However, I believe something has happened that jeopardizes her reign. If she is not consulted, we may lose this war before she wakes."

Tension thickens the air. The last thing anyone wants is for Oberon to gain control over the watergates.

The druid replies, "The flower required for communal

enchantment is rare. Our supply has dwindled to almost nothing."

"I understand. I would not be here if it were not a matter of life or death."

They stare for too long. The smaller druid on the left irritatingly notes, "The seals are still intact. There is no danger."

I grit my teeth. To speak of such things out here in the palace, where the Knight Inquisitor prowls, borders on negligence. Regardless, I give them what they need. "The ravens reported the Wild Hunt has doubled in size."

Another pause. Panic unfolds in their shadowed eyes.

"In addition, Sylvanar has reported his son—a Radiant—is missing, and he suspects the House of Shadow. Do you need me to connect the dots?"

"Very well. You are her most trusted advisor. If you believe this is worth the risk, I will prepare the dew."

For an organization older than Titania, they are incredibly slow on the uptake. Before allowing me entry, the second druid reminds me of the risks as the first leaves to prepare. "You may not remain inside her dreamscape for longer than three minutes. You must not use more than the required dose on her eyelids. You must not—"

I hold up my palm. "I'm well aware of the process."

A pause. "Very well, you may enter. We will be watching."

They hand me the prepared flower essence and usher me inside. The heavy doors close, leaving me alone with my queen in the twilight-lit room. It takes me a moment to desensitize from seeing my beloved with her hands clasped as though she were in a coffin. There is no woolen blanket covering her body, just lashes of greenery. The vines, foliage, and moss of her pillow emit a pungent scent, but she draws power from nature.

She also draws power from the thousands of gemstones twinkling above her bed, dripping essence extracted from dream webs around the city. The Weaving Hunt sleeps at her side and barely lifts an eyelid as I walk through the dragon's misty substance. As I near, I slide my hand along her bare leg until the foliage blocks me. Such a beautiful queen. So perfectly crafted from dreams.

I place a drop of dew onto each of her eyelids. The effect is immediate when I do the same for my eyes.

Titania's incorporeal form materializes beside me. My gut lurches at her disheveled appearance. The lustrous brown locks are matted. Her tiara slips. A strange dress of sculpted lily and rose petals is wilted and torn. Finger-shaped bruises encircle the delicate flesh around her neck.

"Puck," she whispers, as though she is not alone. "You place me in grave danger."

I bow. "My queen, I would not be here if it were unimportant."

Her visage appears to run and glance over her shoulder as if chased by her nightmares. She turns a corner, leans against a wall, and then meets my eyes. "Tell me."

"The Wild Hunt has finally been revealed. It is a baby."

Her eyes widen with relief. "'Tis the sweetest news."

"Can we kill it like this?"

"All things are possible in dreams," she sings hysterically.

"I know you would want to strike the killing blow." I frown. "But I fear we cannot wait for this Interlude to run its course. The Hunt has already doubled in size."

Her eyes widen with mania. "How is that possible? Are the seals broken?"

"The Keepers say they remain intact."

"No." She shakes her head. "Are you sure the seals are intact? When was the last time you checked the Cabinet?"

"It is as before. Their Sixth is a statue inside."

"Then another has removed his collar and must be feeding.

There is no other explanation. It would explain why they've retained their strength for so long." She pauses and frowns. "They have resisted our attempts to draw out the Wild Hunt before. The exhibition was concocted for this reason alone. But to reveal a baby? Why now? What changed?"

"They sponsored a Shadow."

She looks at me as if I've gone mad. "The devils have never been interested in such matters. What has prompted this risk?"

"I don't understand either. They chose a Nothing with a face as ugly as my left testicle."

The blood drains from her face, and I fear I have been too distasteful with my words.

"I apologize, my queen. I did not mean to offend you."

"Tell me what she looks like," she whispers.

*She?* I straighten. How does she know the gender of the Nothing?

"She is ugly," I scoff. "What more do you need to know?"

"Do not test my patience," she hisses and glances somewhere I can't see. Her breath hitches. "Be quick. My nightmare is closing in."

I am thrown. I thought I was her trusted advisor, that she kept no secret from me, but clearly, I am still not trusted enough for her to reveal everything.

"Puck!"

"Uh . . ." I mumble, swiping my fingers over my hairless brows. "She has silver hair, faerie ears, yellow eyes, yet she is mortal. No doubt about it."

Horror fills her eyes. She starts pacing, babbling reassurances to herself I don't quite understand.

"We are almost out of time," I prompt.

Her delicate features harden into the sharp, ruthless queen to whom I pledged my life.

"If the public discovers what we harbor in their midst," she says, "they will know the truth about the war and turn on us. This chaos is exactly what Oberon hopes for, what we strive to suppress. You must neutralize the one who has slipped his chains."

"Understood." I lick my lips, darting a glance at the timer. "Who is the Shadow, my queen?"

"Exactly what you said. An ugly Nothing."

"Then why do the Knights of the Queen's Hive insist she lives at the keep?"

She freezes. Blinks. The nightmares must be terrifying this year. That she refuses to let me reveal the extent of her suffering is a travesty, but questions of her fitness to rule would be raised.

Titania shakes her head and starts babbling again. "No. She is nothing. They will not see the truth. So long as she believes she is ugly, she is in the dark. Yes, yes. Then how can it be light when they see her face?" She laughs manically. Flinches. Twitches. To me, she says, "She is the key to baiting the rogue. Ensure she remains a Nothing."

"And Sylvanar?"

"Do what you must."

"My queen, you have my word." My lips stretch into a wicked smile. "I will neutralize the threats, and your dearest court will be none the wiser. When you wake in spring, all will be in harmony, and your trust in my worthiness to serve will be unequivocal."

She steps toward me and reaches out. "My dearest Puck. If you can do this, you will be worthy of more than serving. You will be—"

A nightmare rips her away, screaming in terror.

I still smile at the memory of Bodin's baffled expression as I walk through the overgrown, damp indoor garden. That hint of a massage had been tempting. I sigh and stretch my aching muscles. Despite the mixed messages with him, today was the best day I've had in a while.

The small dragon runs ahead and whines at the door to the castle main, but I'm in no rush to leave the sweet-smelling, woodsy room. Natural light filters through the limescale-covered glass segmented roof. Garden beds and pots are filled with weeds, but a few stubborn, deadly flowers remain.

It's messy and chaotic and needs loving attention to bring it back to life. But it has potential. A space in the middle is large enough to serve for indoor training if the place is cleaned up. All we need is a little elbow grease and more help.

The garden certainly isn't going to maintain itself, and Finch has enough to do around the estate. I glance outside to where Bodin rubs his forehead pensively by the stables.

His confusion over the Guardian blessing isn't right.

The wildling whines and scratches at the door.

"Settle," I mumble. "I'm coming."

I follow the hungry beast through the castle corridors and into the lower-level dining room. The table is empty, so we continue to the cellar level toward the kitch. I haven't been in here yet. Cricket has looked after me so well that I haven't needed to.

"Come in!" an unfamiliar voice calls when I knock.

Is there a cook here after all? I poke my head through the archway. Bouquets and garlands of dried herbs decorate the bulkhead over a central butcher's block. A pot sits on a soot-covered stove by the wall. Vegetables, fruit, and other food items are stored around the room. Two doors lead to what is likely more storage space. A series of three oil paintings decorate another wall.

"Here!"

Okay, that definitely came from in here, but I still can't find anyone. The dragon runs laps around the butcher block, impatient for his treat. He lifts on his hind legs and flaps baby wings to help him sniff the wooden countertop.

"Get down!" I click my fingers and point at the ground. "You *really* need some training. What have they been doing with you all these years?"

"That's exactly what I said to Cricket!"

My eyes widen. "Who said that?"

"Me!"

My gaze snaps to movement inside an oil painting, and I gasp. A pretty mermaid combs her long red hair while basking on a rock.

"Was wondering when you'd come to see me," she pouts and raises her brows. "Told Cricket it wouldn't take long. Try the sack in the cool room if you want his treats."

She waggles her pearl comb toward a door. I pinch myself to ensure I'm not dreaming. Ouch. Okay, not dreaming.

"Um. Thanks." I use the time searching the cool room to process the fact a painting is talking to me. I've never seen anything like it in Elphyne. But I've also never seen a castle that moves rooms while I sleep.

I can't find the sack, but strips of fresh meat sit on a top shelf —a little for me and the beastie. When I return to the kitch, I pop a piece in my mouth and point my finger to the ground when the wildling tries to scamper up my legs.

"You need to sit if you want a yum-yum."

It takes a few attempts, but eventually, he understands and is the picture of obedience. When I'm out of treats, I dust my hands and say, "All gone. Off you go."

"Ooh yes," the painting says, combing her long tresses to cover her breasts. "I had a feeling you were the right one. Told Cricket that when Master Fox was pining over you. And that was years ago."

"You're the chatty gossip." I laugh, realization dawning on me.

She purses her lips. "I am *not* a gossip. That is illegal."

"Sorry."

"But I know it's what Miss Hoity Toity calls me. What else can I do here all day, stuck inside a painting? Without my dearest Captain Jubal Rackham, I'm bored out of my mind."

I sense a long tale coming on, but before she launches into it, I pinch myself again. Still hurts. No prickling ants crawl over my skin, so it can't be a dreamscape.

"Not dreaming," I mutter.

"Oh, you won't find dreamscapes here." She nods knowingly. "The masters have ensured our secret fantasies are protected. It's a bit sad if you ask me. I was so entertained by a dream or two wandering into the kitchen in the early days."

"What's your name?" I ask with a friendly smile.

"Marina," she replies. "You must be Willow."

"Yes, I'm Willow. It's nice to meet you, Marina. That's a pretty name."

Her face sours. "Far prettier than that faerie cow queen. It's her fault my baby Jubal has been sent away."

"Jubal?"

She sighs and glances to her right. The neighboring painting is an empty turquoise ocean. "He was the finest pirate captain this world has ever seen."

"You must miss him. Have you been here for a while?"

"Since the Awakening." She proudly lifts her chin and then narrows her eyes. "Why?"

"I was just wondering if you knew why the House of Shadow picked me as their protégé?"

The more information I can learn, the better.

She cocks her head. Intelligence flashes in her eyes. "Master Fox wanted you, of course."

"Oh? That's not what I heard." Something tells me she knows exactly what I'm doing, but she shuffles closer on her rock. I drop my chin into my hands and rest my elbows on the counter, the picture of riveted as I say, "You must hear a lot around here. I'll bet you're the most knowledgeable person in the castle."

Her lips flatten.

So, I push some more. "Last night, for example, when we returned from Burn After Reading. I heard there was an argument in here."

Cricket had grumbled about moody males when she handed me breakfast. The mermaid covers her mouth, eyes bulging.

"You know something, don't you?"

She shakes her head.

"Come on, let me know. I'll share gossip in return."

"Like what?"

I waggle my brows. "I remember *everything* from my trip into Burn After Reading."

She gasps, scandalized. "You're not supposed to."

"I know, but I do."

She barely takes a second to consider. "Okay, but you didn't hear this from me."

"You sound like Peablossom." I snort, amused.

"Oh, she's a darling. I like her. Except when she flutters her lashes at our Number One." Marina shuffles forward on her rock again, almost close enough to leap from the gilt frame. "So, about last night. Number One and Two were very cross at our poor little Mister Foxy-woxy." She combs and combs, off in her own little world, recalling the event.

"Angry because . . ." I prompt.

"Because he ate that horrible Radiant, of course." She flares her eyes at me, annoyed. "Do you want to hear the story or not?"

"Sorry. Please go on."

"Well, Mister Foxy was beside himself over your friends not looking out for your well-being. He was all worked up about it, and Number One and Number Two insisted he tell them who, but then they went quiet for a bit, and I couldn't hear the rest."

Oh. Okay, well, that's not helpful.

"But then Number One shouted so loudly, 'Who the fuck is Alfie?' that I dropped my comb, and it fell in the ocean. It took me five minutes to find it. Would you believe it?"

"They spoke about Alfie?"

"Mm. Master Fox was down on himself because he should have monitored minds, but he's been so good at staying out of people's heads without their permission since you got here." She pauses, thinks, then adds, "Oh wait, that was before Number One shouted. He's been doing that a lot lately. Never used to. But they're running out of time to save Number Six, and if you get turned to stone before the tournament, then you obviously can't be turned to stone in Number Six's place, now can you?"

Does this mean they'll still go ahead with that plan?

She pauses, mid-comb. "Mister Foxy is *very* against that plan. Don't worry, he told them he's changed his mind. He's very *not* on board with sacrificing you anymore."

Done with his snack, the baby Wild Hunt sniffs around the floor and wanders out. I lean back against the cold stovetop and chew my nails. The chatty gossip has just validated Fox's confession.

"You're good for them, you know." Marina's comb slows to a halt. "Having their fated queen here has breathed new life into each of them."

"How so?"

"Before you arrived, Number One had grown quiet and withdrawn. Number Two refused to have fun. Anything that took him away from his duties was a waste of time. Even Number Three has visited more often. And Number Four, goodness, he used to wander the halls naked, rambling hysterical nonsense before you arrived. Now he lets them clean, shave, and feed him."

"There's a lot of complicated history between us."

"Mm. And a lot of reasons to fall in love," she agrees, misreading my meaning.

"Their obsession with me ruined my life."

She gasps. "Did it? You seem very real to me. Are you dead?"

"No," I grumble. "I'm right here."

"Oh. Are you ruined, then? You seem very much in possession of all your limbs and wits."

"Fighting for them robbed me of magic."

"Did it?" She cocks her head. "Where did they put it?"

I see what she's doing, and it won't work. "Because of them, my Aunt is dead."

But she drags in a shocked, dramatic breath. "Did they *feed* on your aunt?"

"No!" How dare she insinuate they've done nothing wrong.

"Well, who did?"

"No one. It was . . ." Images flash in my mind—Rory choosing me. Cloud's outrage, his fury that he wasn't the one to kill her. He wanted revenge so badly that he considered letting me fall instead of her. I had nothing to do with their drama, a fact Rory knew.

And if I had nothing to do with their drama, then . . . then Marina is right. The Six had nothing to do with her death.

"Oh, there you are, love." Cricket bustles in, wiping her hands on her apron. "My apologies. Had to go to the little lady's room for a spot. Now, what can I get you? I have a soup waiting to reheat."

She opens a cupboard and reheats a ceramic pot on the freshly lit stovetop.

Marina says overly loud, "I was just telling Her Majesty how it's been so much brighter here since she arrived."

I blush. "Please, just call me Willow. Even if I wanted to be their queen, I have no magic."

"Oh, hun." She gives me a sympathetic pout. "Who said magic has anything to do with it? Right, Cricket? Oh no, Cricket! You need more pepper than that."

"Nonsense. It will be too bitter." Cricket dashes in another pinch, regardless. "I'm the cook here, not you. And magic has to do with everything here."

"But—"

"Fine. Here's your spice." Cricket deliberately stares at Marina while adding another dash but then winks at me when most spills out of the pot.

"Oh, yes," Marina sighs. "We love our spice, don't we Cricket?"

As the mermaid launches into a lurid story about spice on the seven seas, Cricket sends me a secret smirk and explains quietly, "She doesn't understand that adding more bitterness will only make it taste more bitter."

A few days before Tinger's death, my mother was cooking soup in the kitchen. She never cooks. Ever. I assumed because, as the Prime, she's too busy. My father confessed she was never good in the first place. She spent too much of her life stealing and living off the streets, ordering takeout with her gambling ex-boyfriend, and . . . well, she hated it. So it struck me as odd that she invited me to the stovetop to have a taste.

*Annoyed at being interrupted from my skulk toward my room, I storm over, take a sip from her spoon, and spit out the horrible flavor.*

*"No offense, Mom, but maybe you should forget about cooking. It's just not your thing."*

*"Oh well," she sighs. "I guess adding bitterness to an already bitter soup doesn't make it taste any better."*

I touch my heart. There are no coincidences where my mother is concerned. She must have seen this moment in a vision. Despite vowing to let me make my own mistakes, she wanted me to know she knew about my journey as far as this moment . . . and still trusted me to come alone.

I've been holding onto my bitterness over the Six for so long, using it as armor to get through each day, but it's not improving my life.

"Here you go, love," Cricket says as she ladles soup into a bowl.

I take a sip. The broth is surprisingly well-balanced. "It's not bitter at all."

"You like it?" A blush hits Cricket's cheeks. "Master Fox said your wolf blood makes you a rabid carnivore. So I've been—"

"We've been!" Marina corrects.

"Ahem. *We've* been chasing down meaty recipes for you."

"I'm touched." My eyes sting. "Thank you for being so welcoming. The soup tastes perfect."

"Pull up a seat." Cricket drags a stool from behind the stove and sets it beside the butcher's block.

LANA PECHERCZYK

"And while you eat," Marina says, "You can tell me all about Burn After Reading. Who wore what, and which of the gentry behaved deplorably? Oooh, and who shagged who when they shouldn't have!"

At the end of my second helping and a good dose of faerie society gossip, I glance up to see Fox leaning against the doorway, a half-smile on his lips.

"How long have you been standing there?" I ask, licking my spoon.

"Long enough to know someone called Irisa wore a see-through dress." He pushes off and walks to me.

*"Someone?"* I send my outrage into his mind. *"How can you not remember? You fed from her."*

*"Did I?"* The force of his kiss knocks me off balance, but he cups the back of my head and keeps me from falling. My finger hooks into his waistband and I tug him closer. I can't help it. The soup was amazing, but Fox tastes better. And when he adds, *"I only remember details about you,"* I melt.

A pot clanks. Cricket pipes up. "And that's my cue to leave, folks."

I gently push Fox away and raise my brows. "So you think you don't need permission to kiss me anymore?"

A sheepish grin. A flash of dimples. "Do I?"

"Scoundrel," Marina shouts. "Tell him he's a scoundrel, then rip his shirt off!"

Our gazes snap toward the painting. Marina's eager eyes are glued to us.

I give a nervous laugh and scratch my head.

"Maybe next time, Marina." I slide off the stool and take Fox out.

"Don't tease me," he groans.

"Or me!" Marina's shout filters out.

An annoying heat creeps up my neck. I keep walking, shaking my head, but smiling despite myself.

In the corridor, I turn to Fox. "I want to help."

He waggles his brows. "Just say when, little wolf."

"Not that kind of help." I pat my cheeks. Why am I so flustered all of a sudden? Maybe because this has become real. Staring at his handsome, troublemaking face, I know I won't be able to deny this pull between us much longer. I take a step back for clarity and clear my throat, but my body cries at the distance.

"I mean, I want to help with Styx," I explain. "Bodin was on edge during training. I tried talking to him about being a Guardian, and he blanked about many things. You're alone trying to save your hive, and I want to help. So tell me what you all planned for me. Tell me everything. Perhaps the two of us working on a solution is better than one."

The tension leaves his shoulders. "I'm so happy to hear you say that."

"You are?"

"Of course." He pulls me close again. "I need you, Willow. We all need you."

"I think . . ." My heart sings at his nearness, at his words. "I think I need that too."

Maybe.

His lips press against the curve between my neck and shoulder. For a long moment, he breathes through his nose against my skin. My hands slide around his waist and up his spine. It feels so good to touch him. I don't know what this means, but I'm done fighting the pull of destiny. Maybe I'm their queen. Maybe I'm not. But I'm here, and it feels good. That has to count for something.

"I smell Bodin," Fox whispers.

I bite my lip. "I kind of . . . well, we . . . kissed."

He straightens, the whites of his eyes showing. Oh no. Why is he shocked? But then his lips slowly curve in a self-congratula-tory smile. "My job here is done."

"What job?"

His lips flatten. "Nothing."

"Do you need another visit from the tickle monster to spill your secrets?" I threaten, holding out my clawed hands.

"Ooh. Speaking of secrets, I came to find you because the Baleful Hunt has left his post guarding the Cabinet of Curiosities."

His comment is off the cuff, but it's laden with significance. Before I mentioned I wanted to help, he was already on his way to ask me for it.

"Where Styx is held?" I ask.

He nods. "The dragon rarely leaves his post without due caution taken to cover the guard. Sylvanar is on the rampage, interrogating anyone at Burn After Reading." His mood turns serious. "Unless I can find enough wisps to pay Cait for an ancient mirror blocking the Baleful's powers, we might not see a better chance. We have to go now."

"Now?" I gape. "Like, *now* now?"

After my entire weekend derailing, I'd hoped to spend the afternoon at the Nexus.

"Now." Fox gives a grim nod. "I can tell you everything else on the way."

Shit. It makes sense to go now. Hopefully, the others will forgive me. I'll make it up to them tomorrow.

"Does the rest of your hive know we're going?"

"No." He rubs the back of his head, irritated. "They're increasingly confused with each passing day. Your arrival has triggered something. Perhaps the binding seals are wrapping tighter around their hearts whenever their true desires shine through. They might even force me to go through with the plan for you to switch places with Styx. We need to do this alone—you and me."

If this opportunity is as rare as he says, then this might be my only chance to see the truth with my own eyes. I nod. "Let's do it."

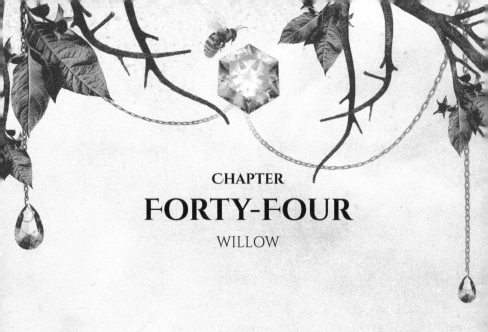

# FORTY-FOUR

### WILLOW

Fox *flickers* us into Titania's private gardens inside the palace grounds, unnoticed by guards on the boundary walls. New snow falls in lazy whorls as we crouch behind a tall column of frost-hardy roses and take stock of our surroundings. Another column stands ten feet away. It's high—at least three stories—and marks the entrance to a maze of hedges. Nero's private garden was similarly landscaped. We did most of our death training at the maze's center, away from prying eyes.

*"These hedges protect Titania's Cabinet of Curiosities,"* Fox sends.

The enormous Ivory Palace dominates the rest of the grounds. The manicured garden stretches onward, mainly water features and pretty marble statues. Sparkling webs decorate the trees. Guards roam the high curtain walls, thankfully peering outward, not inside. I doubt they'll do that for long.

*"How much time do we have before the guards are a problem?"* I send Fox.

He points down the maze path toward a tall, craggy rock

looming above the hedges a few hundred feet away. *"The Baleful Hunt keeps watch from its nest up there. As long as it's with Sylvanar, and we don't cause a disruption, the guards shouldn't be a problem."*

*"That sounds almost too easy."*

His lips flatten. *"The problem isn't just getting past the Hunt. It's getting inside the temple where I believe Styx is held. We need a mortal for that. Punishment for the public discourse of a Radiant is petrification for one year."*

*"I thought you said he would be permanently trapped as a statue."*

*"Titania doesn't plan on releasing him."* His jaw works. *"The truth is, his twelve-month sentence was up two years ago. The spell's narrative is making my hive forget him."*

I suppress a gasp. *"Two years! So if you don't rescue him by the end of this Gentle Interlude . . ."*

*"I might be alone in the knowledge of his existence."*

His sadness wraps around my heart. How can anyone holding this much pain, while still putting me first, be wrong for me?

*"We'll figure it out,"* I promise.

*"Prepare yourself. The Cabinet is . . . confronting."* He takes my hand and *flickers* us further into the maze.

We land in a lawned clearing between two stories of stone pillars surrounding a giant uneven boulder. Slabs on the pillars help create archways, each holding a different statue.

"Oh, my. They're all . . . I mean, they *were* real." From their expression of fear or resignation, it's obvious each statue was once a living creature. From faerie to mortal to nightmare, this Cabinet holds many species, like a menagerie. It's yet another parallel to Nero that makes my stomach revolt. He had a room at the top of his Sky Tower filled with fae wings pinned on walls like butterflies in a box. As I walk around and inspect each statue, I read the inscription on a plaque beneath. A rare one or two mention a crime, but most are simple species labels.

"After the Awakening five years ago," Fox explains, "Titania had Sylvanar collect as many different creatures as he could. For research."

I snort. "She's insane."

"Unfortunately, you may be right. Her madness grows each year when she rises from her winter slumber."

"Why?"

"She makes out like her sleep freezes the watergates and ceases hostilities, but it's a bargain struck with Oberon." He gives me a dark look. "Her dreams are locked in the realm of nightmares for the duration."

"Why would she lie about that?" The truth would only add to her martyrdom for her realm.

His lips curve. "It would mean admitting her sordid love affair with him continues."

"Are you telling me she's down there . . . you know?"

"I suspect he likes to punish her just as much as he likes to fuck her."

That sounds . . . complicated.

We keep walking. My animal side helps me withstand the cold more than others, but I'm nowhere near as resistant as Fox. He dusts snow from his shoulder as though it's a mere hindrance to his fashion, whereas I'm freezing my nipples off. Blowing my hands to keep warm, I go left around the central rock while he walks right. We meet on the other side, where a single, hedge-lined pathway leads into the maze.

"Fox," I ask, having mulled over his words. "If your hive is so dangerous to Titania, why doesn't she use the Baleful Hunt to turn you all into statues?"

"Clever little wolf." His eyes twinkle as he tugs my braid. "She still needs us for something."

"Does this *something* have anything to do with the Corner-twister calling Legion a prince?"

A quietness falls over him. He wears the same haunted expression as in the library when he showed me their history . . . when he shut down after mentioning the Unseelie noble who worked with the Morrigan to steal them from the Keepers.

Is Oberon that noble? That would explain why a Nightmare addresses Legion as a prince. On my first day here, Bob relayed his theory about the war. He'd overheard a Nightmare demanding that a Radiant—I gasp—*give back what they stole.*

"Fox, is this war because of you?" I blink. "Because Titania stole you from Oberon?"

He nods and starts inspecting the rock's surface. "He's a dangerously unhinged faerie with access to ancient dark magics gifted by Mother Dearest herself. If Titania can't kill us, then she needs us alive . . . likely a last-resort hostage exchange." He stops two feet down and taps his fingers on the rock, tilting his head to listen for something. "She might be a bitch, but she's trying to keep her people safe the only way she knows how. Here." He points at a particular section of rock. "This is the entrance to the one place I've been unable to search."

It looks the same as the rest of the bluestone, but when I place my hand on the surface, fire ants scuttle up my arm, and my hand phases through solid rock.

I jump back, horrified. "What just happened?"

"You're mortal." He attempts to push his hand through the same place but goes nowhere. "The wards block any faerie from entering."

"Even your wraith form?"

He nods.

I ask, "Have you tried holding metal to simulate being disconnected from the Well?"

"Guardian." He gestures to his blue teardrop.

"Oh, of course." His flow of magic isn't blocked. Frowning, I test the wards again. The sense of magic is ripe as my fingers phase through the surface. But there's something else, something extremely familiar, and I can't put my finger on what. I plunge my hand in deeper and shudder as the sensation rolls through me.

This magic is friendly.

Fox misreads my unease and pulls me back. "Are you well?"

"I'm fine."

A scowl darkens his features. "We'll leave right now if you sense something wrong."

His angry face shouldn't be so attractive, but his eyes light up with passion.

"Quit worrying." I reach over my shoulder and pull my serrated bone sword from its scabbard. "I get why she wants the Folk kept out of her temple, but why would she allow mortals inside?"

Fox shrugs. "Either they're no threat, or she needs something inside cared for."

"You don't think Styx is alive in there, walking around . . . starving, do you?"

"He won't eat you."

"Wow," I intone, "you sound so convincing."

"Trust me. It's against our very nature to harm our queen."

I wish I shared his confidence. We stare at the rock for a long moment. I'm unsure what he's thinking, but my mind is filled with questions. They chose me as their Shadow partly because a mortal can get through, and I'm a thief.

"Did you expect me to carry a life-sized stone statue out?" I ask. "I don't understand where the thief part comes into play."

He snorts. "We were to convince you to break into the temple to pilfer a powerful artifact, then trick you into completing the ritual that swaps Styx's stone prison to you."

My brows lift. "That's a big assumption that I'm greedy enough to want treasure."

"I was to plant the greed into your mind."

I swallow. "You can do that?"

"I can do many things, Willow." His dark gaze settles on me as he raps his knuckles against the rock. "But I can't get inside here."

"So why don't you enter Titania's mind and force her to release you?"

He faces me with amused eyes. "Does that pretty little mouth ever stop asking questions?"

"Never." Why do people keep asking me that?

His head dips to mine, filling my space with his sweet, woodsy scent.

"Good," he murmurs as he trails his fingers down my long braid, resting it against my breastbone. "It will be a sad day if you ever lose your spark of curiosity."

"Ahem." I raise my brows. "It's nice you're being cute and all, but you haven't answered my question."

Roguish lips curve, flashing dimples. "Like you, she's my queen. We can do her no harm."

"I can do many things, Willow," I mock. Frustration wells inside me. "How can you have two queens?"

"Neither bond works as it should." A brief storm gathers in his gray eyes before they soften on me. "But I have faith you'll figure it out."

"Me?"

He presses my hand against the chest of his brocade coat. My breath is hard to draw when he stands so close, touching me. His next words are low and intimate, almost precious.

"There's something about you, Willow O'Leary-Nightstalk, something disruptive and magnetic. You're smart, ruthless, and yet full of compassion for strangers. You are a natural-born queen, with or without magic, with or without a hive. If this all turns to ruin, and all we're left with is the pleasure of your company for this single heartbeat in time, I will consider myself fortunate."

"Fox," I warn. "You're being very serious. It's unlike you. Is there something you're not telling me about this temple?"

He swallows and rakes his fingers through his hair. "This is where we were originally bound. The site is an ancient, powerful convergence of feylines flowing directly from the Wellspring. I'm unsure if Styx is inside, but I've looked everywhere else."

He's nervous, I realize. Maybe even worried that I'll be harmed inside, and he won't be able to reach me. That knot around my heart tightens. It's almost as though I *feel* his concern as my own. And . . . his fear. My thoughts flick to my parents' Well-blessed mating bond. It allows the sharing of emotions and mana. I shut down the traitorous hope rising in my soul. This isn't that. It can't be. We would have matching blue glowing marks . . . and I could share his magic.

Fox's worry intensifies. "If you wish to turn around now, I'll take you home."

"I choose to enter freely. You're not manipulating me, forcing me, tricking me. I am here because—" I take a deep breath. "I want answers. I can't wait around for you to act or for the others to confess their true intentions. That's me reacting to someone else's choice. I'm tired of living like that. If all I find in here is an empty space, then at least I know I did something. I *chose* to do something because I wanted to."

My fingers scrape down his jaw as he steps away with a determined nod. "I'll be here waiting. If the Baleful Hunt turns up, I'll still be here—you just won't see me."

I give him the most confident smile I can muster and salute him with my sword.

"Let's get this over with, then." I raise my hand to the rock, but he captures my wrist and yanks me hard against his torso. He slants his lips over mine, demands entry with his tongue, and kisses me with a passion bordering on desperation.

When it's over, I'm left wanting more. And wet. He gives me a wolfish grin, knowing exactly what he's done, teasing me with those charming dimples again.

"It might be cold in there," he notes. "Thought you needed something to keep warm."

"Right." I roll my eyes and press my hand to the rock. "Because your lips are *so* hot."

His chuckle follows me as I step through the wards. Tingling, jittery ants scuttle over my body. But more of that familiar feeling embraces me, too.

On the other side, glimmering light blinds me. Sparkles. Stars. It's too bright. I drop to a crouch and use my other senses while my eyes adjust. A few sharp whiffs of the damp air tell me nothing living is here. The twinkling stars take shape on the ground around the cave's outer wall—jars of manabeeze. Holy shit. *Hundreds* of jars of manabeeze. Tables of artifacts are pushed against the outer wall, but it's the single, solitary silhouette in the center that steals my attention. *Wings.* Great draconic wings stretch the entire span of the cave, hitting each side with a sharp-taloned tip.

The statue's muscular back is to me, head down, so I can't see if he has horns. My brows lift. *He's naked.* A long tail sprouts from the top of his toned buttocks. It sure looks like it might be Styx, but Fox said he was sealed like the others. Why would his devilish features be on display?

Only one way to find out.

Gripping my sword's handle, I duck beneath his wing and spin to view his front. My boot slips on gravelly dirt. I lose balance and grab the closest thing to stop me from falling. *Well-damn* . . . that was close. Falling into hundreds of jars of manabeeze could be cataclysmic to my health.

I freeze, still crouched, blinking at the stone penis an inch from my nose—with my hand wrapped around it.

"Sorry," I whisper, blushing like a teenager. "So sorry."

I scramble to stand before him but cover my face, shaking my head. I almost broke his penis off. I peek through two open fingers. Styx is . . . yeah . . . well, he's ripped. Every muscle and tendon is defined as he prepares to attack. That *part* of him is definitely proportionate to the rest.

*Get a grip, Willow.*

No! Don't get a grip.

He's not standing here flaunting his body. He's a statue. No penises were harmed today. I pat my flaming cheeks and reassess him like a mature adult. Dangerous curved horns sweep from his forehead, half buried in short, wavy hair. A row of conical spikes decorates the skin above his eyebrows as they're smashed together in fury. Larger curved spikes, resembling Fox's horns, erupt along his collarbone in two rows—more spikes along his knuckles.

Feeling braver, I step closer and inspect his face. Stone sharpens the lines into something fiercely dangerous. Stepping back again, I sweep my gaze over his wings. Something doesn't add up. I need to tell Fox.

He jolts in surprise when I poke my head through the wards.

"He's here," I announce.

His audible exhale of relief tugs at my heart.

"There's something else," I say, still stuck halfway through the wards.

The fire ants scurrying over my body still feel oddly friendly. The notion distracts me, and I find my mind drifting inward, taking stock of the sensations. It's almost like the magic knows me. I feel around the rock's opening, testing more areas of the warding to check if the familiarity continues.

"Willow?" Fox breathes. "What's wrong?"

"Nothing." I shake my head. "It's . . . it's . . ."

Why would this magic feel like this? It's almost as if it was . . . mine.

"Willow." The concern in his tone startles me. I reach through the ward and take his hand, intending to allay his worry, but when we connect, tingling fire ants scuttle from my arm onto his. My lips part as I sense them continue to coat his entire body.

I gulp. "Are you okay?"

"Smashing. Are *you* okay?"

"You don't feel the fire ants? The prickle of magic all over you right now? Where we touch?" I squeeze his hand.

He gives me an odd look. "I don't sense magic like you do. It's not a visceral sensation against my skin. It's more intrinsic."

"Yes," I muse, recalling how I used to connect with the Well when I had access. My inner well was filled with a personal mix of elemental mana. Then there was the Cosmic Well, the mana in nature. Sensing that magic was both inside my soul and a visceral, physical response. "I always thought this physical sense was how everyone reacted to magic."

"We've never heard of it in anyone else."

My intuition prickles as an idea forms. "So . . . you can't get sliced in half or anything from walking into these wards, can you?"

His brow arches. "I simply hit rock . . . why?"

"Because you should come in here." I yank him into the cave and grin when he arrives in one piece. "Ooh, I was right."

"You were . . ." Utterly astonished, he blinks repetitively for a long moment. "You didn't know that would happen?"

"I mean, I had an inkling." I shrug. "What's the worst that could happen? You'd face-plant the rock." I point with my sword to the center of the cave. "Styx doesn't appear to be sealed."

He stares at me for another beat before turning.

"Styx." He rushes forward but slows as he takes in the wings, talons, and nudity.

"I'm guessing you didn't know about this development?"

"He's not supposed to be . . ." His eyes widen. "I wasn't there to witness the Baleful Hunt petrifying him. The others were, so I never thought to delve into their minds to clarify. We have an unwritten rule never to impose on each other's private mind space if the hive door is closed."

He starts pacing before Styx, wearing a line in the dirt.

"So what does this mean?" I ask. "That he found a way to break his seal?"

"I don't know." Fox's footsteps halt. He faces me. "But he's still stone."

My sigh collapses my knees. I land hard and hack the ground with my sword, frustrated. "We failed."

A sad smile touches his lips. "You pulled me inside. That's far better than I've managed alone in five years."

I lean back, intending to rest my head against the bumpy wall, but a jar of manabeeze digs into my spine. Scowling, I pull it out and shake it. "And what's the deal with these? Is Titania hoarding all the manabeeze?"

Fox takes the jar and narrows his eyes at it. "You might be right."

"I am?"

"She shouldn't need them, but since we're not policing forbidden items so the Wellspring can flow, it's . . . weakening."

He lowers beside me, stretches his long legs, and crosses his ankles. Together, we stare at his stone—

"Do you call them brothers?" I ask, curious.

His face lights up with affection for Styx.

"I do," he answers softly. "But we're more than brothers. We are one at times, and at others, we are six. I don't know how else to explain it."

"You haven't been connected for a long time." I hack the ground again, clenching my jaw. "I'm sorry. That must really suck."

I feel his eyes on me. "Do you miss your family?"

"Yes." My throat thickens. "I miss them so much, but . . . we have a complicated history."

"Because of your time with the humans?"

"In a way." I keep hacking at the dirt between us with my sword, making a mess, but not wanting to stop. It's hard to admit I've been a jerk to my family. "I spent so much time resenting them, but I accept now that keeping me alive meant I had to stay in Crystal City. It's not like they had a choice, I mean —" *Hack hack hack.* "Who can fight the devious plans of gods, right? But they did their best. Along with Rory, they supported me and taught me the skills I needed to survive." *Hack hack hack.* "It just sucks to have missed out on a proper childhood."

Fox's hand snaps over mine, halting my next chop. His fingers displace the hilt, then he presses my knuckles to his lips.

"We told them," he confesses, breath fluttering against my skin. "We warned them to leave you there, or Maebh would hunt you down and kill you."

"I know." It's valiant he wants to take the blame, but it is what it is. None of us truly had freedom.

"I want to say that I'm sorry, but—"

"You're not." My lips curve, eyes crinkling. "If there's one thing you're consistent with, Fox, it's wanting to keep me safe."

"Your amusement is misplaced." His sharp tone startles me. Black, fathomless eyes lock with mine as his dark side flickers beneath his skin. Spiky fangs scrape against my knuckles as they elongate. His voice is harsh with promise. "Make no mistake, my queen, we will steal every star in the sky trying to outshine you. We will ravage every heart pumping to hurt yours. We will devour the world if it means keeping you safe."

*We.* Not I.

I glance at Styx's beautiful, angry face.

Fox's breath on my hand skates shivers down my spine. His pledge wraps talons around my heart, armoring me with something I've not felt in a long time. Security. Belonging.

"I'm not sorry about protecting you," he murmurs. "But I am sorry I can't figure out what Titania has cursed you with."

"She's my problem too." I shuffle closer and sweep a lock of hair from his furrowed brow.

Tension rides his posture as his black, unwavering gaze holds mine. Then his tongue darts out to taste me. It's so unexpected that a tingle shoots up my arm. His next flick of wetness heats my blood, reminding me of how that tongue felt between my legs. I stifle a moan.

"Fox . . ." I don't know what I'm protesting. No words form as he slowly kisses up the back of my hand, heading for my wrist. His fangs pierce my sleeve, and he drags it up my forearm. The scrape, the soft kisses, steal my breath. Our noses touch when he looks at me, waiting for me to say when.

"Kiss me," I whisper. "Kiss me now."

His lips curve. "As you wish."

# FORTY-FIVE

## FOX

Willow's mouth tastes like the stars. When she parts her lips, inviting me in, I catch every last one with my tongue. Each time she whimpers, my cock hardens another impossible increment. I never knew it could feel so heavy, so full of desire for one person, but I need to be inside her, to feel her all around me. It's driving me mad.

I claw at the bindings of her cape. She arches impatiently into me.

"Take this off." I forgo her cape for the buttons on her shirt. Not buttons—a leather strap first. A baldric and a vest. It's also too much. I snarl and tug her shirt down. "What is all this?" The pieces mystify me. "Why are there so many layers?"

"Shut up. Keep kissing." She yanks off her cape, then slides her cool hands beneath my shirt. My sharp exhale is captured by her mouth. Hungry, insistent lips devour my own. She nibbles. Licks. Bites. Clashes teeth with my fangs and doesn't slow. My queen's impatience is a heady drug coursing through my veins.

"I love it when you get like this," I growl between kisses and attempts to remove our clothes.

389

"Like what?" she pants.

"Like you don't give a fuck about anything but having my mouth on you." She pulls away to fumble with the buttons on my trousers. "Like you'll let me do all the nasty things I've dreamed of doing to you, no matter where we are, no matter who watches."

Playful, golden eyes flick to mine, ceasing my heart. But the damage is done. I've seen her interest twice now. I'm dead. A soul levitating from a body. She's perfect for me. For us. The gods knew exactly what they did when they spilled her soul from the Cauldron's Wellspring. She is the—

Her frustrated snarl cuts me off as she fists my shirt and shakes me. "Stop. Composing. Well-damn poetry. In your head. And start *fucking* me." Her face softens with a whimpered, "Please."

"So needy for this body. Now I have no choice but to take this torturously slow." I unbuckle her cumbersome baldric with punctuated flicks. She throws her head back and seems to pray to the cave for patience. I suck on the hollow of her throat, satisfied when goosebumps erupt over her flesh.

"Fox," she begs, fisting my hair until it pulls.

"Yes, my queen." My hoarse whisper makes her shiver. "I'll fuck you now if that's what you want. I'll fuck you so hard they'll hear you scream my name from the palace."

She freezes. "Shit. We shouldn't be doing this here."

I glance at my brother's statue with a wayward smile. "Styx won't mind."

Her adorable, bashful squirm jerks my cock.

"I mean here—this temple. The Baleful Hunt might return at any moment. Can you *flicker* from here?"

A quick check of my senses confirms the wards block me from using magic to leave. We'll have to exit first.

"No," I reply, "but Sylvanar is on the warpath. He'll still be interrogating people tomorrow."

"Good. I can't wait any longer." Flushed cheeks and bright eyes, she bites her plump lower lip and plucks another button on my pants. "I don't know what's come over me. I feel like I'm in heat."

"Heat?" My brows pinch.

She is so focused on my pants that she barely lifts her gaze. "It's a wolf thing. I get all feverish with the irrational need to mate around my cycle, or when I meet my . . ." A flash of chagrin crosses her features. "No, it's not that."

"What?" My mind reels. "Wait. How often has this heat already happened? With who—" My throat tightens at the thought of any other than us touching her like that, of having their mouth on her slick pussy, of seeing to her needs.

"No one," she mumbles, popping the final buttoned obstacle to spring my cock free. Her eyes light up as if she's been waiting for this moment, then she moans, pumping my shaft. My mind blanks as pleasure barrels through me. I barely hear her next words through the cloud of bliss. "I'm still a virgin."

# CHAPTER
# FORTY-SIX

## WILLOW

"You're what?" Fox halts my fist pumping his cock.

For a heart-wrenching moment, I fear he'll deny me.

"Fox . . ." I close my eyes and shake my head. "If you dare say we should wait until we're in a bed or somewhere romantic with flowers and satin sheets or some shit, I'll—"

"You waited for us?" His voice is so quiet I barely hear it, and now I'm too afraid to open my eyes.

"I . . ." No one else felt right, but this does. It's never felt more right to give this part of myself to him.

"You waited for us as we waited for you?" His tone is now deeper, husky . . . aroused.

My eyes flip open to raw, haggard desire commanding his handsome features.

It flicks a switch inside my soul. "I waited."

I'm on my back in an instant, my pants dragged down my hips. Before he tugs them off my feet, I remove my vest and pull my shirt over my head, but I get stuck. I only see fabric when he parts my thighs and drives his tongue deep into my pussy. Gasping, I flex into him. He grips my bottom and lifts me to feast with hard, fast, ravenous strokes.

Every nerve in my body is on fire. Pleasure coils in my lower abdomen. My arms flop beside my head, shirt covering my nose, but I don't care. Without sight, my senses narrow down to that one spot. Every sensation is magnified.

Two fingers invade me, sliding in deep, triggering a sudden, intense orgasm that has me screaming his name. He licks me through my throes, savoring the slickness he's wrought like it's ambrosia.

"This pussy is ours," he murmurs against my intimate flesh, still fluttering.

Breathless, I try to make sense of my limbs enough to pull off my shirt. But his tongue and fingers slide and slip, distracting me. When I finally do, he's watching something beyond my body . . . Styx's statue. He stares for so long that I wonder if he's mentally conversing with the Sluagh inside the stone.

"He's not . . . in there, is he?" I ask.

"He is, but I can't read him." He sits back on his haunches and looks down at me with lust-drenched eyes, the picture of hedonistic sex on legs. Tousled, come-fuck-me hair. Shirt open. His fingers trail down his defined abdomen to where his trousers open enough to tease the tip of his erection. "But if he is, darling, let's give him something to remember. Come here and show me what that pretty mouth can do."

Another wave of heat shudders through my body. I prowl to him on hands and knees, empowered by his breaths growing stilted in anticipation. "Where do you want my lips? Here?" I drop a kiss against his pectoral. "Or here." I circle his nipple with my tongue.

"Pet," he groans, wrapping my braid around his wrist. "Lower."

"Mm, here." I lick around every valley between the slabs of

clenching muscle, hit the side one angling down to his hips, and follow it to his groin. I whisper over the tip of his cock, "Or here."

His grip tightens on my hair. He flexes his hips, chasing my lips, but I pull away with a smirk when he bares spiky fangs in frustration. Whoever thought sucking cock could be so much fun? I don't really know how it's done, but it can't be that difficult.

I palm his crotch, fondling over the fabric around the bulge of his testicles. Each little gasp he makes is fuel to my fire. When I witnessed Irisa's sordid desperation on his lap, I thought sex had to be a little frightening to feel good, but this is only good. Only thrilling and addictive. I yank on his waistband, freeing the full length of his erection.

"Yes," he mutters hotly. "Finish what you started in the library."

I take him into my mouth until he hits the back of my throat, and then I take him deeper, curious how far I can go. His body bows over mine with a sharp, hitched intake of breath. He curses and moans and shudders. Turns out, pretty deep. When I slide back off and don't gag, he quietly praises the gods for building my body like this. I lick him, up and down, around and around, before asking, "Like what?"

"Fucking addictive," he rasps and fucks my throat, once, twice, and then makes a pained sound as he draws out. He cups my jaw and lifts my eyes to his. "I should warn you, Bodin is going to love this mouth."

My eyes widen as I recall Bodin's wild dominance over me—the bite. I moan and touch my aching breasts, needing relief from this insistent desire. Fox's gaze smolders as my fingers rolling and pinching my nipples. He enjoys watching me a fraction longer and then takes over with his mouth. His hot, wet suction shoots bolts of heat to my core. I'm so wet, it's down my thighs.

"I need you inside me," I beg.

Strong hands drag me onto his lap. He hooks my legs around his waist. I thread my fingers through his short hair and meet his eyes.

"You ready?" he asks.

I nod, and he fits his cock to my entrance, coating the length with my desire. My moan of encouragement causes a muttered something about not lasting, about needing more time to show me everything he's learned, his special move. But his hips give a small thrust. The first small breech is a shock, a stretch. I drop my teeth to the tendon between his shoulder and neck.

"Yes," he hisses. "Bite me hard. Make me yours."

I whimper and press harder.

"There's no easy way to do this, love. It's going to hurt." His hands return to my hips. "Just say when."

"When."

He fills me with short, fast thrusts. Each motion is a contrast of pain and ecstasy. Once seated, he gives me a moment to adjust. Then he lifts and slams me down to meet another powerful thrust. Stars in my eyes. A flash of pleasure in the pain. Another still moment. He bites off a ragged groan as I squirm.

"You feel so fucking good," he rasps, lidded gray eyes lifting to mine. Gray, not black. He's being careful with me. "Is this okay?"

My answer is a slow drag off his cock and a flex back down. He kneads my bottom. I feel him inside, so deep. Hot, prickly animal need washes over me. The tightness in my chest expands to the breaking point, urging me onward.

*Harder. Faster. Take him. Claim him.*

I must have shouted in my mind. He flips me onto my back and the soft cape. Then he loses control. Again and again, he pumps into me hard until the initial pain eases, and it only feels good. Then he braces on one forearm, changes his angle of entry, and hits me differently, teasing my nipple with his mouth until I whimper and arch into him, begging for more.

"Tell me what feels good," he pants. "Tell me everything."

"This. You." My fingers flex on his shoulders, still half covered in his shirt. "Just you."

Somewhere, in a distant part of my mind, I know this changes everything, but I'm too far gone into lust to care. All I want is for this to last forever. Right now, he desires me. My eyes dip to the indents my teeth left on the area between his neck and shoulder.

*Mark him. Deep. Make him bleed. Keep him.*

I yank his collar aside. A possessive snarl lurches me forward, and I bite and pierce tender flesh. Hot, coppery blood spills into my mouth. Something primal inside me eases, something animal that wanted satisfaction. He's mine now. All fucking mine. Fox releases a hoarse groan and slaps his hips against mine, fucking me relentlessly until another orgasm starts to build. I lose all sense of my limbs as stars converge in my vision.

"Fox," I plead, grappling for purchase during his drives.

Horns erupt from his head. I grip them hard, anchoring myself against the primeval storm threatening to obliterate my being. He buries his face in the crook of my neck, hands cupping my head, sheltering me from the ground. Sharp pinpricks of pain beneath my jaw make me gasp. His fangs pierced my flesh— marking me too, branding me as his. Forever.

I combust with an earth-shattering cry as ecstasy consumes every fiber of my being. He rears back to witness my undoing, male satisfaction lurking in his eyes. Only after I'm done does he allow himself to come. He seats himself, drops his lips back to his mark, and rides out his pleasure, body trembling under my hands, groaning and grunting with labored breaths.

In an icy cave, we are a pile of hot, sweaty, tangled limbs. Half our clothes are on the ground—well, all of mine, half of his. His trousers are still around his thighs, and his shirt is crooked. His look of contentment hits me hard with affection. That savoring, relishing thing he does begins anew as he licks his way down from my lips to the aching wound at my neck.

"Mm." Raspy laves against the mark. "Nice and high, so the others see who claimed you first."

"What?" I press up on my elbows.

His mouth trails down my body on a one-way track to the single place I don't think can take any more attention.

"When their memories return," he explains. "I won't be number one anymore. I'll have to wait in line. So I want to remind them"—he nips my lower belly—"that I was here first."

I scowl. "I won't be bossed around. If I don't want a line, then I don't want one."

His lips curve on my skin, and I realize I just admitted I'm open to having all of them.

He frowns and looks up at me. "Pet, I made you bleed."

I blush and try to pull away. "That's normal. It only happens for the first time."

His palm flattens on my stomach and pins me down. "More firsts for me."

Before I can stop him, he buries his face between my legs and cleans away every last drop of my virginity with his tongue.

"You're an animal," I moan, tugging his horn.

"You love it." His chuckle tingles my tender pussy, and I gasp. He might be right.

I love this. All the darker urges, doing the things I'm not supposed to be doing. Admitting that feels freeing and arousing. His complete, utter devotion to every part of me is grounding. Somehow, I know no curse, threat, or lie will sway his feelings for me. He'll never leave me on purpose. He never did. My fingers flutter to the wound at my neck. This lover I once called a monster is my mate.

*My mate.*

The word doesn't sound frightening anymore, nor is it foreign. With Fox, it's just right. It's home.

When we're dressed again, the cold seeps in with reality. Styx is still frozen. We're no better off working on a plan to release him. I touch his wing as Fox scours the treasure trove of ancient artifacts, lifting, shaking, and sniffing items.

"Maybe I should do it," I mumble. "Take his place."

"What?" Fox's head whips my way. "Absolutely not."

I round on him. "It's what your true queen would do, right?"

"No." He gestures at Styx. "He would never approve, especially now we know he's somehow broken his seal. In fact, he'd be your most avid supporter."

My brow arches indignantly. "You mean my most obsessive, possessive, macho-protector who thinks he knows what I want better than me?"

His lips part. "I, ah . . ."

"I'm kidding." My brief laugh sobers as his complexion blanches. "Fox, you need to lighten up if we're to survive being mates."

"Mates?"

"Yeah, well." My cheeks heat. I look away. "I figured if we both marked each other, that's what it meant. And, I mean, I, um, feel a connection to you so—"

He strides over and cups my face, shutting me up. "You're beautiful when you bluster."

The heat in my cheeks now burns. "Thanks?"

A full belly laugh throws his head back.

"Shut up, Mr. Abs and Dimples, and . . . *shut up.*"

Fox's heart-stopping smile remains as he returns to his treasure hunt, and I refocus on Styx with butterflies in my stomach.

"But seriously," I say. "What if I activate this swapping spell?

CASTLE OF NEVERS AND NIGHTMARES

What would happen? Would it give you another year to devise an alternative plan?"

I trace the hewn shapes of Styx's arms, the dips and valleys, and the spiky collarbone. I rest my ear against his stone chest and listen for a heartbeat. I've never met him, yet it feels like I have. Maybe it's the portraits I carried around for years or what we did in this temple cave, but he feels familiar. They all do.

"I'm going to tell him you hugged his naked statue," Fox taunts me.

Ha! If he only knew I almost broke his penis. I slide him a wry look. "You're going to be impossibly vexing now that we've fucked."

"Naturally. Who else knows which buttons to push on you?"

Despite myself, I smile, then tell him to shush while I stretch my senses and listen against Styx's chest again. There. A sluggish beat. "He's alive."

Fox comes up behind me and swipes his finger around my nape, shifting my braid to the other side. His melancholic reply steals my breath. "I know, love. We can't really die. I don't think."

"Do you think it hurts him?"

"Pain only comes from being apart from you."

"So dramatic." I grin, then rap my knuckles over the statue, listening for resonance. A ripple of fire ants scuttle over my hand. I knock again, expecting another wave, but I receive a tsunami. The sharp sensation hurtles me back into Fox.

"What happened?" he asks, catching me.

"The magic latched onto me."

He scoffs. "Maybe Styx knows you're here."

"Maybe." But I'm not sure. That sensation was . . . "It felt familiar, like my old magic. Like the wards and the seals. But the gods took back my magic as punishment for what I did. How can I feel it here?"

Fox stares at me. "You think the gods did what?"

I pick up my sword and clang it against Styx's thigh, annoyed Fox is making me repeat it. "They punished me for raising an army of the undead that killed half of Elphyne."

"Willow," he intones, "The gods *never* take back what they give. They can't. It's the reason we're in this mess."

"What mess?"

"Me, him—" He gestures at Styx. "Our hive and the Wild Hunt. The gods can't take back the power they used to make us. Unfortunately for them, how we feed increases it."

My jaw drops. "Then who stole my magic?"

The answer hits us at the same time.

"Titania," we say.

"When I felt my power being ripped away," I quickly add, "the taint still poisoned the Well. I always wondered if maybe I had something to do with this civilization waking up. What if I raised everyone when I just wanted to raise the dead?"

"Will you show me?" he asks, frowning. "Will you allow me to relive the memory?"

I nod. "How do we do that?"

He lifts his hands to my head. "Just think about that day."

# CHAPTER
# FORTY-SEVEN
## WILLOW

**Five Years Ago**

Across the battlefield, someone wants me dead.

The hand of fate reaches into my soul and pulls out an insatiable urge to dominate. My wolfish fangs elongate. My ears flatten. My hackles raise. My fist plunges into soil soaked with blood. I claw at the essence of creation and then do what Nero has trained me to do, what I vowed never to do.

I violate nature.

And it feels good.

Freeing. Cathartic. A rite of passage. This is what I am made for.

A slave to my instincts, I pump the world's veins with my almighty, churning soul.

*Rise.*

*Wake.*

Like the birds I have summoned from the other side of death, fae corpses twitch with life, rising stiffly with jilted movements.

*Kill the queen,* I decree.

Each dead thing on the ground, even those buried beneath, awaits my bidding. They hunt. They rip and shred. But then my rival queen fights back.

I must destroy her. The need is in every fiber of my being, ripping apart my will. The murderous compulsion teases my parched bones, making me thirst for something I don't understand.

But then my gaze pulls again, toward a group of hauntingly beautiful men. My need shifts in tempo and becomes feverish, pulsing, and demanding. It feels like those times when I have to numb my "beastly needs" with iced water in Crystal City, hiding in the bathroom from the humans so they don't call me a freak.

I lock eyes with one of the men and fall into the fathomless night. The impact of his appearance steals my breath. Dark, sculpted brows. High cheekbones. A sharp, masculine jaw but soft, sensuous lips. Long, silken black hair cascading from a widow's peak. He is made for seduction, but there is sadness in his eyes. He tries to hide it behind a hotter, darker emotion.

Others besides him steal my attention: fallen angels, each as hauntingly beautiful as the first but different in their own way. Unique. Precious. Caught in the between, like me. Belonging to neither place but forged from both.

*Not enough,* my dark friends whisper in my mind, urging me onward. *She must die for you to live.*

"Not enough," I reply, agreeing.

And so I reach into that other place beneath the first, the midnight behind the ink. The place I fear to touch. But somehow, with them so near, I feel safe. Home.

*More,* they whisper in my mind. *Close the gap between life and death. Tear a hole in the veil.*

The gap.

Buzzing. Humming. Souls swarming and begging, waiting in the wings.

The gap.

The space between. These fallen angels are just like me. Different, never quite fitting in. Even my parents sometimes look at me strangely. Oh, how they love me. But they misunderstand me. Even as a small child, I have felt different. So when Rory stole me away, and the voices told me it was okay, I believed them.

But as I grew, so did the taunts.

*Halfling freak. Tainted One. Ugly. Weird. Beastly. Bitch. Nothing. You don't belong here. They don't want you.*

I feel a thicker kinship with these beautiful monsters than with my family. I see understanding, acceptance, need, and desire—beings trapped in the dark who want a slice of the light.

*Yes, little wolf. It is not night when we see your face. Tear a hole in the veil. Close the gap. Be our skin.*

The whispers are so familiar. They comfort me in lonely times. They dream alongside me. They wipe my tears. And now, they need me to save them.

Defiance burns through me. I submit to my instincts. The world falls away. Sound dims beneath the roar of buzzing wings until my heart pounds like a drum, and my power shoots into the stars.

There, I find what I need. I latch on and claw into it. Then I tug it back to the earth. I bring it closer, closing the gap.

*Wake.*

*Rise.*

There is no between, only life—one existence for all.

I lose all sense of reality. There is nothing after that but blood, buzzing swarms, screams, and the sense something isn't going according to plan. The taint in the Well changes my intention and mixes everything up. Pain, agony, and the horrifying realization that my power leaks from my body like blood from a gaping wound.

Worse than leaks—something sucks it out like a vampire,

and it isn't the queen across the battlefield. It is someone far, far away, ancient and hungry. Greedy. Righteous.

I fight, scramble, lash, and try to hold on. But it is as futile as catching air. I am not experienced enough. This ancient entity is borne of stardust, and I have woken it from slumber along with everything else.

An ear-piercing scream rips from my throat. A tether snaps inside of me. And then there is nothing but the dry, crumbling hole inside my body.

# CHAPTER
# FORTY-EIGHT
## WILLOW

Fox's hands drop from my head. The visceral memory of my worst moment has left me breathless, dizzy, and feeling nauseous. I look up at him, afraid he'll see my worst parts. His eyes soften with affection as his thumb grazes my scarred cheek.

"You fought for us," he whispers, brows lifting. "And she stole your magic."

"You think it was her?"

He yanks me to his chest and hugs me. Tight. It takes me a moment to relax, but when I do, I'm sobbing silent tears and hugging him right back.

"Willow. . ." He strokes my braid in soothing, repetitive sweeps. "You woke her up. You woke everyone up."

The blood drains from my cheeks. "This war. This tournament. All these deaths. . . are my fault?"

He holds me at arm's length, disbelief on his face. "I just told you that you woke up entire civilizations, and the first thing you worry about is what they did to each other?"

"It wouldn't have happened if I didn't—"

"Try to save us? Try to free us from Maebh?"

A helpless whimper slips out of me. "I don't know."

"Stop second-guessing your choices. Start listening to your heart. It will never steer you wrong."

My mother said something like that the night before I left. "How can someone who's eaten hearts for eons know more about them than me?"

He winces.

"I'm sorry," I mumble. "I didn't mean it as an insult."

"I'm trying, Willow."

"I know."

I help Fox exit the temple but linger to speak with Styx.

"I don't know if you can hear me," I whisper into the cave. "But on the off chance that Fox is right, and you're in there right now—" I bite my lip, wanting to yell so many things, but settle for a promise. "I'm coming back."

I nab a jar of manabeeze and shuffle toward the exit, but kick something on the ground. The object rolls beneath a table. I put down the jar and get on my hands and knees to chase it. My fingers latch on and burn with the intensity of magic vibrating into me. I hiss at the sensation but back up as fast as possible, placing the disc before the jar to inspect it better. Runes are carved into the flat stone. This feels important, so I pick up the jar and disc and take them outside.

It's stopped snowing again, but night has fallen. Fox's pale, worried face is a beacon in the darkness two feet away. I head toward him, but the disc refuses to cross the wards, and my arm is yanked back at the socket. The surprise change in momentum almost has me dropping the jar from my right hand, so I let go of the disc in my left and catch the manabeeze.

"Phew. That was close." I exhale a shaky laugh. "The last thing we want is a thousand manabeeze floating in the sky, announcing to the guards that I just raided the queen's Cabinet of Curiosities."

"What took you so long?" he grumbles.

"Relax. I found something."

He lets me pull him back into the cave, and I show him the flat disc with carved runes.

"It burns with so much power, I almost can't hold it."

"A seal." His eyes widen. "You found a seal."

"It was under a table. Maybe the others are in here too." I gasp with an idea. "Maybe we can break them!"

We attack the seal with everything we've got. I chop it with my sword. He tries to crush it, to obliterate it from the inside with his phantom, and to toss it around with shadow against the cave's inner walls, but nothing we try makes a dent in it. And we're getting perilously close to breaking jars.

"What the fuck is this made from?" I groan.

"It's the runes," he pants, hands on hips, eyes wild. "Only the person who made them can break them."

"Titania?" I ask.

"Maybe. Or a Keeper." He pauses. "Or, if she's using your stolen magic, then maybe if we get your powers back, you can break the seals."

"It might not be possible."

He renews his attempts by scraping his fangs across the runes. I crawl under every table and hunt for the other seals. To my surprise, I find all five of them. One is marred.

"Look!" I hold up the one with a crack splitting the runes in half. "This must be Styx's. But it still tingles."

His gaze swings between Styx and the disc. "He must know how to break them."

We're so close to figuring this out that my heart races excitedly. Then I realize, duh, we can't ask Styx, and I deflate. "Look, it's getting late. We should go and tell the others. Maybe . . . I don't know . . . maybe it will trigger a memory."

Fox nods, disappointment flexing his jaw as he returns the discs to the shadows beneath a table.

"Or perhaps it's time for me to rifle through their minds," he says.

"They won't like that."

"No. They won't."

I take his hand and pull him through the wards. Outside, he freezes and scours the darkness.

*"Is someone here?"* I send him.

He holds up a finger and narrows his eyes at the hedges rustling with the arctic breeze. After a few more heartbeats, he takes my hand. I hug the jar of manabeeze like a life raft. We *flicker* through space, eventually landing in the center of his bedroom.

The disorienting travel sickness abates after a few deep breaths, and I put the jar onto his dresser. Joy fills me. I can activate the portal stone home now. Any Nothing who wants to leave can. My hand flies to Tinger's pendant, and I squeeze the bulk beneath my cape. I didn't get a chance to spend time with my new friends as I promised, but hopefully, this makes up for it.

Fox stabs his hair with his fingers and renews his pacing like a caged animal. "I looked everywhere, even below the tables. Why didn't I see the seals?"

"Maybe it's another mortal thing."

"But I should have seen them." He pounds his chest. "If I'd found them earlier, we could be done with this madness already."

"Hey." I gather his hands and hold them still between us. "We can try again later. You said the Baleful Hunt won't be there until morning, right?"

"I don't know." A faraway look enters his eyes. "I'm sure I sensed someone there. Something feels off."

"Let's call this a win." The warmth spreading in my heart agrees. Fox trusted me enough to bring me. I trusted him to go. Together, we achieved something remarkable. "I know Titania stole my magic. We know Styx is there. And we know he broke a seal."

Exhaustion drops his shoulders. "Yeah."

"We should call it a night and start again tomorrow."

His mood perks up with a glance at his bed. "You're sleeping here."

It's not an order, not a request, but a fact stated.

The last time I slept in his bed, I woke feeling the most rested I've been in years. I keep waiting for the moment of regret, the guilt or remorse to weigh me down, reminding me not to trust them.

But it doesn't come.

# CHAPTER

# FORTY-NINE

## WILLOW

When morning arrives, my muscles ache, and I'm not alone. Fox's legs and tail are twisted around mine. No horns or wings, though. It's a miracle I got any rest in this position, but his embrace was so soothing that I slept straight through.

Excited thumping somewhere in the room jerks my head up. The baby Wild Hunt sits on the floor beside the bed, staring at me, wagging his little dragon tail.

"Seriously?" I mumble, scrubbing my face. "How long have you been sitting there staring at me?"

His tongue lolls, and the thumping intensifies. I groan. "You want yum-yums, don't you?"

I've created a monster.

Glancing at the clear sky outside tells me it's just after dawn. Before Bodin decides to attack me with another training session, I'd better dress and head into the Nexus early.

I slide out of bed and wrap my arms around my cold, naked body. Shivering, I tiptoe toward the door, praying it leads to my room as it did last night. Yep. Still there.

After dressing in clean training attire, I inspect my collection of treasures on my dresser. The jar of manabeeze now sits between the two gemstones I stole from dream webs, and my portal stone back to Elphyne. Fox told me to look after it. Over the weekend, I added an old trowel from the conservatory, possible options for new portal stones, and some spindly wire coiled in a loop. It would make a useful garrote in a pinch.

When I braid my hair, I check the mirror and notice my ugliness still remains at a minimum. Leaning in close, I test my brows and pat the angles of my cheeks. The scars are still small and silvery, as they were before the curse.

I open the door to Fox's room.

"Tell me I don't take your breath away." He waits on the other side, arm braced on the doorframe, naked body holding a pose that accentuates his physique. No tail now, but all male. His biceps are defined, his abdomen is tight, and his cock juts out proudly, ready for attention. When I stare appreciatively, he shoots me a lazy grin, tilting his neck to draw my attention to my mating—*what!*

"My mark is gone!" I grab his neck and yank him down to inspect.

"Whoa." He stumbles into me.

"You healed!" I accuse. There's nothing but red, tiny pinpricks.

Talons erupt from his rapidly blackening fingertips. He raises a clawed hand to his neck and growls, "I'll bring it back."

"Don't!" I tug his hand down, scowling, hating the heat prickling my face with inadequacy. "I'm mortal. You're a demigod. This was bound to happen."

"And Titania has your magic." Gray eyes flick to black. "Perhaps it's time we pay her a visit. Together."

Meaning he can *flicker* me into her room, and I can kill her while she sleeps. She is a rival queen. Perhaps killing her would work.

"The queen's assassination will take a lot of planning," I point out.

"Why?"

I give him a warning look until he groans in capitulation.

"Fine. We'll *plan* it." He pouts as he registers my clothes. "Going into the Nexus already?"

"I don't want trouble today." I bite my lip, thinking of how much attention my theatrics threw on my friends last week. And then gnaw at it when I think of Alfie. "Do you think Milford's death will be forgotten now?"

He rakes a hand through his hair. "Definitely not. But I have no reason to believe you'll be at risk. Cait won't betray us. Actually—" His gaze lands on the jar of manabeeze. "I was hoping to give five hundred wisps to her as payment for that special mirror she promised to hunt down for me. It belonged to another demigod eons ago who used it against a female bonded to the Baleful Hunt."

"Five hundred?"

"Unless you need the wisps for something else?" Fox's tone holds a hint of nerves.

How can I explain to him that manabeeze are my safety net? My mark didn't stay on him, but that doesn't mean anything, right?

"Willow?"

"Um." I scratch my head. "I was saving them to use on a portal stone back to Elphyne."

His face pales. "You were?"

"For the others," I quickly add. "For the Nothings who will die in this stupid exhibition. Maybe."

He offers quietly, "I can activate the stone any time you want."

Shit, now I feel like an asshole. Maybe we've jumped too quickly into this. I let my body think for me at the temple. It might not be the right choice.

Fox steps back. "I know what will cheer you up."

He jogs to his pile of messy clothes, tugs on some black pants, and then scrummages around for something. He returns and drops a gemstone into my palm.

"What's this?"

"Milford's charm. Cait let me keep it."

"It's not keyed to anything." Usually, mana stones or charms feel tingly in my palm. This is just a stone. Maybe he can enchant it to hide my curse, but I can't come out and say that, so try another leading question. "I'm a Nothing. What can I do with it?"

He shrugs as if it's obvious. "You can put it with your collection of gemstones."

Hopeful eyes watch for my reaction. I don't know whether to laugh or cry.

"I have those stones, Fox, because I hope to turn them into enchanted charms. To use them to help win the tournament."

"But you don't need help. You have me."

"I don't want to get into this now."

"I thought you would be happy." He cups the back of his neck, honestly perplexed.

My irritation inexplicably grows. I know it stemmed from the shock of seeing my mark gone, the reminder of our differences, but I can't let it go.

"These are only useful if I can use them. Without being activated, they're plain rocks. Pretty, but plain. They can't even glamour a Nothing's flaws away to prevent them from being deported after the tournament."

His hand drops. "You want me to do that?"

I exhale, close my eyes, and wish I knew which of their

deities to pray to for patience. If he could create charms all this time, and he's only thinking of giving me a secondhand one—that I almost earned myself—then. . .what the fuck?

"I'm sorry." I close my eyes against the onslaught of hormones raging through my system. First, it was the heat outside of my cycle, then the petty jealousy or whatever this is at my mark disappearing. Now I'm being dramatic over a gift. I'm acting like I've just hit puberty again. "Yes, I would love for you to turn these rocks into charms that hide a Nothing's flaws. Thank you."

"No problem." He collects the stolen gems, adds them to Milford's, and stares at me. "Who am I keying these to?"

I briefly consider saying me, but then glimpse the dream web over his bed. I need four stones to cover Max, Geraldine, Bob, and Peggy. Five to include me. I'm here now—may as well go all the way. "Could I take a few stones from your web, too?"

"You know the answer," he replies.

Why is he being so nice? Grumbling, I move further into his room and aim for the bed, but his warning stops me.

"But removing a charm from a web can impact its efficacy. Do you want Avorlorna to watch a replay of my favorite moments between your legs every night? Because"—he laughs quietly—"that's all I dream about."

Heat rises up my neck to twitch my ears.

"I mean, I'm okay if you're okay with it." He gives a half-hearted shrug. "But I'd hoped we only share those moments with the hive."

A slight flutter of arousal pulses through me.

"Um. It's fine. I won't take any more. Thank you." Now that I know he can make them, I'll figure out how to find another stone. "Do you want their names?"

His mood lifts a little. He seems so genuine about his feelings for me. I shouldn't worry about the mark. Or my choice to be with him. I give him three names and vow to find a stone for the fourth. As he holds each, I sense the familiar tingle of magic, and my outrage at Titania grows. All this time, I thought it was my fault that I lost it.

It was her. It's always been her.

He hands me the keyed charms, but I'm too numb to feel them hit my palm. He stares at me for a long, hard minute and then asks, "Are you well?"

If I mention her, he'll get all possessive and growly. She's an ancient faerie who stole the six most powerful creatures to walk the earth and bound them to her. She stole my magic. Taking her down won't be a walk in the park.

"Yeah. These help."

"Take my coat. It's freezing out there."

I let him slide his black brocade coat over my arms. It's the same one he wore to the temple, is fur-lined, and smells like him. I deposit the charms in the pockets.

"Pet," he murmurs, lifting my chin. But before he can say anything else, his eyes grow distant, as if someone else speaks into his mind.

"What is it?" I whisper.

"There's been another attack." He scrubs his face. A sigh. "We're called out of the city to investigate."

"All of you?"

He nods. "After what happened at Burn After Reading, Legion strongly suggests I'm not at the Nexus to draw attention."

"I can see the wisdom in that. You might trigger someone's memory."

"We'll be out all day," he says, "but I'll check in if distance permits."

"You act like I can't take care of myself." I clench my fist around the gems. "But thank you for this."

# CHAPTER
# FIFTY

PUCK

My tailored leather loafers are ruined. The frost-encrusted lawn outside the Cabinet's inner temple is wet, icy, and unforgiving. But worth it.

I crouch to collect one of the resonance recorder stones I placed around the temple earlier. It's hot. So we had visitors, after all.

I hold out my palm and activate the stone. The air above it shimmers and fills with flickering light. The picture of the silver-haired Shadow flickers into existence. I watch as she exits the temple with a glass jar of wisps tucked under her arm. She becomes stuck halfway through the wards and almost drops the jar.

*"Phew. That was close."* She exhales a shaky laugh. *"The last thing we want is a thousand manabeeze floating in the sky, announcing to the guards that I just raided the queen's Cabinet of Curiosities."*

I toss the stone into the air and catch it, then return to the palace, whistling a merry tune.

# CHAPTER
# FIFTY-ONE
## WILLOW

The brisk walk into the Nexus does the opposite of clearing my mind. I ache in all the wrong places from the training but all the right places from Fox.

*Listen to my heart.*

Right now, it's telling me to help the Nothings. Both my parents and Rory instilled a sense of justice for the oppressed. They had different ways of going about it, but the point was the same. Not only do I have some charms, but I have news of a way to get back to Elphyne. This is a good day.

Focusing on that, I stroll into the registration building with my head held high, my hands in Fox's coat pockets. Peablossom sits at the desk, leaning on her hands with a bored expression on her dainty face. Upon seeing me, she perks up with her usual mask of polite pleasantry.

"Oh. It's you." Her shoulders slump.

"'Tis I." I pirouette with a flourish. "The constant thorn in your side."

It was meant as a joke, but her pout grows. This melancholy is very unlike her.

"Is everything okay, Peablossom?"

"We are smiling, oh yes, we are." Her merry laugh is so forced that she sounds hysterical. "All is well, dearest confection."

My lips purse, then I notice her missing eyebrow is growing back. "You're almost back to your usual stunning self. That must be a relief."

Tears glisten in her eyes, and she gives a dramatic sigh. "If only such tidings were enough to elevate the fortune of us all, yet the Earl is stirring disorder. Puck insists I prepare a change in the schedule. Your Knights are away again! Even Lady Selene has changed the curriculum. No one wants to clean the constant messes in the Nothing dormitory. Everything is out of control!"

A knot of dread tightens in my gut. "What messes?"

She shivers, and then her mask is back on, her voice once again whimsical. "Shadow O'Leary-Nightstalk, while we take pride in avoiding tardiness, you are rather eager to prove this point for your first class. Please ensure you do not add to the brewing chaos, lest we devolve into our enemy. We are smiling, yes?"

She grins and points to her cheeks.

Okay, then. I return a tight smile and continue onward. So many things could have gone wrong over the weekend. I should have been here. I'm still lost in my thoughts when I open the door between the commons and the dormitories, so I'm not prepared for the figure running out. We clash. I'm knocked backward and skid on my spine across the wooden floor. The wind knocks out of me. It takes a moment to gather my wits. Heavy breathing in my face. A whiff of cologne. Male. He carelessly scrambles over me in his haste to leave. My fist comes up, but I miss and barely recover to see him rush through the exit leading into the woods.

A scream from the dormitories jolts my heart into my throat. I'm running toward the Malachite suite without a second thought. The hallways are empty as all other exhibitors are now roomed in the Towers.

The suite's door is wide open. The instant I cross the threshold, someone swings a knife at my face, but this time I'm ready. I deflect, forcibly twist their wrist, and disarm my attacker. When I round on them, I point my stolen weapon at Geraldine's tear-stained eyes.

It's Rory's dagger. I lower it. "What happened?"

Her lips open and part, gasping for words. Too distraught. I spin and find blood everywhere. This suite is the largest and most simply furnished. Five rows of six bunks line the space. All but five bunks are made with fresh linen and haven't been slept in. Two bunks are covered in blood with lumpy, body-sized shapes beneath the blue sheets. A quick calculation tells me only three slept-in, untouched bunks remain.

Three left alive.

"Geraldine?"

She drops to her bunk, head in her hands, and sobs, "You weren't here."

My throat tightens. "Where are the others?"

A choking sound at the door turns me. Max and Peggy, freshly showered and wrapped in clean towels, faces ashen. Three. That means . . . I glance at the lumpy, bloody bunks.

"Bob?" It hurts to speak his name.

Geraldine's shaky nod releases a keening wail from Peggy's lips. She limps toward one of the bunks, and I'm ashamed to realize I don't know which one belongs to Bob. I'd planned on coming into this room to help them set up an alarm system or to teach them to protect themselves. But instead, I was partying it up with Alfie and his self-involved crew, fucking Fox in a cave, and . . . there is no excuse.

"I'm so sorry," I whisper, stricken.

After Peggy drops the sheet on Bob's slack face, she rounds on me with more vehemence than I thought she owned.

"You," she hisses. "You act like you're one of us, but you're not."

"Peg." Max gets between us and tries to push her away. "That's not fair on Willow. This isn't her fault. I'm sure she had a good reason for not being here."

Guilt shreds my heart into ribbons. I dig into the pocket and then hold out my palm with the three charms. "I know this won't bring him back, but I found a way to activate a portal stone home to Elphyne if you want to go there. I also had these keyed to hide your flaws. Well—actually, one is for Bob." My breath catches in my throat. The charms blur as I stare. "I'll have it changed. I'm sorry, Max. I only had three, and I thought . . . I thought . . . "

"I would have insisted the others went first. You were right to pick them." His kind eyes give me far too much credit than I deserve. He turns to the two women and adds, "Let's not forget Willow owes us nothing. We all chose to enter this exhibition. We knew the odds."

Sniffing, I kneel before Geraldine and hold out Milford's red charm. "If you secure this to your uniform, always keep it on you. The glamour will hold in place. Just speak your name as you touch it, and it will activate for you."

Red-rimmed, shell-shocked eyes blink at me. "I don't have a chain."

"Shit. I didn't think that far." I'm still unsure why the charms work around metal, anyway. But maybe I've been thinking about it all wrong. Perhaps the isolated magic inside the stone still works regardless of being connected to the Well—like how I still sense magic without an active connection.

"I might have something." Max jogs to his bunk, gripping his towel to stop it from unraveling. After rifling through his rucksack, he returns with a Chaser chain equipped to hold four charms. Sheepishly, he explains, "I stole it from Peablossom's desk."

While Peggy and Max dress in uniform, I hack the chain in half and clamp a gemstone onto each. I make holes in Geraldine's pocket with my dagger and securely weave in the chain. When it's Peggy's turn, she tries not to look ungrateful but can't hide her bitterness.

"I don't blame you for hating me over this," I murmur as I fix her chain to her pocket. "I'm living in a castle while you're here. I get it."

"Honey," she says, voice tight. "I don't mean to be rude."

"It's okay. Send your bitterness my way, then at least it's not directed at trouble."

"Maybe you can tell us more about your home later?" she asks hopefully.

"Of course."

I give the room a puzzling glance, remember the figure who collided with me, and realize how close I came to apprehending the culprit. My mind scrambles over the memory to hunt for evidence of their identity. Besides knowing he's male, a heavy breather, and clumsy, I have nothing. It happened so fast.

*"Details are important,"* Rory once told me. *"Scour every corner twice. Commit it to memory."*

Shaking off my self-deprecation, I start combing the room for clues.

"Don't bother," Geraldine says. "The assassins are different every night. Sometimes there's more than one. We know it's the Shadows. It has to be."

"This is completely unfair," I growl, refusing to stop my search.

Bloody footprints leading from the bunk are more prominent than mine. Before I lift Bob's sheet, my consciousness peels away, distancing itself from what happens next. For five years, I avoided this feeling. It's the part that took over when Nero made me murder, touch dead flesh, and reanimate.

But I must look at everything, even the parts that make me uncomfortable. The clue could be in the wound patterns. Could be anywhere.

I lift the sheet.

For the first time in my life, disassociating doesn't work. In every wound, every drop of blood, every line of Bob's body, I feel his pain. Biting my lip, I force myself to finish the job.

With each inch studied, I let the hate in. This was not a quick death. This was not clean. It was cruel, pointless, and completely preventable if I had been here. The stab wounds are sloppy and fast but brutal. They hit no vital spots. His body is still warm. He would have woken and bled out, knowing exactly what his fate was.

I would have been here if I hadn't stopped to talk to Fox.

Just before I recover his body, a strip of red that doesn't belong stands out in the blood pooling at his throat. Slowly, I pick it up and know exactly who I crashed into. The heavy breather from Burn After Reading. If Fox had allowed Cait to burn my memories away, I might never have known Ryder killed my friend.

As I stand, I kick something white and wispy on the floor into a pool of blood. My hand snaps out to save it from destruction. Wobbly handwriting on paper. "Bob's Theories, Part One."

*"You should write all your theories down, Bob. I'm sure they'd make for interesting reads."*

*"Good idea. Maybe Peg can help me."*

He took my advice.

A tear spills from my eye. I crush the paper so hard that blood leaks from my fist. It takes me a long, painful moment to rein in my emotions. When my courage returns, I find Peggy and Max watching Geraldine gaping at her reflection in the mirror behind the door. She touches her face in awe. "The scars are gone."

*Your scars are what make you beautiful.*

I'd almost forgotten Fox said that to me when he thought I was sleeping. Swallowing, I hold the words dear to my heart and walk up to them. "You were already beautiful, Geraldine. You all are. If they can't see that, then that's their problem."

She frowns, almost as if she's summoning the courage to tell me I'm wrong.

"I know this stupid exhibition tells us otherwise," I continue. "And I know giving you this charm strengthens their claim. But I don't give a fuck what they think. I think you're beautiful without it."

"So do I," Max blurts, his cheeks reddening, but he stands tall. "Furthermore, you're smart and sexy and inspire me."

"Max." Her eyes soften with affection for him.

"Buggers out there wouldn't know beauty if it bit them on the bollocks." Peggy herds them into a group hug, kissing them on the head. "You lot are *all* beautiful." She waves me over. "Come on, hun. You too."

I join the hug, squeeze them tight, and vow that next time, I'll be here to protect them. Lost in the feelings of bliss this friendship gives me, I almost miss my reflection in the mirror.

My ugliness is gone.

# CHAPTER
# FIFTY-TWO

## WILLOW

We approach a commotion on the way to the House of Embers. A crowd has formed around the woodland path further down. Alfie's red hair flashes amongst the gray uniforms. Tensing, I consider bypassing them altogether. But then his head swivels our way.

Instinctively, I step in front of the others. I'm unsure whether it's my reflection, Fox's whispered words when he thought I was asleep, or knowing I'm making a difference, but I feel at home in my skin for the first time in days. I feel like I used to when it was just Rory and me training in Nero's garden. My muscles ache, but in a good way, the way they are meant to ache.

When Alfie arrives, his grin broadens when he takes in my face. He attempts to pull me aside, but I plant my feet. A flicker of confusion passes in his eyes, but he murmurs, "Lord Sylvanar is questioning everyone who went to B.A.R. after the Holly King's feast."

"Bar?"

He smiles tightly. "Burn After Reading."

"Right."

A part of me retains so much loyalty to him; I long for the naïve friendship of our youth. But this newer, scarred, and thicker part of me draws away from him. I search his face for a sign of his belief that I am a spoiled princess, but the same the same green-and-brown-flecked eyes peer back at me. It's a marvel how some faces reveal every ounce of emotion, like Fox's. But others use their faces as masks to hide twisted secrets and ugly lies.

Why does he want to marry me at all? Does he expect I'll grow my powers back? That I'll be his magical tool for world domination, just as Nero hoped I'd be for him?

Ultimately, I settle for asking, "How can anyone confess if they can't remember?"

"He's grilling everyone here, asking if they went, who they saw on the way, and when they exited the establishment." He frowns. "You weren't with us when we left. I was worried."

"What's the commotion?"

His jaw clenches, and then he steps aside. Exhibitors stand around a stone statue that wasn't there last week. The statue's broad-shouldered back faces us, frozen in his attempt to flee the Baleful Hunt. Half-glimpsed images from when he crashed into me confirm his identity.

Alfie glances at my face once more. "Lord Sylvanar's son, Lord Milford, is missing."

I tense. "Okay . . . so why are you warning me?"

"Willow," he admonishes. "I know you can't remember, but with your beauty returned, you obviously went to see him. He was well known to—"

His gaze snags on something behind me. Geraldine stands a few feet back, eyeing my interaction with suspicion. But it's the red charm Alfie noticed. Milford's charm. *Shit.*

"Clever," he praises me, tapping an almost identical charm

on his Chaser chain. "Kill two birds with one charm. It's good to see you're finally getting with the program."

Outrage consumes me. I can't believe he thinks a night of socializing with his friends would make me someone who kills innocent people because it's what's expected of Shadows. Who is this man? Or the better question is, who am I? Because I'm certainly not the same person who kills on command anymore.

"Off to class!" Peablossom's raised, shrill voice pierces the cold air as she approaches along the path. "Embrace the flutter, oh sweet mortal blooms."

"See you in class." I don't wait for Alfie's reply. I'm too busy racing down the path, dragging Geraldine with me, trying to find somewhere quiet to explain why she needs to return the charm I gifted her. It never occurred to me that Milford had a signature gemstone, but it makes perfect sense. Every House probably has a unique type or set. It's how they send coded messages from Burn After Reading.

"What is he talking about, Willow?" Geraldine asks.

"Who?"

"Your Chaser friend."

"He's not my friend." Not anymore.

I can't believe I haven't put two and two together. The Radiants convince a mortal to take a charm, then out here, when a House member notices they're wearing it, they direct the mortal to speak with the gentry or whoever uses that type of gemstone.

My stomach turns to jelly when I realize anyone wearing that red charm has likely suffered Milford's violating attention, only to be forced to forget it and have another so-called favor thrust upon them out here. Knowing that Cait must be complicit in this knowledge makes me feel sick.

*You think you know moral depravity, pet. You haven't even touched its sides.*

Fox knew, too. They all must.

Fuck, I hate this place. Rushing the others behind the House of Embers Tower, I quickly explain. "Take the charm off, Geraldine. It's making you a target."

She stiffens and covers the stone with her hand. "What?"

A glance over my shoulder, then at Peggy's charm as she arrives. "You should take yours off as well, just to be safe. I stole them both, and I'm worried that it might cause trouble for you. I'll find more."

They all look at me with suspicion. We don't have time for this.

"That statue," I whisper, "was the person who killed Bob. Sylvanar must have caught him fleeing the commons, and I don't know, maybe Ryder was worried they'd punish him despite Radiants encouraging Shadows to cull Nothings on the sly. So he kept running. Maybe that was enough for Sylvanar to turn the Baleful Hunt on him."

Geraldine's expression darkens. "How did you know Ryder was the assassin?"

"I bumped into him as he ran out. I—"

"Right," she says, sarcasm dripping off her tongue. "You just *happened* to bump into him. Like you just *happened* to bump into your red-haired Shadow buddy there on day one."

"What?" The word barely leaves my lips. "I told you, he's not my friend anymore. I—"

"Are we a part of your cruel game?" Peggy snaps, crowding me with her body. She's a little frightening when she looks down at me. "Pretend to befriend us so you can build up our hopes and tear them down. You almost had us fooled."

"You think I had something to do with Bob's death?"

"I don't know." Max's eyes are no longer kind. "Did you? Because I'm starting to wonder where you were on the weekend . . . how come your *not*-friend over there warned you about

Burn After Reading? Everyone knows that's where Chasers earn their Lucky Charms."

My jaw drops at his insinuation. They heard everything, including Alfie's praise, insinuating I used the gemstone to hurt Geraldine.

"What's the matter?" she sneers. "We weren't good enough for an invite too?"

I have no answer. I can see how this looks to them. Why trust me when I've walked in, claiming to be a mortal outsider who also looks fae? Someone who gives them hope about another land where they won't be ostracized for how they look. Someone who snags the coveted spot of Shadow in a powerful military house.

"Let's go," Peggy says to Geraldine. "No use wasting our time here."

I block her. "Hate me, fine. But for your own safety, throw away those charms. Please."

"Fuck off. Come near us again, and I'll gut you myself." She shoves me.

I stumble. The woman has more power in that arm than I expected. More moxie behind her smile, too.

Geraldine cuts me a glare as she passes. "If you try to attack us like your friends, I'll be waiting."

It's no surprise she's one of the three Nothings left standing. I'm almost proud of their resilience. But then Max leans toward me and whispers, "Don't expect me to save you a seat this time."

My heart breaks. If that's the worst insult he can come up with, he's truly the kindest person I know. They don't deserve this.

I'm powerless to stop them from leaving. They've lost their friend. This entire week has left them in a constant state of traumatic stress. At least my mom had my dad when she woke in this time. She had the Order of the Well, a safe place to recover and catch her bearings after realizing her entire world had been obliterated. Now, they work to help other Well-blessed humans to assimilate. That's how it should be here, not throwing them into the deep end, expecting them to swim with smiling sharks.

I refuse to sit near Alfie when the Marquess starts his combat class. I also ignore his attempts to talk to me on the way to Tactical Warfare at the House of Stone Tower. I'm saved from explaining myself when Robin Goodfellow flags down his Shadow for a conversation.

The eyebrowless, auburn-haired Radiant swings a distrustful look my way, lifting the hairs on the back of my neck. But then his gaze drops to Fox's coat around my body, and he turns his sneer back to Alfie.

"Tell me what you know." Goodfellow's voice recedes as I continue inside the building.

*Shit. Fuck.*

Alfie won't protect Geraldine if he thinks I gave her the stone to deflect attention from me. I climb the staircase, tugging my braid when I read the motto beneath the house shield: Forged in Will.

There's no way Sylvanar will give up the hunt to find his son.

I sit on the outer ring of the lecture-style circular room, ensuring I can watch Geraldine and Max. Peggy has an alternate class. We all look outside the arched window when a beastly screech rattles the foundations. The Baleful Hunt flies overhead, spilling pebbles and rocks over the woods like falling cannon-balls. The crunch of breaking branches makes me cringe.

Not long after, the Earl descends the staircase. The stocky, chiseled leader walks to the side of the curved room, where they use different varieties of gemstones for teaching. An atmosphere of defeat clings to him. He rearranges the collection. It seems an innocuous task, but I can tell from the tension in his posture that he uses it to calm himself down.

The Tactical Warfare class is the most redundant. It's all about using fortifications and barriers to withstand enemy assaults. But a frozen watergate is the only physical barrier that stops a Nightmare from attacking. It almost feels like this class was just a filler when they made the schedule.

When Alfie arrives, he's accompanied by Goodfellow, who stands to the side and watches proceedings with a careful eye. Sylvanar notices him, scowls, and snatches a stack of pamphlets from his lectern. He strolls around the room, tossing one at each student.

"Given whispered stirrings of . . . disquiet . . . the Court of Dreams has graciously proclaimed a merry celebration to lift spirits to the delightful and sweet amusements for which the Solstice Exhibition is renowned."

Murmurs of excitement ripple around the room. Anticipation rides my nerves, filling me with twitchy energy. When I receive mine, the room is almost in an uproar. It's just another feast.

Sylvanar's footsteps stop. Heart seizing, I glance up from the pamphlet. He stands before Geraldine, eyes cold like granite, chiseled features unmoving.

"*You*—Nothing. Where did you get that charm?"

Geraldine's eyes widen. He grabs her by the scruff and lifts her unceremoniously from her seat.

"Lord Sylvanar." Goodfellow's warning tone slices through the air, but the Earl ignores him.

He shakes Geraldine like a rag doll, snarling, "I remember your scarred face from last week. This charm is new. Who gave it to you?"

"Me!" I shoot to my feet. "I gave it to her."

He drops her, rips the charm from her pocket, and stalks toward me. Goodfellow continues to bark warnings for him to cease his subterranean behavior. I give Sylvanar an explanation before he reaches me.

"I don't know how I got it, so don't ask. It was simply in my possession when I left the, ah, place that shouldn't be named?"

Even though I'm sure everyone knows of B.A.R., I don't want to be the one who says the name aloud and appears foolish.

"You lie." He shakes his fist in my face. "If it is yours, then why is it keyed to her? The gods know you need it more with that face."

My face? But I thought the curse was gone. My fingers probe the skin and slide along the scars. To my horror, the thin slivers feel knotted and engorged again. The angle of my nose is incorrect.

A glance at Geraldine proves her glamour has fallen and her burn scars are back on display. She won't look at me. Max tries to console her, but every strained line in her body tells me she struggles to hold it together.

"I don't know," I answer. "It's a mystery."

He leans in until he's an inch from my face. "Tell me now, or I'll fetch the Baleful Hunt. Then we'll see how fast you—"

"Earl Lord Sylvanar!" Goodfellow's bellow rattles the walls. He tugs at his vest and visibly calms. "Unless you wish to face irreversible consequences for breaking the code, cease your unsavory behavior immediately."

Sylvanar turns on him, a manic, unhinged glint in his eyes. "I am the one who dishes out punishment, boy. You cannot threaten me with consequences."

Goodfellow approaches him and whispers so low I'm sure he doesn't think anyone can hear. "Your dragon bond can be passed to another. You are not irreplaceable. Now, kindly calm yourself, read the pamphlet, and remember there are more civil ways to get what you need."

He holds out his palm, and Sylvanar begrudgingly hands over the gemstone.

431

"Continue proceedings," Goodfellow says, more loudly this time. "See me afterward. We have much to discuss."

I settle into silence for the rest of the class. When it's time to leave, I chase after Geraldine.

"Don't expect a thanks," she snaps. "I never would have been in that position if it wasn't for you."

I balk at her tone. She takes in my reaction, my face, and sighs. "Look, I'm sorry I snapped. I don't know what to believe. Just . . . leave us alone."

She walks away with Max, leaving me to head to the House of Moonlight's Tower solo. Her words leave me stunned. My trembling fingers flutter to my face and test the angles of the curse. They've been worse. And better.

I drop my hands and vow to stop touching my face. It shouldn't matter if the curse is broken or not. She's wrong. I'm not like the others.

I'm the fucking spider.

CHAPTER

# FIFTY-THREE

## WILLOW

E ven spiders wait in the shadows for the right time to strike, so I keep to myself as I enter the House of Moonlight's Tower. Just a few more hours and the day is over.

Taking a desk in the second-story classroom, I'm surprised to find a new copy of the Monster Codex on my desk. The ink smells fresh. Peablossom mentioned something about a new curriculum, but to have books printed on short notice is unusual.

I open the cover with a mix of curiosity and apprehension.

The first entry is the Sluagh—my heart races.

A hand-drawn picture depicts a standard male with horns, taloned wings draping like a mantle from his shoulders, and the impression of a bright skull beneath his skin. This is most definitely *not* the picture Fox showed me in his library. He said they evolved from a monstrous appearance after being enslaved to a long list of queens, so this handsome-faced rendition is new. In fact, Maebh killed all the other Sluagh in Elphyne.

Someone planted this for today's lesson. Someone who wants to target the Six.

Known as the most ancient Nightmare, the Sluagh is listed as an unrepentant, ravenous, and heartless monster who will just as soon pillage your mind as feed on your soul. They have two forms to frighten you—the physical and the invisible form. Both can be used simultaneously. After they are done toying with your emotions and body, they leave it a desiccated husk devoid of a heart.

No mention of the Wild Hunt.

*Interesting.*

Also, no mention of needing a queen to control their hive. As far as this entry is concerned, Sluagh are solitary creatures . . . who eat babies!

This is clearly fiction. I'm halfway down the entry when a gentle breeze caresses my neck. I glance over my shoulder. No one sits behind me. No windows are open. Frowning, I face the front and resume reading, but another tickling breeze brushes my skin, this time on the other side of my neck.

*"Miss me, pet?"* A ghostly touch trails down my jaw, heading down my top. My startle kicks the bottom of the desk.

When others look at me, I smile tightly. "Thought I saw a spider."

*"Fox?"* I send, dropping my gaze and focusing inward. *"Is that you?"*

*"In the flesh, well . . . the spirit flesh."* His self-amusement somehow translates through my thoughts.

The invisible pressure curls around my body, twirling until I feel him in the minuscule layer between my clothes and skin. A tingling shiver runs over my skin.

*"What are you doing?"* I send, trying not to let my arousal show, but after my day, his playful mood makes my heart sing.

*"I'm terribly bored on this expedition, pet. Rescue me."*

*"I'm in class. You can't just feel me up."*

*"Why not?"* Hot breath tickles my ear like he's standing behind me. He nips my earlobe.

I squirm. *"People will notice."*

*"I sense you're upset, little wolf. Is something wrong?"*

*"When are you back?"*

*"Likely the evening."*

*"Why are you bored?"*

*"Fine. Avoid the question."* His mental sigh skates over my skin, erupting goosebumps. *"Given the outcome of my recent Midnight Adventure, I am forbidden to flicker in public. Not that I was technically allowed before, but now we must travel by horse. The journey is tedious. No one appreciates my game of 'Guess what our queen's pussy tastes more like?' Honey, or—"*

*"Fox! You didn't."*

His laughter is like sweet wine, warming my insides. *"I did. Legion refused to partake, but Bodin surprisingly grumbled a list of ingredients, all from the fruit category."*

*"You don't even eat proper food."*

*"Which made it even more entertaining."*

I cover my mouth to stop the chuckle, glance down at the Sluagh entry, and note that sensing sadness is listed as a skill. They are attracted to forlorn and aching souls, *so be warned to guard your heart around them.* They love to increase the suffering of those already in pain.

Except Fox just went out of his way to make me smile.

*"A lot has happened this morning."* Swallowing, I tap the page. *"Have you seen this bullshit?"*

Lady Selene takes the lectern and starts speaking about increased Nightmare activity—more than is usual for this period of the Gentle Interlude. Focusing is almost impossible when Fox nibbles the sensitive skin beneath my ear while simultaneously reading over my shoulder and turning the page with his phantom hands.

The feeling on my skin dissipates. A silence extends.

*"Fox?"* I check to see if he's disappeared. *"Have you ever seen the Sluagh in the codex before?"*

*"No."* His reply is curt.

*"You don't sound happy."*

*"It's a message and a warning. The queen knows one of the Six has broken their seal, someone other than Styx."*

Shit. *"What's the warning?"*

He hesitates. I sense he's considering hiding the information from me. Or perhaps his physical form consults with the others.

*"To remain hidden,"* he admits. *"Educating the public means if we expose our true natures, we will be hunted and killed. Or rather, they will attempt to kill us. I see this listing needs an update regarding our weaknesses. So sad they struggle to get anything right."*

My quill lifts, dips into an inkwell, and scratches a line through the weakness listed as "Sunlight."

*"Stop it."* I snatch the quill and glance around to see if anyone noticed. But the class is enthralled with Lady Selene's lecture. Geraldine, however, sits back in her seat, not bothering to open her codex but staring into space.

A band constricts around my chest. She looks defeated.

*"Hmm."* Fox's mental tone is amused. *"Our feeding habits also need updating."*

*"Updating?"* I glance at the codex. *"You mean you actually used to eat babies?"*

He gives a wistful sigh. *"Those were the days."*

What?

*"But you don't now, right?"* No response. *"Fox. You don't now, right?"*

At first, his silence is worrisome, but then I feel echoes of his amusement pulse through my mind. The bastard is laughing and trying to hide it.

*"You're so dead when you get home."*

*"Promise?"* A nip over his mating mark shoots heat down to my lower abdomen.

*"Who was the worst?"* I ask to distract him.

*"That depends on your definition of worse."* He pauses. *"And 'was' is such a dubious tense."*

*"No, it's not! It's clearly a past tense. Wait . . . are you teasing me again?"*

*"Your buttons are too easy to push."*

*"You should know,"* I fire back, *"that Sylvanar confiscated his son's charm from me, or rather, Geraldine, but I told him it was mine."*

The temperature drops to arctic, and I immediately regret my words. I sense his wraith move about. Brushes of wind and phantom tingles pass my face. Codex pages on desks flutter, one book after another. Is he pacing?

*"Relax,"* I tell him. *"Sylvanar tried to intimidate me, but Goodfellow reminded him that breaking the code has consequences. After the Baleful Hunt left a petrified exhibitor in the woods this morning, I think we're safe from code violations for now."*

*"I'm coming home,"* Fox insists.

*"Honestly, it's fine. I'm more concerned about Geraldine and the others. Someone killed Bob this morning right under their noses. If I'd arrived five minutes earlier, I'd have stopped the attack."*

*"I'm so sorry, little wolf. This is your source of pain? Give me a name, and I'll feast on their soul tonight."* His tone returns to calm. *"Wait. Who's Bob?"*

A small laugh chuffs from my lips. I can't expect them to pay attention to everything I do.

Because hearing his mental voice is still better than the lecture, I explain who the Nothings are, how they've been kind to me, and how I promised to help them survive the tournament. When he listens, sympathizes, and brushes his ghostly hand against mine, I blurt out everything, including why they hate me now.

"*Willow,*" his voice feels like velvet again, soft and comforting. "*I didn't know they meant so much to you. Let me see what I can do to help. Leave it with me.*"

"Really?" I fight my smile.

"*For you, I would rearrange the stars.*"

I add another point beneath the list of descriptors on the Sluagh entry: *Hopeless Romantics.*

"*Who eat the hearts of their queen's enemies,*" he adds. "*Write that one down too.*"

I scratch out the romantic part with a silent eye roll, but then tap the quill against my lips and reconsider. Okay. Maybe I'll write that part back in.

"*Of course you will,*" he teases. "*You love my taste for blood.*"

A flash of his head buried between my thighs.

"*Get out of my head!*"

He chuckles and gives me what feels like a metaphysical kiss on the cheek. Then his presence slips away from my mind. Grinning like a lovesick fool, I resist the urge to etch little love hearts around the Sluagh picture. We're not perfect, but we're mates. I feel it in my heart, curling around that little place always vibrating when they're near.

I add a curly mustache to the Sluagh's face, then admire my handiwork. A large hand slams down on the book, shocking my heart into cardiac arrest. Glancing up, I'm pinned by Lord Sylvanar's dark, stony eyes promising retribution. Beside him, Lord Ignarius watches with a matching expression. Only his eyes are filled with smarmy self-satisfaction. Behind them, Robin Goodfellow raises his lumpy eyebrows as if to say—*gotcha.*

"Uniform violation." Sylvanar's voice is devoid of emotion as he presses his finger onto the desk—on the written violation paper he slammed over the codex a moment earlier.

"*Fox?*" I send. "*You still there?*"

Silence.

Shit.

Ignarius drops another violation onto the desk and struts back to Goodfellow, who gestures toward Alfie and says, "Shadow Alfred, kindly recite the punishment for repeat offenses and failure to show for disciplinary action?"

"This is the first time I received these violations." I clench my fists. "How can I fail to appear if I never knew?"

The entire room turns to Alfie, who stands and recites, "Violators are subjected to public humiliation, their flaws recounted in a grand procession through the streets."

I jump to my feet. "The House of Shadow handles my punishment. You know this."

Goodfellow gives a tight grin. "None are here."

The blood drains from my face. "You planned this."

"Go on, Shadow Alfred."

Alfie refuses to look at me as he straightens his spine and continues. "The guilty party is stripped of all glamours, magical enhancements, and clothing, exposing their natural vulnerabilities for the procession. If the offense is severe, the guilty party will be temporarily stripped of their status and demoted to a lower rank until they can prove their decorum has been restored."

# CHAPTER
# FIFTY-FOUR
## WILLOW

To maximize the public humiliation, the bastards wait until class is over, then drag me outside. People still exit the building when they demand I stop and strip in the thoroughfare. As bodies knock into me, my consciousness retreats deeper into my body. There's no avoiding this. Fox is too far away and on horseback. He won't hear my scream.

This is my fault, anyway. Sylvanar, Ignarius . . . Goodfellow. Who the fuck knows why he hates me so much? Maybe I showed up and ruined his day.

I have no other option than to take my clothes off and suck it up. Facing the woods, I keep my vision unfocused. I undo the buttons on Fox's coat. I try not to think about the whispering crowd, urging others to step up and watch the revelry unfold. The coat comes off, then my boots, trousers, and panties, but I freeze as I pluck the first button on the shirt.

The pendant.

My expression must convey my fear because Sylvanar glances at Goodfellow, who then returns a haughty nod.

440

CASTLE OF NEVERS AND NIGHTMARES

"What are you hiding, Nothing?" Sylvanar rips my shirt open. Buttons scatter to the dirt path.

My heart falls to the floor. I am exposed, naked, for all to see. Every pore on my skin contracts from the cold. But it's not my breasts or vagina they lock eyes with. The overcast sky provides the perfect condition for Tinger's glowing manabee to twinkle like a star, catching the attention of everyone watching. Shocked gasps ripple in the air.

"A wisp!" someone exclaims.

Mesmerized by the light, Sylvanar's meaty hand wraps around my precious friend. He snaps the cord from my neck.

"You took something from my son," he murmurs darkly. "It's only fair I take something in return."

Someone yanks the shirt from my arms. Another person shoves between my shoulder blades. I stumble forward, my bare feet cutting into sharp twigs and rocks on the path.

"Smile, Nothing." Goodfellow sneers. "And march."

He gestures with his hand. Tingling fire ants crawl over my body. They head down my legs and wrap around my feet until they walk without permission. Jerking forward, I am powerless to change my fate—a naked puppet on strings.

I thought I could hold my head high, but each step shoves insecurities into my mind without Tinger's presence against my skin. People laugh when Goodfellow riles up the spectators, urging them to cheer up because sour moods are for subterraneans.

They point at my face. They point at my nakedness. They veil insults within creative jokes. My fingers flutter to my face, to the deformed and bulging cheekbones. Unshed tears blur my vision. My curse is worse again, thick and ugly.

"What's colder than a witch's tit?" someone shouts.

"A Nothing's tit!"

"Hm, yes," Sylvanar's voice filters above the rest. "She looks cold. We're not monsters. Shall we keep her warm?"

Applause breaks out when torrential, scalding water falls on my head as though I'm standing beneath a faucet. I splutter and choke, trying to breathe as it follows me. Any way I turn my head, water is there. Panic strangles my lungs. Blinking rapidly, my instincts take over and I find an angle that helps me breathe.

Goodfellow's enchantment forces me over uneven terrain, heedless of twigs and stones cutting into the soles of my feet. I'll bet even my stilted gait looks ugly. Every step becomes torture. I try to lift my chin, but the water gets in my eyes. I try to wipe it from my face. Immediately, a malevolent magical force pins my arms to my side. Terror fills me. Coughing, I glare at the path ahead and refuse to give them any more signs their cruelty affects me.

Fuck this. Fuck the fucking queen. I refuse to drown.

But the further I walk, the more numb the cold makes my feet, the hotter the water feels, and the harder it is to deny what they call me. My mother wanted me to learn from my mistakes, but I'm here again, flailing in the middle of one, drawing in the air, alone and despised.

"Look at her face."

"She gets uglier with every step."

My eyes sting.

*I will not cry. I will not cry.*

But then I hear a word from my old nightmares.

"Freak!"

I scour the spectators with a trembling bottom lip, but the laughing faces blend into one through the stream running down my head. Even behind me, I see no sign of the Radiants who decreed my punishment. It's as though I'm too pitiful for even them to taunt. Not a single person has defended me. All jeer me. Without nobility to remind them to have fun, to laugh, or whatever excuse makes this okay, their taunts descend into vicious insults.

"Ugh. She's so disgusting I want to puke."

"No wonder no one likes her."

Their laughter becomes a chant. "Freak freak freak."

Hot tears spill from my eyes, but the scalding water makes everything burn. I don't know how, but the House of Moonlight's Tower soon appears. I'm almost a full circle along the path around the woods and towers. Someone must have ushered everyone to the next class because the spectators grow thin. When the last person leaves, the shadowed blob of my clothes is only a handful of paces away. It gives me something to focus on instead of the torture.

*Almost done.*

*Almost over.*

The stream of water stops, and the cold temperature spreads as I finish the march. It's getting late. The sky is darkening. Blood and dirt stick to my sore feet. My stomach rumbles, so I must be hungry, but I don't feel much anymore. I am blue, shivering, and numb all over. I reach for my clothes, but they left me with one final horrifying act of cruelty. The enchantment on my body flees, and I kick the trick mound of dirt.

A raven caws high in the trees. It's the giant laughing at the spider.

I don't know what to do. My brain has frozen with my body. Any decision I make is worthless. Alfie was right. I spent my entire time in Crystal City thinking I was special, but I was just a puppet. It wasn't me they wanted, but my power.

I stare at the dirt. At nothing.

Shuffling nearby should make me lift my head, but I have no energy to care if I'm attacked. Then I hear a familiar voice.

"Chin up, hun. We got you." Peggy wraps her arms around my front. Geraldine takes the adjacent side, and Max at the rear.

"Group hug," Geraldine says, a sad smile on her lips.

"So sorry if this is inappropriate," Max mumbles, but tightens his grip to block the cold.

Everyone shuffles closer. My teeth chatter too hard to speak, but Geraldine turns her sad eyes to me and explains, "It wasn't fair we made demands of you when we've hardly given you anything in return."

I look at Peggy. "Y-you're limping again."

She nods. "I took off the charm."

"We need to stick together," Max asserts.

"We sent a message to Peablossom," Geraldine adds. "Hope that's okay. Exhibitors are forbidden to bring you replacement clothes, and no one from your House is around."

Their bodies keep the worst of the cold at bay, but not my emotions. The shivering and chattering makes my sobs feel so much worse, but it's a letdown of relief. I'm not alone. I have friends.

"T-tell me something," I chatter. "While we wait. Tell me about your families . . . back in the old world."

It starts snowing, but they only cluster around me more tightly, reminding me of Varen the night I fell in the moat. It makes me smile.

"I had a daughter." Peggy's voice is small. "She was twenty years old. Such a firecracker. She was always bitching and moaning about something, but anytime I needed her, she was there in a heartbeat. God, I miss her an awful lot."

"She s-sounds amazing," I say.

"My mom liked to bake these little sugar cookies with sprinkles on top," Geraldine says. "It was just dough and frosting with those colored candied balls, but they were heaven."

"You'll have to m-make them one d-day," I chatter.

Max suddenly steps back, and the frigid air rushes in. A warm weight drops over my shoulders—a soothing, melodic voice. "Come on now, precious cherub. Let's get you somewhere safe to warm up."

"P-p-peablossom?" I turn and find her beautiful face pinched with worry. "I'm s-sorry. N-not smiling."

"Smiling is overrated." Her eyes glisten as she addresses the others. "If you have a class, off you go. If not, head over to your dorm and pack your belongings."

"Why?" Geraldine asks, frowning.

Peablossom tugs the blanket around my shoulders. "Lord Fox announced the Nothings as affiliates to the House of Shadow. And since all members of their house are currently situated in Shadowfall Keep, you must relocate this evening."

They all look at me, eyes wide.

"I didn't know," I breathe. "I mean, I asked him to help, but this is . . ." My throat tightens. "Fast."

"Shoo." Peablossom gestures at them. "I'll take care of our frozen petal."

They hurry away while she guides me down the path. At some point, she hums a tune. It's a forced, whimsical song that stutters when she notices my bloody footprints continue. Instead of returning to the keep, she leads me into the House of Shadow Tower.

It's warm, empty, and quiet. Interestingly, the House of Shadow classes keep getting canceled. It's almost as if someone doesn't want them to influence the exhibitors. Somehow, we make it up the staircase to the first level, but she urges me up one more flight.

Using magic from one of her many charms, she lights the lantern sconces and fireplace, and the room fills with warmth. For the next ten minutes, all I hear is the tinkling of her charms as she bustles about and gathers supplies. She returns with a bucket, washes tears from my face and then offers me a hand-held mirror.

"All clean," she whispers.

I take the mirror and stare at my shame. The curse is back in full force, bloating and distending every little angle until I feel like a swollen puffer fish. How can it be back? How can I still feel so ugly when I promised myself it didn't matter?

*Feel so ugly.*

*Feel so ugly.*

My sluggish mind swims around the words.

*She's getting uglier with every step.*

As Peablossom turns her attention to my abused feet, I recall Titania's original curse.

*Your visage will mirror the ugliness lurking within your heart.*

No.

It can't be. All this time and . . . I lift the mirror to peer at my face again, then laugh.

"Oh, you must be ticklish." Peablossom extracts a stone embedded in my foot, but I can't stop myself. The answer was under my nose the entire time. It's so absurd there's nothing to do but laugh.

Her eyes fill with hesitant mirth. "Sweeting, are you well?"

"I control it," I blurt out with a cackle. "Me."

My shoulders shake so much that the blanket slips. I clutch it to my chest and double over in hysterics.

"I haven't the foggiest notion of what you're laughing about, but I am glad you feel better."

My smile cuts short when thunder rolls, growing louder by the second. What is that? Peablossom and I look at each other as it increases in volume and pitch, almost like a roaring, buzzing swarm. An explosion quakes the tower's foundations. Fox's frantic bellow hits my mind with the force of an avalanche.

*"Why can I scent your blood everywhere?"*

Before I can reply, call to him, or even blink, shadows smother every lantern in the room. A howling wind erupts, and a dark, winged silhouette steps from the darkness, dragging a figure behind him. The light flickers and returns. In his Sluagh form, horns, wings, and tail lashing about, Fox's manic black eyes land on me. He discards the figure he brought with him—a disgruntled Legion—and *flickers* to kneel at my feet.

His hands hover over my legs, his panicked eyes search me for injury. "Our queen."

"I'm okay," I insist.

"You are bleeding." His snarl is guttural as he inspects the soles of my feet.

"Peablossom cleaned them."

"May I heal them?" he asks.

"Why are you being so weird?" I sniff.

"I need your permission." His voice is quiet. He won't look me in the eyes.

"Fox?"

"Willow," he growls, jaw clenched, muscle ticking. He is beyond worked up. Every action jerks and twitches, as if he's battling his body to keep it from unleashing a destructive force against us all.

"Yes, please," I whisper. "Heal me."

When he bows to heal my feet, Legion's conversation with Peablossom filters in. She hasn't mentioned Fox's Sluagh form. She's a little nervous, but not afraid. When Legion arrived with Fox, he was disgruntled. Perhaps Fox wrenched him here without permission. But now, as Legion hears Peablossom's recount of my punishment, I feel the atmosphere tremble.

It's as if the world itself shudders from the look of retribution filling his eyes. When she's finished, Legion's nostrils flare. He prowls back and forth, fingers flexing at his sides.

At first, I think his anger is directed at the Radiants. He'd already decreed my new uniform to be the House of Shadow colors. When Fox's menacing eyes land on the hollow of my throat—to the missing space where my pendant should be—I realize Legion isn't angry. He's afraid.

"Fox," he warns. "Don't."

"Where is your pendant?" Fox's tone is cold, devoid of emotion.

I touch my throat. "Sylvanar took it."

Black eyes blink. "Wait here."

Instinct barrels through me. I grab his arm as he *flickers*. "Don't!"

"Yes." He bares razor-sharp fangs.

"The codex," I remind him.

Legion strides over and takes Fox's other hand. "Reveal yourself and jeopardize everything."

"I will *not* stand for her abuse." Fox's frantic growl sends my heart racing.

Oh, no. He doesn't even know about the water.

His gaze whips to me. "What happened with the water?"

"I didn't say anything."

"You shouted it in your head." Danger tightens his expression. "What happened with the water, Willow?"

"Look." I give a nervous laugh. "Let's talk about this. You kind of ate Sylvanar's son." It's the wrong thing to say. It just reminds him of another who tried to hurt me, so I quickly add, "He was a horrible man—I get that. But what happened was my fault. I was foolish and made a stupid mistake."

Legion snarls at me, "Don't ever blame yourself for the deplorable actions of others."

I blink, shocked at the emotion in his declaration.

Fox's otherness suddenly evaporates, and he is the picture of faerie nobility once more. Except the wildness hasn't left his eyes.

"Fine." He stalks toward the staircase leading down. "I won't kill him."

"Fox!" I try to run after him, but Legion blocks me with a palm to my sternum.

Dark eyes look down at me. "Let him go."

"But he'll . . ." My eyes widen. "What will he do?"

"Remind the nobility why the House of Shadow is not to be messed with."

# CHAPTER
# FIFTY-FIVE
## FOX

*Don't kill. Don't kill. Don't kill.*

D on't kill. Don't kill. Don't kill.
I stalk the Nexus path toward the House of Stone. Exhibitors scurry out of the way, their eyes downcast, their minds whirling with fear.

*Don't kill. Don't kill. Don't kill.*

Blood.

I stop and stare. Blood on the footpath.

Hers.

My fingers curl into fists, popping my knuckles.

*Don't kill. Don't kill. Don't kill.*

My neck cracks. My fingers flex. It's fine. I will have a nice little chat with the imbecile. That's all. A manic laugh bubbles out of me. I'm not a monster. I can *chat*.

Straightening my collar, I continue down the path. Quite proud of myself, really. I arrive at the House of Stone Tower the picture of decorum.

But then I stand at the door and sense the souls inside. They humiliated my queen. Hurled insults at her. Forced her to walk naked and laughed at her.

*Don't kill. Don't kill. Don't kill.*

A shaky exhale leaves my lips. No one needs to get hurt. I will simply walk in, up the stairs, and take her pendant back. The one she almost drowned for. Breathe in. Breathe out.

I plant my palm on the door and shove it open. Wood bangs against stone, startling exhibitors inside.

"Leave," I snarl and stalk up the staircase. More souls in my way—more juicy, tender souls.

*Don't kill. Don't kill.* A female bows and apologizes for breathing. My lips curve. *Definitely don't kill that one.*

Another flight up. More steps. More scurrying souls I growl at to leave. I am almost proud of myself by the time I land on the Shadow's accommodation level. He is a bulky thing with more muscles than brains and does not avert his gaze. He stares directly into my eyes.

*Don't kill.*

"Can I help you, sir?"

He knows his Radiant humiliated my queen. What kind of fool would stand in the way of my retribution? I am . . . astounded.

*"The ugly bitch deserved it."* His unguarded thoughts crash into my mind.

My eye twitches. What did he call her?

He schools his face to innocence. "Sir?"

I seize his mind, rifle through his memories, and . . .

*"Look at that ugly bitch's face." My laugh joins the others in the crowd. "Seriously, what kind of slut must she be for them to let her get away with all the rules she breaks?"*

*"Her face makes me want to vomit."*

*"Go on, shout something. Join in the fun." I elbow my neighbor, then throw my voice above the other jeers. "Freak!"*

*She looks our way, ugly, bulbous, deformed features bloated. Her eyes are red and puffy. She chokes and splutters under a*

451

*magical stream of water that leaves steam curling from her raw, red skin.*

There is no word to describe the consuming rage filling me with blinding, murderous hunger. Sylvanar tried to drown her while she walked. Our queen is terrified of water. What's worse is, I finally know what Titania's curse is. All this time Willow suffered insults and judgment. I should have known, should have dipped into minds sooner, but I was trying to be good. Trying to—

*Don't kill.*

My fangs elongate. My mouth salivates for the taste of blood. I drop my head and take a moment. Legion's warning echoes in my mind. *Reveal yourself and jeopardize everything.*

*Don't. Fucking. Kill.*

"Sir, can I help you?"

My hand plunges into his chest, cracking ribs, latching around the pumping muscle. It pumps to hurt her. This is justice. My wraith hurtles into his body. We scrape his wicked soul from the fibers of his being, sucking every morsel. His body emaciates before my eyes. Juicy, tasty mortal soul. So sad it is now over. I devour his heart in seconds, lick my lips, and groan as my wraith returns home with his entire soul.

His corpse thuds onto the floor. I blink. Stare. Smash my lips together and wonder . . . it's only one corpse. It's fine.

The Baleful Hunt's roar above the tower trembles the foundations—grains of plaster crumble from the ceiling. I dust my shoulders, set the corpse on fire, and continue up the staircase to the next level.

*Don't kill. Don't kill. Don't kill more.*

I step onto Sylvanar's floor and scan the circular room. The bed is messy. The desk is upturned. Papers and books are strewn on the floor. An open archway leads outside to the turret, the nest of the Baleful Hunt when it isn't guarding the Cabinet. He stands bowed, hands braced on a table filled with red gemstones and . . . one twinkling star trapped inside a pendant. Flint-gray eyes meet mine and widen briefly before narrowing.

"She had it coming," he sneers. "If you'd done your job and disciplined her the first time, this wouldn't have happened."

I grin.

He steps back. "Your teeth."

Oops.

"Stay there." He darts a nervous glance to the turret. "I'll call my Hunt."

"Too late, I'm afraid."

I am already inside him, consuming his soul. So much tastier than his son's. So much power, and . . . light. I nibble around the edges of it, but want it to remain more or less in one piece for the Wild Hunt. He might have made a formidable ally against Titania. What a shame his son was a molester.

He tries to summon his Hunt—a feeble attempt at freedom. His heart is mine. My fist breaks his chest open. I take his heart and bite. Blood oozes down my throat with such sweet satisfaction.

A jaunty whistled tune cuts through the haze of my feast. My wraith returns to my body in a snap, bringing the Earl's soul into purgatory.

"Goodfellow," I snarl.

Titania's auburn-haired sycophant strolls in. He wears a green floral-embroidered tunic and brown stockings. He casually tosses a stone and catches it in his fist.

"Oh, my," he croons. "What a mess you've made."

He had a hand in our queen's humiliation, too. His heart is mine.

I bare my fangs.

"Oh, my," he repeats, unperturbed, as he sits gracefully on the sofa and crosses his legs. "What big *teeth* you have."

I prowl toward him.

A familiar baleful look flashes in his eyes, stopping me in my tracks. His pompous rouged lips stretch.

"You bonded with the Hunt," I say, eyes narrowing. "I'm impressed."

Sarcasm lifts a single, lumpy brow. "You're not impressed. But you will be."

His confidence makes me twitch. I glance down at Sylvanar's husk, then at Willow's pendant on the table, and back to Puck's unnatural eyes. "Try to stop me and see what happens."

"Take the wisp." He shrugs. "What do I care?"

I cross to the pendant, wrap the cord around my wrist, and slide him a wary glance. We both know I've stepped over the line. Covering this up is an impossible feat.

"I've never tasted dragon," I note, cocking my head, studying the whirling mass of power in his core.

He opens his palm, and a moving picture of my queen materializes in the air above the stone he holds. Her sweet face, her stirring voice. *"Phew. That was close—"*

He closes his fist around the stone, cutting the resonance repeat. "We both know what she says next."

My lips curve on one side. "You've just bonded with the Baleful Hunt. These pairings take time to master. What makes you think you'll be faster than me?"

*"It only takes a second."*

*"I can enter your mind in less,"* I send to him.

Fear flashes in his eyes. My grin widens as I step over the husk toward him.

"And then what?" he asks, nostrils flaring. "Kill me, fine. But the Hunt will go to someone else, you know that. Every other dragon out there still exists for one purpose only—to keep your hive caged."

A snarl rips from my lips. My wraith splits from my body,

pins him down. Black, taloned fingers wrap around his throat.

*"The last thing we want is a thousand manabeeze floating in the sky, announcing to the guards that I just raided the queen's Cabinet of Curiosities."*

I pause at our angel's voice, our falling star.

"There is a way we all walk out of this victorious," he rasps against my chokehold. "A way you can save her."

"We are all she needs."

His arm moves at his side. My wraith tightens its grip.

"Just want to show you something. That's all."

I allow him the freedom of one arm. He digs into his pocket and holds up another stone. I ease my grip to hear his offer.

"I activate this," he says, "and that resonance will play out on every receiver in Avorlorna. You won't be enough to save her. She stole from the Crown. She will be executed . . . or banished immediately to the subterranean."

"If this is meant to sway me, you're doing a nasty job."

"It's either you, or it's her."

An incredulous laugh huffs out of me. "Do you not feel my hand around your neck?"

Stone-cold, dragon-bonded eyes lock with mine. "You might be fast enough to avoid the Baleful gaze. You might even be fast enough to stop me activating the stone. But if I don't return tonight, the Keepers have been instructed to activate the copies."

I could rifle through his mind and find out who he gave the copies to, but the druids wear masks to hide their identities.

"Agree to my terms," he says. "Accept responsibility for taking a dragon-bonded's life. We can spin it any way you want, say a Nightmare influenced you, who gives a shit as long as you're in the Cabinet, encased in stone, and no one knows what you really are."

I lean in to snarl, "And what am I, Puck?"

"A monster."

# CHAPTER
# FIFTY-SIX
## WILLOW

It's been three hours. I'm back at the keep, and still no sign of Fox. Cricket is about to dish up dinner in the main dining room, but I'm down on the basement level, pacing in the corridor outside the servant's dining room, the portal stone to Elphyne in my hand. Geraldine, Max, and Peggy opted to room down here with Cricket and Finch.

I don't blame them. The Sluagh are all a little scary if you don't know them.

When he arrived back from his military mission, Fox healed their flaws. That was when he learned of my punishment and raced to the Shadow Tower.

Geraldine's skin is now smooth as silk. Peggy's limp is gone. Her eyes are now free of every wrinkle that formed over the years. Max is no longer balding. I do not know how Fox did it, but they're not Nothings anymore.

They're Nevers.

No . . . I shake my head, pacing.

They're people. *Good* people.

456

"Stop wearing a groove in the carpet, hun!" Peggy shouts from inside. "Come in and join us."

I walk into the room and they barely glance at Fox's coat wrapped around my body. I needed to smell him, so I immediately raided his closet after arriving here. But when I place the portal stone on the table, they give it a curious look.

"This is a portal stone to Elphyne," I explain.

Three sets of eyes snap to me, then they all share a look I can't decipher.

"Are you going home?" Geraldine asks warily.

"No. I need to be here. I feel like it's my responsibility to do something about Titania."

"Why?" Max asks.

"Because I was the one who woke you all from . . . from death."

They stare at me with unblinking eyes.

"For real?" Geraldine asks. "You necromanced the shit out of us?"

Max turns to her. "It's like when Dr. Doom went back in time and used a shard of Excalibur to reanimate everyone it killed."

"I don't know who that is," I say. "But you're not *really* dead. You must have been frozen like my mother was, and, I don't know, maybe you were all going to wake at some point anyway."

Peggy asks, "Do you want us gone?"

"No!" I shake my head vehemently. "I would never ask you to leave. You're my friends."

"Good." Peggy nods to the others. "Then we're staying."

"You're our friend, too," Max adds. "We need to stick together."

My eyes water. Before I cry, Peggy gestures for Geraldine to dish up, and just like that, we're in this together.

"Did you hear?" Geraldine waggles her brows as she scoops

soup into her bowl. "The House of Stone Tower burned to the ground."

She almost spills the soup and pouts. Max smiles at her, takes the ladle from her hands, and finishes. The affection blossoming between them swells my heart. Wait.

"What?" I breathe, perching on a stool. "When did that happen?"

"Not long ago," she replies, then notes the concern in my eyes. "Your Radiant still hasn't turned up?"

I shake my head. I love how they don't blink when they call Fox *my* Radiant. The possessive beast in me preens. I rub my mating mark and press all the aching bits so the pain knocks out my worry.

"Do they know who's responsible?" I ask.

They look at me and my heart sinks. Peggy reaches across the table and squeezes my hand, reminding me of my first day here. "Just because he strolled out of the tower seconds before it crumbled down, doesn't mean he did it."

Oh shit.

"Yeah," Max adds, ladling soup into his own bowl. "It could have been anyone. They need proof right?"

I bite my nails. "Yeah."

"You sure you don't want any soup?" Max asks.

"No thanks, I'll—"

Cricket bustles in with Finch hot on her heels. She stops upon seeing me. "Poppet, what are you doing down here?"

"Visiting my friends." I smile at them. "You sure you guys don't want to room up with me? Or even eat with the rest of us? I feel weird with you down here."

"Nonsense," Cricket says. "You lot need your privacy."

"They sure do," Geraldine adds, hiding her smirk with a spoonful.

"What's that supposed to mean?" I gasp. How much do they know?

Max giggles.

"Max?" I shoot him daggers. "What have you all been told?"

I swing my gaze to Cricket, and she raises her palms. "Don't look at me. They visited the chatty gossip, that's all."

My head drops into my hand with a groan. Cricket doesn't wait for my embarrassment to cede. She bustles me off the stool, saying, "Your dinner is going cold and you're the only one who actually eats it. Off you go."

"But . . ." I walk to the doorway, pouting. "Maybe I want to stay here."

"Master Fox has returned," Finch announces rather abruptly.

"Oh." I suck my lips. If I run out now, it will just prove the chatty gossip's . . . whatever she gossiped about.

Geraldine laughs and tosses a balled napkin at me. "Go!"

Before another word utters, I'm out the door and jogging up the stone staircase to the next level. When I burst into the dining room, five sets of eyes snap my way. Legion, Bodin, Emrys, Varen, and Fox. Everyone is here but Styx. The scrape of chairs against floorboards is deafening as they respectfully stand. I scan Fox for evidence of . . . I don't know . . . signs he'll be taken away from me.

He is the same suave, sexy Fox I am in love with. My heart bursts at my silent confession.

I love him.

*"I love you,"* I shout in my mind.

Shock splashes over his features. I run to him and launch. Strong hands latch around my waist. My legs hook around his hips. Our mouths clash. When our tongues meet, a snarl of potent, primal need rips from his throat. Talk about pushing my buttons. I am a hot, needy mess for him in an instant. He cups my head, swipes dishes, and slams my back onto the table so he can ravage my mouth with his. Whatever happened in that tower doesn't matter. He's here. Safe. And he tastes so fucking good.

"Over several days . . ." Varen reports. "The new hive queen takes over brood care duties and emits the nest's signature pheromone blend."

Our lips stop. Hold. My eyes widen. Someone clears their throat. *Shit.* I forgot we had an audience.

*"No, you didn't."* Fox's eyes crinkle.

I scowl to hide the flutter of arousal in my belly. *"Do I shout everything?"*

*"You have very noisy thoughts."* He leaves my mouth to tongue the mating mark on my neck. *"And your scowl didn't hide it."*

My breath hitches and I squirm. *"Stop it."*

Varen adds, "Worker bees adjust to their new queen by imprinting on her chemical signals."

"Fox." I slap him, pushing him off me. He leans back with a flushed, unapologetic expression. But slides into his chair and pulls me on his lap.

*"You're lucky I'm feeling greedy tonight."* His mental purr causes goosebumps. But the heat in his eyes makes my clit throb.

"What's that supposed to mean?"

"Means I don't want to share."

I scramble in a very unladylike fashion onto the neighboring chair. I awkwardly tidy my hair and try not to notice four sets of eyes staring at me.

Two minutes into shoveling Cricket's delicious brisket down my throat, I still feel eyes on me.

*"Why are they still staring?"* I send Fox.

*"Well,"* he returns with a flash of smolder. *"Bodin is disappointed I didn't turn you over and take you right here on the table. He wanted to join in and fuck your mouth."* His gaze flicks to Emrys,

whose eyes narrow with hate. *"He's wondering how much you'll scream if he bites that mating mark on your neck."*

Oh-*kay*. I reach for Fox's untouched glass of water.

He glances at Legion, whose knuckles are white as he clenches his cutlery. *"Our First is deciding which punishment is best to handle your disrespect. Shall he have Emrys spank you over his lap while I fuck you, or should he tie you up with shadow, then spank you while I fuck you."*

I spray water everywhere. "Sorry!"

*"And Varen . . ."* Fox's gaze softens on him. *"One guess."*

*"Stop messing with me,"* I send Fox. "You told me you don't go in their minds unless you're in the hive state."

I smile at the rest of the table and then steal his napkin to mop up my mess.

Now Fox stares openly at me, too. Deadly serious. Wait. Was he telling the truth? Then he laughs so hard, he rocks back on the chair and pats his stomach.

"Yeah, you're real funny." I point to my lips. "In case you didn't realize, that was my sarcastic tone."

"Fox," Legion barks. "Enough."

He shoots his leader a careless glare. The tension in the air thickens. No one is smiling now. Even Varen looks disgruntled. I try not to worry and continue my meal, but it's creepy when no one else eats.

"Did you tell them about Styx?" I ask Fox.

"Who's Styx?" Bodin asks.

Time stops.

Fox warned me this might happen, but I never expected them to forget their Sixth. Fox stares hard at the air before him. He takes a deep breath. Then another.

"It will be fine." I squeeze his hand.

Legion moves on, as though Styx's name was never uttered. "Explain yourself, Fox. What happened at the tower?"

Fox abruptly stands. "I'll explain in the morning."

He takes my hand and lifts me from my seat.

*"Let's go,"* he sends. *"I don't have the energy to deal with this tonight."*

Fair enough. I give the others an apologetic smile. Varen jumps to his feet, eyes wide. "When a worker bee stings a threat to the hive, it rips away part of their body."

*"Varen,"* Emrys warns. "Sit back down."

But Varen jogs after us. At the door, he takes my wrist in a painful grip, forcing me to look at him. My heart aches at his sadness. "They die," he insists, shaking my wrist. "They die!"

"No one is dying." Fox's smooth, calming voice washes over both of us. He gently cups Varen's jaw and stares deeply into his eyes. "I promise. No one is dying. Now, be a good little honeybee and let the others clean you up. I'll give you some more bee bread tonight."

"Bee bread?" Varen repeats with a frown.

*"Is he okay?"* I send Fox.

*"Just a little confused, that's all."*

"Bee bread," Fox repeats.

Varen nods. He relaxes but then says with a warning tone, "After drone bees copulate with their queen, their explosive climax *rips* their genitalia out."

Fox's hands slide off Varen's jaw with an unsettled look my way. "Shit, pet. My cock will blow off if you're not careful."

Flames scald my cheeks.

"Fox," I chide.

Bodin arrives to corral Varen back to the table, but first warns Fox, "Tomorrow." He slides his glare to me. "And you. Training at dawn."

Fox threads his fingers through mine and walks me back to his room. We fall into companionable silence, but an unsettled feeling remains, even when we arrive.

"You don't think Varen was trying to tell us something, do you?" I ask at his door. "He makes sense sometimes."

His lips twitch. "You worried about my cock, pet?"

"Har har." I squeeze his hand. "You know what I mean."

He tugs me into his room and spins to face me with a heart-stopping grin. "If you could do anything tonight, what would you do?" He pulls me close, assumes a dancing pose, and swings me deftly around his room. "To fly? A dance in the clouds?"

I laugh, shaking my head. "I can't believe I told you my dream."

We stop dancing, and he dangles something sparkling before my eyes. "Or would you like to reunite with your special friend?"

"Tinger." Tears burn my eyes. "Thank you. Again."

My heart aches as he turns me and loops the cord around my neck. I hold the glimmering ball of energy to my heart. My inability to let go of my friend has caused so much trouble. The guilt gnaws at my soul.

When he's done, Fox brushes the hair from my nape and presses his lips to my skin. He asks again, "What would you do?"

I am filled with raw emotion. Trembling with it. First Varen. Now this strange offer to go out and have fun? Twisting in his arms, I slide my hands around his neck and look into his eyes.

"Do I need to be worried, Fox?"

His smile broadens until his dimples pop.

"Not at all." His eyes flare suddenly. "But I do wish to return to the temple before dawn. I have a feeling the Baleful Hunt will be back tomorrow."

Sylvanar must be alive still. The thought makes me relax a little, but not enough to risk a trip outside for the sake of enter-tainment. A flash of my humiliating walk around the Nexus hits me. When the water fell on my face, my terror made it so much worse.

"You know what?" I ask quietly. "There is one thing I'd like to do."

"Whatever you need." Unwavering gray eyes make me blush.

"It's kind of embarrassing. I was hoping you'd help me take a bath. You know, like you did the other night?"

I figure the more attempts I try, the less afraid I'll be.

Something dangerous flickers in his gaze before a roguish twinkle replaces it. Fox glides his hands down my back and grabs my ass. "You need me to drink the bathwater if you feel like you're drowning?"

"Forget it." I scrub my face. "I know it's irrational to think I'll fall and drown in a tub."

"Willow." He holds me at arm's distance, showing me he's serious. "It will be my honor to catch you."

"Good." Smirking, I shove him and wrench off my coat, almost tripping in my haste to get past him. "The last one in the bath is a rotten egg."

# FIFTY-SEVEN

## WILLOW

I shouldn't be doing this.

I'm standing outside Fox's bath while he's sitting inside the steaming water, holding my hand and trying to convince me I won't drown. Tinger's pendant is the only item on my body. There's no excuse not to get in, but I glare at the water and hunt for sharks. Or Well Worms. They're the fuckers that ate Rory.

"Willow, relax," he murmurs. "I'm right here."

I haven't moved in five minutes. I keep remembering how the constant stream of water over my head felt suffocating. But if I can't get past this, the fear will control me for the rest of my life.

"I'm not going anywhere," he reminds me. "If you want to stand there all night, that's okay."

My gaze flicks to his. I see no hate, no anger. Just patience. He deserves a medal for it.

My shoulders drop. I can do this.

"Yes, you can," he agrees.

"Seriously," I mumble, letting him help me climb into the

bath despite the warning my galloping heart gives me. My eyes squeeze shut as my toe hits the water and I hold my breath.

"Good girl." He guides me down onto his lap and tightly wraps his arms around me. "See? You can't go anywhere."

I nod and try not to think. Definitely not about hot water feeling like it's suffocating me.

"Open your eyes, Willow."

Nope.

"You don't trust me to keep you safe?"

I twist to scowl at him. "Of course I do."

"Good." His dimples flash. "Just checking."

I take a moment to appreciate how damn attractive he is. Steam makes his skin glisten with luminosity. Heat gives his cheeks and lips a rosy color. Damp black hair. Gray eyes sparkle with joy.

Is this really my fate? To be linked to six beautiful, passionate males who only dream of my happiness?

"You know," I murmur and swipe my fingers down his nose. "You're incredibly sexy in the bath."

His eyes crinkle. "You're *in* the bath."

My heart leaps. "I am."

"What's the verdict on the bathwater situation? Do I need to find a drinking straw?"

I cover his lips with mine. His growl is low, breathy, and dripping with need. His cock stiffens beneath me.

"Tell me, Willow," he mutters against my lips. "Have you been fucked in a bath before?"

"You know I haven't."

"Do you think my cock is safe from falling off?"

I laugh. "Better watch out."

His face deadpans. "I'm actually serious."

My hand glides down his front, wraps around his shaft and

strokes. His eyes grow unfocused, but he keeps them locked with mine. Watching his downfall is the most erotic thing I've witnessed. My hand, my touch, is doing this to him. Need simmers in my blood.

"Turn around," he whispers gruffly.

It hurts to look away from the raw desire on his face, but I turn. His splayed palm presses against my sternum until I recline against his back, mostly submerged in the water. Fear flutters in my pulse.

My hands slap on the bath's edge. I try to pull myself up, but he holds me firm.

"I'm here," he says. When I stop resisting, he slides his hand down my stomach, between my thighs, and circles the heel of his palm against my mound. "Relax."

"I am," I whimper, resisting the arousal. It will distract me too much.

His chuckle trembles down my spine. He swipes a finger through my slit, flicks my clit. Sparks of pleasure shoot from his touch. *Fuck*, that felt good. I let go of the tub.

"That's better." He kisses my neck, fingers my pussy, and kneads my breast. Stimulation overloads my senses. A shuddering, helpless moan slips from my lips, and I melt against him. My climax breaks in what feels like seconds and I whimper when it's over.

Fox's shuddering, stilted breath has me twisting. I need to see what I do to him, need to see that desire on his face. This curse might be around forever. It won't matter if I know he doesn't see it. I'll survive. Water sloshes as I slide around on his lap. My pulse quickens and I clutch his biceps, tensing. My bottom rubs his erection, and he bites his lower lip to stop a groan. When I look at his face, I'm not disappointed. He is agonized with need for me.

"I love seeing your thoughts on your face." I swipe condensation from his brow.

Lust-drenched eyes hit mine. He seems to want to speak but can't. A plea enters his eyes. He also can't seem to voice his desire with thoughts, either.

"I know what you need, baby," I murmur against his lips and straddle him.

I undulate against him to roll my hips into position. When my breasts glide against his wet chest, we both moan. So slippery. So much sensation. His cock is so hard, so ready to fuck, it must hurt. Holding his heavy-lidded gaze, I impale myself on it. He hisses, whimpers.

I bite his neck to anchor myself through the sensation of him filling me, stretching me, and threatening to annihilate me.

His fingers flex on my hips. "Willow, you're so tight."

The sight of this ancient demigod undone by the feel of me is a heady aphrodisiac. I rock gently on him, roll my hips, and glide up and down his length, but the water sloshes. Reminds me it's there. I can't find a rhythm.

In a flicker of light, we're suddenly on his bed, dripping and soaked on the sheets. Panting for breath, I take a moment to adjust. He's inside me still, beneath me, waiting until I'm ready.

I plant my hands beside his head on the pillow. An aching need grips my heart.

"Fox?" My brows lift in the middle.

"Yes, pet?" His husky, sex-laden voice melts like butter. His hands drift up my hips and circle my waist. Galaxy eyes meet mine.

"When."

But he doesn't unleash his dark, primal desires on me. He lifts his lips to mine, kisses me with loving tenderness, then gently rolls us so he's on top. Fox makes love to me with a slow, savoring tempo. He cups my head between his hands and catalogs every reaction on my face. His leisurely glide out makes me whimper. His slow re-entry is torturous . . . until he slams the last inch. I gasp. He kisses me, drives his tongue in, dominates me, takes what he needs from me.

My fingers spear his wet hair. "You must have watched a lot of people fucking," I moan, "To be this good."

"You haven't even seen my special move yet." Raw ecstasy consumes his humor as he thrusts in with a grunt.

"Who'd you steal that from?" I tease.

His breathy, self-assured laugh flutters in my stomach. Treacherous eyes meet mine. "It's all mine, pet."

Another thrust. Another moan coaxed from my lungs.

"I don't think you're ready," he says.

"You mean, that wasn't it?"

He shakes his head. Drops his face to the crook of my neck and relishes a few more languid thrusts. But I can't stop thinking about it now. He knows I'm like this.

"Show me." I scrape my nails down his back. "Fox."

His hissed breath is cold against my damp skin. "Fine. You asked for it."

Triumph drags my lips into a grin until he rears back, and I see the devilry in his expression. A flash of panic hits me. What have I asked for?

Fox's skull flickers beneath his skin, then stops. It does that when his wraith leaves his body, but I don't feel the signature air brush against my skin. Is his wraith going to join in? Pin me down? The mystery drives me insane. Makes me hotter. Makes me beg.

"What are you going to do?" I breathe.

A wolfish grin is my answer.

His skull illuminates again. And keeps flickering. A flutter of air down my entire body makes me gasp. Anywhere his body touches mine, I feel it . . . including between my legs. He's pushing his wraith out, taking it back, and pushing it out again. Over and over. Faster and faster. The fluctuating pulses of wind stimulate every nerve ending in my body. Then he fucks me hard. I'm so damn wet, so aroused it hurts. Another orgasm is quick to build, coil, but refuses to break. A keening wail catches in my throat. The need to come has me in a chokehold.

"Come for me," he groans, slams in deep. "Come *hard*, Willow. Let it out." Then his voice in my mind: *"Let the hive hear how good you are for us."*

I explode, shatter, break apart. Still, he fucks me. Still, he flutters my sensitive nerves with his special move, drawing out my climax until tears stream from my eyes. He finally seats himself and snarls a deep, bone-shuddering growl as he submits to his release. Collapsing on me, he moans with satisfaction.

We lay there for what feels like hours, trying to muster the strength to move. When he finally draws back to look me in the eye, his face is all his—no skull.

A very pleased, very smug male look enters his expression. "What did you think of my move?"

My mouth opens. Closes. "I mean . . . it was okay, I guess."

He wraps me in his arms, and whispers, "Go to sleep, little liar. You earned the rest."

I WAKE TO DARKNESS, DELICIOUSLY COVERED IN FOX'S MUSKY SCENT. HE woke me up twice, craving more. I can't say I'm disappointed. Being so blatantly worshipped made me feel like a queen.

Smiling to myself, I roll and reach for him but find the bed empty. Frowning, I sit up. Something feels wrong. My fist rubs my sternum.

"Good, you're awake." Fox sits in the shadows on his settee, wearing black.

"Is everything okay? Why are you sitting alone in the dark?"

He walks over and sits on the bed, affection twitching his lips. "It's almost dawn."

"Oh, right." I rub the sleep from my eyes, then stretch my sore body. "The temple."

"I wanted to wake you . . ." His tone becomes distracted as I arch my chest, completing my arm extension.

"But?" I prompt.

He clears his throat. Lifts his gaze to mine. "But you needed your rest."

I toss the sheets off. "I'm good now. Let's go."

It takes no time to get dressed in warm clothes. I wrap a scarf around my head to keep the temperature from hurting my ears. Last, I tuck Tinger's pendant beneath the shirt and reach for my sword.

Fox stops me. "You won't need it."

"Oh?"

"We won't be long."

That's right. It's almost dawn. "Okay."

He gathers me into an embrace.

"So tense." I wriggle. "No one would ever believe you'd just fu—"

We *flicker*. Changing landscapes flash around us. It only takes a heartbeat, and then we land on the crisp, frost-covered lawn inside the Cabinet of Curiosities. After catching my bearings, I look around. The stone statue silhouettes seem more macabre before dawn. A shudder runs through me. Fox is already at the rock, testing for the entrance.

"So what do you hope to do?" I ask, jogging over and then blowing on my hands.

He glances at me. "Wait until we're in to talk."

My brows knit together. "You're acting odd."

"Here." He taps a spot on the rock.

I place my palm and feel the itch of fire ants against my skin. Taking Fox's hand, I walk in.

## CHAPTER
# FIFTY-EIGHT
### WILLOW

The light of thousands of manabeeze blinds me. I wince, shield my eyes, and wait for them to adjust. Nothing has changed inside the temple. Styx stands frozen in the middle, taloned wings flared and ready to attack. The scent of moss, rock, and dirt surrounds us.

Fox exhales a shaky breath and starts emptying his pockets onto a table.

"What are you doing?" I ask warily.

He takes another deep breath. Another shaky exhale, as if he's summoning courage.

"Fox?"

Jaw working, he stares at the table and plucks open buttons on his coat. It comes off. His shoes are next.

I laugh nervously. "I think sex in here once is enough, don't you?"

As his shirt comes off, he finally lifts his eyes to mine. Monumental sadness strikes me. My throat closes. The walls cave in.

"What's happening?" I breathe, dread filling me.

"I'm so sorry," he croaks. "But there's no other way."

"Put your clothes back on."

He unbuttons his trousers and nods at the items he put on the table. "Those spectacles are enchanted, allowing the wearer to see through magical bindings. No one will suspect because it's brass. Who you choose to wear them is up to you, but the enchantment won't transfer to others. Choose wisely."

"Stop."

He pulls his trousers down, collects his clothes, and drapes them over the table.

"My clothes might be too small for him," he mutters, "but it's better than him turning up naked."

Tears blur my vision. "I said stop!"

"Between Styx and the spectacles wearer, you'll be safe."

"Fox!"

He grinds his teeth. "It has to be like this. Puck had a resonance stone holding an image of you leaving here, a jar of wisps in your hand, confessing to stealing them. I would have killed him if it made a difference. Instead, I made a bargain."

I choke back a sob. My mind whirls. Resonance stone? No sense. No logic. Bodin's voice telling me, *There are charms that relay images.* I can't think of a way out of this. I fucked up. Again. *I'm* the curse. It's me. I close the gap between us, take his face, and beg. "Please don't go. Don't leave me."

Long lashes flutter closed. He leans into my hand, brows lifting in the middle. "I'm not leaving you. I'll be right here."

"No," I accuse. "You're leaving me. You said you wouldn't."

"Willow . . ."

"Is it because I keep getting into trouble? I'm sorry, okay? I'm calamity, a jinx—a magnet for trouble. I'll change. I'll do whatever you want, but don't leave me."

Pain is etched all over his face, in every line of his body, his stilted breath. I try to latch onto him, to lock him in my arms, but he pries me off with ease. I fall to my knees, head bowed, tears splashing onto the dirt.

"Is it my face?" I whisper.

"You're the most beautiful creature I've ever seen."

"Fox . . . we can figure a way out of this. We have the manabeeze. We can portal home and get help."

"You are our *queen*. This is your home," he growls, eyes flashing. He slams his palm on Styx's solid chest. "I ate Sylvanar, Willow. I ate his Shadow. I'm the fucking monster!"

"You're not."

"But I am." He laughs bitterly. "I tried so hard not to be. But in the end, I made it worse. Puck bonded to the Baleful Hunt and said it was either you or me. I fucked up, not you. But I can make it right. I'll trade places with Styx."

The blood drains from my face. "I thought it had to be a mortal."

"We only need a mortal to gain access to this temple. But then you found a way to pull me in."

"You didn't tell Puck you were coming here, did you?"

"He thinks I'll turn up tomorrow for my sentencing." His sad, wry smile breaks my heart. "I bargained for the night, for the evidence he holds over you, and for the jar of wisps you stole. Use it to pay Cait for the mirror, or use it to—" He chokes up. "To return to Elphyne."

He doesn't mean that. He just said this is my home.

Fire ants crawl over my skin, itching me as he chants a spell. Panic squeezes my heart. I try not to let my emotions break me, not to fall apart, but I can't lose him. Can't lose another person I love. My fist wraps around Tinger's pendant. I yank it over my head.

"Is it this?" I shake the pendant. "I'm ready to let him go. It won't cause any more trouble. Fox, I promise!"

My last word is a shriek. Horror fills me as tiny cracks appear on Styx's body and transfer to Fox's skin as slivers of stone.

"It's not the pendant, Willow." His voice is strained. Pained.

"I'll get rid of it."

"He's a part of you." He struggles to speak. "Cherish him. Don't get rid of memories that define you."

"*You* define me, Fox. You!"

The tears are free flowing now. The cracks appearing in Styx are deafening, like thunder. My fist clenches so tightly that a stress fracture forms in the vial.

"*Cherish me,*" Fox whispers into my mind. "*Wait for me.*"

My mother's voice rises from a memory—the night I was cursed. *Cherish his memory, and he'll live in you forever.* I open my palm. My blood is black against the buzzing ball of Tinger's light. *He'll live in you forever.*

I came here because of Tinger. He saved my life, but I thought I wasn't worth the sacrifice. This pain has followed me around ever since, feeding Titania's curse. And it will keep following me until I let it go, let *him* go.

I lift my gaze to Fox—to the ribbons of stone slicing over his body.

A manabee has power. If Titania's magic is half mine, maybe I can save Fox and Styx. All I need is a spark, and my fire might reignite. I crush the glass vial in my fist. Pain slices into my palm. Tinger's memory melts into me.

*Bounding down into the gully, I sniff the dirt for danger and stop. Another whiff, just to make sure. Then I lift my twitching nose her way and flap my wings. Here. I'll do it. I'll be the bait.*

*Her brows lift. "You want to be the bait?"*

*Perfect lady. She understands me. We belong together. What a fierce mate she would make. But then she hesitates. No, she's not like the others. She sees my heart and believes.*

*But sometimes she forgets. I snarl to remind her of my fierce worthiness as her protector.*

"Okay," she agrees, and I puff my chest in pride. "People keep telling us what we're not capable of. So, if you want to sit there as bait, be my guest. We have another fifteen minutes, then we'll—"

*I dare the hound to come for us. Let it try. We are unstoppable. She is mighty, and she believes in me.*

The memory shifts. Blurs. Blinks as Tinger's eyes open and close. I see my face, sobbing over him in the forest, but it's my little friend's thoughts I hear.

*I am whole. My purpose is filled. I have saved her, my mate, all because she dared to believe in the heart of a broken monster. And now she has freed me.*

Tinger's next blink is his last.

I open my eyes, and I'm back in the cave, clutching broken glass to my chest. The stupid, adorable wolpertinger thought I was his mate, but he loved me.

Pebbles drop on my head, crumbling from Styx's wings. Fox is almost completely riddled with stone. And I'm still empty—no dizzying, drunken effect from the ingested manabee. No spark. No power inside me with which to save my hive. Nothing.

I was wrong.

I failed.

*Nothings don't have names.*

*You're such a pathetic, disgusting waste of space.*

My fist tightens. Pain radiates up my palm. Blood drips onto the dirt.

*You belong with the other nightmares. It's high time your realm acknowledges that too. When you rise on the morrow, your visage will mirror the ugliness lurking within your heart.*

Titania's voice fills me with hot, trembling rage. She doesn't know my heart better than me. I am the only one who holds that power. I control my destiny, my choices, my fate. She might have stolen my magic and left me empty, but I'm not nothing.

I'm something.

Time to let it out. Time to let it all go. I refuse to let my life end like Rory's, filled with a never-ending vendetta. I want it to end like Tinger's, in service to those I love, those who love me in return. Taking a deep breath, I scream. I let it go. My rage, my fear, my insecurities. I scream until my throat is hoarse, and then I scream some more.

"I'M NOT NOTHING!"

I was something to Tinger. I am something to my family. I am something to my friends. I am something to *the Six*.

If Fox believes this is the best choice, then I trust him. I'll wait for him. I'll be the spider—No! I'm not the spider, not when I raised civilizations from death and slumber. I'm the fucking *giant*. Always have been. I just never believed it before now.

A snap inside my chest. A twang around my heart. My hand flutters there as something changes, something dissipates.

The curse is gone.

I have a moment of peace, and then pain flays every inch of my body. Power consumes me, dark and intense. What is happening to me? My eyes bulge, my muscles lock, and I seize. There's nothing I can do but ride it out and hope I don't die. It's not my magic. Not mine. But it's blinding and willful, and it comes from Fox. From Styx. From four others in the distance. Theirs is a smaller trickle instead of a torrent, but it's there filtering into my soul, latching around my heart, linking us together.

Blue light fizzes in the brightness of white manabeeze. Luminescent blue tiny marks appear on Fox's neck, glimmering defiantly through the solid stone consuming his beautiful face and body. And Styx . . . blue marks glimmer on his neck, too.

Somehow, I sense it on all six of them. I hold my hand above

Fox's mating mark on my neck. Blue light reflects onto my palm. Same color as their Guardian teardrop, as my parents' Well-blessed mating mark. It's not the same beautiful, identical pattern on their arms. It's something more me.

Teeth.

The hive's magic flows through me. I am the center of their universe, their star. Their one true queen. One by one, their emotions slam into me. Sorrow, pain, confusion, hunger, anger, listlessness. Love. I gasp and look at Fox's frozen face. I can feel him in there. Trapped.

Styx's wings shift away with a rustle. His skin is blueish with a hint of blush. His horns go next. Then his tail. He hunches over himself and falls to a knee, choking and gasping for air. Slowly, the blue fades. All signs of his otherness are gone, as if they never existed.

"Let me help you." I try to lift him off the dirt.

A strong arm swings at me, slaps me away. Sharp fangs gnash at my face—a flash of blue startled eyes. I stumble backward and give him space, holding up my palms in surrender. This would be disorienting after being trapped in stone for over a year.

Slowly, he catches his labored breath and straightens to his full, towering height. Fuck, he's strong. All those bulging stone muscles are more frightening in the flesh.

Having dismissed me as no threat, he moves with the grace of a fighter around the room, inspecting items on the table. Fox's clothes. Wasn't Styx petrified for brawling with another Radiant? I try not to breathe, to draw attention from the caged wild animal finally freed.

He narrows his eyes at Fox, then faces me and asks, "Who are you?"

# ACKNOWLEDGMENTS

Thank you to all the Fae Guardians Team Sluagh fans who encouraged me to write this book. It would never have happened without you. Thank you to all my amazing Patreon supporters. You helped me craft this story and brainstorm and lifted me up with your enthusiasm during a difficult time in my life.

Thank you to Erika Robles for beta reading for me in a pinch. Deadline-mode came into full force with this book.

Thank you to Kelly Messenger for also shoving me into the gaps of your proof-editing schedule last minute. You are a legend.

Thanks to my structural editor, Ann Harth, for helping make sense of the word vomit this book started as.

To my sister, Heidi Pecherczyk, you've rallied to take on far more than you should but have saved my bacon more than once.

You're the bee's knees.

# ABOUT THE AUTHOR

**OMG! How do you say my name?**

**Lana** (straight forward enough - Lah-nah) **Pecherczyk** (this is where it gets tricky - Pe-her-chick).

I've been called Lana Price-Check, Lana Pera-Chickywack, Lana Pressed-Chicken, Lana Pech...*that girl!* You name it, they said it. So if it's so hard to spell, why on earth would I use this name instead of an easy pen name?

To put it simply, it belonged to my mother. And she was my dream champion.

For most of my life, I've been good at one thing – art. The world around me saw my work, and said I should do more of it, so I did.

But, when at the age of eight, I said I wanted to write stories, and even though we were poor, my mother came home with a blank notebook and a pencil saying I should follow my dreams, no matter where they take me for they will make me happy. I wasn't very good at it, but it didn't matter because I had her support and I liked it.

She died when I was thirteen, and left her four daughters orphaned. Suddenly, I had lost my dream champion, I was split from my youngest two sisters and had no one to talk to about the challenge of life.

So, I wrote in secret. I poured my heart out daily to a diary and sometimes imagined that she would listen. At the end of the day, even if she couldn't hear, writing kept that dream alive.

Eventually, after having my own children (two firecrackers in the guise of little boys) and ignoring my inner voice for too long, I decided to lead by example. How could I teach my children to follow their dreams if I wasn't? I became my own dream champion and the rest is history, here I am.

When I'm not writing the next great action-packed romantic novel, or wrangling the rug rats, or rescuing GI Joe from the jaws of my Kelpie, I fight evil by moonlight, win love by daylight and never run from a real fight.

I live in Australia, but I'm up for a chat anytime online. Come and find me.

*Stalker Links*
www.lanapecherczyk.com

f facebook.com/lanapecherczykauthor

instagram.com/lana_p_author

a amazon.com/-/e/B00V2TP0HG

tiktok.com/@lanapauthor

g goodreads.com/lana_p_author

patreon.com/lanacreates

# ALSO BY LANA PECHERCZYK

THE FAE GUARDIANS WORLD

**Fae Guardians - Elphyne**

*(Fantasy/Paranormal Romance)*

*Season of the Wolf Trilogy*

The Longing of Lone Wolves

The Solace of Sharp Claws

Of Kisses & Wishes Novella (free for subscribers)

The Dreams of Broken Kings

*Season of the Vampire Trilogy*

The Secrets in Shadow and Blood

A Labyrinth of Fangs and Thorns

A Symphony of Savage Hearts

*Season of the Elf Trilogy*

A Song of Sky and Sacrifice

A Crown of Cruel Lies

A War of Ruin and Reckoning

**Fae Devils**

*(Fae Guardians Sluagh Spin-off)*

Castle of Nevers and Nightmares

Trials of Dusk and Dreams

# THE DEADLYVERSE

**The Sinner Sisterhood**

*(Demon-hunting Paranormal Romance)*

The Sinner and the Scholar

The Sinner and the Gunslinger

The Sinner and the Priest

**The Deadly Seven**

*(Fated Mate Paranormal/Sci-Fi Romance)*

The Deadly Seven Box Set Books 1-3

Sinner

Envy

Greed

Wrath

Sloth

Gluttony

Lust

Pride

Despair